BOUNDED RATIONALITY

— The America Incorporated Saga —

MIKAEL CARLSON

WARRINGTON
PUBLISHING

Danbury, Connecticut

Novels by Mikael Carlson:

– The Michael Bennit Series –
The iCandidate
The iCongressman
The iSpeaker
The iAmerican

– Tierra Campos Thrillers –
Justifiable Deceit
Devious Measures
Vital Targets
Revealed Secrets
Decisive Endgame

– Watchtower Thrillers –
The Eyes of Others
The Eyes of Innocents
The Eyes of Victims

– America, Inc. Saga –
The Black Swan Event
Bounded Rationality
Boiling the Ocean

BOUNDED RATIONALITY:

It is an idea that in decision-making, an individual's rationality is limited by the information they have, the cognitive limitations of their minds, and the finite amount of time they have to make a decision.

For all those willing to risk everything to chase a dream.

CHAPTER ONE

AMERICA, INC.

Human Resources Center
Rikers Island Geographic Area
New York City Municipal Corporation

One of the most recognizable prisons in the United States once consisted of ten separate jails capable of housing up to seventeen thousand inmates. Riker's Island was plagued with bureaucratic inefficiency, inmate brutality, and corruption that contributed to an ongoing public relations nightmare. Before the collapse, a staff of over ten thousand officers and civilians managed a hundred thousand admissions per year. Times have changed.

The Rikers Island Human Resources Corporate Detention and Reeducation Facility continues that long tradition by maintaining its status as a void of misery in the middle of America Incorporated's most prosperous metropolis. Only a fraction of the original facility is in use. The operations against the urches and the search for Liberteum have pressed several more structures into service.

"Handling this one personally, Chief Guardian?" a guard asks as Teman enters the interrogation building.

"I watched the raid on his shop and want to see it through."

Interviews of employees suspected of wrongdoing are typically conducted at One Guardian Plaza. Once charged with a violation of corporate policy, employees are brought before Human Resources for a hearing. Most infractions are adjudicated at the hexagonal stone structure that was once home to the New York State Supreme Court. Cases involving serious offenses, like providing material support for urches, are heard here.

Teman enters the dingy, water-stained room to find Shopkeeper Stevwil manacled to a steel table. Harsh fluorescent overhead lighting bathes the room in an unnatural light, undoubtedly making his experience more uncomfortable.

Stevwil launches into the usual litany of denials as the chief guardian sits down opposite him. Teman doesn't find anything he says compelling. They already know he's guilty, so this will be a short conversation if he isn't willing to give up Liberteum. Then again, he would've bargained that information away by now if he had it.

"Shopkeeper Stevwil, the evidence against you is overwhelming. Make this process easier on yourself, and tell me where I can find Liberteum."

"I've told you," he says, his face twisting in frustration. "I don't know anyone in Liberteum."

"Then I can't help you," Teman says, rising and staring at the camera. "Take him before HR."

Corporations rely on Human Resources to make the critical employment decisions that keep their economies humming. America Incorporated takes it further by placing HR in charge of disciplinary matters, making these executives among the most powerful in the corporation.

Teman follows the guards escorting Stevwil into a finely appointed room filled with rich cherry furniture. They proceed down the center aisle past the lines of wooden chairs to a small circular rostrum near the front of the room. There are few witnesses to this proceeding as the records clerk reads the case from his tablet.

At the front of the room, the HR executive sits at an elevated desk, much like a judge would have. His high-tech workstation is replete with computer displays showing the charges and Stevwil's personnel record. He studies the subject as the clerk finishes his announcement.

"I have read the charges against you and weighed the evidence provided to me by Public Safety and Security. It's compelling. As a result, I find you in violation of corporate mandate, to wit: providing material support to the scofflaw population. Given the seriousness of this transgression in light of recent events, I order your immediate termination from employment by the New York City Municipal Corporation."

"No! God, no. Please, I beg you—"

"I hereby remand Shopkeeper Stevwil into America Incorporated custody. Guards, escort the former employee to the Delta Building for out-processing."

Teman rises following the brief pronouncement. The out-processing facility is one of the newest buildings on the island. The large, square structure comprises four three-story wings designated Alpha, Bravo, Charlie, and Delta. The first three areas are designed to handle routine terminations, while Delta is dedicated to more sensitive ones. Among employees, it's known as "Delta Doom."

The ride over to out-processing is a short one. At the main entrance, a guard scans Stevwil's biojack and confirms the termination order. Everything here is efficiently verified and then re-verified.

"Take him to Section C, Room Thirteen."

"You don't have to do this," Stevwil protests as the pair of guards the size of bears drag him down the corridor. "I have information that can be of great value to you."

"Then you should have shared it when you had the chance," Teman says, dismissing the blatant lie.

"There's still a chance! We can undo this."

"Decisions rendered by Human Resources are final. You've known that since you were a registrant."

Stevwil's eyes sweep left and right. The guards recognize the action for what it is. They know the drill. They've seen it countless times before.

"Don't even think about it," one of them warns. "Running will only make this worse for you."

"Please, I beg of you. Bring my case to the CEO. He can override—"

"Save it!" the guard barks.

Stevwil spins and tries to bolt back down the corridor after the door to room thirteen opens. He doesn't make it two steps. The guards manhandle him as he wails in protest. Silence envelops the hallway after the soundproofed door closes behind them. Out-processing won't be pleasant for him.

The sound of Teman's boots clacking on the polished tile floor reverberates off the corridor's sterile white walls. He climbs a flight of stairs to the second floor and turns the corner toward the gallery. Only a few people sit in the five stadium-style tiers of padded blue seats.

Teman selects a seat in the middle front with a good view out the slanted, one-way mirrored window that provides a commanding view of the courtyard. He buries his face in his tablet and studies the latest reports from the RTCC. Four more possible Libertcum locations have been identified. That will make tomorrow a long day.

A buzzer sounds and strobes flash about fifteen minutes later as guards escort Stevwil to the courtyard center. They lash his ankles to the bottom of the steel T-shaped apparatus and input his measurements into a tablet. The position of the wrist restraints automatically adjusts, and the crossbar aligns to match the height of his shoulders. Once he is secure, the detail moves off to the corner of the yard.

The decree is read to Shopkeeper Stevwil once more as five special members of the BCS assigned to the prison march in lockstep to their positions on a concrete pad. They assume a low-ready stance, balancing on the balls of their feet. The terrified man stares at them wide-eyed.

"Make ready...aim...."

On command, the agents level their rifles. Their laser optic sights form five distinct glowing red dots on his chest. A beat later, they converge over Stevwil's cold, traitorous heart. Each illuminated dot from their rifles is steady and unmoving.

Stevwil looks down at the red lights on his chest. He is blubbering like a fool, but his final pleas for mercy fall on deaf ears. The drugs he was administered may have pacified him, but they don't override the will to live. Teman watches as the traitor unleashes a primal scream. It's the last thing he'll ever do.

"Fire!"

Each shot hits its mark. The sound of the rounds echoes off the courtyard walls before dissipating. A moment later, a doctor checks the limp body for vital signs. Satisfied, he nods to an administrator, who uses a device to scan the man's biojack for the last time.

Teman rises and straightens his uniform. One more urch supporter is gone, and there are plenty more to catch. For now, he can rest knowing that the final entry in the man's personnel file will read:

Stevwil, Shopkeeper
New York City Municipal Corporation
Terminated for treason on 14 April 2088
Rikers Island Human Resources Center.

CHAPTER
TWO

INTERCORPEX

ICX Backup Datacenter
Hafnarfjörður Municipality
Independent Territory of Iceland

The taxi's electric engine whines as it passes the guardhouse and turns onto the road leading back to Reykjavik. Zyree faces the plain white data center that houses the historical record of every transaction and spot price from the Beijing, Frankfurt, and New York trading sites. Plentiful geothermal power, coupled with the cool ambient temperature, makes Iceland a perfect place for the thousands of servers that require an abundance of both.

"You finally took my advice and spent a night in town?" a familiar voice asks Zyree as he enters the lobby of the building. He turns to see the man who picked him up in Keflavik the first time he was here. "Did you have fun? I mean…did you learn firsthand that our women are far hotter than our weather?"

"Chief Inspector Zyree. Please follow me," the ICX Security guard interrupts.

He gives the driver a thumbs-up and passes through the mantrap and redundant security safeguards implemented to deter authorized access. Once on the other side, they walk through the immaculate data center to the back office. It's a perfect place to hide if someone doesn't ever want to be bothered.

"I'll be right with you, Chief Inspector," Ortan announces as Zyree enters.

Diminutive in stature, if not personality, he is still as white as snow. Ortan's most prominent feature is the exoskeleton that provides him the mobility an accident stole years ago.

"At least I'm not looking at bare walls this time," Zyree says, patiently waiting.

"Huldufólk was expecting you."

The text that pops up on Zyree's contacts reminds him that Huldufólk is the elf that runs Ortan's displays. There's no point in claiming that elves don't exist. The chief inspector would either lose the argument or regret bringing it up. Probably both.

Each wall displays an infrared projection that only Ortan's contact lenses can interpret. His exoskeleton negates the need for a chair. This time, there is an old army cot in the corner of the otherwise empty office with a dozen empty Chinese power drink cans strewn beneath it.

"Are you sleeping here?"

"What little I get. I haven't left in…what day is it?"

"Wednesday. It would have been easier if we talked over a VidLynk."

"Easier, but not safer," Ortan says, turning to acknowledge him for the first time. "You look well."

"How else would I look?"

Ortan cocks his head. "Singed…maybe slightly charbroiled."

Zyree ignores the odd little man's attempt at humor over his almost getting killed in the Broad Street explosion.

"Safer how? They know I'm in Iceland."

"No, so far as Intercorpex is concerned, you're in Paris. *Ça te dit?*"

"I don't speak French. How did you…? Actually, never mind."

It's a stupid question. Ortan hacked into the PSS emergency operations center in ten seconds and put himself on their main screen – twice. There's no doubt he can make it look like Zyree is someplace he's not.

"I asked you to come here because…wait. You don't speak French?"

"Ortan!"

"The work orders. The last time you were here, we found three that moved the circuits in Secaucus to intersect at a location leaked to Liberteum. They detonated the explosives that forced ICX to use the microwave transmitters."

"I don't need a history lesson. Get to the point."

"I am. Do you need caffeine? I have these great Chinese drinks—"

"Ortan!" Zyree snaps again.

"All right, all right, suit yourself. Those unsecure microwave transmissions were intercepted and used to copy our trade message format. Liberteum placed phony ones on the wire that nearly collapsed the exchange."

"That was all in the investigation report. Explain how they beat the encryption."

Ortan frowns. "I haven't figured that out yet."

"Then at least tell me something I haven't already learned."

"Director Lyris wet his bed until he was nine."

Zyree raises an eyebrow. "That explains a lot, but it's not what I'm looking for."

"Then try this: The two ICX backups were corrupted beyond repair. Whoever wiped them tried to make it look like a hardware failure. The saboteur didn't know that I keep backups of administrative documents on a separate yottabyte solid-state drive."

"Yottabyte?"

"It's a million times larger than the common exabyte drives. It holds a trillion times more data than the terabyte drives used before the collapse."

"Whatever," Zyree says, waving a dismissive hand. "Do you realize what will happen if you get caught making unauthorized copies of files by someone in, say, *Intercorpex Security*?"

"What could they do, send me to Iceland?"

Zyree takes a breath and closes his eyes. He's trying to be patient. Ortan is a good guy, but he has a unique ability to wear on his nerves.

"Get to the point…please."

"The 'please' was a nice touch – you should try it more often. I found the work orders and restored them. The administrator-general generated the requests."

"Hold on…you're saying that Raimius is behind this?" Zyree asks, astonished. That's one twist that he didn't expect.

"No, I'm saying someone wanted us to think that. These records should never have been recovered. In case they were, a safeguard was put in place. It was a clever misdirection," the engineer muses.

"I'm getting a headache, Ortan. Who did it?"

"I'm getting there. When I realized I was being led down the rabbit hole, I cross-referenced the system information from the first work orders against the missing one for the network turn-up and turn-down in ICXNY that allowed Liberteum to tap our circuit."

"And what did you find?"

"The key to the lock."

"Damn it, Ortan…who did it?"

"I don't know," he declares, refusing to make eye contact.

Zyree takes a menacing step toward him. He'll break Ortan's arms to match his legs if he dragged him to Iceland for nothing.

"I thought you said that you knew!"

"There's no way to know," he says, pointing to some strings of numbers and letters on the wall. "I do know the hexadecimal IPv6 address where the request originated from. That led me to the physical location on the network."

"Where?"

"The office of the man who wet his bed until he was nine."

Zyree's mouth hangs open as Ortan smirks at him. "Okay…say that again."

"The man they just gave a medal is behind everything. There is a one hundred percent certainty that the work orders and deletions originated from the computer in Executive Director of Global Operations Lyris's office."

CHAPTER

THREE

THE PATRICIANS

The America Building Memorial Complex
Financial Geographic District
New York City Municipal Corporation

Most United States commemorations were removed or destroyed long ago, including its war memorials. The exception is the September 11th Memorial at the southern end of Manhattan.

Terrorists killed nearly three thousand people in an attack on corporate interests, or so the narrative establishes. Artifacts from the tragedy were recovered following the Great Collapse, and America Incorporated rehabilitated the museum as a reminder of past dangers, and the safety and security corporatism provides.

Farron enjoys his early evening stroll between the illuminated twin reflecting pools. The manmade waterfalls cascading from the courtyard down the walls are still the largest in North America. Every person who died on those fateful days in 2001 and 1993 has their name inscribed on bronze panels along the edge of each pool. He wonders if the victims of the Liberteum attack will garner the same respect. Probably not.

"If you told your peers that you needed to stretch your legs, you shouldn't make it so obvious you're waiting for someone," Farron whispers into Fiolla's ear as he comes up behind her.

"If you'd been on time, I wouldn't have had to," she says, scolding him.

"Patricians keep their own time. You know that as well as anyone."

His dazzling smile, well-groomed appearance, and intelligence are among his most alluring qualities. Farron also has a distinguished family name and fortune to match. Even if he weren't a patrician, he'd be the total package that girls dream about.

Farron provided critical information and guidance twice during Liberteum's attack. Chief Executive Valen owes his job to Farron, although he doesn't know it. The appreciation Fiolla has for his support is only surpassed by how deeply she has fallen in love with him. There is give and take in any relationship, and now it's her turn to return the favors.

"I'm neurotic enough about doing this. Please don't make it worse," Fiolla pleads. "I don't like doing this in public places covered with surveillance cameras. I'm going to see you later tonight. Why is this so urgent?"

Farron frowns. "My sources tell me the PSS are planning a major sweep in the underground tomorrow. I need this information sooner, not later, my love."

"Stop with the terms of endearment in public," Fiolla demands. "People could be listening."

"Nobody is listening," he reassures her.

He reaches into his pocket and pulls out a device about the size of an old coin. The "disruptor" is an electronic emitter that saturates the surrounding area with interference, making audio eavesdropping impossible. Senior executives have ones that are the size of bricks. This device is far more advanced and probably a hundred times as costly.

"I'm taking a huge risk giving you this information…and you still haven't told me why you need it. And please don't say it's for business dealings with the urches."

"We've been through this, Fiolla." Farron moans.

"I know, but you deflect the question with the same canned response every time. I work in the *White House*, Farron. I know how lying works."

"Do you think I'm protecting Liberteum?"

Fiolla stares at the ground. As much as she loves Farron, she can't be sure he isn't. Relationships between patricians and employees are exceedingly rare, and she's navigating unfamiliar waters. If she gets caught, Farron can quickly move on. Fiolla could get terminated.

"Or the urches who are protecting them. Look, Chief Guardian Teman isn't getting results. The chorus of people asking why is growing louder."

"Is Valen asking?"

"Not yet, but his enemies see an opportunity. Talya Bettancourt is applying pressure on the board. It's only a matter of time before they make a move."

Talya Bettancourt is the *prima* patrician, owning the majority stake in America Incorporated. She is powerful, influential, and relentless. Valen thwarted her first attempt to remove him, but that doesn't mean she'll give up. It was a minor victory in a long war.

"The way corporate executives talk, you would think society had progressed since the Great Collapse. The truth is, it hasn't. The same political games from the old world are played in the new one. It's just done less openly."

"I work with patricians, Farron. You aren't above politics, either."

"You're right. We only play the game at a higher level. Sweetheart, you're not going to get caught, and if by some chance you do, I'll protect you," Farron adds, getting back to her initial concern. "They wouldn't dare haul off and terminate the future wife of the heir to the Keating fortune."

Fiolla's heart flutters. A warm sensation sweeps over her body, right down to her fingers and toes. Did he just say what she thinks he did?

"Are you asking…?"

"No, not now…not here," he says with a laugh and a glance at the reflection pool beside them. "But I will. I love you, Fiolla. I think you question that, so maybe putting a diamond on your finger will convince you once and for all."

"That's an old tradition. Employees can't afford diamonds anymore."

"Patricians can. And a man sealing his promise with a ring adorned with an indestructible gemstone is a tradition that never should have been lost to the ages."

"I…I don't know what to say," Fiolla stutters.

"Then don't say anything. Just know what you're doing isn't for me. It's for us."

"Okay," she says, dipping her hand into her pocket and pulling out a device the size of a fingernail.

The solid-state drive has a capacity that far exceeds the size of the document that details public safety's plan for the underground raids, security sweeps, and sensor placements. She hands it to him, and he tucks it into his pocket.

"Thank you, my love. I'll see you later tonight?" he asks, looking into her eyes.

"Absolutely."

He winks at her and heads off in the direction he came. His father would be livid to hear that he's marrying down, considering their conversation on the day of the attacks. But that's not what's bothering him. Fiolla knows that the information she's providing is getting into Liberteum's hands. He frets the day she learns precisely how.

CHAPTER FOUR

REGISTRANT RYKOS

Essence Ristorante
Upper East Side Geographic District
New York City Municipal Corporation

Being a teenager in America Incorporated isn't easy. The miserable stipend earned as registrants is just enough to cover the cost of a lower-end restaurant once every couple of weeks. It would take six months of saving every Bytecoin to afford the Essence Ristorante. Fortunately, I'm a celebrity now.

"Good evening, Registrant Rykos. I'm Maître d' Ambrozio. It's a great honor having a hero of the corporation and his beautiful guest at our establishment this evening."

I feel Mollae clutch my arm as she blushes at the compliment. "We're grateful to be here."

"We have a special table ready for you. Please follow me."

"This place is amazing," Mollae says in a hushed tone, taking in the décor of the fine restaurant as we're escorted to our table.

The dining room is adorned with sophisticated wall sculptures and crystal chandeliers hanging from the vaulted ceiling. The dimmed lights give the room a warm ambiance, and the faint sounds of a string quartet complete the setting. Casual restaurants have modern, futuristic themes consistent with the corporation's message of a bright future. This restaurant embraces an old-world appeal and is first-class all the way.

"Everybody is staring at you," Mollae whispers as we follow Ambrozio.

"I know. They're wondering how a guy like me managed to land a date with a beautiful woman like you."

Mollae giggles, but she already knows that she's the prettiest girl in any room. Her five-foot-five height is the only thing average about her. She is toned with long legs, flawless skin, perfectly coiffed long blonde hair, and a pair of eyes made for seduction.

"I'm so excited to finally have some alone time with you," she genuinely says.

"Me too," I respond, desperately trying to sound authentic.

I should be excited. There isn't a guy who wouldn't sell his soul to take her on a date. A month ago, she wouldn't have given me the time of day, let alone drop hints about wanting to get romantically involved. That's how much my love life has changed.

"My father says the food here is amazing," my date says, grasping my hands on the table. "Especially the desserts. He says the crème brulee is to die for. My brother isn't allowed to have dessert. He's in the fat kid program."

Mollae is talking so fast that I can barely decipher what's coming out of her mouth. The rant continues about how her brother is twenty pounds overweight and was inducted into the Corporate Weight Reduction Initiative. Her parents came up with the name "fat kid program" to shame him. That kid will need therapy, assuming he doesn't allow himself to get terminated to end his agony.

"I'm sorry to interrupt," an older gentleman says, stopping at our table with his wife in tow. "I wanted to shake your hand, Registrant Rykos. It's a great honor to meet such a remarkable young hero."

"Thank you, sir. I appreciate your words."

I hear them all the time. Everyone recognizes me from my AME News interview or the full documentary running on an endless loop on one of the AME Entertainment channels. The parent company held me up as an exemplar of the conduct it expects of all employees. Then they bestowed upon me an award and the title "Hero of the Corporation." If they only knew the truth.

"You know, Career Day is on Friday," Mollae says, visibly pleased with the attention that comes with being around me. "Can you believe it's only two days away? Everyone in school is so nervous. Well, everyone except us, that is. We know we're going to the Ivy League. I think there's a good chance we'll be going to the same school. Do you know what that could mean for the future? I mean, we make a great team."

Mollae couldn't be more transparent in her motives. I used to think she was the perfect girl – bright, pretty, and destined for an executive career. Then I met Michele, and my perceptions changed. That woman is the complete package: tough, intelligent, loyal, and beautiful beyond compare. All are attributes I would never have assigned to an urch who's a wanted terrorist.

"I guess we'll see what the future brings," I say, smiling weakly as our waiter arrives with the appetizer.

I glance up and see a passing acquaintance of my father's waiting for a table. He's a top executive within Human Resources and might be able to provide the elusive answer to a haunting question.

"Will you excuse me for a moment, Mollae? I need to say hi to someone."

"Of course," she says, poorly hiding her disappointment at the abrupt interruption.

I thank her and walk over to the man standing with his wife or mistress. I ask for a word in private, and we move to the tonic bar where patrons get their nutritious drinks as their tables are prepared. Even influential executives don't get seated as quickly as a hero of the corporation.

"What can I do for you, Registrant Rykos? If this is about Career Day, I'm afraid I can't spoil the surprise."

"It's not about that. It's about a friend of mine who was a registrant at Dinsmore. His name is Balin."

The tension contorts Executive Kenady's face as he pulls me away to a quieter spot along the wall. Scanning the restaurant nervously, he checks for microphones and cameras hidden in the ceiling and walls.

"Don't mention his name. Not here, not anywhere."

"I don't understand. I—"

"Just don't mention his name. Even in private. I can't talk about him, Rykos."

"Please, sir. Everyone congratulates me on killing a terrorist mastermind but ignores me when I inquire about my best friend. He was a victim of Liberteum just as I was. Tell me, did he go to West Point?"

West Point is on the Hudson River at a campus that used to be home to a military training academy. It was repurposed for training agents in the Bureau of Corporate Security not long after founding the parent company.

"You didn't hear this from me. He did but was pulled out before training started."

"Thankfully, someone realized he's not suited for that," I say, relieved. "Human Resources should have known that from the beginning."

"HR didn't send him there or remove him," Kenady admits.

"What do you mean? Where is he now? Is he okay?"

"I don't know."

"What do you mean you don't know?" I snap.

Kenady's eyes check around us again. Nobody is within immediate earshot. This guy is making it look like we're exchanging corporate secrets. It's a harmless question, or at least I thought it was.

"He's no longer listed in any corporate directory, nor is he a registrant at any academy. He belongs to the Pentagon."

"I'll ask there, then."

"Rykos, let me give you a piece of advice: Stop searching for him. When the BCS creates their agents, they do it from the ground up. If they pulled him out of West

Point, they have something special in mind for him. Making too many inquiries will only land you in trouble."

"Okay," I croak.

"You'd better get back to your lovely date. She's getting impatient." Executive Kenady shakes my hand and leans in. "I know all too well how the BCS operates. If you ever see your friend again, he won't be the same. Please, let it go."

I came into this conversation with one question. Now I have a hundred. When the BCS questioned me, I wondered if they were the good guys. The heavy-handed interrogation tactics were not what I expected, at least not from someone on my side. I can't imagine what's happening to him.

CHAPTER FIVE

AMERICA, INC.

Waldorf-Astoria Hotel
Midtown Geographic District
New York City Municipal Corporation

Chief Executive Valen sits across from AME News's most distinguished and recognizable reporter at the posh Waldorf-Astoria Hotel and scans the room. The landmark is one of the few structures that maintained its original name following the Great Collapse. Its fine furniture, splendid décor, and luxurious old-world spaces make it superior to a sterile television studio or his America Tower office.

The seven a.m. news hour is the corporation's most-watched broadcast, but it delivers critical and timely news to employees before the workday begins. This eight p.m. interview may have a lighter viewership, but it guarantees that the crucial clips will be replayed in the morning for full effect.

"Good Evening, Chief Executive Valen. It's an honor having you with us tonight."

"Thank you, Journalist Kassaya. It is a pleasure being here."

This entire interview is scripted, just as most dialogues between corporate executives and the reporting arm of the corporation are. Unfortunately, things don't always work according to plan, especially with this journalist. Her off-script adventure with Fiolla in an interview the morning of the New York attack nearly ended her career. This is her chance to atone for that.

After Fiolla announced that Liberteum didn't exist, the terrorists set off a total of eight explosions in the city. The timing was unfortunate, and the results were tragic. The first four severed secondary and tertiary data links that transmit trading information to the Intercorpex exchange on Wall Street. Two minor explosions in Times Square and Grand Central were a distraction. The final two blasts decimated the PSS's attempted breaches of the abandoned subway station and allowed Liberteum to escape.

"It's been a week since the terrorist group Liberteum crippled the city and murdered more than a hundred employees, including more than two dozen New York Public Safety and Security guardians. How is the search for the perpetrators coming?"

"Not fast enough, Kassaya," Valen says, using a soothing voice. "We have dedicated considerable resources from the BCS and PSS to find and eliminate the threat. Unfortunately, it takes time, and the coming justice isn't as swift as we would like it to be."

"Have they had success in identifying or capturing members of the group?" Kassaya asks.

"Key members of Liberteum have been identified, and as you know, during the attack, their leader was killed by the son of New York City's chief guardian following his kidnapping and subsequent escape."

"Yes, we owe Registrant Rykos a great deal of respect and gratitude," she adds, using her radiant smile and lacquered-on cosmetics to mask her apparent doubts about the official story. "He is truly worthy of recognition as a hero of the corporation."

"He did a great service to America Incorporated, but there's work to be done. The terrorist organization's remnants have been driven deep underground, and we need to root them out."

"How can they hide considering the manpower dedicated to locating them?"

"The New York City underground is a labyrinth. Fortunately, the number of hiding spots is also finite. It's only a matter of time before we find them."

In many respects, the underground is a city in itself. The urches have transportation networks, a black market economy, and even residences that sometimes include electricity and running water. Despite having no freedom of movement above ground, they live better than most executives imagined before this manhunt began.

"Is there anything that can be used to speed up the search?" Kassaya presses.

"We are using all available technologies, including various sensors and drones. Unfortunately, there are limits to what can be used. I cannot provide operational details, but stealth and the safety of our personnel are of utmost importance. We will prevail in the end, but it will take time and effort to eradicate the terrorists once and for all."

"Do we *have* time?" Kassaya quizzes.

The question is on the script, but the inflection makes it a challenge more than an inquiry. Valen narrows his eyes, and Kassaya takes a deep breath.

"Let me ask that another way: Does Director Virtari fear another attack in the coming weeks?"

"Operations are underway to apprehend urches and their sympathizers. By eroding Liberteum's support base, we're confident we have inhibited their ability to conduct another attack."

"Chief Executive Valen," Kassaya says, leaning forward in her chair, "we were previously assured that Liberteum didn't exist. How can employees be confident that what you're saying is true?"

Valen glances off-camera at Employee Communications Director Jenizee. The six-foot, three-inch raven-haired Amazon has her arms welded across her chest. Her scowl would make the most fearsome BCS agent wither.

She worked with the AME News producer to agree on the questions but not their precise wording. To ensure an authentic appearance in the interview, flexibility in the questioning encourages a less-stale dialogue. Kassaya has leeway but was warned to be careful. That advice isn't being heeded.

"Liberteum was effectively destroyed several years ago during a BCS raid. While their capabilities were decimated, Quarren escaped and was able to reconstitute his group with men and women who wanted to destroy our way of life. With him dead, that's no longer the case."

"And you're sure that Quarren was Liberteum's leader?"

"There is no doubt about it," Valen states.

"An attack of this nature would lead most employees to believe that the BCS would play a wider role in the search. Why is New York City's Chief Guardian spearheading the effort, and given the unimpressive results, are there discussions about making a change?"

Valen's blood is boiling. Does Journalist Kassaya think his orders are up for debate once final? He already knows what her next question will be and needs to shut her down before she can ask it.

"'There are always spirited discussions among executives in Washington. This is no different. I weighed my options for this operation and made my choice. *Everyone* supports that. Chief Guardian Teman has a vested interest in destroying this group. They kidnapped and almost killed his son. I can't think of a better man for the job. Can you?"

Kassaya wants to ask a follow-up, glancing off-camera at Jenizee, who is busy burning a hole into her with a frightful glare. "No, of course not. Intercorpex had reported market anomalies that day. Do you have any information about that?"

This is the most critical part of Valen's interview, and he hopes that Kassaya doesn't screw it up. The glowering head of Intercorpex has rebuffed his overtures for a face-to-face meeting over the past week. Everyone is hoping this interview forces the issue. If Kassaya doesn't ask the intended questions, her next interview will be with Human Resources right before they terminate her.

"No. I have not spoken with Administrator-General Raimius, and no other CEO has either to my knowledge."

"Is that unusual?"

"He's likely busy determining what happened to his systems and repairing the damage to the facility. I'm certain a meeting will be forthcoming."

"There's a rumor circulating that he blames America Incorporated for the attack and the problems with the exchange that day."

"Administrator-General Raimius knows better than to conflate the two problems. He also knows that blaming the parent company for the acts of desperate terrorists is counterproductive."

"You said in your speech following the attacks that Liberteum believes that this society must be destroyed. That what they preach is anarchy. Can you explain why Liberteum would turn to terrorism to accomplish their goals?"

"Their ideology was born of violence in the American Revolution and perpetuated through centuries of wars and conflicts. They don't look at corporatism as an achievement, despite our eliminating war, poverty, and corruption. They would rather erase fifty years of human progress."

Kassaya nods, but Valen can see that she's only pretending to listen. Part of him wonders if she buys into what the terrorists are selling. It would explain her tone throughout this interview.

"The world was once ridden with poverty, income inequality, racism, homelessness, and lack of opportunity. People weren't free – they were slaves to governments that hampered them from reaching their full potential. The notions of liberty and self-determination have a romantic appeal but have failed throughout history. When they did, people suffered. Corporations replaced the broken nation-state system with one that works. Democratic rule and the notion of unalienable individual rights are a myth and the single greatest fraud ever perpetrated. They never existed."

"That has to be the last word because I'm afraid we are out of time. Thank you, Chief Executive Valen, for sitting with us this evening," Kassaya concludes.

"We're out," a producer bellows from off-camera as the bright lights around them dim to a comfortable level, and Kassaya offers a cold, formal thank-you.

"Excellent interview, sir," Jenizee says. "We have plenty to work with for the seven o'clock hour tomorrow morning. Do you think the administrator-general will take the bait?"

"It will depend on how the patricians react. Either way, we had nothing to lose. Kassaya went off-script. Her tone was challenging and accusatory."

"I noticed," Jenizee agrees, folding her arms. "I will talk to her about it."

Talk. It's all people do anymore. Following the Great Collapse, America Incorporated became a company of doers that built the most productive and resilient corporation in the world. Valen has tried to recapture that in his time as CEO. Employees have forgotten the hardships that previous generations had to overcome. They've grown soft and entitled, and Journalist Kassaya represents the worst of them.

"No, Jenizee, say nothing to her. Call a meeting with Public Affairs and executives from AME News. I have a new task for you."

"Certainly, sir. What do you need me to do?"

Valen grins. "Find Kassaya's replacement."

CHAPTER
SIX

LIBERTEUM

Safe House
Tribeca Geographic District
New York City Municipal Corporation

Michele hasn't spent this much time above street level in her life. It's a fascinating experience. The tinting on the window is turned to privacy mode so that she can stare at the city street below in relative safety. She wonders how strong these windows are. She's about to throw Haven through one.

Her father recruited the former ICX Security goon because of his skills as an inspector. His value comes with a downside now that Quarren is gone. Haven's a loose cannon that Michele must corral on her own. He responds only to strength, and right now, she has to summon hers before he embarks on a rampage that will ruin everything.

"Haven, you're not listening," Michele says when he finally ends his rant.

"And you've had a break from reality. How long will you stick to this ridiculous plan before realizing it isn't working?"

"What are you talking about? Archimedes is working as planned," Michele counters, wondering if he's provoking her or too stupid to understand.

"Really? We dropped the IGI by over half its value, and it's already recovered. Everyone is acting like nothing even happened. That's your plan?"

The first phase of the operation was preparatory, culminating with the attacks on Secaucus circuits. That forced Intercorpex to use their less-secure microwave transmission system so that Liberteum could intercept the data. A strategic series of subsequent explosions in Manhattan allowed Adiz and Jasper to plant fraudulent trade data on the wire. It was a means to an end. The data they accumulated for phase three will deal Intercorpex a fatal blow.

"Nobody ever said we would collapse the market in the second phase," Michele explains after a calming breath. "I'm surprised we caused as much damage as we did."

"That's why it's named after Archimedes," Adiz says, spinning around in the ergonomic executive chair he's seated in. "It took the—"

"Shut your mouth before you lose your teeth," Haven snaps.

The two men glare at each other, but Adiz is physically overmatched and lacks the fighting skills to compensate. Small in stature, confidence, and physical strength, his value is behind a computer. He isn't wrong, though. "Archimedes" was chosen as the codename for precisely that reason.

"What do you want, Haven?" Michele asks softly.

"What do you mean?"

"We're all here for the same thing. We hate what corporatism has done to this world. Liberteum was created to bring change. Everyone here signed on for that, including you."

"Don't tell me what I signed up for, Michele," Haven says, taking a threatening step toward her. "My allegiance was to Quarren."

"And his allegiance was to Liberteum and this mission. America Incorporated, Intercorpex, the patricians… none can be defeated by brute force alone."

Haven grins and shakes his head. "Violence is the only thing they fear. You can play all the computer tricks you want. It's meaningless. We're on the path to failure because you don't have what it takes to finish the job."

"We're still in the middle of the job, Haven."

"No, you had them on the ropes and let them off because you're weak. Hell, they're hailing that kid you took as some kind of hero. I should have killed him when I had the chance. Or was he part of your plan, too?"

"Part of Quarren's plan, actually," Michele says, invoking the name of the only man who commanded Haven's respect.

Michele's father compartmentalized the details of Archimedes to maintain operational security. Only three people in this safe house know the overall operation—Michele and the two hackers. Haven was only told his role, and that's all he's cared about.

"Bullshit. He was the son of the chief guardian. We should have ransomed him."

"Rykos warned us of the impending raid at the urch rave. We owe him our freedom and maybe even our lives."

Haven thrusts his jaw out and clenches his fists. "We wouldn't have gotten caught. I wouldn't have allowed it."

"You think too highly of yourself if you believe that."

"Careful," Haven says, taking another two steps toward her.

Michele pulls the knife off her belt and taps it on her hand as a reminder of the last time the two nearly came to blows back at the Broad Street Station. Haven eyes the blade but shows no signs of being intimidated.

"Remember?"

"Oh, I haven't forgotten."

A loud knock at the door interrupts their standoff and sends Adiz and Jasper scrambling for their weapons.

"Relax, guys. Damn, do you really think the PSS would bother knocking? You're late," Haven says after opening the door and sliding out of the way to let their host enter. He takes a quick peek in the hallway before closing the door, which auto-locks once shut.

"Yes, well, appearances must be maintained, and the most direct route is not the best one," Farron says, looking around their spacious digs. "Besides, I come bearing a gift."

"Is that the new sweep target list?" Jasper asks after the patrician reaches into his pocket and produces a microdrive. He answers the question with a smug look.

"Someday, you're gonna have to tell me how you're getting these," Haven muses.

"It's a trade secret." Farron hands the drive to Adiz, who inserts it into his workstation and brings up the file. "I see you guys are making the most of my old bachelor pad. I hope you're finding it comfortable."

The Tribeca section of Manhattan was once known for trendy coffee shops, overpriced retail outlets, and the city's most expensive residential real estate. Following the creation of the patrician class, many young members of esteemed families flocked here to avoid their parents' stuffy estates and bourgeoisie uptown brownstones. Farron is no different.

"Uh, Haven, you may want to look at this," Jasper says, looking over Adiz's shoulder at the display.

It takes him only a moment to identify the problem. "Half of my soldiers would've gotten caught in their dragnet."

"I'm glad the intelligence is useful, even if it was *late*," Farron responds, heavy on the sarcasm.

"I'm going to get my men out of harm's way," Haven says before turning to Michele. "We're not done with our talk. Not by a long shot."

CHAPTER SEVEN

THE PATRICIANS

Safe House
Tribeca Geographic District
New York City Municipal Corporation

Farron has a pit in his stomach as he watches Haven leave. He makes eye contact with Michele and nods toward the study when he's sure the psychopath isn't coming back. The small nook is being used as a planning room for the next phase of Archimedes. Michele follows him in and closes the door behind her.

"What's on your mind?" Michele asks.

"I was just thinking about how refreshing it is to walk into one of my old domiciles filled with terrorists dressed in urch goth clothing who would rather kill me than work with me."

Urch goth is the corporate moniker for the style of dress in the underground. Usually black, layered, and harsh, the clothing is fashioned using material from discarded corporate tunics. Michele grimaces, clearly uninterested in discussing either fashion or their violent dispositions.

"How do you know your source isn't giving us false intel?" she asks, taking a seat at the edge of the desk.

"Trust me, I know."

"Why? Because you think that woman loves you, or because your love for her blinds you?"

"I know that she loves me. I'm not blinded by anything. Are you afraid any feelings I have could compromise the mission?"

"Maybe," Michele says with a shrug.

Farron leans forward. "And what gives you the right to question me about that?"

"Because we both have a lot to lose, and you did the same thing to me after we kidnapped Rykos."

Farron nods. He avoided interacting with Liberteum to the extent possible during the first part of Archimedes. A conversation was warranted once he learned that they had the chief guardian's son chained up under Broad Street.

"You have enough to deal with. Let me worry about Fiolla. Now let me ask you a question. What were you and Haven arguing about?"

"The usual," she moans. "He wants to set New York on fire, thinking it'll be more effective than what we're doing."

"He's a rabid dog, Michele. We've known that for a while. With your father...." Farron hangs his head. "What are you going to do about him?"

"Whatever's required to keep him in line."

"*Whatever's* required? You know what that could mean. You can't let him keep challenging your authority. He doesn't respect you."

Michele scoffs, picks up a blown glass paperweight from the desk, and studies it. "Haven challenges everyone's authority. Even my father wasn't immune to that."

"You won't be able to control him with Quarren gone. Maybe it's time to cut him loose."

Michele shakes her head and gives him a stern look. "It's not that simple."

"Isn't it? I'm simply saying he has operational knowledge of Archimedes. If he goes to the PSS—"

Michele bursts out laughing. "First, he knows almost nothing about Archimedes. Second, you are drinking too much scotch in your ivory tower if you believe he would do that."

"My family didn't get to where it is by ruling anything out. My great-great-grandfather told everyone who would listen in the 2020s that the world economy was in danger of collapsing. But there is an equally terrifying scenario: Haven goes rogue and takes matters into his own hands."

"We're on the verge of starting the next phase, and we need Haven. That must be our focus, not worrying what he may or may not do."

Farron gently removes the glass ball from her hand and grips it in his own. "I know, and I agree. There are already countless variables we can't control. Not everything is bound to go our way. I need you to eliminate as many risks as possible. Haven needs to be dealt with, and now is better than later."

Michele lowers her eyes. Farron's message is getting across. She's an urch with little to lose. He's a patrician with a sizable fortune who could lose everything. They have a symbiotic relationship, but the consequences of failure are inequal.

"I'll take care of it on my timetable," Michele finally says after a long silence.

"Good enough," Farron concludes, placing the glass ball down on the desk. "I need to get back up to Greenwich. There's one thing you need to know. If Haven becomes a problem and you don't act, Narik Covington will. He won't play it so fast and loose with the fate of his family on the line."

CHAPTER
EIGHT

INTERCORPEX

Global Network Operations Center
Manhattan Financial District
ICX New York Exchange

The Board of Regents is Intercorpex's governing body and meets biweekly via secure VidLynk to discuss policy and growth. It functions similarly to a corporate board, although its members have more influence and control over the strategic direction of the exchange. Based officially in Zurich, they select the administrator-general similarly to how the Catholic Church elects a new pope. Their conclave undoubtedly has more shouting and fewer prayers.

Marggerie, Borix, and Vijai are three prominent regents on the Intercorpex board. The trio from the Russian, Indian, and French spheres of influence often agree politically but are rarely seen together due to their geographic separation. Lyris is surprised when they stroll into the NOC.

"Good morning," Lyris says as he approaches them on the NOC floor. "I apologize. I wasn't made aware that we were hosting distinguished guests today."

"That's okay, Executive Director Lyris. We didn't inform anyone that we were coming," Marggerie says, a smile making her wrinkles more pronounced. "We wanted to see things for ourselves instead of reading reports."

Since the attack, the Wall Street NOC has been a revolving door for stakeholders. Corporate CEOs, high-level executives, and countless exchange officials from headquarters and Zurich have inspected the repairs and the operation. Everything has returned to normal, except the introduction of intrusion detection safeguards to stop a recurrence of that horrible day.

"It's still a mess outside," Borix says, pointing a chubby thumb over his shoulder.

"At least they managed to fill in the massive hole in the street," Lyris says. "As you can see, we've made our repairs. Most of the damage to this facility was superficial, but there were problems with backup power—"

"We're not here to discuss the facility, Director Lyris," Vijai whispers to prevent the NOC staff from overhearing.

"Is there someplace we can speak privately?" Borix asks.

"Yes, of course. We can go to my office."

"I'm afraid that won't work either," Marggerie says with a slow shake of her head. "Let's go up on the balcony. Can you show us the way?"

Lyris nods apprehensively and escorts them past his station and the watchful eyes of Director Wyeth. They take the stairwell to the second floor and step onto the famous balcony where the bell that opens and closes the exchange is rung. The last time he was up here, Liberteum crippled their circuits in Secaucus. He's avoided coming up here ever since.

The three regents take a moment to enjoy the view. The modern network operations center doesn't have the bustle the NYSE trading posts that once occupied this space had. With the enormous displays on the walls and a cadre of dedicated men and women monitoring things below them, the NOC appears to be a well-oiled machine.

"Raimius has a listening device in your office," Borix finally offers.

"Excuse me?"

"You're being monitored, and what we are about to discuss is sensitive," he continues. "For appearances, make it seem that you're explaining the repairs to us."

Lyris does as instructed and points to the newly rebuilt windows on the east side. He feels stupid doing it.

"What did you want to discuss?"

"Raimius."

"What about him?"

The three influential decision-makers look at each other before Vijai speaks. "My colleagues tell me your relationship with him is strained."

A hundred questions flood Lyris's mind, and most of them set off alarm bells. Did Raimius send the regents here to test his loyalty? Did Denali Keating, for the same reason? Can they be trusted? Is this a trap?

"Let me speak plainly. Momentum is building to remove Raimius as administrator-general and replace him with someone more reliable."

"More reliable or more malleable?" Lyris asks Vijai, eliciting grins from the three regents in return. "How much momentum?"

"We're only a few votes away from sending him to sip piña coladas on a desolate beach in the Caribbean Corporation," Borix answers with a wry smile.

There is no set term for the leader of Intercorpex. Once chosen, an administrator-general can hold the position for life or be replaced after a month. Some AGs have maintained long, healthy relationships with the Board of Regents, and others haven't. Modern leadership is a political dance where the music never stops, and the partner who tires first loses. Raimius is fading fast.

"What do you need from me?"

"Your support when we make a move. Several regents don't need to be swayed. Several are ardent supporters of Raimius, for whatever reason. The rest are sitting on the fence with their finger in the wind."

"I'm not sure how anything I could say would matter," Lyris says, still fuzzy about their request.

"You're the executive director of global operations and were awarded the Intercorpex Service Cross. Your opinion carries incredible weight," Marggerie explains.

Lyris smiles weakly. He is only the third person to receive that highest honor. It must have killed Raimius to hang that medal around his neck. Now he realizes that the regents may have insisted on the award for this reason and not for his actions that fateful day.

"You want to use me as leverage."

"We want you to lend your voice to the proceedings," Borix explains.

Lyris turns and gestures around the NOC. He needs to organize his thoughts. There is too much at stake if he's wrong about their intentions.

"You risked a lot coming to me with this. I'm more than Raimius's operations director. I'm his right-hand man. He trusts me."

"If that were true, he wouldn't have bugged your office. He doesn't trust you, Lyris, and you know it," Borix says, turning his attention to the displays on the opposite end of the NOC floor. "Raimius is a paranoid tyrant who needs to control everything and everyone. How long before you're a threat he can no longer ignore? We're offering you a solution to that problem."

"You're not offering anything. I've already been granted the privilege of becoming a patrician when my Intercorpex service ends. What more do I need?"

The regents smile at each other.

"Patrician status is a great honor, but to enjoy the perks, you must have wealth. It's no fun being in the bottom ranks of the *gentez-minorez*," Marggerie says. "We have benefactors that can make your support…let's say, worth *your* weight in gold. We can even arrange an early release from Intercorpex service to enjoy it."

Lyris does some more pointing and gesturing. When he accepted Denali Keating's offer, it was because he offered something otherwise unattainable – Raimius's job. Regents have always selected the administrator-general from their ranks despite no policy specifying it. Denali wants to break that tradition. There's no doubt one of these regents has designs on Raimius's office, and they're ready to move. Lyris wonders what Denali is waiting for.

"What do you need me to do?"

"We'll be in touch," Marggerie says, a satisfied smile creeping across her lips. "Good job on the repairs, by the way."

"For obvious reasons, this conversation never happened," Borix adds, with a stern look of warning after Lyris nods goodbye to Vijai. "Your discretion is expected."

"I understand completely. You'll have it."

The three regents depart, and Lyris leans against the railing. The meeting was an unexpected development, and he will uphold his promise of discretion, at least insofar as telling Raimius is concerned. His other benefactor is another story entirely. Denali will be keenly interested to hear what was said.

CHAPTER
NINE

AMERICA, INC.

Underground North of Grand Central Terminus
Midtown Geographic District
New York City Municipal Corporation

The PSS has conducted dozens of underground sweeps and hasn't located a single terrorist or uncovered a clue about their location. The guardians are getting frustrated, and Teman's superiors, from Chief Executive Safmor on up, are getting impatient. Even the chief guardian's optimism is waning.

"I feel good about this one, boss," Captain Spirak says in a hushed voice.

"What makes you think it will be any different than the other raids?"

"A gut feeling. I think this is the one that changes our fortunes."

"Let's hope so. Deploy the microdrones," Teman commands.

The smaller, faster, modular drones are shiny new toys lent from the BCS. They can land in the palm of someone's hand, be outfitted with different sensor suites, are maneuverable in tight spaces, and are whisper-quiet. Teman knows that they're not the top-of-the-line equipment stashed away in corporate security's inventory, but it's better than anything they have.

"Microdrones away," the captain relays, intently watching his portable display. "All teams report with a final equipment check."

Teman turns his head to the grainy helmet cam feeds on the tactical displays as the forward-most team does as instructed. Each guardian is outfitted with body armor, ballistic head protection, ear defenders against sonic weaponry, throat mics with burst radio transmitters for communications, standard night vision, thermal and infrared goggle sets, and automatic rifles.

"Drone now fifty meters forward and approaching the target area off the rail siding. No contacts."

Track Sixty-One is a unique rail line leading out of Grand Central closed to the public long before the Great Collapse. United States President Franklin D. Roosevelt used to enter the Waldorf-Astoria Hotel from it during visits to the city. When

Grand Central was reconstructed during New York's first revitalization project, the old line and rusting train car were left in place. It's become a popular transit line for urches in the years since.

"What's that?" Teman asks, pointing at the thick concrete lip raised above ground level on the screen. As the drone approaches it, he sees that it's much more than just a poured slab.

"I…don't…know. It looks like stairs to a sublevel," Spirak says, cocking his head to study the display. "Old ones."

"Old, but recently used. Look at the treads. The layer of dust has been disturbed."

Spirak nods. That's good enough for him. "Alpha and Bravo teams, be advised that we have possible confirmation of an active site sixty meters to your front. Stand by for instructions."

"Send that to the RTCC for analysis," the chief guardian orders. "I want to know where those stairs lead. In the meantime, send a drone down there."

"Roger that."

The technician pilots the drone cautiously down the stairwell, avoiding the walls that would destroy the rotors and render it inoperable. Instead of a corridor, there is an open space at the bottom. The pilot spins the drone around the blackness and fires up the infrared to enhance the night vision.

"Chief Guardian, RTCC. We have no record of any access in that area. We'll keep digging through the archives to see if we can uncover something."

"Acknowledged."

Teman closes his eyes. With so many records and blueprints destroyed during the collapse, he isn't surprised that nothing was found. Still, something feels wrong about this.

"Chief Guardian, we have a problem. There's a cement block wall."

"What?"

Teman strains to see their cameras on the small tactical display. He misses the command truck, despite it not being practical in these circumstances. It's hard to catch terrorists if they know you're in the area, and that thing is unmistakable.

"Any sign of activity?"

"Nothing on thermal, infrared, or night vision. Should we hit the lights? It's low risk."

The micro LEDs on the drone can provide illumination despite its small size from an intense light beam. It will also advertise its presence to anyone down there.

"Low risk, but not no risk. I'm not going to make assumptions. Send two men from Alpha forward to investigate. Tell them to do it quietly."

"Roger."

Teman watches their feeds as they stealthily move through the darkness. One man provides security as the other surveys the area. Satisfied, they retreat up the stairs and down the train tunnel.

"Chief guardian, that wall doesn't look like part of the original structure. Someone erected it and installed a door."

"I don't care how it was built. Is it rigged?"

"We don't see any sign of booby traps. I think we heard sounds in the room."

Teman takes a deep breath. This is it. He tries to temper his enthusiasm but can't help himself. Maybe Spirak was right after all.

"Captain, move your men into position."

"Alpha team, prepare for entry. Charlie team, forward with the breaching gear. Bravo team, pull rear security."

The three teams of guardians move forward through the tunnel and down the stairs, careful not to scrape the walls.

"Prepping breach," the team leader says.

One of the guardians applies a thick silver bead of foam to the doorframe from a cylinder on his back. The plastic explosive will cut sheer through the steel in a nanosecond. A second charge is applied to the center of the door and will ignite a millisecond later. Battering rams are last century technology.

"Entry team ready. Breach, breach, breach."

The explosion blasts the door out of its frame. The team launches countermeasure grenades through the gaping hole in the wall to stun anyone inside. The bright light and piercing sound they emit disorients anyone not wearing protective optics and ear defenders.

The team crashes into the room, and Teman expects to hear gunfire. For a long moment, there is only the sound of silence.

"Clear!"

"Clear!"

"Clear!"

"You have to be kidding me," the chief guardian moans.

"Command, the room is secure. Chief Guardian, you need to see this."

When Teman arrives, the men have the room's lights flipped on. They are not hastily rigged construction lighting. They're fluorescent lights probably original to some pre-collapse building.

The rectangular, roughly thousand-square-foot space has empty industrial-strength metal storage racks along the walls and some rickety old office furniture. Trash litters the floor, and Teman angrily kicks an empty container across the room.

Captain Spirak walks over to an arms rack along the back wall and pulls the lone rifle out of it. It was left here for a reason. He verifies that no round is chambered and hands it to the chief guardian.

"Brand new, sir."

"That explains how they're so well-armed. This is a munitions plant."

The ambient noise comes from an old stereo system located on the industrial shelving along the wall and wired into the building's power supply. The recording makes it sound like people are talking and moving around. Teman begins to walk over to silence the infernal sounds when a guardian signals him to the center of the room.

"Chief Guardian, take a look at this. Heavy machinery was recently removed, from the looks of these scratches," he says, tracing the gouges on the floor with his fingers.

"I'm betting they were 3D printers," Teman mumbles. "Pre-collapse industrial ones. Somehow the terrorists found a few and managed to get them working."

"From where?" Spirak asks.

"I'm sure you can find just about anything in the bowels of this city, Captain. They could have produced thousands of weapons down here. We could be facing an army that we can't even find."

Alpha and Charlie team guardians stand around, dejected. The past week has been hard on everyone. They're the ones risking their lives crawling through the underbelly of this city every day without any measurable results. There's nothing Teman can say to them to boost morale.

"Move them out, Captain. And kill that stereo."

"You heard the chief guardian. Move out. Sergeant, turn that recording off."

Teman takes one last look at the room. Liberteum couldn't have gone too far with this equipment. It's big, bulky, and heavy.

The stereo clicks off, and a loud noise fills Teman's head as his ear defenders kick in. The oxygen is sucked out of his lungs as he's blown off his feet. He lands hard on the concrete floor and chokes on the smoke and dust permeating the room.

Bravo team rushes in and drags their leader out of the makeshift factory. He's brought back up the stairs and laid alongside the tracks above. Most of the men return to help their wounded comrades.

"Are you okay, Chief Guardian?" the Bravo team leader asks.

"I'm fine," he says between coughs. "See to your men."

Medics begin arriving from down the tracks to treat the wounded. Some are only battered and bruised. Others have more severe injuries and are immediately evacuated.

"What's the count?" Teman asks Captain Spirak when he sits down next to him.

"One sergeant is dead, and three others are seriously injured. The rest of us have lacerations, bruises, and concussions. It could have been worse."

Teman closes his eyes and rubs his forehead. "It took a lot of effort to get that machinery out of there. Then they made a recording to make it sound like the room was occupied and rigged the stereo with explosives. Why would you do that if you were them?"

"Sir?"

"They knew we were coming, Spirak. Someone is tipping them off."

"Who would do that?"

Teman shakes his head. "I don't know. We need to revise our plan and adapt to a terrifying new reality."

"What reality is that?" he asks as Teman struggles to his feet.

"One where Liberteum has infiltrated America Incorporated."

CHAPTER
TEN

INTERCORPEX

ICX Administrative Annex
Zurich Banking & Commerce Center
Switzerland

Zyree walks into the Intercorpex Administrative Annex that once served as Zurich's Rathaus, or local town hall. The modest box-shaped, gray, four-story structure that's foundation sits in the Limmat River is the birthplace of the world's only stock exchange. It is one of the world's few government buildings that survived unscathed when governments collapsed.

Intercorpex outgrew the structure and moved its operations to the former site of the United Nations, but this building is still its spiritual home. It is also the base of operations for ICX Security. Technically speaking, this is also Zyree's home, although his duties require extensive travel. Inspectors often forgo anchors like a permanent residence or a family.

A pleasant administrative assistant shows him into the office of the commissioner-general. Plucked from the ranks of the chief inspectors, the CG is more bureaucrat than a security professional. Most of the good inspectors are passed over for the job. Jurghen is an exception.

Lured away from the ranks of the *Unternehmenssicherheit*, the German equivalent to America's Bureau of Corporate Security, Jurghen was a brilliant chief inspector. He plays the political game, but not as adeptly as the previous men who sat behind this desk.

"*Guten tag*, Commissioner-General. *Veritatem et honorem.*"

"Zyree! *Fratres in armis. Kommst du rein,*" the German says, clearly pleased that the chief inspector addressed him in his native tongue.

"*Danke.*"

In his mid-fifties and completely bald, Jurghen has intelligent brown eyes behind thick, black-framed glasses. He is a throwback that values grunt work, doesn't rely on technology, and still believes in antiquated concepts like honor and integrity. Surprisingly, he ascended to such an important position by adhering to those principles. He's also one of the few people Zyree is willing to trust.

"Congratulations on earning the Medal of Gallantry, Zyree. I didn't ever think they would award one of those. I wish I could have made it to New York for the presentation."

"Thank you, sir."

"I trust your flight from Paris was good?"

"Air travel is always brutal on my body," Zyree says, careful to avoid outright lying to him in case Ortan isn't as good as he thinks he is.

"Excellent. Did you get a chance to read the communiqués I sent you about the patricians?"

"That they're building personal security forces? Yes, I've read them."

The reports were dismissive of their impact, but some of the more powerful families command forces outnumbering the militaries of small countries before the collapse. Nothing in the Zurich Canon forbids them from having them, although none of the drafters ever thought there would be a need.

"The patricians claim they are simply a deterrent," Jurghen says, plucking an old baseball off his desk and spinning it in his hand.

"Since when does a patrician invest in something they don't expect to return a dividend? You aren't afraid of a war between the elites?"

"I wasn't until recently," the CG says, leaning back in his chair. "The rhetoric between the *gentez-majorez* and *gentez-minorez* has become increasingly heated. If it continues unchecked, I fear somebody will do something stupid."

Various corporate media outlets have reported that the different classes of patricians are blaming each other for the attacks on ICX in New York. Each accuses the other of conspiring with Liberteum to use targeted attacks to damage the other's ability to conduct trades. How long before one of the families decides to retaliate?

"Is my next assignment to investigate the patricians?"

"I don't think that would be a good idea," Jurghen admits. "You're my best chief inspector, but you lack the required political skills to deal with the elites. I don't need Raimius breathing down my neck because you're pissing off the patricians. I'm sending you back to New York to assist America Incorporated in eradicating Liberteum."

Zyree checks for deception in the hopes that he's joking. He isn't. Lyris made it clear that he never again wants to see him in New York. There's no way he made that request.

"I don't think you summoned me to Zurich only to catch a plane back to New York. That wasn't the assignment you were planning to issue, was it?"

Jurghen stares at him. "It's the assignment I'm giving you."

Biological computers interface with ICX systems to provide a constant information stream on a pair of contact lenses. They have real-time analytic abilities, like determining deception based on a subject's voice and body language. The unemotional response is meant to defeat Zyree's voice stress analyzer. Jurghen may be old school, but he knows how their technology works. Zyree has something that can't be beaten: instincts.

"Based on whose orders?"

The CG straightens in his chair at the challenge to his authority. "Does it matter? I expect you to do your duty with the same proficiency that earned you the medal Raimius hung around your neck."

"The search for Liberteum is an America Incorporated issue," Zyree argues.

"Is it? I read your report. Most inspectors would have been thumping their chests at stopping a major attack on the exchange. Your tone was…muted."

Zyree's report on the incident was detailed, minus a few items he chose not to include. Details about the missing work orders, Rykos's involvement with the group, and suspicions about what Liberteum was doing in that subway station were omitted. He fully expects the terrorists to attack again but couldn't state that in the official record.

"Sir, I think there are—"

"You're going, Zyree. It's not a suggestion. Given the sensitivity of the mission and your reluctance, I'm assigning you some company. That's also not open for discussion."

"Who?"

"Chief Inspector Chiana."

"Please tell me you're kidding," Zyree moans. "Is this some sort of sick German joke?"

Everything has an opposite – yin and yang, good and evil, night and day… and she is his. Notoriously stiff and by the book, their styles are diametrically opposed. It's a match made in hell.

Chiana conducts many of the Far East operations for Intercorpex Security. Her beauty is only surpassed by her ruthless desire to occupy Jurghen's chair. She ruthlessly maneuvers for every promotion to ensure that will someday happen.

"We have no sense of humor in my part of the fatherland. Chiana is more than capable, and everyone else is on assignment."

"The woman despises me."

"*Everyone* despises you, Zyree," Jurghen says with a devilish grin. "Consider her an angel to sit on your right shoulder. You already have the devil perched on the left one."

"Commissioner-General, chief inspectors are never assigned to the same mission. When did that change?"

"When I posted the orders two hours ago for Chiana to meet you in New York. Now, if there's nothing further...."

The look he gives Zyree through his thick eyeglasses is a direct challenge to continue the argument that only a fool would accept.

"No, sir," Zyree says. *Veritatem et honorem.*"

"Report in when you get to New York and make contact with Chiana. *Fratres in armis.* And Zyree? Try to stay out of trouble."

Zyree nods and makes his way out of the office, wondering what just happened. Not only was Jurghen's behavior bizarre, but his willingness to flout established security protocols is unprecedented. None of that matters. His mind is made up, leaving Zyree no choice but to fly across the Atlantic so he can get this over with.

CHAPTER ELEVEN

REGISTRANT RYKOS

Chief Guardian Teman's Domicile
Upper West Side Geographic District
New York City Municipal Corporation

Career Day is the most critical moment in a registrant's life. Its significance ranks ahead of marriage and having children. What happens today is the culmination of every educational endeavor since elementary school and will set the course for the rest of my life.

I remember my sister's well. My parents hosted a party for friends and family as Varella paced back and forth, checking the clock every ten seconds. Career Day is traditionally the Friday before Sunday's commencement ceremony and is when graduating registrants learn how the next chapter of their life will read.

For Varella, it was nerve-racking. For me, what's about to happen is a foregone conclusion. My status as a hero of the corporation means the Ivy League schools all lobbied human resources to secure my attendance. The only question to be settled is which institution won the battle.

Our Upper West Side residence is filled with family, close friends, and people my father works with. Several of my mother's former colleagues have also joined us. My father isn't here, of course. He helped arrange every detail of my sister's Career Day but can't be bothered to attend mine.

The relief of saving his only son from the clutches of deadly terrorists lasted about two days. I can't help but wonder what his priorities are. The CEO of New York City doesn't share the duties keeping my father preoccupied. Chief Executive Safmor is one of our distinguished guests, and he's spending more time talking to my mother than my father does.

"You know I was on the fast track before I got pregnant with Varella," my mother informs him in our dining room as I slide into earshot. "You know what skills I bring to the table. I would be an asset to your office."

"I know you would, and believe me, I would love to have you. But you've been out of the corporate world for a while. I'm afraid installing you in such a lofty position would be viewed as favoritism," Safmor says.

"It would look like a shrewd executive decision given what's going on in this corporation. I'm not asking for an immediate decision, Chief Executive Safmor. Think about your needs and whether I would be the strong voice from your office that people can trust during these trying times."

"I'll give it some thought," he assures her before she turns and notices me standing here.

The CEO is about to launch into a stale congratulatory oration when the elevator doors open at the other end of the domicile. The lone occupant glides into the foyer like medieval royalty. I almost expect the Maester to blare trumpets over the sound system, followed by an old rendition of *"God Save the Queen."* Undergraduate Varella has returned to the castle.

My sister would be the archetype if America Incorporated could ever figure out how to clone executives. Varella is physically fit, intelligent, armed with natural business savvy, and fits the corporate image perfectly. She's also as cold as ice. For her, relationships are only useful if they provide her unequal value in return. That's why I don't have much of one with my older sibling.

"Well, you are quite the celebrity around here, aren't you, *little brother*?" She sneers. "A true, genuine corporate hero."

"It's so good to see you too, *sister*," I fire back. "Although I'm surprised you came down off Mount Olympus just for me."

"Mother made me come," she says. I give her a cynical look. "All right, father insisted on it. I'm not sure why since there won't be much excitement surrounding your Career Day."

"What's in it for you? Father's pleading wouldn't have been enough to compel you to come here."

"You're right. I'll be spending the summer semester working for the Office of Corporate Affairs in the America Tower and wanted to stop in to introduce myself. The internship was one of the most highly coveted internships Harvard offered. I'm the one who earned it."

And there it is. "Good for you. You must be quite a *hero* up there, then," I say with a beaming smile. I may detest my sister, but I'll never say that she isn't sharp. She got the implication immediately.

Varella drops her bubbly façade. "You're not Ivy League material, Rykos. You never were."

"And yet I'm still attending one of them," I point out, forcing her to acknowledge the inconvenient truth.

"You never would have gotten admitted based on your grades and attitude. You're getting accepted because you were lucky, not because you earned it."

"I accomplished more for this corporation than you probably ever will," I say, fighting to control my temper given the stature of our esteemed guests. "It doesn't matter how I got into the Ivy League, only that I did."

The elevator doors open, and a uniformed messenger materializes in the foyer. He looks around at the crowd and then back to the tablet with the hardened, industrial-strength case in his right hand.

"Good afternoon, everyone. I'm looking for Registrant Rykos."

"That's me," I say, abandoning my sister as the crowd in the living room parts.

"Please scan your thumb here," he says, which I do until the small LED light turns green when the verification completes.

"Here you go," the messenger says, presenting me with the scroll. "Happy Career Day. Good luck."

In a world reliant on digital communications, this is one of the few messages still written with ink on paper. The scroll is sealed with wax pressed with America Incorporated's logo. It's a document that most parents frame and then hang on a wall. Varella's scroll is in the hallway leading to the bedrooms.

Under different circumstances, I would be terrified by its contents. Despite knowing my future is secure, I still take a deep breath and exhale it slowly as I trace a finger over the seal. I pinch the wax between my fingers and squeeze, splitting it down the middle with a distinctive crack.

The Ivy League universities train the executive managers for the parent company. Their graduates will never do grunt work – they are the leaders of their fields. Each of the eight schools has a primary discipline. For Harvard, it's business leadership; Yale promotes corporate law; Pennsylvania has a world-class international trade program, and Princeton fosters brilliant engineers. Cornell has a renowned pre-med institute; Brown focuses on business operations, Dartmouth is well-regarded for its economics, and Columbia for the sciences.

I unroll the scroll as everyone watches. It's not a memo or other generic business document. It looks like it was hand-written by a monk during the Middle Ages. The word in the center is unmistakable.

"Harvard."

"Congratulations, Rykos! I knew you could do it," Mother says, hugging me.

The mood in the room becomes instantly festive at my announcement. Varella only offers a couple of polite claps and a scowl. I always thought we were competitive with each other growing up. I was wrong. Our rivalry is only just beginning.

CHAPTER TWELVE

LIBERTEUM

Safe House
Tribeca Geographic District
New York City Municipal Corporation

Haven isn't a big guy but is giant compared to the two mousy hackers. When he violently swings the door open to the safe house and storms out, the two men are unfortunate enough to be entering. Haven flattens Adiz and effortlessly shoves Jasper out of the way before heading for the stairs.

Jasper recovers and helps a stunned Adiz back to his feet. They shuffle in and turn to Michele, who's watching from the kitchen.

"What the hell was that about?" Jasper asks.

"Haven being Haven. We lost the Foundry in a raid. He's upset over it."

"I didn't raid it. Why did he take it out on me?" Adiz grumbles as he walks over to the workstation in the corner.

"Did they get our weapons?" Jasper asks, apparently less bothered by Haven's behavior than his counterpart is.

"Haven distributed them to caches throughout the city," Michele says, moving to the living room sofa and taking a seat.

"Any casualties?"

"None. Haven knew that the PSS was coming, thanks to Farron's information. Not that he offered any thanks for it."

"What about theirs?"

"Same answer," she says with a smirk that turns into a frown. She'd be surprised if he didn't leave some small present for them. "It'd be out of character, wouldn't it?"

"Then why's he so upset?" Adiz asks, spinning around in his chair. "He almost killed me on the way out."

"Haven's sentimental. He loved that place. Now he wants to ambush the PSS as payback. I gave him a laundry list of reasons why that was a horrible idea. He didn't take it well."

"Clearly," Adiz mutters.

"Michele, he's becoming a problem," Jasper warns.

Michele stares at her hands. She knows that the hacker is right, just as Farron was. What can she do? Like it or not, she needs Haven. They are sitting ducks against the PSS without him and his men to protect them. The problem is, Haven knows that, too. It's only a matter of time before he decides to dictate terms.

"I don't expect Haven to understand Archimedes, much less support it, but he will. We share the same goal."

"You want to kill everyone, too?" Adiz asks, picking up the argument. "Because that's what he's about. You're fooling yourself if you think otherwise."

"He made a promise to my father."

"Quarren is dead. That promise died with him."

It was a callous comment. Michele hasn't had the chance to mourn her father's death. He was the only family she had, and his loss has created a hole in her life that may never be filled. Despite the pain his words brought, there is truth in them. It's nothing she wants to face right now.

"Do you have everything you need here for the next phase?"

"Yeah. These rigs that Farron bought are faster than anything we have," Jasper says, stroking his fingers over the new computer like he's petting a cat.

Soldiers have their rifles. Employees have their tablets. Rescue teams have their trucks. Hackers have their computers. They are prized possessions that are treated like The Crown Jewels.

"The bandwidth is also better, but we're very exposed here," Adiz says, restating the same complaint he's had since they arrived here following the evacuation of Broad Street Station. "I still don't understand why we aren't doing this from the safety of Valhalla. The PSS is locking down this city. There's no escape for us if things go south."

"They're focusing their efforts on the underground. We're safer here than anywhere else," Michele says, prompting Jasper to give her a confused look. "I know…it's counter-intuitive."

"They'll notice the massive increase in data usage," Adiz whines. "There's no disguising it."

"Farron is a high patrician, and everyone fears his father. They won't question anything he does. By the time they have cause under the Zurich Canon to search his premises, it'll be too late."

"Yeah, but that will implicate the Keatings, won't it?" Jasper asks.

Michele grins. "It won't matter if we succeed."

"No, I guess it won't. We need to perform some tests before we launch the second phase," Jasper says. "We need a trading account."

"Farron says we can use one of his father's. We can also use one of Shalius Covington's if a second test is needed," Michele says, having worked the logistics earlier.

"Speaking of our benefactor, where is Farron?"

"At their Greenwich estate. He'll be back tomorrow afternoon. He may want us to do a test when he returns. Make sure everything is ready."

"You got it."

Michele rises from the sofa and retires into the bedroom. She has a headache, thanks to constant quibbling with Haven. They are at a critical point...and a dangerous one. What happens in the next seventy-two hours could determine the fate of their movement. And their lives.

CHAPTER THIRTEEN

AMERICA, INC.

The America Tower
Manhattan Financial Geographic District
New York City Municipal Corporation

Teman's first time here was a bad experience. This isn't shaping up to be any better. He stares out one of the floor-to-ceiling windows of the America Tower, wondering how he will break the bad news to executives unforgiving of failure. It's his first duty, and one that comes with sacrifice. Not that he expects Rykos to understand why he's missing Career Day.

Varella always understood when he was absent for birthday parties and school events. She understands obligation, while Rykos has always been more selfish. He thinks everybody owes him something. The world doesn't work that way.

Thanks to the stars aligning at just the right time, his son's acceptance to the Ivy League is assured. He would never have gotten in with his abysmal marks alone. A true hero of the corporation will take his rightful place among the corporate executives in the parent company. Teman can't decide whether he thinks Rykos deserves that title, regardless of what the White House and AME News might say.

"They'll be ready for you in a few moments, Chief Guardian," the receptionist says.

"Thank you."

Teman's wrist tablet chirps, and he looks down at the display. It's a simple one-word message from Ilaria: *HARVARD*. Wow, his children are two for two. Any parent rarely gets to send a child to the Ivy League, let alone two attending the same school.

"They're ready for you. You can go on in."

The big doors leading to Chief Executive Valen's office ominously swing open.

"Come over and take a seat, Chief Guardian Teman," Valen says from the head of the conference table.

This is a C- and D-level meeting, meaning the titles of the people around the table begin with those letters. Along with Chief Executive Valen are New York's chief operations officer and director of Urban Development, Director Virtari of the BCS, Executive Fiolla of Corporate Affairs, and the chief information and Public Affairs officers from America Incorporated. Safmor is nowhere to be found.

"Teman, you know why we're here," Valen says as the chief guardian takes his seat. "It's been almost two weeks since the attacks, and you've yet to catch a single terrorist. Your city-wide dragnet has some holes in it."

"Sir—"

Valen holds up a hand to stop Virtari. "I'm not here to pass blame, but we need results. What percentage of the city has been swept so far, Teman?"

"Thirty-seven percent of the island of Manhattan has been fully swept."

"That's it?"

"Sir, we are searching every basement, sewer, and old subway line on the island. There are fifty thousand structures in Manhattan and over three-quarters of a million in the five boroughs that make up the city. Each one of them needs to be searched."

"Is it possible Liberteum is hiding in Brooklyn or Queens?" the director of Urban Development asks.

"It can't be ruled out. For now, we're focusing on Manhattan. It offers the most hiding places and transit options."

"How many personnel have you dedicated to the effort?" Valen asks.

"Over seventy-five percent of my force is tasked with the mission. Those protecting the population are working double shifts to cover."

"Is the BCS assisting?" Fiolla asks, probably wondering if the two rival organizations are playing nice with each other.

"We are," Virtari chimes in, eager to control the conversation. "We have focused on cutting off means of travel underground. Tunnels are monitored with motion, video, and thermal sensors. We're confident that we have locked down all main transit options on the island and have Liberteum isolated."

"Unfortunately, that isn't entirely accurate."

"What do you mean?" Virtari asks, vitriol dripping from his voice as all eyes focus on the chief guardian.

"Technicians conducting an audit of our systems following the hack at our EOC made a disturbing discovery. Liberteum possesses coded transponders that allow them to move around the city in vehicles without scrutiny."

The room bursts into a firestorm of yelling and accusations aimed at Teman. He remains stoic in the face of withering verbal assaults, knowing nothing will make the truth more palatable.

"I find it inconceivable that an *urch* hacker compromised your EOC, to begin with," Virtari spews.

"The hacker's name was Freya, and she was a highly trained computer programmer for the German corporation before being purchased by Intercorpex. She worked on Wall Street and specialized in intrusion detection. That urch was capable of hacking any system in this corporation, including yours, Director Virtari."

"She would never get access to *our* facility, Chief Guardian."

"Enough," Valen decrees. "Explain these transponders to me."

"Sir, to maintain positive control of the vehicles, the city uses transponders that sync with a database monthly," the director of Urban Development explains. "If there's a match, a code is sent to the vehicle that authorizes its use for the month. An array of sensors throughout the city monitors these signals, especially on major avenues and river crossings. When a vehicle fails transponder code authentication, the vehicle is disabled with a kill command, and the PSS is called to investigate."

"So, you're telling me that known terrorists could be moving around freely on surface streets?" Valen asks.

"They would still have to avoid drones and static video monitoring," Virtari interjects, "but it's possible. We instituted facial recognition, thermal, and infrared monitoring with our enhanced security measures at the river crossings. They may be able to travel around the island, but they can't leave undetected."

Valen frowns, clearly finding Virtari's posturing annoying. The director of the BCS wields an incredible amount of power, so his grandstanding is tolerated. At least to a point.

"Chief Executive, the PSS is—"

"Riddled with shortcomings and a lack of experience," Virtari says, interrupting Fiolla. It's time to revisit the conversation about the BCS assuming control of the hunt for Liberteum."

The table erupts in a cacophony of grumbling and side conversations before waning to a hollow silence. Teman knows it's getting harder to justify not ceding control to Virtari. He also knows what that will mean for the city's employees, qulis, and even urches. It would yield dramatic short-term results and long-term ramifications nobody can foresee.

"I need results, Virtari, not body bags. Are you going to argue that BCS tactics aren't heavy-handed? Is your recollection of what happened during the Catharsis that fuzzy?"

Harsh corporate edicts in the early 2050s led to thousands of employees fleeing the strict controls of their jobs for a life on the streets. Dirty and dressed in rags, the name "urchin" began to be used with greater frequency until shortened colloquially to "urch." Executive action was taken when a group of them savagely beat the CEO of Boston.

Catharsis is an old Greek word meaning "the purification and purgation of emotions—especially pity and fear." The Bureau of Corporate Security spearheaded a vast operation to apprehend the urches and summarily execute them. Tens of thousands were murdered in only a few weeks.

"Those were desperate times, Executive Valen," Virtari retorts, muffing his title on purpose.

"*Chief* Executive Valen, and yes, they were. So are these. I'm not going to sanction a repeat of those dark days."

"Rounding up and killing every urch and every employee who supports them is the only way to put an end to Liberteum once and for all," Virtari argues.

"And murdering untold thousands of people in the process."

"This is a security issue, Fiolla. You're speaking out of place."

"What place is that, Director? The kitchen? I'm sitting at this table, same as you."

"Don't delude yourself into thinking that makes us equals."

"I would never confuse us for equals, Director. But I don't mind you staying anyway."

The snarky comment elicits some snickers around the table.

"We're getting away from the point of this meeting," Valen says. "Our security sweeps are not seeing results, and I'm no closer to understanding why."

"Simple," Teman says after a prolonged silence. "There's a leak. Liberteum is being passed information."

Virtari gives Teman a death glare that the chief guardian returns as Fiolla stares at the table.

"Chief Guardian Teman, if there's a leak, it's coming from the PSS. Chief Executive Valen, I must insist that the BCS assume command of this operation."

"Director Virtari, this is already a joint venture between our two organizations," Teman points out. "Public safety is charged with protecting the employees of this city, and Liberteum is their biggest threat. If someone is sharing information with them, it's not us."

"He's right," Fiolla says to everyone's surprise. "It's most likely coming from within the BCS."

"Young lady, you'd better think long and hard about the accusation you're leveling," the director warns.

"Sir," she says, ignoring Virtari and turning to Valen, "the BCS has been angling to assume command since the attack on the exchange. It's not inconceivable that intelligence is being passed into the underground in an attempt to make the PSS look bad—"

"You're out of line!"

"We've been through that already, Director. If you can't remember, check your notes."

Valen raises both hands to shoulder height to command silence. Virtari looks like he's about to explode.

"From this point forward, all operational details are restricted on a need-to-know only basis to critical personnel. If that doesn't solve our problem, I'll enact stricter measures. In the meantime, I want a top-down investigation of both your organizations and all anomalies reported to my office. Questions?"

Heads shake. Valen has spoken, and the discussion is over once he issues his orders. Executives who violate that simple principle do so at their own risk.

"That's all."

* * *

The group rises and begins exiting the office. Valen makes his way over to his desk without lingering for post-meeting chats. Chief Guardian Teman wastes no time in heading straight for the door. Fiolla is about to beat a hasty retreat when she's grabbed and escorted into the outer office.

"What do you think you were doing in there?" Virtari asks, pointing his crooked finger at Fiolla's face.

"My job."

"Oh, really? I didn't realize Corporate Affairs concerned themselves with security operations. I'm sure Valen appreciates the insights from his lap dog. You'd better hope that's always the case. Someday, it might not be."

"Director, you almost sound like you're advocating for his removal. That's dangerously close to subversion."

"Do you know the difference between a subversive and a devotee? Timing. You made a huge mistake in that meeting, Fiolla," Virtari says with a devious smile that sends a shiver down her spine. "You made an enemy out of me."

CHAPTER FOURTEEN

INTERCORPEX

Bettancourt International Airport
Ozone-Rockaway Geographic District
American Air Transit Corporation

Modern air transportation rarely experiences delays. There are fewer flights and aircraft competing for slots at airports and far less security for travelers to deal with than existed before the collapse. So long as the weather cooperates, there's little chance of not arriving at the appointed time.

Zyree departs the airliner as soon as it pulls up to the gate. Once known as John F. Kennedy International, Bettancourt was redesigned using a mix of new and existing structures to meet the needs of modern air travel. He hustles past displays espousing the merits of America Incorporated in what he refers to as "Propaganda Hall" as he heads into the arrivals area to find his new partner.

"Chief Inspector Zyree," Chiana says from behind him, bowing slightly once he wheels around to face her. "*Veritatem et honorem.*"

Chiana is beautiful, athletic, intelligent, and deadly. She's called "the ninja" by inspectors in ICX Security for her appearance and fighting ability. Skills aside, she is better known for her political savvy and ability to outmaneuver and destroy her enemies before they know what hit them. That's what made her one of the youngest chief inspectors in history.

"*Fratres in armis.*" Zyree doesn't bother returning the bow.

"It will be a pleasure to work with you on this operation. Congratulations on earning the Medal of Gallantry…very impressive."

"Thanks. Did you just arrive?"

"I've been here for a couple of hours."

"All right. Let's go."

"You're heading the wrong way, Zyree. I noticed that you didn't arrange transportation to ICX headquarters so I took the liberty. It's waiting at the other end of the terminal."

Zyree smirks and keeps walking. This one's a real go-getter. "We're not taking that car because we aren't going to headquarters."

"Chief Inspector, Security Field Operations SOP, Section One, Paragraph Seven, Subparagraph B-9 requires us to check in once we arrive at a location," Chiana says, hurrying to catch up to him.

"I don't care about protocol."

Chiana rushes ahead and stops him with a hand against his chest. "I'm afraid I must insist."

Zyree hears a chirp in his ear and sees Malkor's request for secure video. His timing is perfect.

"Connect," Zyree says. "What's the word, Malkor?"

"I have his biojack position courtesy of Bird's Nest's willingness to hack into the PSS again. He's at a Midtown restaurant."

Zyree smiles, happy that the ridiculous moniker stuck. The kid looked like he didn't know how a comb worked. Tsinnial is a network engineer assigned to the NOC and worked with him following the Secaucus attack. He was one of the few people not reporting his activities back to Lyris.

"Nice work, Malkor. Keep me posted on his location."

"Is the ninja with you?" he asks.

"For now," Zyree says, disconnecting the VidLynk.

"We're going to check in at Wall Street. That's final," Chiana says. Zyree turns and walks away from her. "Zyree!"

"I don't work for you. Jurghen assigned you to this case, and that's fine. He's in charge. But we're going to do things my way."

"Under the auspices of Security Field Operations SOP, Section Thirteen, Paragraph Three, Subparagraph A-5, deliberate disregard for protocol and duty to inform, I will report you for this infraction."

"They can add it to the list."

Zyree joins the end of the queue and waits for a StreetRyde taxi. Pay-for-ride car services fell out of fashion with this city's focus on mass transit. Most of the patrons are business executives and visitors who find the SpeedRail inefficient for their schedules. In his case, StreetRyde provides the flexibility to change destinations if his target moves.

"Where are we going?" Chiana asks a split second before the driver makes the same inquiry.

"Central Park," Zyree says, answering both of them.

"Why?"

"We're going to conduct an interview and beat the grass to startle the snakes, so to speak. You know that adage, don't you?"

"First, it's a stratagem, not an adage. I'm from the Beijing City Conglomerate. So, yeah, I know it. Second, that's against protocol. Security Field Operations SOP, Section Five, Paragraph Thirty, Subparagraph A-3 states that we are not to conduct interviews without the proper equipment."

Zyree sighs. "Please tell me you read that off your contacts and didn't memorize the SOP."

"You didn't?"

"I'm too busy winning Medals of Gallantry," Zyree says, offering a mischievous grin.

"Fine. How do you want to approach this?" Chiana presses.

"With a great degree of tactical prowess commensurate with our superb training. I'm going to walk up and say, 'hi.'"

"That's it? That's your plan? What do you need me to do?"

"Stand behind me and look imposing."

"That's not funny."

"You're right. It isn't. You can go get us some ice cream while I work."

Chiana glares at Zyree. He would never treat other chief inspectors this way, but they also wouldn't have the audacity to quote procedures to him. It's rare for two chief inspectors to work together for reasons like this.

"So, what's the point of this?"

Zyree stares out the window at the Manhattan skyline as the StreetRyde approaches the city. "I want to relive some of the old times."

CHAPTER

FIFTEEN

THE PATRICIANS

Keating Family of the Gentez-Majorez Estate
Greenwich Geographic District
Southern Connecticut Municipal Corporation

Denali watches from his patio vista as the pilot performs his pre-flight checks on the helicopter. The sleek machine sits gracefully on the concrete pad, reflecting the light off its shiny black paint. The patrician checks his antique Rolex watch and notes the time. Farron is due back in the city, but he needs to have a conversation with him before departure.

He retreats into the house and makes his way to the foyer. Farron shuffles down the grand staircase from the upper level and meets Denali at the bottom. He looks well. Optimism and eagerness are weapons in the war that's to come. He's happy to see his son embrace them.

"It will be a new world when we see each other again, Father. Wish me luck."

"Come have a word with me, Farron."

His son looks at his watch and frowns. "I need to leave."

"You have time. The helicopter won't leave without you. Come."

It was an order, not a request. Farron follows his father into the study. Instead of heading straight to the bar, Denali turns to face him.

"Are you ready for this?"

Farron cocks his head slightly at the question before straightening it on his shoulders. "It's what we've been working toward."

"That wasn't my question. Are *you* ready for this?"

"Yes, I'm ready."

Denali nods. "You remember our conversation from a week ago, don't you?"

"Of course, Father."

"And?"

"And I will do what's necessary. Did I give you a reason to doubt that?"

Denali takes a deep breath and looks away. Loyalty. It's impossible to measure, hard to earn, and tough to realize it's lost until it's too late. Many great leaders have met their end through betrayal and disloyalty. Denali is determined not to join their ranks.

"No, you haven't. But I also know that Michele is a beautiful woman. There's nothing more dangerous on Earth than a potent combination of feminine beauty and intelligence."

"I'm not interested in Michele," Farron answers quickly.

"And Fiolla?"

Farron stares at his father blankly. "She's a useful idiot. Nothing more."

"That usefulness will end with the week if all goes as planned. I expect you will do your duty and sever your contact with her."

"As we agreed."

"You know what is likely to happen to her when the dust settles," Denali says, the acidic tone leaving no doubt about the meaning of the words.

"I do."

"And you're okay with it?"

"Fiolla isn't a patrician, and she isn't family. She's a source of information, nothing more. She isn't my future."

Denali nods. Farron is saying all the right things. Now, if he could only convince himself to believe his words. This generation is impressionable. He gave his son the best of everything, but he hasn't toed the line quite like Narik Covington or his other peers. The elder Keating can't shake the feeling that Farron is hiding something.

"I expect you to remain in contact with me once Liberteum starts its next phase."

"You will be informed every step of the way, Father. I understand the need for coordination."

"Very well." Denali extends his hand, which Farron shakes. "You are correct. The next time we meet here, it will be a very different world."

Farron nods and releases the handshake. He disappears out the door and hustles out to the helicopter. Denali follows him as far as the doors leading to the patio and watches as the aircraft's blades start their graceful circles. Farron climbs aboard, and the door closes.

They are so close. After Saturday, Denali will no longer need to rely on outside influences to ensure success. He will hold all the cards and can play them at his leisure. He just needs the world to play its part for a little longer. Most importantly, he needs his son to do the same.

CHAPTER SIXTEEN

REGISTRANT RYKOS

Central Park
East of Lincoln Square Geographic District
New York City Municipal Corporation

After a quick dinner at a much more affordable restaurant than we visited on our first date, I asked Mollae to take a stroll with me through Central Park. She accepted the invitation, eager to lobby about our future as a couple now that we're both attending Harvard. I managed to change the subject, but that failed to slow her talking. Everything coming out of her mouth is about her, and none of it is interesting.

None of that matters. I had ulterior motives for coming here. We sit on a park bench, a mere stone's throw from the large rock I used to sit on with Balin when we would lament the state of the world. I miss my friend. If what Executive Kenady said is true, I'll never see him again.

"Rykos? Honey?"

"Yeah?"

"Are you listening to a word I'm saying?" Mollae asks.

"Uh, sorry, I zoned out for a minute there. I guess I have a lot on my mind."

"So long as it's about us, I don't care," she says, adjusting her grip on my arm and letting out a flirtatious giggle.

I notice a shadow shift along the ground and realize that someone is standing next to us. It scares the crap out of me. Where did they come from?

"Good evening, Rykos," the dark, imposing figure says.

"Can I help you?"

"You don't remember me, do you?" he asks, moving into the streetlight until it illuminates his face's etched features and two-day-old growth. He does look vaguely familiar, but I'm not sure how.

"No, I'm afraid I don't. Are you a friend of my father's?"

"We've crossed paths," he says, light on the details.

"We're having a conversation here that you're interrupting," Mollae chides, never willingly accepting interruptions to our alone time.

"Leave," the ominous man commands her.

"Excuse me?"

"I said leave. As in, have a pleasant evening."

She looks at me before glaring back at whoever this guy is. "I don't know who the hell you think you are, but—"

"I'm Chief Inspector Zyree of Intercorpex Security. The constipated Asian woman brooding behind me is Chief Inspector Chiana. I'm not going to ask you again, Registrant Mollae. Leave."

"How do you know—?"

"You have an impressive record at Dinsmore if you ignore the low marks in basic chemistry. Congratulations on getting into Harvard. That's quite an accomplishment. Now, unless you want this obstructionism noted in your personnel file, run off back to your Lennox Hill domicile before your father gets another visit from the PSS. That last incident was *ugly*, wasn't it?"

I remember him now. I have no idea what he's talking about or how he knows any of that, but Mollae does. The blood drains from her face, and she leaves without another word. We all watch as she hurries east through the park towards home without looking back.

"You just ruined my date."

"You're not that into her," Zyree says, taking Mollae's seat on the bench next to me. "She wants a commitment you won't give."

He's right. There are two benefits to keeping the lie about my hero status. One is that I'm still alive, and the second is the resulting popularity has made me a chick magnet. Girls who never paid me any attention now swoon, Mollae among them. She's more interested in being seen with me than actually being with me. I'm not complaining. She's beautiful enough to make it worth the effort to see how far I could take things.

"What do you want, Chief Inspector?"

"I read the reports about what happened in the station before the explosion. At least the ones the BCS shared. Your interviews were enlightening."

The last thing I want to do is to relive that nightmare again. Chief Inspector Zyree is studying me the same way the interrogators did. I force myself to relax. I got through this once and can undoubtedly do it again.

"An 'interview' is a polite way to put that ordeal. So what?"

"You were lying," he leans in and whispers before retreating. "You didn't fire the gun that killed Quarren."

My heart skips a beat. Nobody has ever challenged me on that before with that degree of certainty. I rehearsed the story of how events unfolded in that dingy old subway station so many times that I convinced myself it was the truth. It was easier since nobody questioned whether I shot the terrorist mastermind. Until now, that is.

"If he were here, he'd argue that. But he can't because I killed him."

"I swabbed your hand with a swatch, Rykos," the chief inspector says, staring into the darkness blanketing the park. "When I shook it at the makeshift triage. There was no gunpowder residue. None at all. How can you explain that if you had just fired four bullets into his chest?"

"Three," I correct. I'm used to authorities trying to trip me up on the details. "I can't explain it. I only know what happened, and it's just as I said."

"Sure it is, Rykos. The executives at America Incorporated may have deluded themselves into thinking that you're a terrorist-slaying superhero, but we know better, don't we?" He stands and straightens his jacket before looking back at me. "I'm going to find out what happened down there one way or another."

"You spoiled my evening just to tell me that?" I ask with as much defiance as I can muster.

"Yes. See you around, Rykos," he says, grinning. "Say hello to your father for me."

I watch as he walks down the path and disappears into the darkness of the shadowy park with the Asian woman alongside him. I wanted to put all of this behind me and get on with my life. Now it appears that those events will never leave me. The man who saved me that day is now hunting me. Thinking about what that means makes me sick to my stomach.

CHAPTER SEVENTEEN

INTERCORPEX

Lyris's Domicile
Battery Park City District
New York City Municipal Corporation

Most of Lyris's meals are delivered from restaurants that cater to Wall Street. On the rare days he leaves work early, he orders something on the way home. Recent developments compelled him to dust off his apron and cook. Lyris isn't a half-bad chef when considering the dearth of opportunities to practice the culinary arts.

The buzzer rings, announcing the arrival of his guest. He refuses to allow one of those infernal Maester systems to be installed, even for the home automation convenience. As an Intercorpex employee, he doesn't need a computer annotating and reporting his every move.

"Hello, beautiful," Lyris says as he greets Nevala at the door and gives her a soft kiss. "Nine p.m. on the dot. Please, come in. Did you have any problem with the back entrance?"

Nevala is breathtaking. Petite, with amazing eyes, porcelain skin, and shiny black hair, Raimius's admin is also keenly intelligent. The complete package comes with a chip on her shoulder and an ambition to do more than menial administrative tasks.

"I didn't take it. I came through the front door like normal people."

"Nevala, what did I say?"

"I deal with enough paranoia working for Raimius. I don't need it from you too," she moans, taking a seat on the sofa and crossing her long, gorgeous legs.

Their rare evenings out are spent in a quaint bistro across the river in the Brooklyn District and away from the prying eyes of Intercorpex. Lyris is convinced that it's becoming too dangerous for them to chance being seen together, thus his adventure in cooking.

"I'm not being paranoid," Lyris says. "Raimius bugged my office."

"I would know about it if that were true."

As Raimius's senior executive assistant, almost everything he sees crosses Nevala's desk. It's a sensitive position that warrants constant scrutiny by ICX security personnel. It's why they keep their relationship a secret. Since the day he met with Denali Keating, it's even more critical that nobody learns they share information, let alone a bed.

"He would never ask you to arrange surveillance on one of his directors."

"What makes you so sure he did?"

Lyris explains his reasoning as he uncorks the wine, starting with the three regents who visited the NOC. He pours her a glass as the summation finishes. Nevala waits for more evidence and, receiving none, sighs loudly.

"That's flimsy. Besides, if he bugged your office, he could've easily bugged your domicile."

"I had it swept by ICX Security. It's clean, and I installed defeaters just in case. This may be the most secure place to talk in all of Manhattan."

"Defeater" is the colloquial term for audio jammers designed to confuse listening devices or directional microphones. They broadcast background noise in the same spectrum as human speech, creating an audio camouflage against eavesdroppers. It's a remarkable piece of technology.

"Those are pretty extreme measures for someone who only *thinks* he's being monitored."

"What more proof do you need? An e-note saying, 'Hey, Lyris, by the way, I have someone watching—"

"Don't patronize me! I didn't come here to be scolded like a schoolgirl who doesn't understand my multiplication tables."

Lyris is about to launch into an apology when the oven chimes. Without a word, he moves to the kitchen and plates their meals. Nevala sits in silence at the small dining room table as he serves dinner and lights the candles.

"My intent isn't to start a fight with you tonight," Lyris says, taking a seat and searching for something that will salvage this romantic evening before she decides to end it.

"What is your intent?" Nevala asks, sipping her wine.

Lyris plants his elbows on the table and interlaces his fingers. "Raimius sees me as a threat. He knows I met with Denali Keating and have access to visiting regents. They forced him to award me the medal to make my voice in internal political affairs stronger and louder. It doesn't take a paranoid mind to believe I'm conspiring against him."

"You are."

"Yeah, but he doesn't know that. He only suspects it and is trying to find proof."

When Denali Keating summoned him for a face-to-face meeting at the patrician's Greenwich estate, Lyris could never have imagined he'd redline the treachery meter. Not reporting the meeting was insubordination. He was guilty of subversion for listening to the powerful patrician's proposal to depose Raimius. When he agreed to the scheme, it became sedition.

"You're still being paranoid."

"I'm being cautious…and prudent. We're entering a sensitive time. Big changes are coming, and I don't just mean for the exchange. Power is shifting between the patricians and the corporations. We have to be ready."

"If constantly looking over our shoulders is how we're going to live, I'm not sure I want to be a part of it," Nevala complains.

"You already are. That's why you need to use the back door. Raimius can never learn about us. If he does…."

Lyris allows his voice to trail off. Nevala's duplicity would be viewed as the ultimate betrayal. He wouldn't reassign her – she would disappear and never be seen again. Intercorpex does not have sanctioned terminations as most corporations do. That doesn't mean they don't exist.

"Lyris, you know that I want you to be administrator-general. Everybody knows you would do a far better job than Raimius. I just don't know why you need to involve me."

"Because I need to stay ahead of him. You have access to information I can't get on my own. I need someone close to him that I trust."

"You want me to spy on him?" Nevala asks. Lyris sees a mixture of surprise and bewilderment on her face.

"Raimius is planning something. I need you to find out what. This is about more than just me becoming administrator-general. Both our lives might hang in the balance."

Nevala dabs the corners of her mouth with a napkin and sets it on the table. Lyris thinks she might get up and leave, but she remains seated. It's a big ask but a necessary one. There was no easy way to ask this of her, and he didn't do the best job. All that matters is the answer, and it feels like he may need to wait an eternity for it.

CHAPTER EIGHTEEN

LIBERTEUM

Carnegie Hill Brownstone of Narik Covington
Upper East Side Geographic District Location
New York City Municipal Corporation

Farron's driver pulls the four-door luxury conveyance up to the curb in front of a row of majestic brownstones in the Carnegie Hill section of the Upper East Side. This area always belonged to the wealthy and elite. While the area just to the south is home to corporate executives, patricians dominate the neighborhood lying next to the reservoir in Central Park.

"Have you ever been in this area before?" Farron asks as Obvir punches some commands on the dashboard's touch screen display.

"Urches avoid this area. Patricians have a lot of personal security."

"That we do. Obvir, are the counter-surveillance measures active?" Farron asks.

"Coming up to full power now, sir."

The display changes, showing the vehicle superimposed over a neighborhood map. Waves emanate from their position, and several dots begin to blink. He studies them a moment before looking at Michele.

"Let's go."

"What was that?" Michele asks after Obvir lets them out of the conveyance and returns to the driver's seat to wait.

"The dots were aerial drones. They're out of range for the time being. The car has a device installed that scrambles wireless signals and emits infrared light to make video surveillance impossible. They can't see inside the car on its normal setting, but it's a different story once you step outside. At maximum power, the coverage halo extends to thirty meters. The PSS is completely blind to our presence, even out here in the open."

"Impressive."

"We have the neatest toys," the patrician says with a broad smile, climbing the small flight of stairs leading to the brownstone.

"I assume you didn't have any problem getting here," Narik Covington says after swinging the heavy oak door open.

"It's risky bringing Michele here by conveyance. This had better be good," Farron tells his friend as they pass into the foyer. Narik closes the door.

Underground passageways are becoming heavily monitored by the PSS and BCS. It takes an infuriating amount of time to traverse the island now. Traveling with a patrician is cake by comparison. The elites are never stopped by public safety, and no executive would believe that they are consorting with the likes of "terrorists."

"I thought you lived in the Village, Narik."

"I did. My father acquired a new residence in the city, so I decided to move to this one."

"A new residence?" Michele asks, wondering why anyone would willingly leave this beautiful space.

"A penthouse that doesn't have any stairs," Narik says, pointing over his shoulder as they walk into the living area.

"Must be nice," Michele whispers to Farron, who rolls his eyes in return. "Patricians wouldn't last thirty seconds in the underground."

"Would you like a drink, Michele?" Narik asks from the small bar on the far side of the spacious room.

"Sure," she says, checking her appearance in an antique mirror.

The underground is cold and dark. Although her olive complexion makes Michele less pale than most urches, living beneath the streets does nothing for her color. For once, her hair is washed, shiny, and smells like flowers, thanks to the shampoo Farron bought for their stay at the safe house. She tied it into a long, single braid for this meeting.

"Here you go," Narik says, handing her a scotch. The three of them clink glasses and take long sips. "I apologize for asking you both here. I know the risks, but we need to have a conversation. Please, sit."

The two patricians take seats in overstuffed armchairs while Michele runs her hand over the finely upholstered sofa. She still marvels at how soft and comfortable modern materials are.

"What's on your mind, Narik?" Farron asks.

"I'm concerned about the prospects for success of Archimedes."

"Things are right on schedule," Michele says. "We'll be ready to launch the second phase according to plan."

"You need to accelerate the timetable."

"Narik, we've talked about this," Farron warns.

"Yes, we did. And my father wants the timeline moved up. Did your father have a different opinion?"

"No, but neither of us has told our fathers the whole story, either."

"The time for that will come," Narik says, steepling his fingers. "The pace of these security sweeps is concerning. It's only a matter of time before the PSS starts looking for Liberteum aboveground."

"I have that under control," Farron dismisses.

"Yes, thanks to your seduction of the pretty redhead. Quite a feat to use your status to seduce a desperate employee."

"Could you have done it?"

Michele stifles a grin. It's a rhetorical question. Narik is not an attractive man. If not for his stylish clothing, last name, and family coat of arms affixed at the opening of the collar of his shirt, it's doubtful that he would ever be identified as a patrician.

"She's an executive in Washington," Narik says, ignoring the barb. "How long before she figures out you're using her?"

"I'm not using her."

"Oh, sure, okay. You love her and are going to marry her. Remind me to be up in Greenwich when you tell your father."

"Get to your point," Farron snaps, genuinely annoyed at having his motives questioned.

"What are we going to do if Liberteum gets caught?"

"We? They're hiding in my old apartment, not yours. It's my problem."

"That's where you're wrong. They'll get names, associates—"

"Boys, I don't need to be here for this conversation and would rather not be," Michele interrupts. "You can lament over how bad your lives will suck if I get caught in a PSS dragnet on your own time. At least you'd still be alive."

Narik stares at her coolly. The glare is more comical than intimidating. Urches don't have much reason to respect elites. They may be high and mighty up here, but in the underground, they wouldn't survive long.

"Haven."

Michele stares at the patrician. "What about him?"

"I understand that you two aren't getting along."

"Michele," Farron says, trying to be diplomatic, "Narik is saying that we both have concerns about your ability to control him. I've already shared mine with you."

Michele rises and begins strolling around the large living room. She spots a strange-looking gun in a cabinet hung among the nautical-themed décor and paintings depicting sea battles. Curious, she removes the weapon and admires it.

"You don't control Haven. You channel his rage. He respected my father, and that made it easier. Unfortunately, we need Haven, and you need us. What is this thing?"

"It's called a blunderbuss. Naval officers and privateers carried it for its effectiveness in boarding actions. It's an heirloom, and it's probably loaded, so be careful."

Michele sniffs it and glances over at Narik. "It's a fine weapon. You shouldn't store it loaded."

"We don't need Haven. We don't even need you anymore. We only need the hard drives to make Archimedes work."

"It's my plan," Michele says, resting the weapon's barrel over her shoulder as she continues strolling around the room.

"We can execute it without you and your hackers if needed. Farron may consider you a friend, but this is foremost a business arrangement. If the deal no longer advances my interests, I no longer need you as a partner."

Michele studies the two men. She trusts Farron, but her relationship with Narik is more of a tenuous alliance. His constant meddling can be tolerated, but advocating for Haven's assassination crosses a line.

"I hope you're not suggesting what I think you are."

"It can be arranged," he replies smugly before sipping his scotch.

"You know, I wasn't born into this world. My parents had the good sense to risk starving in the underground rather than raise a child in a corrupt society. I've lived in the shadows my whole life."

"What's your point?"

"I learned hard truths about what is and isn't realistic. It's key to survival. Take your best shot if you think you know someone dumb enough to take on a highly trained former Intercorpex security inspector on his turf. Reality will set in after that: If you try to take out Haven, you'd better succeed."

"I don't fail, Michele. Ever," Narik states flatly.

"Since when?" Farron argues. "You forget, I've known you since we were both toddlers. You need to reconsider this."

"This is a nice boat," Michele says, wandering over to the intricate wood model of a sailing ship perched on a pedestal.

She studies the model. The sails of the two main masts and triangular jibs almost look real. No detail was missed from the riggings to the individual planks making up the deck.

"Thanks. It's our family yacht," Narik says, admiring it himself.

The Covingtons have a long naval tradition. Generations of the family served king and country in the Royal Navy before becoming wealthy shipping tycoons in the United States. They used their resources to rekindle global trade when America Incorporated was first chartered. The rise of Intercorpex and the adoption of the

Zurich Canon instantly made them one of the most powerful families in the *gentez-majorez.*

"I've never been on a boat but have always wanted to go sailing. It's an amazing metaphor for life. Every part of the ship has an important function. Every crew member has a responsibility they need to fulfill to ensure a successful voyage. The stronger the crew, the more likely the ship survives the storm and makes it into port."

"Haven could ruin everything," Narik says to Farron, ignoring Michele's whimsical observations as she walks back toward the sofa. "Containing him is no longer an option. He must be eliminated. Either the Sewer Princess does it, or I will."

"Sewer Princess? That's not nice, Narik."

Michele spins and levels the blunderbuss at his chest, putting her finger on the trigger. Shock registers on his face. Now she has his attention. She swings the weapon at the model ship and pulls the trigger as Narik dives behind the chair for cover. The muzzle belches smoke and lead as the intricate yacht explodes into wood splinters.

"What the—? You're crazy!" he screams as the smoke dissipates and shreds of fabric from the tiny sails float gently to the ground.

"I'm not crazy, Narik," Michele says, cocking her head slightly for effect. "I'm a terrorist."

"Why the hell did you do that?"

"To prove a point. That ship over there is our plan. We each have responsibilities to get it through the storm and into port, including you. If you decide to take out Haven and fail, the whole thing will blow apart and sink faster than you can scream for help. That's the end of this discussion."

Michele tosses the blunderbuss at Narik, who almost drops the antique weapon. She storms out of his brownstone and is let into the car by Obvir. Farron joins her in the back seat a moment later. He lets out a heavy sigh before looking at her and starting to laugh. She smiles and joins him. He enjoyed that as much as she did.

CHAPTER NINETEEN

AMERICA, INC.

Chief Guardian Teman's Domicile
Upper West Side Geographic District
New York City Municipal Corporation

This is becoming a routine. Teman returns home well after nine to find his wife looking like she was hit by a car. Deep bags have formed under her eyes, and her hair hasn't been touched since she did it yesterday for Career Day. Ilaria has become a far cry from the woman he dated and a hollow shell of the passionate one he married. This is destined to be another bout with her drunken logic. She's halfway through the jug of urch shine.

"Where's Rykos?"

"Why don't you ever ask where your daughter is?" Ilaria snipes at him from the couch.

"Varella sent me an e-note saying she was going out to dinner with some executives she met at the America Tower. She's courteous that way, unlike my son. So, where is he?"

"Why don't you check his biojack and find out?"

"I've had a long day, Ilaria," he moans, flopping onto the sofa. "I'm not in the mood to fight tonight."

"He's still out with Mollae."

"Still? I've never seen him spend this much time with a girl. This must be getting serious."

"Have you ever *seen* her?"

Teman frowns. He hasn't met Mollae in person but did check her personnel file for red flags that he should know about. There were none. Well, none except for one incident. She was an awkward girl who blossomed into a beautiful, intelligent young woman. That means she's way out of Rykos's league and only uses him for attention.

"He hasn't introduced her to me."

"That's because you're never home."

Ilaria is as determined to have a confrontation as Teman is to avoid it.

"How many times do you need me to apologize? I'm sorry I missed Rykos's Career Day. It couldn't be avoided."

"Apologize to your son, not me."

"It was a meeting with the CEO of the *parent* corporation. I shouldn't have to ask anybody for forgiveness."

"Ah, yes, the C-E-O of Am-er-i-ca In-corp-or-ated," she muses, drawing out each syllable as she swirls her drink in the glass. "Must have been one hell of a meeting. You were gone all day."

Teman wonders how much of that jug she's swallowed tonight. Urch shine, along with all alcohol, is forbidden for a reason. People are ugly drunks, and Ilaria is the worst.

"I was doing my job."

"Being a father is your job, too. Rykos is your son, in case you forgot. You would never have missed your daughter's Career Day. Hell, even *Varella* came down from Boston to be here for him."

"I get it, okay! Now, drop it."

Ilaria takes a couple of long sips of urch shine. The silence is welcome. Teman leans back into the couch and tilts his head toward the ceiling to relieve his throbbing headache. Several doses of painkillers haven't put a dent in it.

"Chief Executive Safmor came. We spoke about my returning to work at his office. He seemed amenable to the idea."

That gets Teman's attention. "You did *what*?"

"Rykos is graduating. Two weeks after that, Human Resources will assign me to some random job. I thought I would ask the CEO if he could make a by-name request for me to work at Corporate Hall."

Teman shakes his head. "You shouldn't have done that, Ilaria."

"Why not?"

"Because it could look like undue influence and damage—"

"What? Damage your career? You forget that I was on the executive fast track until I got pregnant with Varella."

Both parents in most households were working to make ends meet in the decades before the collapse. To combat the resulting breakdown of the family unit, America Incorporated instituted a policy whereby one parent must leave the workforce when they have a child. That parent assumes the title of "homemaker" and starts their new job raising the next generation of employees. Except in rare situations, it's the wife who accepts that responsibility.

"I remember," Teman sighs. She has never let him forget.

"Then why is it so surprising that I want to pick up where I left off?"

"You should have discussed it with me first. You're not taking a job at Corporate Hall," Teman says, rising from the sofa and walking toward the kitchen. "Let HR do their job, and take the assignment you're given."

"No."

"No, what?"

"No, I'm not letting some bureaucrat decide what I'm doing for the rest of my life," Ilaria flatly states. "Safmor will give me a job, and I'm returning to work at Corporate Hall."

"You will do what I say you're going to do," Teman insists, storming back into the living area.

She stands, wobbling enough to slosh some liquid left in her glass onto the carpet. "No, I won't."

Teman's head pounds harder. He reaches back and slaps her across the face. The smacking sound of flesh on flesh is crisp. Ilaria spins, catching herself on the edge of the couch. She stares at him with barely suppressed hatred in her eyes as she gingerly touches her cheek.

"You will obey me. This corporation does not cater to the whims of employees who don't like their chosen career path. You will do what they need you to do, period."

"Chief Guardian, you have visitors en route to the domicile," the Maester system announces. It just dawns on him that the entire incident with Ilaria was probably reported.

"Refuse entrance."

"I'm afraid I cannot deny the request," the system informs him.

"Why not?"

"Because we have the override protocol," a guardian says as the elevator door opens and he steps into the foyer with his partner. "Good evening, Chief Guardian. I'm Deyago and this is Trulog. We're from the Department of Domestic Intervention and Arbitration."

"I know who you are and where you're from. What are you doing here?"

"Your Maester system reported a domestic disturbance in progress," he says, looking at the red welt forming on Ilaria's cheek.

"I'm sure it did. It's standard operating procedure that inquiries into domestic transgressions are first made via VidLynk."

"That's true, sir. SOP also states that guardians are dispatched from the DDIA when a second disturbance is reported within ninety days."

"Ma'am, are you okay?" Guardian Trulog asks, studying her red cheek and noticing her inebriation.

"I'm fine," she slurs.

"Yes, she's fine. We're all fine. You need to leave now."

"That's not going to happen," Lieutenant Deyago says. "Under the circumstances, you need to come with me while my partner attends to your wife."

"Ma'am, why don't you accompany me to the kitchen so we can put some ice on that cheek?" Trulog asks gently, leading her into the kitchen.

"Sir?"

Deyago gestures towards the elevator. Teman folds his arms across his chest and stands fast.

"Okay," he says. "You have a decision to make, Chief Guardian. Trulog was generous to let your first indiscretion slide. That is turning into a mistake. You can respect and follow directives you help enforce, or I can make this a 'failure to comply' incident and have ten men carry you out."

The PSS doesn't just deal with low-level employees accused of a corporate policy infraction. They deal with executives, foreign employees, and the occasional patrician. Each requires varying degrees of diplomatic tact and a sense of when to make threats.

"Please, sir, don't make this worse than it needs to be," Deyago says after his leader doesn't respond.

"Fine, let's go."

The chief guardian glances over at the kitchen, where Trulog is icing Ilaria's cheek. Her head is down as if something is mesmerizing on the floor. Teman enters the foyer and climbs into the elevator, knowing that the cooling-off period is twenty-four hours. It will take longer than that to undo the damage to his marriage.

CHAPTER TWENTY

THE PATRICIANS

Keating Family Brownstone
Manhattan Upper West Side Geographic District
New York Municipal Corporation

The well-appointed and opulently decorated Manhattan brownstone is one of Denali Keating's favorite places. It's Farron's least favorite place in the city. Patricians enjoy flaunting their obscene wealth to each other in meaningless ways. This domicile is the perfect exemplar of that.

Farron prefers function over form, substance over style. His domiciles are nice, but they forgo the gaudy décor most of his peers relish. Unfortunately, he can't stay at any of them. If Liberteum is discovered in his building, his places in the city would be their next stop. No guardian or chief inspector would ever be bold enough to intrude here without his father's men hearing about it first.

"Sir, you have a visitor," Obvir says after appearing in the doorway.

Farron's heart jumps. He hopes it's Fiolla. She's in town, although she said work would keep her busy. He told her that he was here in case anything changed.

"Patrician of the *Gentez-Majorez* Narik Covington."

Farron lets out a disappointed sigh. "Show him in, Obvir. Thank you."

Narik enters. No, enters isn't the right word. He struts in, thrusting his head back and forth like a peacock.

"It's been a while since I've seen you at your father's brownstone."

"It wasn't my choice. Believe me."

"Your father wants to keep tabs on you? I can see why. You have had so many domiciles that I've lost track of where you live."

Farron ignores the comment. "What are you doing here, Narik? Apologizing for your behavior today?"

His friend makes himself at home on the opposite sofa. "Are you going to put your pet terrorist on a leash?"

"You were out of line."

"She shot at me."

"She destroyed a model ship. Nothing more. If she'd shot at you, you'd be at a medical center right now…or a morgue."

Narik narrows his eyes. Farron knows that he isn't on the same page as him. Not only about Michele's behavior. About their plan, in general.

"Michele is out of control."

"The only one who appeared out of control was you," Farron says, shaking his head.

"Whose side are you on?"

"It's not about sides, Narik. You called her a sewer princess. She took action. End of story."

"She shot at me."

"Near you. We've already established that."

Narik shakes his head. The closest his friend ever got to shooting a weapon is having one hung on his wall. He's never even been skeet shooting. If Michele had fired the blunderbuss from down the block in the opposite direction, Narik would still complain that it was aimed at him. Or so Farron tells himself.

"I think the Covingtons need to rethink our arrangement."

"Would your father agree with that?"

"I can make him see things my way," Narik snaps.

Farron lets out a laugh. "Please. You have no more control over him than I do my father. We both know that."

"I'm the family heir."

"As am I."

"Farron, we're risking everything with this endeavor."

Farron takes a deep breath. Narik has always had a penchant for dramatically stating the obvious. A blind man could see that they're risking everything.

"You knew the stakes when you signed on. You helped develop our plan, so don't pretend you are ignorant about the possible consequences. You're invested. It's too late to back out now."

"I'll be the judge of that."

"No, *your father* will. He's about to achieve his wildest ambition."

"You're assuming that this plan will work."

"And you're assuming it won't. It's a risk, but most things worth doing are."

He doesn't expect his friend to understand that. Narik and his father are partners in this endeavor because of what it could mean for their family. They want this battle for their ego, not their ideology.

"You're being too cavalier about this, Farron."

"I have bigger concerns than soothing your nerves. We've known each other our whole lives, Narik. I've never once seen you take a risk."

Narik scoffs. "And you have?"

"I've been consorting with urches, supporting terrorists, been busted at an illegal gathering and detained by the PSS, and am in an unsanctioned relationship with a corporate executive. Do you *really* want to compare resumes with me?"

"It only means you're reckless. Liberteum has you wrapped around their little finger."

"I'm filling my role. Our fathers are filling theirs. You need to do the same."

Narik stands and looks around the opulent living room. "The situation is changing. Our arrangement must change with it."

"It's too late for regrets, Narik. We're committed to seeing this through, and everyone has their parts to play. Yours is the easiest."

Narik can't argue with that. He has almost no responsibilities in this plan. All he needs to do is supervise a few important financial transactions. Even if Archimedes fails spectacularly, the Covingtons will face few repercussions under the Zurich Canon. It's the Keatings who will face the worst consequences for failure.

"Rein in Michele and Haven. I will not indulge Liberteum's recklessness. After this next phase, I won't care what happens to them."

"You should."

"I don't. If you were smart, you wouldn't either. Your father expects them to be eliminated. I understand that you don't want that to happen so long as they serve us. Only they aren't. If you follow their siren song, you'll wreck on the rocks."

Farron gets the *Odyssey* reference. "Are you going to plug your ears with wax after tying me to the mast?"

Narik smiles. "If it comes to that, yes."

CHAPTER TWENTY-ONE

AMERICA, INC.

AME News Broadcast Studio
Times Square Geographic District
New York City Municipal Corporation

The men and women in the editing bay are putting the finishing touches on the video packages with complete indifference to their graphic nature. Fiolla watches the violence playing out and can't understand how the producers can remain impassive. It's making her stomach turn.

"Put them on jumbos one, two, and three," the producer orders.

An instant later, the packages are loaded on the three largest displays in the front of the video production room. Each has a surveillance camera feed complete with a timestamp in the corner.

"This is what you wanted, right?" Journalist Kassaya asks, more as an accusation than an inquiry.

Fiolla nods. The first video shows a vicious assault. Several men dressed in urch goth clothing are beating a woman in an AME uniform on a darkened street. There is just enough light to see what's happening and who the perpetrators are, with shadows added to make the faces hard to distinguish.

The second display shows a man getting stabbed outside the entrance of a high-rise residence. The assault is quick, but the assailant remains long enough to strip the employee of anything of value while the victim's blood paints the sidewalk crimson. The look of joy on the ghoul's face when he looks up at the camera is chilling.

The final scene is the longest and most disturbing. Three men pin a woman to the ground in the storage area of a small eatery. Her clothing is ripped open, and the assailants take turns mounting her. It is heart-wrenching watching her anguish, and Fiolla covers her mouth when she's kicked in the face after the predators leave her naked and violated on the dingy floor.

It would be worse if any of this had actually happened. Fiolla's new mission is to turn popular opinion against the urches, and these scenes were created to influence employees. These propaganda videos, or prop vids, will have the desired effect. They are affecting Fiolla, and she knows the truth behind them.

"I can't believe it only took you a day to film these. They look so real," Fiolla utters.

"We had credible actors," Kassaya explains. "It's amazing what urches will do to save their skins."

Without another word, she walks out of the editing bay. Fiolla follows her past the rows of workstations that make up the newsroom floor. It's a hive of activity. Outside of Washington, New York hosts the busiest newsroom in the sphere of influence.

"Word around the office is that Valen is meeting with Raimius tomorrow," Kassaya says as they walk.

"People like to talk."

"Is it true?" she asks as they enter her office and close the door. Fiolla is offered a seat in front of her desk as she moves behind it to her own ergonomic executive swivel chair.

Fiolla grins when she notices that Kassaya's chair is slightly higher. The technique is used throughout the corporate world to place the person in the lower chair at a psychological disadvantage, even if it's recognized on a subconscious level. In meetings between top executives of parent companies, the height of each chair is measured and adjusted to ensure conversations are at eye level.

"Yes, they have a meeting scheduled. That's not to be publicized," Fiolla warns.

"Why not? It's news. You should be selling tickets instead of staying quiet about it. It's going to be the world's greatest physics experiment."

"What do you mean?"

"Are you kidding? After what happened in New York last week? Valen and Raimius in the same room will be like watching an irresistible force slamming into an immovable object. You're lucky to be a part of it."

Fiolla doesn't share her enthusiasm. Valen wanted the meeting to apologize for the incident and repair the relationship with ICX. The fact that he had to publicly shame Raimius on AME News to get the meeting changes things. This is now two mighty titans jockeying for position on the world stage.

"If you say so," Fiolla says, using her best dismissive tone.

"If you're not willing to talk about *actual* news, what are you doing here, Fiolla? Just checking up on the manufacturing of your disturbing propaganda?"

The contempt drips off her tongue. On-screen, Kassaya is a picture of pleasantness. Behind the scenes, she's resentful, brooding, and disrespectful.

"I was informed that you had concerns about these packages and wanted them addressed. I was dispatched here to tell you to shut your mouth before the BCS does it for you."

Kassaya's shocked reaction is priceless. Fiolla rarely uses threats, knowing that the specter of bodily harm or termination isn't a practical long-term approach to resolving disputes. She's making an exception for Kassaya after her antics during the interview on the day of the attack. As they used to say, "payback's a bitch."

"You wouldn't dare. I'm untouchable."

"Don't make me laugh. Human Resources could replace you in fifteen minutes. Do you think your notoriety gives you power? Trust me when I say that you'd be an afterthought in less than a week."

Kassaya leans back in her chair. After a moment of fidgeting and playing with her hair, a smile creeps across her lips. "I don't ever remember you being this aggressive, Fiolla."

"And I don't recall you ever being this obstinate. If you make your stand on this hill, Kassaya, you'll die on it. Get behind this. Per Valen's instructions, stories and prop vids will be reported with unsurpassed dedication to the corporation."

"Fine, I will ensure that the AME propaganda machine churns efficiently. I mean, who cares about the truth, anyway?"

Fiolla stares at her hands for a moment. "You just refuse to see the big picture, don't you?"

Kassaya leans forward. "Once upon a time, journalism was about disseminating information and speaking truth to power. That changed even before the Great Collapse. It dawns on me that media was corporate-controlled back then."

"Careful, Kassaya. That's sedition," Fiolla says, rising from her chair. "You have an idealist view of history if you think journalism was ever like that. There were no high and mighty ideals in broadcasts, except maybe in the minds of the egocentric anchors. There has always been an agenda."

"And now we're advancing yours."

"You are advancing the agenda of every employee who works for America Incorporated, yourself included. You're promoting safety and stability against a terrorist group bent on destroying our way of life. You have your instructions, Kassaya. What you choose to do with them is on you."

Fiolla has done her part and delivered the message. It no longer falls on her to threaten Kassaya into compliance. Valen is determined to replace her anyway. Determined to leave before receiving another high-minded dissertation, she storms out of the office without another word.

CHAPTER TWENTY-TWO

INTERCORPEX

ICX Headquarters
Midtown Manhattan Geographic District
New York City Municipal Corporation

Summits are usually hosted on neutral ground by a disinterested third party when disputes arise between corporations or with Intercorpex. France Limited is notorious for holding them at Versailles, while Scandinavia has also brokered several agreements. Raimius demanded this meeting be held on his turf. It's logical to hold the meeting in New York, but Intercorpex hosting it is a power play.

Fifteen executives accompany Valen up to one of the building's upper floors. Raimius's contingent is equally impressive in size when he arrives five minutes late. Both parties customarily face each other, five feet apart, with a facilitator off to the side.

"Administrator-General," the facilitator says, launching into his rehearsed spiel, "please allow me to intro—"

"We know each other," Raimius interrupts, breaking protocol. "I think we can skip the five minutes of traditional formalities. Wouldn't you agree, Chief Executive Valen?"

The CEO smirks and nods politely. He knows that Raimius is trying to rattle him by skipping the usual ritual. It won't work. Valen doesn't advertise that he finds formal introductions prosaic and tiring. The two men select seats on opposing overstuffed sofas.

"What do you say we clear the room and speak frankly to each other?"

With a flick of his hand, Raimius's staff departs with the exception of his director of operations. The act was too smooth not to have been rehearsed. Valen plays along, nodding at Fiolla, who dismisses his entourage. The once crowded room is down to four.

"I'm glad you finally agreed to meet with me," Valen says, opening the discourse.

"I'm sorry for the delay, but we've been busy putting our NOC back together after nearly being destroyed."

"I sincerely apologize for the *cosmetic* damage it received."

"Well, yes, I suppose it was less than the two gaping holes blasted into your city streets."

None of Liberteum's explosions were more devastating than those that opened up large craters in Nassau and Broad Streets. It was an embarrassment to America Incorporated and an employee relations nightmare.

"What happened that day was unfortunate. I requested this meeting to express that."

"I don't want your apologies, Valen, nor banal expressions of remorse. I want security for our facilities and any known threats to them eliminated. America Incorporated is failing miserably at both."

"I hope you were as hard on your network engineering and security teams as you're being on us."

"The urches are your problem, not ours."

"Terrorists are a global problem. The ones in New York managed to hack into your network undetected and almost crash the stock market. We both know that was the true source of your 'anomaly.'"

"Something that wouldn't have happened if you had eradicated this group when you said you did. Or did you send your executive to AME News to lie on purpose?"

Fiolla's sit-down with Journalist Kassaya may have been the worst-timed interview in history. No sooner did she assure employees that there was nothing to fear than Liberteum launched the worst terrorist attack on the city since the chartering of America Incorporated. It was an unfortunate coincidence, not an outright deception. Raimius can't say the same.

"Is it more of a lie than giving Executive Director Lyris a medal?"

"Valen, is your intent to shift the blame and absolve yourself of responsibility?" Raimius asks with an edge to his voice.

"I want to ensure that responsibility is spread appropriately."

"I will blame who I choose."

"No, I don't think you will," Valen says, drawing the words out to drive them home. "Unless you want the patricians learning the whole truth about the events of that day."

Raimius leans back and folds his arms. Mimicking body language is a technique used by salespeople to subconsciously manipulate a subject. Matching non-verbal signals, including body positioning, movements, and facial expressions, creates a subconscious attachment. The inverse is also true. Raimius changing his body position is a subtle "screw you."

"You think that they will believe you?"

"Patricians will ask uncomfortable questions. When you don't answer them – because you can't – they will lean on your regents for answers. We both know how fickle that group can be."

The Intercorpex Board of Regents has a reputation for being petulant toddlers. They are unpredictable, emotional, and often bloodthirsty for advancement. They all want to be administrator-general and often use available leverage to force the current one out. Raimius should know. That's what he did.

"Do you think you can come into my building and blackmail me?"

Valen shakes his head and leans forward even farther. "This isn't blackmailing. It's a reminder."

"Of what?"

"Your place in the world."

"I'm well aware of it," he snaps, resentment of the implication evident on his face.

"I don't think you are. Corporations created Intercorpex to reward our benefactors for their financial support in helping to rebuild society. Somehow, you think that the exchange has a remit to bully those same corporations with delisting threats. That practice has gone on long enough and will end."

"You're in no position to make demands of me!"

Raimius is known for his volatility. He's teetering on the verge of losing grip on his emotions. Valen knows that it's time to go in for the kill.

"Are you willing to test me on that?"

"You think that just because you're the world's largest corporation, you can dictate anything to me? I should delist you just for the insinuation."

"Then do it," Valen says, leaning back into the sofa after getting the unhinged response he was looking for. "Delist us from the IGI. We can suspend trading tomorrow, and you can move Intercorpex out of New York. All you have to do is say the word."

Raimius glares at his guest in silence. Valen threw down the gauntlet and challenged him to a battle his opponent can't win. Delisting America Incorporated would cause irreparable harm to the exchange and likely end his reign as administrator-general.

"I didn't think so. Raimius, sooner or later, you'll realize that you need us more than we need you. The patricians may rely on you to enhance their wealth, but corporations have no such need. We don't use our stocks to raise capital like before the collapse, and patricians can be accommodated in other ways."

"You're playing a dangerous game, Valen."

The CEO cocks his head slightly. "Liberteum is a problem for both of us," he says, ignoring the warning. "Our organizations worked together to avoid a calamity. It's in our interests to do so again. Privately, you will stop spreading rumors about America Incorporated as retribution against us."

"I have done no such thing!" Raimius shouts.

"You have, and it will stop. There is no reason for the patricians to hear the truth if it does."

Valen rises to let the administrator-general know that he considers the conversation over. It's a power move and a little showmanship as repayment for interrupting the introductions. Raimius isn't the only one who can break protocol.

"And if I don't agree to any of this?"

"Then we will see which one of us is carrying the biggest stick."

Lyris watches Valen and Fiolla rejoin their entourage outside. Raimius came to this meeting with all the advantages and was still outmaneuvered. Lyris watching his boss get humiliated would usually make his day, but in this case, he made them look like bumbling oafs.

The administrator-general gets up and begins pacing around, mumbling to himself. He stops at a half wall that juts out into the room to inspect the relics perched on it. Picking up a vase with an intricate black and gold animal frieze, he runs his fingers over the lip. It's but one artifact in a room awash with them to show the multicultural makeup of the modern exchange.

"Who the hell does Valen think he is?"

"The CEO of the world's largest and most powerful corporation," Lyris deadpans.

"He's nobody! Our facilities get attacked, and he has the audacity to stomp in here and lecture me?"

Raimius launches the piece of pottery across the room. It hits the far wall with more than enough velocity to explode it into a hundred pieces. That decorative vase is as fragile as the administrator-general's mental state.

"That was an Etruscan vase from the fifth century B.C."

"Do I look like I give a damn?" Raimius snaps, seething with anger. "He's into something with Keating and Covington. I know it. Zeykala is working with *Prima* Bettancourt to convince the board to oust him. He's allying himself with strong patricians to save himself."

"Why would they help him?"

"To embarrass me. The Liberteum attacks made me look weak and inept. It's a coordinated effort to destroy me, and those two bastards are behind it."

Lyris closes his eyes. How paranoid can this man possibly be? It takes a special kind of egotism to believe that this is about him. To think that Valen is involved with Denali and Shalius requires an excess of imagination.

"You don't sound angry at this. It makes me wonder just how committed you are to your work."

"I would do anything for Intercorpex," Lyris says, making this about the exchange and not the man running it.

"Anything? That's good to hear, Lyris, because I have a special assignment for you. Accumulate all the data we have on the New Jersey attack and manipulate it to finger the patricians of the *gentez-minorez* as the instigators."

"What?"

"I will slow this down so you can understand," Raimius says, walking over and getting uncomfortably close. "Link the terrorist attack on our circuits to the wealthier families of the *gentez-minorez*."

Rumors that the lower patricians somehow urged Liberteum to conduct that attack are circulating around the globe. The notion is laughable, but Raimius is counting on leveraging the fear-mongering over the notion of such an unholy alliance.

"To what end, sir?"

Raimius grins. "Proof of how far we're willing to go. If Denali Keating and Shalius Covington don't back off, we'll orchestrate a second leak that claims the anomaly was an attack on our trading systems by the *gentez-majorez* in response to the incident."

"I don't think anyone will believe that, sir."

"It's 2088, Lyris. People will believe whatever corporate media tells them to. Corporations will demand an investigation under the auspices of the Zurich Canon. Keating and Covington will become toxic and Valen will be exposed. I will take care of things from there."

The world's bourgeoisie already has a healthy resentment of Intercorpex and the Zurich Canon. Now Raimius wants to use it to blackmail patricians to guarantee their silence.

"What's the matter, Lyris? I thought you said you would do *anything* for the exchange."

"I'll do it," the director croaks, seeing no alternative that doesn't include smacking the grin off his boss's face.

"I know you will," Raimius says. "Don't think that I forgot about your meeting with Denali Keating just because I hung a medal around your neck. If you want to earn back my trust, this is how you're going to do it."

He slaps Lyris on his shoulder and storms out the door. There is no earning Raimius's trust because he doesn't trust anyone. This plan is all upside for him. If it works, he gets what he wants: patricians at each other's throats. If the ruse is sniffed out and backfires, he has a stooge to blame and will remove Lyris from his position. It's the kind of shrewd political move that he should have pulled on Valen instead of a subordinate.

CHAPTER TWENTY-THREE

REGISTRANT RYKOS

Radio City Music Hall
Corporate Entertainment District
New York City Municipal Corporation

The chancellor-educator of the New York City Municipal Corporation opens the ceremony with greetings to the distinguished guests, parents, and the graduating registrants. He only attends a few graduations a year and is likely here because of me and our last-minute guest speaker.

"We are gathered in this beautiful hall to mark a transition; a rite of passage that began twelve years ago with learning the A-B-Cs now ends with the foundation needed for executive education. Dinsmore Preparatory Academy is the preeminent institution in this city charged with molding tomorrow's corporate leaders.

"Through its dedication to unsurpassed instruction, Dinsmore boasts the highest Ivy League placement rate in the entire sphere of influence. It is the cradle of corporate leadership, and I'm honored to send the graduating class of 2088 off on its next journey to fill their ranks."

Applause erupts through the cavernous venue. Many significant landmarks changed names when America Incorporated came to power to reflect their new governance. Others, like the Empire Building, were only tweaked. Radio City Music Hall joins a select few historic places that didn't, and I have no idea why.

The chancellor-educator prattles on, and I'm bored enough to hazard looking around. The seats in the center are reserved for the registrants. Parents and relatives flank us on each side and fill up the lower level. Corporate executives and other interested parties sit in the three mezzanines above us.

My class is dressed in ridiculous hats and traditional gowns with the school's logo embroidered over our hearts. Those attending the Ivy League wear double intertwined honor cords with the school's colors they will report to in a couple of months. The top ten percent of graduates wear graduation stoles with Dinsmore's secondary color. The valedictorian wears a sash with the distinction of the primary color and is afforded a place of honor on the stage.

Of my graduating class, thirty-five are going to the Ivy League and will be joined by graduates from preparatory schools in other major cities. The rest will head to secondary universities to become subsidiary corporation executives. Occupational academies will send their graduates forward to become physicians, scientists, engineers, manufacturers, and business administrators. Vocational schools will ship the least educated registrants to the ranks of the qulis to become plumbers, electricians, farmers, and other tradesmen.

The valedictorian gives a speech filled with the usual optimistic nonsense she was known to pontificate about in the school cafeteria. She is a tailor-made executive: equal parts oblivious follower and ardent cheerleader. She has the privilege of introducing Chief Executive Valen to thunderous applause.

He is widely considered one of the greatest CEOs in modern history, and the riotous ovation only fades after several long moments. He chose to give this speech in the presence of a hero of the corporation, or so the story goes.

"You live in a remarkable age—one that has never been seen before in human history," Chief Executive Valen begins. "We left behind the wars and poverty that consumed the old world. We matured from the violence and corruption that were once commonplace in it. You are free from the yokes of suffering and despair that monarchs and presidents, despots and tyrants thrust upon their people. We unlocked humanity's true potential."

I reconcile Chief Executive Valen's words with what Quarren told me in the subway station. It's all a lie: my heroics, my future, and the whole world. Everything is a lie.

"There are those who want to tear down what we have labored so hard to build. They would return to a world of racial inequality, sexism, and discrimination. They would instill fear in your hearts and then play on them to achieve their sick, twisted goals.

"We will never bow to their threats or cowardly attacks. We have faced them in the past and will eliminate them in the future. Their legacy will be that of the corrupt ideology they idolize: abject failure."

I watched Liberteum tap into Intercorpex and almost crash the market. Intercorpex called it an anomaly as America Incorporated informed the world that the incidents weren't related. People were told these lies without hesitation. Whose ideology is actually the corrupt one?

What would happen if they didn't blindly believe it? What if critical thinking skills were turned against our corporate masters? Is that even possible? People rely on the corporation for everything. Employees have a career assigned and are told where to work and live. What if employees finally realized that the company isn't looking after their interests but its own?

You are freer locked in this room down here than you ever were up there. Quarren's words rattle around in my head. I now know what they mean. Our lives aren't ours. We gave up our independence and traded our individual destinies to be part of some centrally managed master plan. We bartered our souls away for the perception of stability and safety.

"You are a few short years from taking your place among us. You are on the precipice of ascension to institutions where you will learn to be more than who you are. You are part of a bigger plan that has defined the rise of America Incorporated for decades. On behalf of all executives and employees of America Incorporated, congratulations. This is a world you will conquer. Our future is your future, and it is a bright one."

The speech ends with enthusiastic applause. My fellow newly minted undergraduates pose for pictures on stage in their academic regalia. Others talk with classmates they may never see again. As the chief guardian's son and hero of the corporation, legions of parents congratulate me for killing Liberteum's leader. My father is commanding his share of attention, as well.

Something happened between my parents, but neither has said what. If Varella knows, she isn't sharing either. She's too busy burying her nose up executive asses. My father approaches and is about to say something when his tablet chirps.

"This is not a good time."

"I apologize, Chief Guardian, but the RTCC just got a priority message. One of our tactical units took an urch into custody an hour ago who wants to meet with you."

"I don't meet with urches."

"You're going to want to meet with this one, sir. He's at Rikers for interrogation and is claiming that he knows where Liberteum moved their weapons fabricating equipment."

Teman looks at me. "I'll be there in under an hour."

"Leaving already?" my mother asks in disgust.

"I don't remember you rushing out of Varella's graduation ceremony," I pile on.

"Stop being so selfish!" my sister scolds.

"No, Rykos is right," my father admits. "I didn't run out of yours, but this is different."

"Why? Are you the only one capable of hunting down Liberteum?" my mother says through clenched teeth.

"In this case, yes."

"One day," I mutter. "I can't manage to get you to spend one day with me, even if it's my graduation."

Varella rolls her eyes and scoffs.

"Why don't you do us all a favor and shut your damn mouth for once, Varella."

"Don't talk to your sister that way, Rykos," my father demands.

"And don't scold your son while you let your daughter's behavior slide, Teman," my mother says, glaring at him.

My father shakes his head. "I'm sorry, I have to go."

"Good luck, father. Go get them," Varella encourages as he strides away without looking back.

I don't try to disguise my anger. Nothing has changed between us – nothing at all. I will never measure up to the son my father wishes he had. It would take something extraordinary to change that, because being a hero of the corporation and getting into Harvard clearly isn't enough.

CHAPTER TWENTY-FOUR

LIBERTEUM

"The Bastille"
Midtown Geographic District
New York City Municipal Corporation

Haven relishes his return to this place. Michele has Valhalla, and although he likes the security of the Alamo, the "Bastille" has always been his. He arranged for its construction and named it after the Saxon Bastille. That fortification had strong outer walls built by Saxon Kings in the 16th century, giving it a reputation for being unconquerable. He designed this place to be equally secure.

The conversation with Michele put him in a foul mood that the long trek north to Midtown did little to change. He's impatient and growing more disillusioned with each day that passes. She looks at the PSS intrusions into the underground as an inconvenience. Haven sees them as an opportunity to deal painful blows to his enemy.

"How did it go?" Nyvar asks after Haven takes a long drink of water from a canteen.

"Just like I expected. Michele said no."

"Why?"

Haven shrugs. "Weakness. She doesn't want us doing anything that could jeopardize Archimedes. That includes antagonizing the PSS."

Nyvar grumbles a few words to himself before looking up at Haven. "Stupid."

"Her whole plan is stupid," Haven admits.

Quarren chose to keep him in the dark about what their intentions were. Haven resented being out of the loop despite understanding the reasoning. He's a frontline soldier in the cause. His capture could betray their intentions and put Intercorpex, the BCS, or even Public Safety and Security in a position to thwart them.

He also knows that whatever Michele is doing won't work. He's explained that a thousand times. The people of this world are irredeemable. He's lived in it. She hasn't. There is no way to experience what life above ground is like to someone who has spent theirs below it.

"So she's just going to let us get hunted? That's bullshit. Sooner or later, Farron's intelligence will be wrong. It's not if, it's when."

"I know, Nyvar. I'm surprised that the guardians haven't changed tactics yet. It's lazy work. Sloppy."

"What are we going to do about it?" he challenges.

Nyvar is a man always itching for a fight. Scivix was the same way. He had the perfect warrior's death near Broad Street – sacrificing himself to protect his comrades from an encroaching enemy. There is little doubt in Haven's mind that his last remaining lieutenant is jealous about that.

"We're making our own path. The wheels are already in motion. I made the decision before I even met with her."

"What will Michele say about that?"

"I don't care," Haven says, looking around his stronghold. "She doesn't understand that this is a war. We're the ones fighting while she's comfortably ensconced in Farron's building. She's happy to let us run for our lives. I'm not willing to accept that. We're taking the fight to them right here."

The Alamo and Valhalla rely on their location and lack of approaches for defensibility. You can walk right up to the Bastille, but it would be a bloodbath. It's the perfect place to ambush the PSS.

Nyvar looks around. "I'm good with that, but we'd be giving the Bastille up. We can't hold it forever. Even if we decide to, how will the PSS find us? There ain't no sign pointing them to this place."

"I already arranged to leak its location."

"That ain't gonna work. They'll sense it's a trap."

Haven runs his hands over the thick wall. They put a lot of effort into reinforcing this place. It would be a shame to lose it unless the result is spectacular.

"I spent years in Intercorpex Security. The political pressure up there gets intense. The PSS raids have resulted in nothing since the attack. Corporate executives must be screaming, and they'll be desperate for results. The guardians will act on plausible intelligence."

"And if they send a small army?" Nyvar asks.

Haven pats the wall. "That's what I'm counting on. We plan for the worst and take them all out."

Nyvar nods. "The men have been itching for a fight. They want payback."

Haven gets it. They lost some good men during the siege of Broad Street Station, including Scivix. He was popular with the guys and is revered for his heroic actions. That reverence has turned to bloodlust. Scivix was worth any hundred guardians.

"What about Michele?" Nyvar asks.

"This is our operation. We are the Liberteum splinter cell. It's our fight."

Nyvar grins. "Then let's work through the details and make arrangements."

Haven returns the smile. The "leader" of Liberteum is about to find out just how powerless she really is.

CHAPTER TWENTY-FIVE

INTERCORPEX

Radio City Music Hall
Corporate Entertainment District
New York City Municipal Corporation

Zyree rubs his chin as he stands along the wall. The stress indicators on Rykos and his parents show significant duress. The only one not embroiled in the family drama is the daughter, who has returned to flitting around from executive to executive like a butterfly hopped up on opium. It doesn't take a genius to see that she's clearly the favorite.

It explains some of his experiences with the chief guardian during the search for his son. He wanted to find Rykos, but the raw emotional passion Zyree would have expected from a distraught father was absent. His fateful plunge into the first tunnel that led to a devastating ambush was more of a response to Liberteum killing his first assault team than a desperate need to rescue Rykos.

"Not exactly the perfect family, are they?" Zyree asks his cold-hearted cohort as Teman heads for the exit.

"Who?" Chiana asks, watching the scene unfold from next to him.

They moved down to the orchestra section from the second mezzanine once the ceremony concluded. He would never get spotted up there, and visibility is the point of being here.

"We're wasting time," Chiana says for the fifth time since they arrived.

"No, we're not. We're conducting research."

"Research on what? The kid's graduating. Big deal. This is an inappropriate use of ICX resources."

"Isn't there some part of the SOP you should be quoting?"

The answer pops up on Zyree's contacts courtesy of his biocomputer. As useful as the device can be, it doesn't understand sarcasm. He blinks the worthless information away.

"We've been in this city for eighteen hours. Instead of pursuing leads on Liberteum, you're obsessing over this kid."

"Wow! A whole eighteen hours? Your complaining makes it feel like a month."

"Despite what you think, he isn't going to contact the terrorists, or vice-versa."

"So you say. I think that's exactly what's going to happen."

"Why, because you have a *gut feeling* about it?" Chiana says with a sneer.

Zyree grins. For a woman with designs on the big chair in Zurich, she's volatile when someone doesn't adhere to her line of thinking. There is no place for narrow-mindedness as commissioner-general. Jurghen has continued the long, infuriating tradition of being disassociated and dispassionate, and now Zyree knows why. Chiana running ICX Security would be a disaster.

"I do, which is why you'll never be as good as I am," Zyree says, losing interest in this conversation.

Chiana steps in front of him and sticks a finger in his face. "You're a dinosaur whose final day should have been after you had that medal hung around your neck. You're old, tired, and too stupid to quit the game. I'm ICX Security's future."

"You're in my way," Zyree says, calmly and evenly.

"No, you're in mine. I'm going to be the commissioner-general. I will never let you get that chair over me."

"You're still in my way," he states again. She cocks her head at him when he moves her out of his vision. "I can't see Rykos with you blocking my view."

She looks back at their targets and slides back over to his side, gnashing her teeth in anger. Rykos and his mother cut across the hall and are walking straight at them. Zyree makes eye contact with the graduate and sees surprise register on his face, followed by anxiety. It was the precise reaction that the chief inspector wanted. Rykos averts his eyes as he passes by without an acknowledgment.

"Okay. We can go now."

"Finally! I was thinking we should go back and start looking—"

"I was thinking about dinner. Investigating makes me hungry."

Zyree heads up the aisle toward the exit, failing to suppress a smile. Whatever words Chiana is muttering to herself behind him aren't nice ones. That makes this even more fun for him.

CHAPTER TWENTY-SIX

THE PATRICIANS

Keating Family Brownstone
Manhattan Upper West Side Geographic District
New York Municipal Corporation

Farron rolls back onto his side of the bed, out of breath and sucking all the available oxygen out of the room. Fiolla is panting equally heavily. He glances at the clock on the wall. Where did the day go?

Fiolla came to meet him at the brownstone right after wrapping up her work with AME News. She didn't tell him what she was doing or how it went. Instead, they fell into bed and have been there ever since. Now it's one o'clock in the morning and she has to be at work in a few hours.

"Are you okay?" he asks, kissing her bare shoulder as he strokes her hip.

"I'm fine."

"You don't sound fine. You're usually more playful than this."

"Why am I here, Farron? Why would a handsome, wealthy, young patrician from a prestigious family settle for a corporate executive?"

"Settle?"

"Let's be realistic for a moment. You could get any woman you want."

"That's true," he admits, "but none of them are you. Fiolla, you don't get just how remarkable you are. You're just as beautiful as anyone, but you are also so much more. That's why I'm with you and always want to be."

Fiolla doesn't seem satisfied with the answer. Farron can feel her tense up. He has a feeling about what's coming next.

"I'm going to ask you a question, and don't lie to me no matter what you're afraid I'll think. Are you a part of Liberteum?"

"Fiolla, do you really want to have this conversation again?"

"I've heard you deny it before, and I know you're going to deny it again. I also need to know if the denials are real. I need to know the truth. You've all but asked me to marry you, and there's nothing in this world I would love more…"

"But...?"

"But if you lie to me and I find out later, it will hurt. It will destroy...it will be the end of us."

"I would never risk what we have," Farron assures her, taking her hand into his. "Look at me. No, I'm not a member of Liberteum."

Fiolla closes her eyes, finally relaxing. She explains what happened with Valen, the PSS, and the BCS at their meeting. They are convinced there is a leak, and she needs to ensure it's not her.

"Is it possible the information I'm giving you is finding its way to them?" she asks him, looking for one more assurance.

"It's possible," he admits after pondering the question. "What happens once I use the information to protect my family interests is out of my control."

"Then it has to stop. I can't risk it anymore. There are too many eyes watching now. I'm sorry."

"I understand," he says with resignation in his voice. "I would never want to place you in a more compromising position than I already have. I appreciate you taking risks as long as you did."

"Does this affect your...interests?"

"Considering the speed at which public safety is rounding up urches, it's inevitable. This saved us a lot of headaches."

"Do you mind me asking what those interests are?" Fiolla asks, turning over to face him.

"Information. What the urches do best is gather intelligence on our rivals. They are especially effective at reporting their underground activities. You'd be surprised how many wealthy families are involved in the black market."

"I'm not sure anything surprises me anymore. This is getting bad, Farron."

"Maybe this will help. You've done so much for me that I need to return the favor. My father arranged for an urch with a loose affiliation to Liberteum to inform the PSS of one of their locations."

Fiolla's eyes light up. "When will he share what he knows?"

"He may already have. It's not as simple as just walking into One Guardian Plaza."

"That's amazing, Farron! Thank you!"

Fiolla grabs him, and they kiss. With a few more hours until she needs to leave, there is still time to enjoy each other's company. Sleep is overrated, especially when they have so little time to spend on the more pleasurable activities in life.

CHAPTER TWENTY-SEVEN

INTERCORPEX

Global Network Operations Center
Manhattan Financial District
ICX New York Exchange

That man is a walking, talking, perpetual motion machine that could power a small city with his boundless energy. Lyris finds the way Wyeth conducts New York exchange operations inspiring. It's also why he's wide awake and raring to go at six a.m., when all the global director of operations can think about is a strong cup of coffee.

"This must be important if you called me up here this early," Wyeth says after Lyris's office door swings open. "You look like hell. What time did you get here?"

"I never left," Lyris says, leaning back in his chair and taking a long sip from his mug.

"Problems overseas?"

"Let's go for a walk. I need a refill."

Instead of heading to the break room or traveling to the little coffee shop on the ground floor, the two men exit the building and head down Wall Street. Most employees don't leave for work until around eight, leaving the sidewalk sparse at this hour. Lyris still looks around, ensuring the few people he sees are not within earshot.

"My problems are actually all in New York. We work for the biggest one."

"Yesterday's meeting with Valen was that bad? What happened?"

"It's not important. Let's just say Raimius showed his colorful side after it. What I'm about to tell you can never be repeated. I've been ordered to release information that implicates the *gentez-minorez* in the attack on our datacenters."

"Wait," Wyeth says, stopping. "Nothing definitively links them to that attack."

"Exactly."

"So, he wants you to lie about it? Why?"

Lyris nods for him to keep walking. "Raimius wants to divide the patricians. He's convinced that they've allied with Valen and want to remove him from power."

"That sounds exactly like some fiction that Raimius would conjure up. What's the real reason?"

"Preventing patricians from rallying against his move to broadly enhance Intercorpex's power. I think he wants to open trading up to employees."

"You can't be serious," Wyeth moans.

"It would simultaneously strip corporate power over their employees and dilute the patricians. It's genius. I just can't figure out how he plans to do it."

"If you're right, Raimius is playing a dangerous game. If the patricians find out, it will undermine our credibility and end the exchange as we know it."

Lyris shakes his head. "I don't think he cares. Raimius is becoming more neurotic by the day. He became AG by convincing the regents that his predecessor had lost control. Irony has a sense of humor."

Lyris and Wyeth enter the small bakery and get their coffees. He pulls out his e-fob embossed with the ICX logo and waves it in front of the scanner to debit his account. Corporate employees have bank accounts linked to their biojacks, but Intercorpex has no such leash.

"What are you going to do?" Wyeth asks after they step back onto the sidewalk.

"Nothing. I can't be associated with the release of that information."

"So, you're going to ignore a direct order from the AG?"

"No, I can't do that, either. Raimius would replace me for insubordination in a nanosecond. The information needs to be leaked. That's why we're getting coffee."

He scoffs and then lets out a little disbelieving laugh. "Lyris, with all due respect, that's not exactly in my job description."

"I would never ask under any other circumstances. You're more than a subordinate, Wyeth, you're a friend. You defended me after the attack. That Intercorpex Service Star I received is as much yours as mine. It's time for me to repay that."

Wyeth rubs his chin as they approach the outside of the NOC. He stares up at the façade. This is the only building he has ever worked in. He rose through the ranks here to one of its most powerful positions by avoiding predicaments like this one.

"A vacation on some island in the Caribbean Corporation would be a better reward."

"You can bask in the sun on some sandy beach with a fruity drink in your hand when this is over. Big changes are coming – the kind that will lead to you sitting in my office and running the whole exchange."

"I appreciate the vote of confidence. I do. But that'll never happen and we both know it."

It's a rare individual who knows his place in the order of things. Most people claw their way up whatever ranks they can in a world where upward mobility is severely limited. Wyeth is content to do the job he has and do it well. That's how Lyris knows that he can rely on him.

"Normally that would be true, but as I said, changes are coming. You're the director of New York operations, and someday soon you'll be the director of global operations. I promise you, I'll do everything in my power to make that happen. First, I need you to do this one thing for me."

Wyeth stares straight ahead as he weighs his decision. Agreeing to get involved is a huge risk despite the deception coming at the behest of the administrator-general. If things don't work out, the regents will sack everyone involved. Lyris understands that a headfirst dive into the deep end of the pool requires an act of courage…and faith.

"Okay," he says, looking over at Lyris. "How do you want it done?"

CHAPTER TWENTY-EIGHT

AMERICA, INC.

The America Tower
Manhattan Financial Geographic District
New York City Municipal Corporation

Valen thanks his assistant as she shows Aris Fontainbleu into his spacious office. The two men exchange greetings, and the CEO takes his arm and helps him to the seating area. He's an old man by modern standards, even for a patrician. Medical care took enormous steps backward during and after the economic collapse. The resulting plummet in life expectancy only began to rise a decade and a half ago.

Frail and suffering from the ailments that come with an aging body, his mind is still sharp. Despite being in the *gentez-majorez*, he's not a significant shareholder of any one corporate stock. His diversified portfolio contains shares of every stock on the IGI and blocks of subsidiary corporations that trade on the secondary exchange.

"Thank you for coming, sir, although you didn't need to rush over. Can I offer you anything?"

"No, I'm fine, thank you, Chief Executive Valen. I don't get the opportunity to meet corporate leaders much these days. My children and grandchildren tend to the family's interests now. Naturally, your invitation aroused my curiosity."

"I just thought we could talk. You've seen things, Aris. More than most people have."

"It's always a pleasure to get called old," he says without a smile.

"I'm sorry. I meant no offense."

"I know you didn't. At my age, my satisfactions include regular bowel movements and making people uncomfortable with sarcastic comments."

Valen looks out the window from his seat. The sunset was twenty minutes ago, and the lingering light is slowly yielding to the encroaching dusk. Lights flick on all around the city, and in another twenty minutes, the view of the towering skyscrapers will be completely different. This is an amazing city. It took decades to get it to the thriving metropolis it is now.

"How old were you during the Great Collapse?"

"I was a young and dumb twenty-year-old full of idealistic optimism. I was in college and planned to change the world when I graduated. It's the same thing every young person thinks when they're about to step foot into the 'real world.' Then that world changed for me. It changed for all of us."

"It was the ultimate test. Your generation was the reason humanity survived." Aris lets out an amused laugh. "What's funny?"

"How history changes perceptions. I suppose it's a good thing the world doesn't name generations anymore. The one I belonged to was known as 'Zoomers.' We were despised by previous generations even more than the 'Millennials' before us. People thought we were coddled and sheltered from the world's harsh realities, and they weren't completely wrong. Valen, you're a busy man…are the ramblings of an old man with a foot in the grave really what you want to hear?"

"I do. I know what's recorded in history. I also know how it's been…finessed. It's a privilege to hear the experience from someone who lived through it."

Aris leans back on the sofa and takes his turn staring out the window. 'Finessed' is an understated word for it.

"My generation was reared on unearned accolades. Winning wasn't valued like it is today. The desire to be a champion was an afterthought. Just showing up was rewarded because everyone was afraid that losing would damage our self-esteem. We were characterized as fragile because we were, so they called us 'snowflakes.'"

"I've never heard that."

"It's not a narrative the early executives promoted. Every generation is different from the one that preceded it, but we were very different. Many of us lived with our parents until well into our twenties. We were addicted to drugs. We were addicted to technology and something called 'social media.' We lacked confidence and ambition. Our whole generation was completely dependent on others for almost everything. And then it all came to an end.

"In some respects, the economic collapse was the single greatest thing that happened to us. In one moment, every support system we relied upon was gone. We were forced to adapt. To become individuals. To fight for ourselves. Those who did joined the corporations trying to restore order and began rebuilding. Those who didn't…well, they perished."

Valen leans forward, paying rapt attention. An alliance of powerful companies joined forces to restore order when the government collapsed. They were an ark of sorts: a vessel in a stormy sea of chaos and despair that was the best chance to avoid prolonged anarchy. They get the credit for organizing the recovery, but it was the people who made it happen. Aris's generation gave birth to the modern corporation.

The youth were the laborers who rebuilt the infrastructure, the farmers who fed them, and the guards who provided them security.

"Corporatism was born from the belief that people were unable to make important decisions for themselves – that the great experiment in democracy was the world's undoing," Valen states, drawing from his own understanding of those fateful events.

"And my generation proved those early executives correct. When given the chance, we returned to our pre-collapse mentality. We sacrificed freedom and independence for comfort and stability."

"You don't think very highly of your contemporaries," Valen observes.

"Those aren't my feelings," he corrects. "Those are the facts. Corporatism rose only because my generation embraced it. I only explained why they did. Do you want to know the *real* reason behind the collapse?"

Valen nods as his guest coughs and waves his hand toward the pitcher of water on the credenza. The CEO rushes over, pours a glass, and hands it to him.

"It was the people. Not just the rich and powerful, or the corrupt governments like history books profess. It wasn't even my 'snowflake' generation. It was the people. All of them."

"How could the people be responsible?"

"Because they stopped believing in institutions they held sacred. In the 1960s, it was the government. Politicians failed the people during the Vietnam War and never stopped failing them. Then, starting in the 1980s, it was corporations. The tech bubble, the housing bubble, countless financial crises, greed, manufacturing shortcuts, low wages…the list goes on.

"Then things got worse. Priests molesting children undermined the Church. Police brutality undermined law enforcement. A growing divide between civilians and service members undermined the military. Parents undermined teachers, school boards undermined parents, and everyone failed to prepare students for the real world. The family unit disintegrated. Personal relationships eroded. All we were left with was faith in ourselves. For my generation, that was a death sentence."

Valen shakes his head. "Aris, government leaders drove us off the cliff with their rampant corruption and ill-advised policies. That's an inescapable fact."

The patrician lets out a laugh. "Oh, there were some beauties running the nations of the world at that time, for sure. The truth is that the people were already in a stampede heading for the edge. Remember, most people chose their leaders back then. Ask yourself why they chose them."

"We solved that problem. The board of directors makes those decisions now," Valen argues.

"Yes, since the inception of America Incorporated, the people have everything they say they wanted: jobs, safety, security, entertainment…. Except most people don't know what they want. They only think they do. The ones who do know cast themselves out of society, and…"

"And we call them 'urches.'"

Aris nods. The headaches caused by urches have superseded the strife from the quli laborers. The debate over what to do with the captured ones is still raging down in Washington. The BCS wants to eradicate them, and Human Resources wants to reeducate and reintegrate them. So far, no worthwhile solution has been found.

"You consider them criminals because they rejected the system you deeply believe in. They also think outside the box. America Incorporated has historically penalized that gift instead of embracing it. For all intents and purposes, those sewer dwellers are this world's greater fools."

Valen understands the reference. 'Greater fool' is an old business theory that states that prices are not determined by the actual value of something, but rather by the irrational beliefs of market participants. A rational buyer justifies paying more because they believe that someone else, a greater fool, will be willing to pay an even higher price for it later. Commerce cannot take place without the greater fools. They are a powerful force of progress. He's not comfortable with its application to urches in this context.

"I think you're giving them too much credit."

"Am I? You're approaching this battle against the terrorists in the wrong way. You're fighting them with conventional tactics, and they're beating you with unconventional ones. The harder you fight them your way, the more spectacular your failure will be."

Valen stares down at his hands as he rubs them together. "Aris, I invited you here for guidance, not to have our shortcomings pointed out."

"I'm too old and tired to measure words, Chief Executive," he says with an edge to his tone. Valen meets his eyes and sees the relentless stare of a man not interested in preventing hurt feelings. "Stop playing into their hands, Valen. They know your playbook. Every time you flip the page, they're a chapter ahead of you. You're doing exactly what they want you to do."

"So, we need to scrap the playbook?"

"No, son, you need to completely change the game. You need to recognize that this fight *against* Liberteum is not *about* Liberteum."

The chief executive inhales deeply. His guest is becoming more and more cryptic. Valen prides himself on understanding vague innuendo, but he's struggling to keep up.

"If this struggle isn't about them, then who is it about?"

"Your *own* employees. Liberteum believes that whatever price they pay in this conflict to sway the sentiments of your employees will be worth the cost."

"I don't believe that," Valen argues. He has more faith in his employees than Aris does.

"Because you're conditioned to think that way. Open your mind and understand that you are fighting for the soul of humanity, and on the verge of losing."

Valen shakes his head. "I'm afraid I don't understand."

"Your true enemy is the same today as it was sixty years ago," Aris says, leaning forward. "If Liberteum causes employees to lose faith in institutions again, we will all relive the Great Collapse. You move a little closer to that with every failure. This time there may be no path to follow out of the darkness."

CHAPTER TWENTY-NINE

UNDERGRADUATE RYKOS

Central Park
East of Lincoln Square Geographic District
New York City Municipal Corporation

The e-note came out of the blue. I hadn't expected to hear from her again. But I was wrong. I replied to the message and told her to meet me in Central Park. She agreed, and fifteen minutes later, I'm watching a vision walk toward me down the sidewalk.

There is a lot that needs to be said. The last time I saw her ended abruptly and left lingering unanswered questions for both of us. We embrace and hold it for a beat longer than is usually acceptable. The end of the hug will leave us face-to-face with little idea of where to start this conversation. The weather is nice. Harvard starts soon. Our families are excited. It would all be small talk skirting the real questions.

"Do you want to walk?" Mollae asks once we separate.

"Sure."

It's a slow stroll between graduates in no rush to be anywhere. We may be the only two people in this city doing that. Life in the corporation is a race. Every employee is constantly on the move.

"I know this is awkward, Rykos. For both of us. I was having such a great time until we were interrupted. Who was that man? And the woman with him?" Mollae asks.

"Chief Inspector Zyree of Intercorpex Security. He was the man who rescued me from the terrorists at Broad Street Station. I don't know who the woman was. He introduced her, but I forgot her name."

"What did he want?"

"To talk. He was looking for intelligence on Liberteum. Something urgent, which is why he was so rude."

"I thought you told the BCS everything you knew."

"I did. Multiple times. The BCS doesn't share information with Intercorpex Security. He doesn't know the story."

"And you told him?"

"The short version, yes."

Mollae accepts the explanation without further question. It was a convincing lie. I'm getting good at that, and it's not something I should feel proud of.

"He knew a lot about me."

I don't respond.

"He knew my grades and my getting into Harvard," she continues.

She glances over at me but I don't react.

"I guess I should explain what he was talking about with my father and Public Safety and Security."

"You don't need to. Whatever happened doesn't matter. The past is the past."

Mollae loudly exhales in relief. That was a source of stress between us. Her first concern was what I thought of her getting in trouble with the PSS. What she couldn't know is that I willingly went to an urch rave. I'm hardly one to judge her.

Unlike our last date, she isn't hanging onto my arm. Outside of the hug, we haven't touched at all. A thought occurs to me. I might not be into her, but she isn't into me, either. She wants to be with a hero of the corporation. That's it.

"I have a question for you. Can you imagine a world without corporatism?"

She turns her head and squints at me. "Why would I want to? Better yet, why would you want to?"

"No reason. Sometimes I wonder what it would be like if I lived a hundred years ago."

"I don't. Corporations are the greatest force of good in world history. They rebuilt a civilized society after the collapse and eliminated the inhumanity of the pre-corporate eras."

"By erasing homelessness, war, poverty, blah, blah, blah. I attended my modules."

"So, why are you questioning them?" she asks, concern dripping in her voice.

"I'm not," I lie. "Only, corporations have been around for centuries. Why didn't they do any of that stuff before?"

"Governments stopped them, silly. They kept passing laws and raising taxes to keep corporations from acting on behalf of the people."

I nod a few times. "Wasn't a corporation's purpose to earn a profit?"

"Sure, but those profits were reinvested in communities. They invested in research and innovation. That's how the world progressed. Think about how much further we would have advanced had governments stayed out of their way."

"What about now? Why don't they innovate?"

"They do."

"For the betterment of people?"

Mollae takes a hard look at me.

"Why are you asking all this?"

"I don't know. I'm just curious what you think about it."

"I think as we all should. Like we need to. We're future executives, Rykos. Employees are going to look to us for leadership. You need to provide it."

"Aren't I?"

"You don't sound like it. Questioning the system is not leadership. It's sedition. It's treason. You sound like one of the terrorists."

How would she know what Liberteum sounds like? Quarren had no voice. Michele has no voice. They are subjected to the narrative the corporations and Intercorpex construct for them. What Mollae thinks happened was drawn from words assembled in an employee relations office and uttered by our chief executive and his minions. None of it is fact, let alone truth.

"I'm not one of them," I argue. "I killed their leader."

"I know. And you're a hero of the corporation because of it. Act like one. You've been handed the chance at an amazing executive career on a gilded platter. You could be the CEO of America Incorporated someday. Don't throw that away with nonsensical talk."

We continue our stroll in silence. There's nothing left to say. Mollae is just like my sister – driven, dedicated, and completely brainwashed. There is no future between us, despite her intelligence and beauty. It would be a power relationship, not a loving one. That's not a unique concept, but not something I'm interested in.

"I should get going," I say, no longer willing to endure the tense silence.

"It was good seeing you again, Rykos."

Mollae turns back for home. There is no hug or kiss. No affection of any kind. Any thought of a relationship is dead, not that there ever was much hope for one. We are different people who want different things. Mollae is an instrument of the corporation. I wonder how many others are just like her.

CHAPTER THIRTY

AMERICA, INC.

Tycoon Park Underground
Midtown Geographic District
New York City Municipal Corporation

Teman studies the map on the oversized tablet and exhales. Tycoon Park was built during the first rehabilitation of New York City following the collapse. The block between Forty-Eighth and Forty-Ninth Streets straddling Second and Third Avenues was once filled with businesses and residences. Engineers deemed the buildings too damaged to be saved. The area was razed and a park was constructed with a traditional surface green space and a special subterranean "lowline" for inclement weather. Somehow, the urches are using a void somewhere in there to run their operation.

"Here we go again, Chief Guardian," Spirak says, looking over his shoulder at the field command unit screens. The feeds display the guardians' helmet cameras, but nothing yet from the target area.

"Let's hope it isn't more of the same," Teman says with a heavy sigh. "Do we have eyes on yet?"

"No, sir, not yet. There is a series of tunnels carved through subbasements that lead to the western edge of Tycoon Park. We have Alpha team staged here," Spirak says, pointing at the map, "with Bravo in support here. Twenty-four men in full tactical load-out."

"Deploy the drones. Let's see what we're dealing with."

"Yes, sir," Lieutenant Aschalai says. Teman remembers her from the EOC the day of the Manhattan explosions. "Drones away."

Teman watches the camera feeds from the small quadcopters as they effortlessly maneuver in the tight underground spaces. He feels the butterflies kicking up in his stomach. He's trying to remain positive for his guardians, but this feels too easy.

"Sir, incoming intel from the RTCC," Lieutenant Aschalai says, pulling it up on one of her screens.

The RTCC used ground-penetrating radar from a drone to image the area. It shows dead space on the western edge of the park. Incorporating an overlay of an overhead map of New York City from 2027, there were two buildings that occupied that footprint.

"Did you know any of this was down here?" Spirak asks.

"Nobody did," Teman mutters. "It was supposed to have all been filled in when the park was constructed."

In the rush to rehabilitate the city, shortcuts were taken and never documented by architects or engineers. The PSS has found dozens of instances of these inconsistencies since their sweeps began following the terrorist attack. And executives wonder why Liberteum is so hard to pinpoint and eradicate.

"They cut that corner. We never would have found them under there. How did the urch who turned himself in yesterday know this was here?"

"He had a falling out with Liberteum. He wanted to trade the information for clemency."

"Do you trust him?" Spirak asks, looking up at his boss.

"Are urches ever to be trusted?"

"Drones have reached our teams…wait a second. I have a thermal image between us and the target area."

Aschalai's fingers dance as she calls up a tracker on a secondary display and overlays a map on it. The map fades to twenty percent transparency so they can see a wireframe with current information. The blue dots are the tactical team members. The single red dot is the unknown subject. It could just be an urch navigating the tunnel, but Teman doubts it.

"Alpha team, do you have friendly personnel forward of your position?" she asks to confirm.

"Negative."

"Okay, then you have company ten meters to your direct front," Lieutenant Aschalai relays.

"Alpha team, go radio silent. Do not let him see you. If he gets too close, take him down quietly," Spirak orders.

The order is too late. Gunfire erupts and is immediately returned. The muzzle flashes show up like fireballs on the thermal camera. They can hear the reports rumble down through the underground. After the brief exchange, the figure disappears behind a wall and is gone.

"Damn it!"

"We're compromised, sir," Spirak says. "We need to pull back."

"No. Order the assault!"

Teman knows this is their best lead. He needs to show progress and can't wait around for another opportunity. Who knows how long it will be before they get one. They have to act. Aschalai and Spirak both stare at him.

"Sir, they'll be expecting us. I don't think—"

"Alpha team, this is the chief guardian. Breach! Breach! Breach!"

The ghostly images dance on the displays as the guardians expertly take turns lurching forward and seeking cover. They enter a larger space and all hell breaks loose. Gunfire erupts in massive volleys from the back wall. The signatures from their muzzles burst like camera flashes on the display. Teman watches as several men go down, and the rest take cover behind their portable titanium shields.

"Drone One just went offline," Aschalai says, piloting the other out of harm's way. She rotates the camera and leads the vehicle along the far wall, where muzzle flashes erupt every five feet. "They built firing ports and are using heavy weapons for suppressive fire."

"They'll get cut to pieces!" Spirak exclaims in a panic. "Their personal shields can't withstand this volume of fire. We have to get them out of there!"

"Sir, we have a blocking force in the lowline beneath the park. That's the only escape route. We can gas them out," Lieutenant Aschalai chimes in.

Although not as common as the high-powered strobes, sonic weapons, or the active denial system used to break up urch raves, gas can incapacitate threats. These lachrymatory agents are chemical weapons that cause severe eye, respiratory, and skin irritation, and can lead to vomiting and blindness after prolonged exposure. They come in grenade form or can be pumped in via hose from tanker trucks on street level.

"We can't assume they don't have an escape route we don't know about, Lieutenant," Teman argues. "I'm going to lead them in."

The two guardians start to protest as he grabs his rifle and bolts forward through the maze of cellars and utility tunnels leading to the underground outskirts of the park. His infrared-enhanced night vision illuminates the pitch-black route.

"What have we got?" he asks the Bravo team leader.

"Alpha is pinned down on the other side of this door. It's some sort of secondary room before the main area. We've tried using non-lethal measures to push them back so we can breach. All ineffective. None of the terrorists budged."

Teman gets in the prone position and uses his arms and toes to rock forward and peek through the doorway. Bullets zip past his head. They were aimed high, but still too close for comfort and he rocks back. Doorways are "fatal funnels" because an enemy can concentrate fire on them during entry. This one is living up to its name, and it's not the only one they need to get through.

"Then we try lethal ones."

The chief guardian pulls out a fragmentary grenade from his body armor. He twists the two halves to activate the soup can-sized black cylinder. Wasting no time, he rolls it underhand through the door and hears it clank against the far door.

"Cover!"

The grenade pops itself upright and a spring activates. The explosive jumps into the air and detonates, blasting shrapnel horizontally and downward. The noise is deafening, even with ear defenders in. The device did the trick. The volume of gunfire drops significantly and the door to the main room blows open.

"Forward!" Teman screams, bounding through the first door.

He takes two rounds into his body armor and collapses, the wind knocked out of his lungs. Bravo team climbs over his prone body, firing rifles at their cyclic rate. Two men drag him across the ground to the sturdy metal table one of the Alpha team members upends to use for cover.

"Are you okay, Chief Guardian?" Spirak asks as Lieutenant Aschalai returns fire. They decided to join the fray.

"Yeah, the armor took the brunt of it."

"I think they pulled back," Aschalai says, leaving her hiding spot and advancing through the room.

The two men follow, steering clear of the rounds being fired through the doorway to the main room. Alpha team is firing in through the softball-sized ports that the terrorists were firing their heavy weapons from. Teman taps the commander on the shoulder as he manipulates a snake camera into the hole. They watch the feed on his wrist tablet.

"What do you see?"

"Heavy machinery. They may be taking cover behind it."

"How many?"

"Hard to tell. There could be three or thirty."

Smoke and dust choke the stagnant air of both rooms. Teman can barely see the team leader next to him. They could be a blocking force covering a retreat or they could be making their last stand. Either way, Teman knows this will be their last mission if they fail.

"Who do we have left?" he asks Captain Spirak.

"Four from Alpha, nine from Bravo, and the three of us," he says, nodding over to Aschalai. "More support is fifteen minutes out."

"Fifteen minutes? Where are they coming from, Brooklyn?"

"Sir, they're moving—"

"We're ending this right now. Drop smoke in through those firing ports."

Spirak relays the order, and Alpha team pushes two smoke grenades through each of the holes and the doorway. White smoke billows out of the firing ports and shattered doorway. The firing ceases.

"Guardians, this ends today," Teman says into his throat mic as he pulls out his remaining grenade. "Alpha goes first and to the right, followed by Bravo to the left. The command team goes up the middle. Move fast, stop for nothing. We will envelop and overwhelm them. Form up."

Nodding at the captain, they arm the grenades and sling them through the open doorway. The teams take cover, not shouting anything that would tip off their adversaries. Five seconds later, the grenades detonate within a quarter second of each other.

"Go!"

The first four men disappear into the room and gunfire erupts. Bravo follows them in, heading in the opposite direction. Teman falls in behind his two officers as they launch themselves through the door to dart through the middle. He takes a step. Then another. Then another.

Two explosions rock the room. Teman feels shrapnel piercing the air around him. Men scream over the radio when another blast hits him like a sledgehammer. Shrapnel slices through the captain and lieutenant as the force blows them backward.

Teman's ears are ringing. He can't move. His vision is blurry...the halos of bright pops of light. Gunfire....

The rifle reports slowly decrease until a blanket of silence grips the room. Everything is still as if time itself stops moving. His senses return, and he finds himself pinned beneath what's left of Spirak. To his left, the lifeless eyes of Lieutenant Aschalai stare back at him. So young and promising.

Wounded men moan. Teman can hear the footfalls of heavy boots on the dingy concrete floor. He tries to pull himself out from under the pile of broken and bleeding flesh to reach his holstered handgun. He's pinned. He can't get to it. With increasing desperation, the chief guardian gropes the darkness for his rifle. Wherever it is, it's not within reach.

He jumps at the two loud pops from a weapon. A double-tap. He doesn't know if it's his guardians or the terrorists and doesn't dare call out. Not until his vision and hearing return. He needs to know what's happening. Two more pops pierce the air and the last of the moaning ceases.

"Clear."

"Clear."

The chief guardian allows himself to relax a little at the sound of standard room-clearing techniques. It has to be his men. Thank God. Despite the tremendous loss of life, they scored their first victory against Liberteum.

Deadweight is called that for a reason. Teman manages to push Spirak off and free himself when a beam of light hits his face, blinding him. He shields his eyes as several other men wielding torchlights form a loose semicircle around him. Something is very wrong.

An injured man limps over. Teman strains to see his clothing—it's not a guardian uniform. He cranes his neck at the ominous figure pointing a handgun at his face. The recognition is instant when the man's face gets illuminated by the torchlight.

"This must be my lucky day," Haven says, grinning from ear to ear. He takes a knee and looks Teman in the eye. "Hello, Chief Guardian. Were you looking for me?"

CHAPTER THIRTY-ONE

INTERCORPEX

Global Network Operations Center
Manhattan Financial District
ICX New York Exchange

The Wall Street Network Operations Center is Intercorpex's nerve center. It not only monitors New York trading but also oversees global operations. The man responsible sits in a swanky office at the top of the building. He practically lives there, except for when he's making lives miserable on the NOC floor.

"I thought I told you I never wanted to see you in New York again," Executive Director Lyris says after Zyree is shown into his office.

"I wasn't listening."

"Naturally. What are you doing here?"

"I'm on orders from the commissioner-general to continue the hunt for the perpetrators of the attack on our facility."

"I'm sure you are, and it's *my* facility. Who are you?" he asks, pointing to Zyree's hostile colleague.

"Chief Inspector Chiana, sir," she says, stepping forward and shaking his hand. "I requested this meeting."

"At nine forty-five in the evening?"

"Please accept my apologies, sir. It was the only time you were available," she says with a slight bow.

Zyree rolls his eyes. She's laying it on thick—what a suck-up.

"How can I help you?" Lyris asks, clearly enjoying the deferential treatment.

Chiana begins briefing Lyris, doing an adequate job other than forgetting important aspects of Zyree's decision-making. That spin would have made a great corporate executive or even better pre-collapse politician.

"Do you think harassing the son of a high-ranking municipal corporate employee is investigating, Zyree?"

"I call it following an instinct."

"I'm sure you do. And you think this 'instinct' will lead you to the terrorists' front door?"

"It led me to yours when I saved your ass a week ago."

"You'll have to pardon us, Chief Inspector Chiana," Lyris says with a charming smile. "Zyree and I have a short but turbulent history. I run a tight ship around here and he's the loose cannon on the deck trying to sink it."

"I understand completely, sir."

He's about to say something in his defense when notification of an incoming priority displays on his contacts. The bureaucratic wrangling will have to wait. This must be important.

"Connect video," Zyree instructs his biocomp. The image of his trusted partner pops up a second later. "Malkor."

"You're taking a call?" Lyris says, insulted and incredulous.

"Sorry to interrupt, but this is urgent. Duckballs and Bird's Nest intercepted some communications traffic from the PSS. Liberteum took chief Guardian Teman after a failed raid."

"What's going on?" Lyris barks.

Zyree resents playing go-between but isn't about to patch Malkor into Lyris's office communications system. He won't subject his subordinate to that.

"Two members of your staff intercepted PSS messages. Chief Guardian Teman is in the hands of the terrorists."

"Two of my staff? Are they helping you? Why wasn't I told?"

"I guess you don't run as tight a ship as you think you do," Zyree says, smirking.

"We're trying to get more information," Malkor continues, "but things are chaotic over there. From what we can tell, they've lost contact with his biojacks. I'll let you get back to your fun and brief you once we learn more. "

"Why are you spying on the PSS?" Lyris demands as Malkor disconnects the VidLynk.

"I told you. I've been charged with hunting down Liberteum. Public safety has the best intelligence on them, so I tapped into it. Now I have the best intelligence on them."

"You hacked into their system?" Chiana asks, probably hoping that she can show off her regulation-quoting skills to Lyris.

"It wouldn't be the first time," the director laments. Zyree frowns. Here it comes.

"You know that's a violation of—"

"Spare me, please."

"She's right. You play hard and fast with the rules. Maybe Chief Inspector Chiana should be running this investigation."

The corner of Zyree's mouth curls up. Lyris has found himself a kindred spirit. They're both ambitious, by the book, and completely useless. They'll make a great team.

"I don't know, Lyris. Why don't you ask Jurghen?"

"It's *Executive Director* Lyris," he says, anger flashing in his baby blue eyes. "And maybe I will. It would get you out of my sight once and for all."

"Good luck with that."

Jurghen hates being told how to run his inspectors, especially by people like Lyris. The request will be listened to and subsequently ignored.

"Is there a threat to this facility, Chief Inspector Chiana?"

"No, sir, I don't believe there is at this time. You'll be the first to know if that changes," she says, causing Lyris to smile.

Zyree is being cut out of the conversation on purpose. Part of him doesn't care, but he is irritated because they're destined to screw things up. This is still his investigation, even if he doesn't want it.

"Please report any and all of Chief Inspector Zyree's infractions to me, and note any that your chain of command fails to act on."

"Yes, sir, I will." Chiana is so pleased with herself that she's bursting.

"Is there anything else, Zyree?"

It's time to go back on the offensive. "As a matter of fact, there is. I'm taking seven of your staff and am commandeering the same conference room as last time. Unless, of course, you want to say no."

He recognizes the dare for what it is. So long as Zyree gets what he wants, he'll let Lyris think he's winning. The poor guy is always a step or two behind with no chance of catching up.

"Anything to help Intercorpex Security. The room is yours. Chiana, check with Nolirah. She'll provide you a list of technicians that can be temporarily reassigned."

"I serve at your pleasure, Director," she says with another bow.

"If there's nothing further, get the hell out of my office, Zyree."

Zyree smirks and walks out. He's not about to bow.

CHAPTER THIRTY-TWO

LIBERTEUM

Safe House
Tribeca Geographic District
New York City Municipal Corporation

Michele dismissed Adiz and Jasper when a wild-eyed Haven showed up snorting like a bull. He's on an adrenaline high that he hasn't come down from. After hearing about the events at the armory, she can understand why he's amped up. It's how he'll channel that rage that's the problem.

That's why Farron chose to stick around, despite the late hour. He's equally curious. The patrician already has reservations about Haven and wants to see if they're confirmed.

"Where is he now?" Michele asks.

"Nyvar and my guys are moving him to someplace safe."

"You're holding the chief guardian of the PSS hostage. He's transmitting. There is no place safe in this city."

"I cut his biojacks out and left them on the floor with the rotting corpses of his stormtroopers. Trust me; he's not transmitting."

Michele scoffs and shakes her head. "Haven, he's the *chief guardian*. He probably has biojacks inserted who knows where."

"That's why we put the mesh net over him before leaving the Bastille. If we missed one, that signal isn't getting out of the underground. He's invisible."

It was a prudent measure. The net looks like medieval chainmail and functions like a Faraday cage. The mesh blanket is constructed using a conductive material that blocks electric fields. It will attenuate biojack signals to the point that the PSS would have to be on top of them to pick it up.

"Where are you keeping him, Haven?" Michele demands.

He narrows his eyes at her. "None of your damn business."

"*Everything* is my business. I'm Liberteum's leader."

"Where were you when the PSS stormed in? Oh, that's right. You're a coward who hides behind a computer because you've convinced yourself that Archimedes will change the world. You're not a leader and don't know the first thing about combat."

Michele clenches her fists as tight as her jaw. "You don't think I feel their losses just as much as you do?"

Haven walks around her in a circle, probably expecting her to stay square to him. She doesn't, but rather lets him make his alpha male orbit to show his dominance.

"The PSS knew we were there. How is it possible that two dozen heavily armed guardians showed up right where I was?"

"How the hell would I know?"

"What about you, Farron?" Haven asks the patrician.

He's leaning against the wall and watching. Michele thinks it was his way of running a low profile. Haven just spoiled that notion.

"I have no idea."

"Yeah, right. Princess here is telling the truth, but you're lying."

Haven was a highly trained Intercorpex inspector. Although his former comrades employ all sorts of technological enhancements to decipher behavior, they are still trained to use their instincts. He thinks Farron is hiding something but Haven should be angrier than he is. That means he's also hiding something.

"You need to check yourself."

"Or what?" Haven asks, taking a menacing step toward him.

"You can't hold the chief guardian hostage," Michele says, pivoting Haven away from answering Farron's challenge. "They'll tear this city apart looking for him."

"He's a prisoner of war, not a hostage. You do remember who the enemy is?"

"Don't presume to lecture me about this struggle. I started it."

"Your father started it," Haven barks. "You're just losing. This plan of yours isn't going to change a damn thing."

Michele glances over at Farron. He shakes his head. No matter what happens, nobody will win this standoff.

"Release the chief guardian."

"No."

"It's not a request," Farron reiterates.

"You're a spoiled little bitch, Farron. You don't give orders around here," Haven says, turning back to Michele. "And *you* don't have the stomach to lead Liberteum. Maybe it's time for a coup."

Haven sweeps his arm against his side and pulls a knife in one fluid movement. Michele sees it just in time to lean back hard and away from his arcing underhand thrust. The blade slices through the clothing and skin on her left shoulder.

He deftly changes the grip and plunges it toward her chest while she's off-balance. Michele recovers in time to narrow his angle of attack and grabs his arm on the way down. She slides under it and uses his momentum to bend him forward at the waist, locking his elbow to the rear.

She thinks about crashing an elbow down on his collarbone in an attempt to break it, but Haven is too strong. It won't work. He's already recovering from the move when she pushes away from him and reaches for the small of her back.

Haven spins, trying to slash her again. He's too slow. Michele ducks and pops upright, swinging her arm and slicing his chest with her knife. He recoils and steps back.

He dabs at his chest with his fingers, keeping his eyes on her. Then he licks his fingers. The pain doesn't faze Haven. The sick bastard looks like he enjoys it.

"I'm going to enjoy gutting you."

"Bring it."

The first rule in a knife fight is understanding that you will get cut. The key to surviving is ensuring that it's not in a critical area when it happens. To win, you must disarm your opponent. That won't be easy against a man with Haven's experience and training.

The pair moves counterclockwise in unison, both crouching low and balancing on the balls of their feet. He has the size and experience advantage, but Michele's quickness is an equalizer. Haven thrusts his knife toward her abdomen. She steps laterally a split second too late. The blade cuts into her side as she drags her own across his shoulder and upper arm.

He grunts as he pivots, and Michele whiffs on a thrust at his torso. She doesn't register his left elbow's movement in time to stop it from crashing into her temple. She falls to the ground and rolls as his boot crashes on the floorboards inches from her head.

Her vision is a galaxy of stars. She's sensing more than seeing. Michele buries the knife into Haven's leg. He bucks immediately, causing her to lose the grip on her weapon. With her disarmed, he has the advantage. She desperately looks around the floor and furniture for anything that can be used as a weapon. Nothing.

Haven yanks the knife out of his leg and tosses it aside. "Now you die."

He steps toward her when a shot rings out. Haven changes direction and dives across the floor. Another shot is fired, followed by a third, both going wide. Farron has brought a gun to a knife fight. Haven has no tactical advantage and scrambles to the door. The patrician fires two more rounds at him and misses both. No longer concerned about Farron's ability to aim, Haven stops at the threshold and points his finger at Michele.

"This isn't over."

"Are you okay?" Farron asks after Haven disappears into the hallway.

Michele sits up, still trying to recover her senses. Farron takes a knee, steadying her with one hand while holding his gun in the other.

"Five shots, and you couldn't hit him once?"

"I don't shoot handguns. I'm a patrician. We go skeet shooting."

"You jumped in just in time. Thank you," Michele says, gingerly climbing to her feet.

"I thought you had him for a while there. I figured you'd want the privilege of killing him."

"More than ever, now. The gunshots…someone could have heard them."

"The walls in this building are soundproofed. It's a reason why I stashed you guys here. Drones won't even pick them up. What do we do now besides getting you some medical treatment?"

Michele checks her wounds and frowns. He cut her deeper than she realized. A few milliseconds slower, and she wouldn't have dodged that first slash. The thought makes her even angrier.

"We wait for Adiz and Jasper to return and pack up the equipment. We need to get out of here in case Haven comes back. Any ideas about where we can go?"

"Yeah, up a floor. I own the building."

"Of course you do," Michele says with a chuckle.

Farron looks around the apartment. "So, we switch floors, deploy security, whatever. Then what?"

Michele closes her eyes and moves over to the kitchen counter. This is what she was afraid of. Without her father, Haven is uncontrollable. He was the only man that the psycho listened to. She had hoped that this fight wasn't inescapable. She was wrong, and everyone knew it except her.

"We find Haven and kill him before he ruins everything."

CHAPTER THIRTY-THREE

UNDERGRADUATE RYKOS

Chief Guardian Teman's Domicile
Upper West Side Geographic District
New York City Municipal Corporation

I step off the elevator into our foyer and am greeted by a living area full of guardians with solemn looks. They wear expressions reserved for funerals, and I instantly fear the worst. One look at my mother sitting motionless on the sofa. That validates my cause for concern.

"What's going on?"

Chief Executive Safmor stands from the chair adjacent to the couch. His face is equally serious. I know mother was looking to get a job at Corporate Hall, but this isn't bad news about a refusal. There's only one thing it can be about.

"Why don't you come over here and take a seat, Rykos?" the CEO says.

"I don't want to sit. What happened to my father?"

It's the only logical conclusion. Safmor confirms it when he looks at my mother, who remains expressionless and completely impassive. The guardians in the room avert their eyes, leaving the municipal corporation's top executive to deliver the news.

"Your father conducted a raid against Liberteum earlier this evening. His teams were ambushed and killed when they stormed in. The terrorists took your father."

"Took him? What's that supposed to mean?" I ask, urging Safmor to state things plainly.

"It means we think that he's alive but is being held captive by the terrorists," one of the guardians explains. "We found three of his biojacks cut out. None of the others are transmitting."

Now I need to sit. I can only hope that Michele has him somewhere. Otherwise, Haven has him. Both scenarios are bad, but one is worse.

"Rykos, the PSS has teams and drones all over the city trying to locate him," Safmor says. "We'll find him."

I don't share his enthusiasm. They didn't find me when I was taken. This society is too reliant on technology and is helpless without it. If not for the attack on Intercorpex, I would still be down there. Liberteum managed to find his biojacks. Without them, they don't even have a place to start.

"I know this is hard to hear, son, but know that we're doing everything in our power to get your father back. The whole city will be praying for the same thing when we release this information."

All people do is pray when something terrible happens. It's all the Church is good for in a corporate world. Meanwhile, executives will use my father's capture as propaganda to illustrate how awful Liberteum is. There's no doubt they have video of the firefight and the dead bodies left in its wake. They'll enhance the footage and splice it into a neat package to coerce the masses.

"Mother?"

"If you don't mind, Chief Executive Safmor, I'd like to have a word alone with my son," she says without flinching from her catatonic state.

"Of course, Ilaria. Why don't the two of you go to a bedroom? We'll wait here to ensure everything is okay before we leave."

"Thank you, Chief Executive," she says politely.

We rise from our seats, and I take her arm. Moving gingerly around the furniture, I guide her down the hallway. Instead of going into the more spacious master bedroom, she nudges me into my room and then closes the door behind us. She leans her forehead against it.

"I feared this day would come. When your father was working night shifts before you were born, I would lie awake at night staring at the ceiling. It's hard knowing that someone you love is constantly in harm's way."

"I'm so sorry, mother."

"Your father has always chosen his job over his family. It's who he is. He believes in his heart that he's part of something greater. You've paid the price for that, same as me. The only one he ever sacrificed for was Varella."

"Does she know?" I may hate my sister, but not telling her something like this would be inhumane.

"She's taking the first available train back to New York. She's devastated."

"How are you holding up?"

"Uh...I'm numb. I should be more emotional, but you know things between your father and me haven't been...good."

"Most of that is my fault," I say, finding the edge of my bed to sit on.

Mother turns from the door and sits next to me. She takes my hand in hers, just like when I was a small child and needed reassurance.

"No, our problems have been simmering for a long time. We just ignored them. Now, we may never solve them."

"Mother, don't—"

"Don't what? Think the worst? Is there any reason not to? You would know the odds better than anyone."

She's right. Haven showed me little mercy just for being the son of New York City's Chief Guardian. I can only imagine what he will put my father through. As much as I might despise him, nobody should be forced to endure that.

"Your father never completely believed your story about what happened in the station."

"What?" I shouldn't be surprised by that revelation, but I am.

"When you escaped. He never said anything," she says, pointing her eyes upward as a reminder that Maester is listening, "especially when the official report calling you a hero was released. But I know he had doubts."

"Did you have doubts?"

"I got you back. I never cared about the how or why. Rykos, I need you to help get your father back for the sake of this family."

I shake my head. "I don't know how I can help."

"You're resourceful. Maybe you can think of something that public safety can't or won't," she says, staring at me hard.

I get the message and know what she wants me to do. She wants me to contact Liberteum. Somehow she's under the impression that I know a way to do that.

"I'm not *that* resourceful."

Her voice drops to a whisper. "They let you live for a reason, Rykos."

"They didn't let me do anything. I had to kill Quarren to escape."

She looks into my eyes and takes my face in her hands. "A mother knows her son. You spent time with them. I know you can figure this out."

She kisses me on the cheek and leaves the room. The door closes, leaving me alone with conflicting emotions. I collapse onto my bed. The stress is making my temples throb like they're being beaten with a hammer. How the hell am I supposed to contact Liberteum? Forget about figuring out why I would want to.

There were days during my intense interrogations under my own father's watchful eyes that I would have loved to see him take my place in that dirty old transportation hub. I never expected it to actually happen. Fate has a morbid sense of humor.

Searching the underground for them is pointless. If the PSS can't find them with all their resources, I won't either. So how do I get in contact with someone who doesn't want to be found? It's not like I can VidLynk urches and ask them to connect me to the beautiful terrorist leader. Even if I could enlist the urches for help, I would need to be a patrician to afford to pay them off.

My eyes click open. A patrician. Who was the guy I saw at the first rave? I never got his name, but he was a member of the elite. If I can find him, maybe he can lead me to them.

I reach for the tablet on my nightstand and power it on. It's a long shot, but it's the only one I've got. This is going to take some digging.

CHAPTER THIRTY-FOUR

AMERICA, INC.

The Silver Eagle Restaurant
Corporate Hill
Washington Corporate Governance District

Fiolla has never set foot in this place. Her salary could never cover the price of the meals served here. With its stained oak appointments, plush leather seating, and crystal chandeliers, this restaurant caters to high executives and patricians. Mere mortals, even ones with a fancy title who work at the White House, only dream of eating here.

"Fiolla! I'm happy you could make it."

"Thank you, Chairman Hammond. I was surprised by your invitation."

The big man smiles. Not obese but chubby by corporate standards, Hammond shows each of his sixty-nine years. He's in the twilight of his career; whether forced retirement or a heart attack ultimately claims him is the only remaining question.

"I thought it was time we talked. Please, take a seat."

A waiter pulls out a chair, and she and Hammond sit. In the usual routine, her crystal water glass is filled, and a napkin is placed on her lap. At high-end restaurants, they do everything except cut your meat and chew your food. Fiolla wonders if they would do that too if asked.

"I know it's unusual for executives to lunch with members of the board, but there isn't any policy against it," he continues, justifying this meeting not far from the steps of Shareholders Hall.

"Yes, sir."

"Would you like something off the menu? Their pasta is fresh, and the sauce comes from an old Italian recipe."

"It sounds wonderful, sir, but my order depends on whether this conversation will cause me to lose my appetite."

"Just water for the lady, for now," Hammond instructs the waiter, answering that question. "Any news on what is happening in New York? Has the PSS located their chief guardian yet?"

Fiolla crinkles her brow. He's stalling. "No, not yet, but you can get that update from anybody. Why am I here?"

"You're a good executive, Fiolla. You like to get straight to the point. I need you to relay a message to Valen for me."

"Sir, with all due respect, you're the chairman of the board. Why don't you just VidLynk him yourself?"

"Things are tense on Corporate Hill right now. There are prying eyes and ears everywhere. I don't want anyone getting wind of what I'm about to say and using it as leverage against me."

Fiolla isn't sure a restaurant like this is any better, especially in this part of town. Maybe the chairman thinks so. Either way, she keeps her objections to herself.

"I can certainly relay anything you need me to."

"Zeykala is demanding Valen testify before the board in a hearing."

"She's been doing that since the attack."

"I know. She hasn't had enough support to push forward, and I've used that as a reason to decline her requests."

"And now that's changed," she concludes. He was right not to order her lunch.

"I'm afraid so."

There are thirty members of the board of directors for America Incorporated, not including the chairman. Each of them is a distinguished former CEO of a major subsidiary. Together, they comprise the most active, invested, and incorruptible governing body in the world. That doesn't mean they aren't subject to political maneuvering or immune to the allure of promises made by outside influences.

"How did that change so quickly?"

"You want me to say blackmail. It may be. *Prima* Bettancourt has been pushing this agenda as well. She has political clout and unlimited resources. Always getting what she wants is a habit, and what she wants is for Zeykala to control America Incorporated."

"Zeykala is a member of the board. She can't become chief executive."

The articles of incorporation forbid any board member from becoming chief executive of the parent company. It was a wise move that has spared America Incorporated from internal turmoil that other corporations – and Intercorpex itself – regularly endure. Zeykala wants to undo that for her benefit.

"Corporate policies change at the will of the board of directors, Fiolla. With enough votes, the charter can be amended. She can fill the seat as a temporary measure until then."

"How close is she?"

"I don't know, but far closer than Valen would like. As chairman, I'm given great latitude in setting the agenda. However, if I want to continue in that role, I need to cater to the majority's interests. You understand what I'm saying, right?"

She leans forward, now understanding the weight of this meeting. "You're going to order him to appear."

Hammond nods solemnly. "We have another two dozen dead guardians in New York and no results to show for it."

"Chairman Hammond, public safety took out their munitions plant and a stronghold," Fiolla challenges, exasperated at his insinuation.

"I'd be excited if they confiscated an arsenal, which they didn't. I'd be even more excited if Liberteum's leaders were killed at that stronghold, which they weren't. Instead, they have the chief guardian of the New York City Municipal Corporation held at gunpoint somewhere."

There's nothing that Fiolla can say. The countless raids and sweeps over the past week have been failures. There's no defending that, so why try?

"You understand the position I'm in. We've spent untold blood and treasure hunting these rogues down. Every mission has failed."

"And yet the economy is booming. Productivity is up. Trade is reaching historic levels, and—"

The chairman holds up his hand and closes his eyes. "Terrorists are running amok in New York and inspiring urches in other cities to replicate their attacks. Nobody gives a damn about another quarter of economic growth right now. The cancer that started in New York is metastasizing across the sphere of influence. There are threats from urches in Boston, Ottawa, Philadelphia, Chicago, Montreal, and Los Angeles. Other corporations are having similar issues. The board feels something must be done."

"So the board will replace Valen, knowing full well the next CEO won't have any better luck?"

"It is a hearing, not a death sentence. He still controls his fate, although I don't think using the word 'luck' is how you want to approach his defense."

He's right, but that wasn't Fiolla's point. History is replete with examples of leaders acting hastily to everyone's detriment. Hammond recognizes that.

"When is the hearing?"

"Four days. He won't get the official notice until tomorrow. I wanted to give him as much notice as possible. I know how he likes to plan."

"Sir, you know this isn't the right call. Valen is exactly the type of leader we need to get us through this."

"I've known Valen since before you were born. He's a great CEO and I consider him a friend. But this is a business decision, not a personal one."

"It's personal for Talya Bettancourt and Boardmember Zeykala."

"We all have enemies, Fiolla. Nobody understands that better than the executive who sits in the Oval Office. Valen can't worry about who is coming after him. He needs to focus on the one thing that will save him."

"What's that?" she asks, taking the bait.

"Eradicating Liberteum once and for all. Unfortunately, if he hasn't made any progress to that end by the time we vote, his reign may be over."

* * *

The cold front approaching from the west over the Potomac River threatens to blanket the city in a forbidding shroud. The bright sun that shines through the Oval Office windows slowly gives way to gray darkness. It's all an apt metaphor for the moment.

"Did he say when?" Valen asks as Fiolla waits for his response.

"Saturday. Sir, may I make an observation?"

"Go ahead."

"This news is a kick in the gut, but you don't sound surprised by it. I was. I never thought Chairman Hammond would betray you."

"He's not betraying me. Hammond is about as loyal as you can expect a chairman to be. Talya Bettancourt is using our cumulative failures in New York to sway the other board members. Under those circumstances, he held out longer than most would have."

"Our problems with Liberteum hardly qualify as 'cumulative failures,'" Fiolla argues.

"They do when that's the only thing people measure success against."

"It's not your fault."

Valen grins. "I'm the chief executive for America Incorporated. *Everything* is my fault."

He turns to watch the approaching storm, and the pause turns into a long, awkward silence. "Do you think it's enough to remove you?"

"A leader is only as good as the most recent accomplishment. It has never mattered whether he or she was called Mr. President or Chief Executive. The occupant of this room grapples with a 'what have you done for me lately?' mentality."

Valen returns to his desk and runs his hand over the back of the leather chair, cherishing the feel of it. This simple piece of finely crafted furniture has a physical power that augments the symbolic.

"I never wanted to sit here. Even as a registrant, when seemingly everyone wanted to be the CEO of America Incorporated, I never did. I wasn't upset when I went to Penn instead of Harvard or ended up in the transportation sector instead of technology or energy. I didn't dream of glory. I focused on planning a strategy, managing its execution, and moving on to the next once I saw the results. I figured the rest would take care of itself."

"And it landed you here anyway."

"I promised myself the day I took over the company: Always do what's best for the employees, no matter the cost. It's not our geography or infrastructure or technology that makes us great; it's them. They're our most valuable asset. Too many of my predecessors didn't think that way. They would have let Virtari butcher the urches because they always valued productivity and profit over people."

Fiolla has never heard him sound like this. His tone reeks of defeat. She needs some assurance that everything will be okay, but Valen isn't offering any.

"Sir, you're talking like you don't expect to survive the hearing."

"There will be a vote to remove me on Saturday. I don't know which way it will fall. Despite what people think, I can't predict the future. All I can do is plan a strategy and execute it, as I always have."

"So, what's your strategy?" Fiolla asks, perking up.

"The best way to win a war is not to fight one. When a battle is unavoidable, the second-best way to win is to strip away your enemy's power to fight. I know Talya Bettancourt and Zeykala's weaknesses. I need to contact an old acquaintance of mine to see if I can exploit one of them. The rest I can do myself."

CHAPTER THIRTY-FIVE

INTERCORPEX

Global Network Operations Center
Manhattan Financial District
ICX New York Exchange

Boredom defines most workdays in the network operations center. The explosions in New York were a notable exception and not a day that anyone cares to repeat. When something of importance does happen, technicians charged with monitoring the environment jump into action. This is no different.

The operators on the floor saw the news flash on the display before Lyris did. The resulting buzz in the cavernous room gets his attention, and he pokes his head up to see what is going on. That's when he spots the breaking news banner.

Wyeth is standing near the network engineering workstations. He turns and gives Lyris an almost imperceptible nod. His mission is accomplished. AME News will get credit for breaking the story, and within an hour, the news bureaus of every major corporation will report that the *gentez-minorez* were behind the Secaucus attack.

Media outlets covet news items outside conventional business or market updates in an unending thirst for fresh content. That is guaranteed to spread the story like a wildfire. Lyris sits down and connects to the GlobalNet. Every corporation has a network that connects employees to information. America Incorporated calls theirs the InterLynk. The GlobalNet is the cumulative repository for that information and is restricted to senior executives, patricians, and exchange personnel.

Lyris glances at the stock display on the far wall. The "big board" shows volume trending downward as patricians digest the reports and contact each other for information. Impacting news slows trading as the elite formulate strategies to capitalize on it. That leads to a rush of activity.

Lyris and Wyeth just took a bat to the beehive. Corporate leaders will begin issuing statements expressing their outrage and demanding proof of the accusation.

Lower patricians, especially the Wilmington, Townsend, and Lockwood families, will scream to defend themselves. The three families were instrumental in founding the United Kingdom Corporation but have struggled to amass the fortunes others did. As a result, they've remained mired in the ranks of the lower elite and harbor a seething resentment of the *gentez-majorez* and the exchange itself. Coupled with their frequent trips to New York, they make for perfect patsies. It's why Lyris had Wyeth specifically release their names.

The director understands that he's playing with fire. If Denali gets angry, Lyris can honestly tell him that he wasn't the source of the leak. If it's welcome news to the patrician, he can take full credit for the move. Either way, Raimius is planning to use this as leverage against Denali somehow.

That will only strengthen the patrician's resolve to force the regents to remove Raimius. This may speed up the process. That suits Lyris just fine. He's tired of languishing in his position. The sooner he moves into the administrator-general's Midtown office, the better. Then he can do some housecleaning.

Zyree will be the first to go. He can't fire ICS Security personnel, and Jurghen would never allow the most decorated chief inspector in ICX history to be terminated. That means Jurghen needs to be retired first and replaced with someone who agrees with Lyris's line of thinking.

The thought causes the director to smile. That's for a later day. Events are transpiring quickly. Everybody has been holding matches to the powder keg. The terrorists dropped theirs in Secaucus, Denali his when he brought Lyris to Greenwich. Raimius just responded in kind. The only question that remains to be answered is how big the explosion will be, and who will be left standing in the aftermath.

CHAPTER THIRTY-SIX

THE PATRICIANS

The Mall
Corporate Governance District
Washington-Arlington Municipal Corporation

Talya Bettancourt is not a woman who believes in wasting time. She doesn't believe in stopping to enjoy the moment or smell the roses. Productivity is life; therefore, every action she takes is meant to further a goal. For that reason, she can understand the puzzled look on Zeykala's face as she walks down the path toward the bench Talya is seated on. It's out of character.

This narrow strip of grass probably hasn't changed much since the collapse. Like the White House and Shareholder Hall, once the U.S. Capitol, it was preserved out of a sense of continuity. Now simply known as "The Mall," it's an area with no specific purpose. The dusty old museums that once lined its side have mostly been replaced. The monuments were toppled and replaced with more appropriate honors for great CEOs and innovators. The Mall itself is just here for people to enjoy, not that Talya sees the point of that.

"You wanted to see me, *Prima* Bettancourt?" Zeykala asks when she finally reaches her.

"It's a lovely day, isn't it, Boardmember Zeykala?"

"Yes, ma'am."

"I should be in a great mood. The sun is shining, the air is warm yet still crisp, and Valen is on the cusp of being removed." She turns to face Zeykala. "Or is he?"

"We don't have the votes."

"How is that possible?" Talya asks, shaking her head slightly.

"Valen has developed several loyal board members."

There are two broad categories for explaining a failure. The first is outlining the reasons for it. Sometimes, you are outmaneuvered, outplayed, or unable to overcome circumstances. The second is offering excuses. They are often portrayed as reasons but are nothing more than hollow words uttered to cover up inadequacies, laziness, or poor decisions. There is little doubt in Talya's mind which category Zeykala's words fall in.

"And you have had every opportunity to sway them."

"I've tried. They won't budge."

"What more do they need?"

"I don't know."

"It was a rhetorical question," Talya says with a sneer.

Some people just will not listen to reason. Loyalty belongs to the corporation, not the person running it. Personal loyalty was on its deathbed prior to the Great Collapse and should have died with the old system. Corporatism has a different set of demands that must be met.

"I'm disappointed in you, Zeykala."

"I'm doing what I can," the board member protests.

"This corporation wasn't built by people trying their best. That's an excuse for failure. It was built by men and women who made things happen. It was a drive that we restored after the collapse. Citizens forgot how important success was. Employees learn from the time they enter their first year as a registrant that winning is all that matters."

"I don't know what you want me to do."

"Start winning."

Zeykala doesn't say anything. Talya understands that she thinks it's an impossible situation. It isn't. She just needs to find the courage to do what must be done. If there is no path to follow, you make one. If people are in your way, you find a way to remove them. It's not complicated.

"Are you the right person to lead this corporation?"

Zeykala's head spins back to the *prima*. "I absolutely am. I've done everything you've asked."

Talya purses her lips. "Except secure the needed votes on the board."

"I don't have the leverage."

"Then find it. You don't get to become CEO by watching slide presentations and attending fancy parties. You need to get your hands dirty."

"I know that."

"You said you were cutthroat and would do what it takes to help me remove Valen. Now prove it."

"I will do whatever you ask, but I need your help. Tell me what to do."

"Stop being scared of him."

"I'm not," Zeykala argues.

"You are. Otherwise, you wouldn't let something like personal loyalty stand between you and your wildest dreams. How many votes shy are you?"

"Three."

"Get two. I will take care of the final one. Then force the others to support a hearing on Saturday."

"Why Saturday?

Talya glares at her and rises from the bench. "Because I said so, and I always get what I want. If you can't make that happen, I'll find someone who can. Always remember that I'm the *prima* and you are replaceable. Make it happen and contact me when it's done. You have until the end of the day."

CHAPTER THIRTY-SEVEN

AMERICA, INC.

Somewhere in the Underground
Manhattan Island
New York City Municipal Corporation

Haven made the mistake of talking too loudly when he described his fight with the group's leader to one of his soldiers. It's been a source of strength for Teman, who knows that Haven is bothered by the incident, and the chief guardian won't stop mocking him for it, no matter how badly he gets hurt for it.

Teman smiles after a hard right cross. "You hit like a pansy. No wonder you got your ass kicked by a girl."

Haven rears back and hits Teman hard in the jaw. Teman winces. That one hurt. He spits blood on the floor and lets out a laugh, desperate not to show the bastard any weakness.

"You think being a wise-ass is a good idea right now, Chief Guardian?" he asks, rearing back and punching Teman hard in the gut.

He coughs hard and strains against his restraints. "My son hit me harder than that once…when he was six."

"Put him back in the chair," Haven orders.

On command, two of his thugs untie the ropes running through steel eyelets drilled into the ceiling and give them slack. Teman's arms collapse to his sides. His ankles are secured to the floor in the same manner, without the eyelets. Liberteum put some thought into this torture chamber. The end result is his being suspended in the air for these torture sessions with no means to resist. Teman is dropped into an old metal chair and manacled.

Every bone in his body aches. His lower lip is split wide open and his left eye is swelling shut. The contusions on his torso have merged into one massive purple bruise covering his midsection and the broken ribs underneath. There is no concept of time down here. They could have been working on him for ten minutes or ten hours. It feels like ten lifetimes.

"You ready to talk yet?"

"Not really," Teman admits. "Every time I say something, you hit me."

"I want information, not insults."

"I don't know anything of importance."

Haven shakes his head and stretches his arms as he circles. "You're the chief guardian. You hold the keys to the castle."

"Sorry to disappoint you. Access is granted via my primary biojack, which you removed. Of course, you didn't get them all. My guardians are already on their way."

Haven's laugh is part sadistic, part ridicule. "If that were true, you'd have been rescued by now. Look around you, Teman. Even if you are transmitting, no signal is getting out of here. You might as well be on Mars for as reachable as you are."

He figured that Haven would call his bluff. Teman scans the room. Made of brick and whitewashed, it is only about one hundred and fifty square feet. Wire mesh covers the walls and ceiling. A single overhead light provides illumination, and there are two entrances: the main one that everyone uses leading into the crypt, and one carved into the wall directly to his front that goes who knows where. It's not Mars but is almost as inaccessible.

"What do you want?"

"Information. It's the coin of the realm in the business world, isn't it? You have it and I want it."

"Anything valuable was on my wrist tablet. I'm worthless to you, so if you're going to kill me, do it now."

"And put you out of your misery?" Haven asks, leaning into Teman's view and wagging a finger before jabbing him hard in his temple. "I don't think so. Not all information is digital. You have plenty in that head of yours. If you don't want to share it, I'll beat it out of you. I wasn't allowed to do that to that soft, worthless Ivy you call a son. Now I call the shots and you're taking his place."

Teman's face registers surprise before he can stop it. His muddled mind begins racing. Rykos isn't connected to Liberteum. He was telling the truth.

"Oh, you thought maybe he was helping us? That's priceless. Some father you are. Employees really are stupid. Rest time is over. String him back up."

The chief guardian is unshackled and lifted out of his chair. The two men secure his wrists with the ropes and move to opposite sides of the room. They nod at each other, hoisting their prisoner back into the suspended crucifix position. The strain on Teman's shoulders is agonizing, but he fights the pain and lets out another laugh.

"What's so funny?"

"I needed to stretch."

Haven walks over and hits him again. His fist feels like a sledgehammer even when he doesn't put his full weight behind it. Teman's coughing fit lasts a little longer this time.

"You're not laughing so hard now, are you? Tell me what the PSS knows about us."

"Okay, okay," Teman says, hanging his head in defeat. "You all have small penises."

Haven hits him in the face before directing a pair of blows to his torso. The chief guardian spits blood.

"How much do you know about us?"

"Everything," Teman taunts with a smile, getting another punch to his kidney for the effort.

"I can make this last forever, Chief Guardian. Every time you pass out from the pain, I'll wake you up. And just when you think you can't bear to take any more, I'm going to slice pieces off you one at a time."

Teman understands his situation. He's not leaving this room alive. It's a fate he's already come to terms with, but for the first time, feels real fear. Not of death, but dying like this.

"Do you really think that torture will get you what you want?"

"Did Freya ask you the same thing?" Haven reaches up and pinches his jaw in a vise-like grip. "I know you tortured her."

Teman's eyes betray him. Freya was the hacker he waterboarded in the emergency operations center when she didn't cooperate. Then he put a bullet between her eyes.

"Freya was a friend," Haven says, planting a pair of sharp slaps to Teman's swollen cheek. "You'll be happy to hear that I changed my mind. I'm not going to torture you for information. I'm going to do it so you know what real pain feels like before you die."

Haven winds up and hits him again. The shot to Teman's kidney sends a sharp pain through his body, followed by an overwhelming wave of nausea. He cries out in agony, knowing it will be far from the last one.

CHAPTER THIRTY-EIGHT

LIBERTEUM

Safe House
Tribeca Geographic District
New York City Municipal Corporation

No time was wasted transferring to a different domicile in the building. Michele wasn't feeling well and rested in the bedroom while Farron moved essentials to the new floor. He then employed some surveillance countermeasures to monitor the approaches. With limited manpower, they need to see a threat coming in advance.

The tasks completed, Farron moves to the bedroom to check on Michele. She's propped up in the bed and is staring at the ceiling when he enters. He hands her a steaming cup of coffee, which she graciously accepts.

"How are you feeling?"

"Better. I'm not as lightheaded."

"You lost a lot of blood. You really should have let me call the doctor."

Michele looks over the dressings covering her wounds. "I'm fine. You said we could trust your doctor friend, but I don't want anyone knowing that we're here. You did a good job patching me up. Where did you learn that?"

"I spent time playing doctor with old girlfriends," he jokes, swiveling his head as he looks around. "I'm sorry. This place is still a little rough around the edges."

The bedroom isn't as nice as the downstairs one, but far better than any place Michele has ever stayed. The construction crew has left the usual detritus and debris from the remodel behind. The bedroom is done, but still wants for a coat of paint. Most importantly, it's warm, dry, and has a bed with an actual mattress.

"Yeah, I'm slumming it here," Michele says, rolling her eyes. "You realize I grew up in the underground, right?"

"I forget sometimes. You're not exactly a typical urch."

Most urches born under the streets of the city barely speak in complete sentences, can't read, and have more street smarts than actual intelligence. Michele's father believed in education and raised her using the best of both worlds: the book knowledge of the corporate world and the street smarts unique to urches.

"Do you think Haven will be back?" Farron asks, changing the subject.

"Haven worked for ICX Security. He knows we won't stay in the domicile. He might check your other residences, but I suspect he's busy with his captive."

Michele knew she would have problems controlling her lieutenant following her father's death. After their countless arguments, she should have seen this coming. Farron did. She's appreciative that he isn't rubbing that in right now. The reality of their situation is bad enough.

"So much work and it's all for nothing."

"All is not lost, Michele," the patrician says, trying to reassure her.

"Haven has our weapons, control of our underground strong points, and commands most of Liberteum's soldiers. I may be the leader, but he's the muscle. Most of our fighters will follow him."

Farron waves away the comment like it was hanging in the air. "Narik was right. We don't need Haven and we don't need the fighters. We have the hard drives, and Jasper and Adiz are loyal to you. The next phase can be launched from here and the final one from Valhalla. Haven can't get to that."

"And then what?" Michele asks, staring at him. "When all hell breaks loose, who will we have to defend us? If you think the PSS manhunt is bad now, can you imagine what it will be once Archimedes runs its course?"

Farron takes a moment to reflect. "My father's men are an option."

"Your father doesn't know the scope and scale of Archimedes. You told me that."

He's delusional if he thinks his father will go along with their plan. Denali Keating wants to control Intercorpex, not destroy it. When he finds out his only son has been colluding with them on something bigger, Farron will have problems of his own.

"Did Narik tell the PSS where to find Haven?"

"I don't know. Probably." He sighs then sits down on the floor and leans against the bed. "I've been friends with him for a long time. He's always had his own way of doing things. I had hoped your little demonstration changed his mind. I guess it didn't."

"I'll never understand patricians. I mean, why are you doing this? Why get involved with us at all?"

"Please don't tell me you're questioning my dedication to all this."

Michele shakes her head. "Not at all. You've proven your loyalty, but it's hard for me to understand. You have everything. Why are you so willing to give it up?"

Farron sighs deeply and is about to answer when there's a knock at the door. Adiz opens it and pokes his head in. Michele grimaces at the poor timing. The answer to that question will have to wait.

"Am I interrupting anything?"

"No. What's the status?"

"The equipment is up and running. The drives are installed and loaded. We're ready to go when you are."

"Good."

"When exactly is that going to be?" he asks, stepping into the bedroom the rest of the way.

"When I say so. We're not ready yet."

"What are we waiting for?" he presses.

Her eyes squint reflexively in confusion and suspicion. Adiz's questions are a little out of character. He can be combative but is never this direct. He's probably unnerved about what happened with Haven, but something about this doesn't feel right.

"I've had enough fights with my people today, Adiz. I'm in no mood for another one."

"If we don't move soon, there might not even *be* a phase two. Haven has gone rogue. The PSS will search every inch of the city looking for him, above ground and below. We can't hide out here forever. It's too much of a risk to wait. There are too many variables."

"Adiz, we'll execute when I say so," Michele snaps.

"All I'm asking is that we set this plan in motion. What happens, happens. You knew that Archimedes would never go exactly like you thought it would. That's why you and Quarren spent so much time in war-gaming scenarios. It's now or never, Michele. Let's do this thing."

"I have to admit, he has a point," Farron says. She glares at him.

"Trading in New York ticks every day between seven and five. I say we execute on Saturday."

Michele laughs when she thinks of Saturday's date. "It is serendipitous."

"What do you mean?" Farron asks.

"The twenty-fourth of April, eleven eighty-four B.C. It's the day the Greeks got past the walls of Troy."

Farron still looks lost. "How does that relate to us?"

"We're about to unleash the modern version of the Trojan Horse."

CHAPTER THIRTY-NINE

UNDERGRADUATE RYKOS

Chief Guardian Teman's Domicile
Upper West Side Geographic District
New York City Municipal Corporation

If I had worked half this hard on my studies, I would have done much better in my modules. Twenty straight hours. That's how long I've been searching for a way to reach Michele. I close my tired and bloodshot eyes and rub them hard. This effort would be worth it if I made any progress whatsoever.

I stare at my untouched dinner on the plate next to me. Mother has checked on me twice and brought me a couple of meals. My stomach is tied in knots, so I skipped them both. Our relationship may be strained, but I can't bear to think about what is happening to my father. It's no doubt worse for my sister who worships him.

Varella arrived from Boston only a few hours after receiving the news. She hasn't bothered poking her head into my room, nor have I ventured out to the living area to see her. I'm okay with her avoiding me. I don't need a confrontation right now.

I push myself off the bed, stand up, and stretch my arms. My spine pops like firecrackers, and my neck cracks when I roll it on my shoulders. I swing my arms in circles and move around the room to fight fatigue. My body is screaming for physical activity. It will have to wait as I mentally review what I've already done in a desperate search for a fresh approach.

I began searching the InterLynk for patricians of the *gentez-minorez* in their twenties. I figured that only low-ranking elites would attend an urch rave. The guys with Michele weren't wearing their family crests. Of course, this is assuming they were patricians. Just because I thought they were doesn't make it so.

"Come on, Rykos, you can do this," I mumble.

Maybe I'm going about this all wrong. I move back to my desk. I sync my tablet to the larger display with a couple of taps. I'm surprised it comes to life. I haven't used it in years. Moving quickly before I lose my train of thought, I bring up AME News.

Every article and video clip is searchable by keyword. I try typing "patricians" and get too many results to be helpful. I narrow it to "young patricians," and again, it is too broad. I enter "young patrician social events," and the number of results is more reasonable. I begin selecting and scanning them one at a time.

The nice thing about modern media is that everything is visual. Articles have at least three pictures or videos. After scanning thirty-three entries, my eyes settle on an image of two men in full family regalia.

Bingo.

I don't recognize the scrawny one, but the other…yes, that could be him. I read the names in the caption. *Farron Keating and Narik Covington.*

"You've got to be kidding me," I moan aloud.

It never occurred to me that I may have started my search at the wrong end of the food chain. Feeding off the surge of adrenaline, I open the AME corporate database and enter Farron's name. Open to all employees, the historical record contains a listing of every past and current America Incorporated shareholder. I select the link to his dossier and study it when it comes up.

"Yes!"

It is definitely him. Energized, I search for him on AME News. Dozens of articles pop up, mainly relating to his family, father's fortune, and involvement with…Intercorpex. Well, that's interesting. Why would he be involved with Liberteum?

The article doesn't delve into much detail, not that I expected it to. The Keatings would have demanded the removal of any defamatory or unflattering information. It doesn't matter. So long as he can get in touch with Michele, I don't care who they're involved with or why.

"Okay, so where are you, Farron?" I ask under my breath. It's one thing to know he can relay a message to me, but it's another to get in contact with him. A VidLynk will never get routed to him. I need something more subtle, and it starts with determining his location.

I exhale loudly into the silence of the room. This won't get any easier, but at least I'm closer than I was fifteen minutes ago. I'm determined to find a way to reach him. I just hope he's in the city.

CHAPTER FORTY

INTERCORPEX

The "War Room"
ICX New York Exchange
New York City Municipal Corporation

Lyris didn't give Zyree the seven personnel he requested, but he isn't complaining. Duckballs and Bird's Nest made up half of the four operations center personnel Nolirah assigned to the war room. It makes sense. Duckballs had explained before the attacks in Manhattan that the pair don't fit in well with the hyper-loyal ICX staff. This has the makings of his kind of team.

"Chief Inspector? I think we have something," Malkor says from over Duckballs's shoulder on the other side of the conference table.

"That would be refreshing," Chiana chirps from the other side of the room.

Zyree has already learned too many things about her. One of them is how cranky she gets when she's tired. Another is that she is even more insufferable when she's bored.

"Whatcha got?"

"Rykos's search patterns have changed."

"How so?"

Duckballs leans back in his chair. "Well, he's been sifting through the patrician database for hours—"

"Oh, we know," Chiana moans.

"Ignore her. I do. Go on."

The technician looks up at Malkor, who stands and straightens his tunic. "Now Rykos is searching through Intercorpex. The focus is on one person: Director of Global Operations Lyris."

"What?" Chiana asks, shooting up out of her chair and rushing over to them.

Zyree crosses the room and joins her. Duckballs and Malkor show them the search history. It's unmistakable. Chiana has seen enough and starts for the door.

"Where do you think you're going?" Zyree asks, already knowing the answer.

"I need to stretch my legs."

"Would that walk include climbing the stairs to Lyris's office?"

Chiana narrows her eyes. It's pointless to lie, and she knows it. "He should know about this."

"Why?" Malkor asks. "There's no threat to Intercorpex operations. If Lyris acts on the information, we risk letting Rykos know we're monitoring him."

"Which clause of the SOP does that violate?" Zyree asks. He blinks away the paragraph that pops up in his peripheral vision.

"I was instructed to report developments to him. That's what I'm going to do. Are you stupid enough to try to stop me?" Chiana challenges.

She glares at Zyree, expecting him to do precisely that. He doesn't. There is nothing to be gained by a confrontation. Satisfied she won this battle, she disappears out the door. Zyree walks over and peers into the corridor. She's gone. Perfect.

"You're one hell of a liar, Malkor. My biocomp didn't pick up the deception."

"It comes with practice. I've spent years covering for you," he says with a grin.

"So, what do you have?"

"His searches are all surrounding a patrician. Farron…" He stares in at the display. "Farron Keating."

Zyree stares at the ceiling and exhales. "You've got to be kidding."

His biography pops up on Zyree's contacts. There isn't much interesting until he reaches the PSS report. Farron was detained at the Chinatown rave – the same one that Rykos was at. There's the connection.

"He's locked onto this guy," Duckballs adds, staring at his display.

"He's learning about where he goes," Malkor concludes. "You think he could be involved in all this?"

Zyree shrugs. "Media reports are linking patricians to the attacks in Secaucus and Manhattan. We have to assume it's at least plausible."

"Boss, Farron Keating is *gentez-majorez*."

"That makes it north of plausible. Dig into Farron Keating's life. I want to know why Rykos thinks Farron Keating is involved with his father's abduction."

The two men nod and get to work. Zyree moves back to the front of the room and rubs his chin as he stares at the displays. Both men were at the rave. Liberteum was there. That can't all be a coincidence. He only needs to figure out what the next move is.

CHAPTER FORTY-ONE

AMERICA, INC.

The White House
Corporate Governance District
Washington-Arlington Municipal Corporation

They are in the middle of a crisis. Terrorists have executed two devastating attacks in New York, and the CEO is facing a formal investigation from the board of directors. Considering those challenges, Fiolla never would have thought Journalist Kassaya would be her biggest headache.

She wishes that she had poured herself that second cup of coffee. It is way too early in the morning to deal with this. AME News is supposed to be working for the White House, not against them.

"I have my editor's blessing to run with it," Kassaya asserts, drawing her line in the sand. "This VidLynk isn't me asking for your permission. I'm extending you the courtesy of a heads-up."

"And your editor ran it past Public Affairs?" Fiolla asks, skeptical that this would have been approved.

"I don't presume to know what he did or did not do. It doesn't matter. I have a story. It's news. *Actual* news, not corporate propaganda. I have permission to run with it from my editor, so that's what I'm doing."

Fiolla goes from furious to irate. For AME News to publish or broadcast anything without corporate approval is unthinkable. It's also disturbing.

"The hell you are. Not without approval, which I'm happy to help you get if you provide me with some details. Where did the information come from?"

"My sources are—"

"Who gave you the information, Kassaya?" Fiolla shouts, cutting off her ridiculous defense that sources are confidential. "I'm not going to ask again."

"You're Corporate Affairs, Fiolla. You're not in a position to demand that information," she growls, fighting her anger. "Let's just call them unimpeachable sources."

"There's no such thing. Are they from ICX?" Fiolla asks, now starting to feel like a reporter.

"One of them is. The other is completely unassociated."

Fiolla doesn't care about the ICX source. It is one of Raimius's minions acting on his behalf. The other source is the one that has her concerned.

"By any chance, is the person who gave your editor authorization to run the story the same one who gave you the information in the first place?"

"We're done here," Kassaya says. "This gets reported at the top of the seven o'clock news hour. I will announce to the corporation that Denali Keating and Shalius Covington were the masterminds behind the New York City attacks. They were directly responsible for the explosions that killed and wounded countless employees and damaged Intercorpex's Wall Street facility."

In deflecting the question, she answered it. Whoever is busy pulling her strings is high enough to manufacture information and compel corporate media to report it. That narrows the list down to a precious few. It also means a change of tactics is in order.

"Go ahead, run with it," Fiolla says, smiling. The sudden change in direction throws her off her game.

"What? You are okay with it?"

"Sure. You trust your sources. Unless they aren't trustworthy, in which case, you'll be forced to issue a public apology and retraction. Then two of the most powerful patricians in the world will demand your termination, which Valen and HR will enthusiastically grant."

"My sources are compelling."

"Or you're blinded by desperately wanting this story to be true. Tell me, why would Keating and Covington set off explosives around Manhattan if they only wanted to hurt Intercorpex? Did you ask that question?"

"I don't need to. Our evidence meets AME journalistic standards. We'll lose credibility if we don't report it."

Fiolla nods. She's listening, but her mind is racing ahead. Valen needs to know what's going on. She doesn't know but has a good guess what this is really about.

"Kassaya, I won't change your mind. Instead, I'm going to tell you the stakes. You're in the middle of an ugly power struggle. It's not a crossfire you want to be caught in."

"Are you willing to elaborate?" the journalist asks.

"No. I will say that the promises you were made hinge on Valen being removed as chief executive." Her face lets Fiolla know that she's on the right track. "I will assure you that he will sign your termination order if he isn't. So, you're rolling the dice running with this story. Your life rests on removing one of the most successful CEOs in corporate history. Good luck with that."

She moves to disconnect the VidLynk. "Wait…just wait," Kassaya says, her voice cracking under the weight of her nerves. "I can't divulge the name."

"Did you learn nothing from your business modules? The time for negotiations is over. I want the name."

"I…I can say it's a *prime* example of how the world works these days."

Fiolla nods and disconnects the VidLynk without another word. Good enough. The source isn't who she thought it was. The reality is worse than what she expected. Farron's family is about to be blindsided, but that conversation will have to wait. Fiolla pings the White House switchboard and waits for the VidLynk to connect. She only hopes that he doesn't shoot the messenger.

CHAPTER FORTY-TWO

THE PATRICIANS

The White House
Corporate Governance District
Washington-Arlington Municipal Corporation

The West Wing colonnade is an open, columned walkway that runs between the offices and the residence. In the early days of the mansion, it was a covered pavilion that led to the stables on the west side of the estate. The stables were removed when the West Wing was built in 1902. After the Great Collapse, architects toyed with the idea of enclosing the passage to stay out of the weather.

The largest shareholder of America Incorporated is pleased that it was left open. Chief executive officers spend too much time indoors already. This offers a chance for them to get some fresh air before the workday. It also provides a valuable spot to ambush one who is avoiding her.

"Prima Bettancourt, you know you can make an appointment with me," Valen says, emerging from the mansion for his sojourn to the office. "There's no need for stalking."

"I wanted to deliver this to you myself," Talya says, handing him a plain white envelope.

Valen stares at it. Printed documents are used only for things of great importance. That can only mean one thing. He hands the envelope to the aide behind him without opening it.

"You should open it."

Valen just stares blankly at her.

"It's a summons to appear before the board of directors on Saturday."

"I know. You came over from Corporate Hill to personally deliver it?"

"And to warn you that a vote to remove you will be held in absentia if you decline to appear."

"On what grounds?" Valen asks, placing his hands behind his back.

"Gross incompetence. Your time running this corporation is over. Your failures against Liberteum are your undoing."

"The board makes that decision, not you. I can't imagine it will be an easy one given my record."

"I'm sure they will make a show of the deliberation. However, do you think I would have summoned you if I didn't have the votes to remove you?"

"No vote is final until the ballots are cast, and results tallied."

"If you think you'll be able to persuade the board to change their minds," she says with a sarcastic laugh, "think again."

Valen turns to face the Rose Garden. "Corporatism was designed to remove the influence of power and money on the system of governance by separating the wealthy from the masses. Only that's not how it turned out, is it?"

"I'm not sure I like what you are insinuating," Talya says, coming alongside him.

"Americans once believed elected officials were acting in the best interests of the populace. Once the global economy collapsed and the truth came out, they dragged politicians out of their houses and put bullets in their heads. I suppose that's why the right to bear arms wasn't included in the corporate charter."

The United States of America had several notorious periods and events throughout its history that future generations would be ashamed of, and "The Cleanse" was one of them. It started innocently enough when the home address of every congressman and senator was posted by a frustrated citizen on an archaic forum called "social media."

A group of unemployed Texans used this information to confront a congressman outside his home to vent their frustrations. The politician feared for his life and shot an unarmed man. The crowd reacted, and he and his family were beaten to death.

The stunning video of the incident was beamed around the world in minutes. Copycat attacks began slowly and then snowballed. Armed mobs set out to find every leader who had failed them. Legislators, governors, mayors, and city councilmen were found and murdered in cold blood. Almost half of the elected officials in the United States were killed.

"You'd better watch yourself, Valen. I am nothing like those politicians."

"No, you're like the lobbyists who controlled them. You've read the old books. You know how influence peddling worked back then. No wonder governments never accomplished anything."

Talya clenches her fists at her side and releases them. It's a technique that she was taught to control her anger, although it rarely works. She finds most corporate executives insufferable. Valen is among the worst.

"Save your philosophical musings for the hearing. I have no interest in listening to them now."

"Fair enough." The CEO turns and starts off to the door leading into the Oval Office. Talya waits until he reaches it.

"Chief Executive Valen, the summons deserves an answer."

"Prima Bettancourt," he says, turning back to her. "Procedure allows twenty-four hours to respond unless you're planning to change that policy as well."

"As I said, this hearing will move forward, with or without you."

"Yes, I heard you. You delivered your message. Since you don't have an appointment, please remove yourself from this place of business."

"It's going to be fun watching you and your ego go down once and for all."

Valen smirks, and Talya watches him disappear into the building. Throughout her studies, she couldn't appreciate the reasons for the Great Collapse. People were blind to realities right in front of them. Leaders used this blindness to drive the world off a cliff. She could never understand how they were capable of that. After watching Valen do the same to America Incorporated, now she appreciates the motivations behind The Cleanse.

CHAPTER
FORTY-THREE

UNDERGRADUATE RYKOS

Essence Ristorante
Upper East Side Geographic District
New York City Municipal Corporation

The building's façade looks different as the last glimmer of sunlight has begun to yield to an inky twilight. Of all the restaurants the patrician could go to for a meal, it had to be the one that I'm familiar with. What are the odds I tracked the man down to the same place I took Mollae on a date? I catch him in the doorway, preparing to leave. I will have to calculate them later.

"Farron Keating?" I ask, stepping in front of him.

"Do I know you?"

"We've met once."

"I'm sorry, you don't look familiar. So, if you don't mind, I'm late for a meeting with some friends."

He starts walking to his waiting car. I wonder if those "friends" belong to Liberteum. It's time to be bold. I haven't searched for dozens of hours to let him walk away.

"I have a favor to ask of you," I finally manage to blurt out.

"I'm not giving you a job because you didn't like what you got on Career Day, kid," he says with one foot already in his town car.

I rush and grab the door as he climbs in the back. The well-dressed chauffeur reaches inside his jacket. I'd better hurry.

"I need you to get a message to a mutual friend."

The driver pauses, looking at his charge for permission to unleash the beating I'm expecting to get. Farron shakes his head slightly.

"I doubt we have friends in the same circle."

"We have one. I met her last week at a dance party. Then we spent some time in an old train station."

I hold my breath, hoping that the code is obvious enough. I can't exactly say what I want. The PSS's video capabilities are well known, but they also have a robust audio surveillance capability.

"Train station?"

I direct my eyes to the skies in the universal sign that somebody could be watching. "Yes, one downtown in the financial district."

"Get in," he commands, sliding over in the seat. The door closes as soon as I'm in, but the driver doesn't move from his position outside the door.

I look around the interior. Damn, this car is nice. Unlike the suburban and rural areas within the sphere of influence, employees in large metropolitan areas are not permitted to own personal vehicles. I've ridden in StreetRyde taxis, but none of them were this luxurious.

"Is it safe to talk in here?" I ask.

"Yes. Now, who the hell are you?"

"Undergraduate Rykos. I'm Chief Guardian Teman's son."

"I see," Farron says, nodding. "I heard about your father. My family is hoping for his safe return. Is that what this is about?"

I suddenly start feeling very uneasy. It's the kind of nervousness I felt walking into that rave. Hopefully, this goes better. If I'm wrong…

"I believe our mutual friend may be of some assistance in the matter."

"The PSS and BCS are more than capable of getting your father back. I don't believe I have any friends who would be able to help you."

I shake my head. "BCS agents can't find their way home after dark with a map and a torchlight. Guardians don't have the training for this. Michele can help, and you wouldn't still be talking to me if you didn't know her."

I see the glint in his eye. Recognition. I allow myself to relax.

"I have indulged this too long already. Please show yourself out of my—"

"All I'm asking is for you to give Michele a message. That's it."

"Michele isn't a friend. She's more of a passing acquaintance."

"It's none of my business how well you know her. If you can reach her, I need you to tell her something for me."

Farron shifts his gaze out the windshield in front of us. He might think this is a trap, but he recognizes me now. He sighs.

"Assuming I can do what you ask, what's the message?"

"Tell her that Quarren was right about everything. I'd like to speak to her about it. You know how to find me if she agrees." I start to open the door and stop, looking back at the patrician. "And then tell her she's a great kisser but hits like a pansy."

Farron smirks and shakes his head. I flash him a smile and climb out of his expensive imported conveyance. His driver closes the door, moves around the vehicle, and climbs into the front seat. They speed off.

I did everything I could. I don't know if he'll give her the message or whether she would agree to see me. Mother is counting on me, but I don't know if my plea was enough. It's the only lead I have, so all I can do now is wait and see if it pans out.

CHAPTER FORTY-FOUR

LIBERTEUM

Safe House
Tribeca Geographic District
New York City Municipal Corporation

Farron stares down three rifle barrels as he enters the apartment. Michele lowers her weapon, prompting the two hackers to do the same. Farron takes a deep breath and moves away from the door.

"That's such a welcome," the patrician says. "I'm going to regret telling you this, but you'll never guess who I just ran into."

Michele leans her weapon against the wall. "You're right, I won't."

"She's more uptight than usual," Adiz says, earning a nasty look from Liberteum's leader.

"Your former hostage."

"Rykos?" That's not what she expected him to say.

"Unless you've had more hostages you haven't told me about. He ambushed me outside a restaurant as I was leaving a business dinner."

Michele is surprised that he could find her through Farron. It's unnerving. If he can make the connection, she has to wonder who else can.

"What did he want?"

"You. I have no idea how he knew I could reach you," Farron says, reading her mind.

"I do," Jasper says, spinning around in the ergonomic office chair. "The rave. You were in the room when Haven and Scivix were threatening to carve him and his friend into pieces."

Farron rubs his chin. "I forgot about that."

"How did he identify you?" Michele asks. "He couldn't have seen you for more than a few seconds. We never used your names that night."

"Haven has his father," Adiz says. "If Rykos knew the man he saw was a patrician, he had plenty of motivation to put a name to the face."

"The son of the chief guardian knows we're connected. That could be a major problem," the patrician says.

"Maybe. Did he say what he wanted?"

"Yeah." Farron tries and fails to suppress a smirk. "He said you're a great kisser and hit like a pansy."

Michele blushes as the two hackers turn to her.

"You kissed him?" Adiz asks.

"He also said that Quarren was right about everything and wants to talk to you."

"That's a bad idea," Jasper advises.

"I can't believe you kissed him," Adiz mumbles.

Michele walks over to the refrigerator and pulls out a bottle of water. She remembers the kiss well. She also remembers hitting him so hard that he went down.

"He thinks I can help him get his father back," she admits.

"Which you can't, so there's no point in meeting him, right?" Adiz asks.

Michele shrugs, considering it. "The original plan for Archimedes required an outsider. We couldn't find the right person for the job…and then we met Rykos."

"Quarren worked on him for days and couldn't turn him in time," Jasper argues. "That's why you sent him back."

"After kissing him, apparently," Adiz mutters.

"Michele, we can't trust him," Farron advises. "We shouldn't do anything that jeopardizes our plans for Saturday."

She stares at the three men. Everyone here is against her. Normally, that would lead her to think she's missing something. Not this time. Her gut is telling her that meeting Rykos is the right thing to do. Michele has learned to trust that feeling. It's kept her alive this long.

"Haven is already jeopardizing everything. Meeting Rykos won't solve that problem, but maybe getting his father back is the leverage we need to get him to help us."

"That had better be followed up by killing Haven in the process," Jasper muses. And to think he actually *liked* Haven.

"I can't go along with this, Michele," Farron says, taking a seat in the chair in the living area. "Today's report linking my family to Liberteum is making things dangerous enough. Please don't make me regret telling you that I saw him."

"Farron's right. We shouldn't even wait until Saturday to launch the next phase. How long before the BCS comes knocking when they realize you own this building?"

"I'm a patrician, Adiz. Only ICX Security can investigate us and they haven't opened a case yet."

"Since when does the BCS play by the rules?" Jasper moans.

"I convinced myself you wouldn't agree to a meeting, Michele. We don't need any more variables in this equation. You know that better than anyone. If Narik was here, he'd agree."

"Narik is afraid of his own shadow," Michele says, pacing the floor.

Nobody in this room would argue with that. Outside of Farron, Narik doesn't have any fans here.

"It's. Too. Dangerous. It's only a matter of time before Intercorpex Security *does* open that investigation, even if my father's stunt tonight distracts them."

"The time for half-measures is over, Farron. If we want Archimedes to succeed, we need to be bold, just like your father. Rykos could solve some problems we know we'll encounter. We could also ensure that he won't confirm the media reports about your family."

"If he agrees to work with us."

He's right – it's a risk. Rykos wants his father back and there is no guarantee that Michele can deliver that. The odds aren't in their favor. But there was something he said in the message that he delivered to Farron. "Quarren was right about everything." Maybe it was meant to convince her to meet, or maybe it was something else. She needs to know which.

"There's only one way to find out. My mind is made up. Set up the meeting, Farron."

CHAPTER FORTY-FIVE

THE PATRICIANS

Keating Family of the Gentez-Majorez Estate
Greenwich Geographic District
Southern Connecticut Municipal Corporation

The helicopter touches down on the pad, and Abbot shows their guest into the bastion-like manor. Instead of being led down the corridor to Denali's study, Lyris is ushered into an enormous dining hall. He's surprised by the sight of the men gathered around the far end of the banquet table.

"Ah, Lyris, thank you for joining us," Denali says, standing and placing his napkin on the table. "Gentlemen, please let me introduce my guest, Executive Director of Global Operations Lyris from Intercorpex. Lyris, my distinguished colleagues: Namyn Wilmington, Yannen Townsend, and Nygehl Lockwood of the *Gentez-Minorez*. Please, join us for dinner."

Lyris knows the names well. What is baffling to him is why they are seated in Denali's dining room. Serious allegations were made implicating them in the Secaucus attacks that crippled high-frequency trading for Denali and the other upper patricians. If that wasn't confusing enough, Lyris wonders why he is there.

The dining room is as regal as the rest of the estate. The vaulted ceilings and gold walls are accented by the warm glow of chandeliers and pedestal lighting positioned between the gilded trim of the enormous windows. The table is long, with seating for thirty guests. The velvet-upholstered chairs, elaborate china place settings, the linen tablecloth and napkins, and floral centerpieces are more luxurious than those found in the finest Manhattan restaurants.

Lyris is shown to his seat and lowers himself into the chair. He eyes the security personnel manning the exterior doors, keeping vigil over the diners. Denali isn't taking chances with his safety. The men are physically imposing, clad in slick black combat uniforms with high-end body armor and weaponry.

"Yannen, will your son be joining us this evening?"

"My apologies, but no. He is still traveling, I'm afraid."

"Shame. Well, let's dine."

The waitstaff brings in a series of gourmet entrees. Dinner is pleasant, with the men opting to ignore the eight hundred-pound gorilla in the room. It's only during coffee and dessert that Denali broaches the subject of the Secaucus attack.

Lyris is a spectator and isn't asked to contribute to the conversation. There is no way Namyn, Yannen, and Nygehl could know that they were implicated in that event by the man they are ignoring. The room is tense enough. Lyris isn't about to volunteer the truth.

"I'm sorry, gentlemen. I find your denials hard to believe," Denali concludes after the three men deny their involvement in the attack.

"It's the truth," Namyn argues. "Just as you claim that the allegations made against you and Shalius Covington this morning are lies."

Denali doesn't appreciate the comment. Instead of lashing out, he takes a sip of his coffee from his bone china cup and gently replaces it in the saucer.

"The media reports trying to implicate us could easily be disinformation you provided to cover your wrongdoings. You see the dilemma I face, gentlemen?"

"We are not insensitive to your position. Someone is trying to divide the patricians by turning us against each other. It's the only plausible explanation. We had no involvement with Secaucus, and we want to believe that you didn't retaliate. Someone is. All we are asking is to work together to uncover if someone is conspiring against us."

Yannen, Namyn, and Nygehl stare at their host. The only people the corporate elite trust less than executives are each other. They have a long history of betraying each other for personal gain.

"Fine. Let us pool our resources to do that," Denali says to the apparent relief of his guests. "Fair warning, though. Don't let me find out you came to my home, dined at my table, and lied to my face."

"I assure you, Denali, that's not the case," Nygehl says with a slight bow.

"Very well. In the spirit of our new understanding, I'd like to show you all something. Lyris, please join us for this."

The men rise from their seats and head down the hall. A sturdy door leads to a spiral stone staircase that descends to a corridor with a heavy vault door. Two heavily armed guards snap to attention beside it.

"Behold!" Denali exclaims as the door swings open.

The room they enter looks like it could withstand a nuclear blast. Unlike the ornate décor in the residence above, the space is absent ornamentation. Large displays line the far wall, and both side walls have power and communications connectivity ports for additional workstations. It is set up much like Lyris's NOC on

Wall Street in some respects. The big difference is the eerie blue light enveloping the room, like encroaching dusk on a cloudy day.

"Very impressive, but we have seen rooms like this before. Why are we here?"

"To witness my latest operation," Denali announces with theatricality.

He points at three large displays showing different green video feeds from what appear to be helmet cameras. The information below shows the time stamp and the operator's call sign. Whatever this is, it's happening live.

"We have served the same master for far too long. Intercorpex created the Zurich Canon to keep us in line. Now, they use it to enhance their power and punish those who dare question them. Gentlemen, it's time that ends. This is the first step."

The men watch as each of the three commando teams breaches a door and quietly enters a structure. They creep down hallways, swinging their weapons in graceful arcs. The three patricians watch as the teams each reach different stairwells. Denali walks over to one of the guards who joined them in the room.

"Wait a second. That...that's my home!" Yannen screeches.

"It is. My men are inside each of your main residences."

"What is the meaning of this?" Namyn demands.

"Do you need to ask? Your houses...my assault teams," Denali says, his back to them. "It is exactly what it looks like. But don't worry, gentlemen. Your loved ones won't suffer any more than you will."

The anger on their faces turns to shock when he spins around and points the guard's rifle at them. He begins laughing as he starts unloading on his unsuspecting guests. Lyris dives to the ground as bullets rip through their flesh. Blood sprays around the room. The three men collapse in heaps as Denali continues to fire into their corpses until the ammunition runs out. A creepy silence grips the room after the firing stops.

Denali tosses the rifle back to his guard, who inserts a fresh magazine into the weapon as the patrician helps Lyris up off the cold concrete floor. His legs wobble beneath him. He stares at the patrician, finding no anger in his face. There is only a cold, calculating grin.

"Now, on to new business."

"You ju...just killed them," Lyris says, staring at the expanding pools of blood and eyes of the three patriarchs frozen wide in surprise.

"Yes, I did. It's the highest violation of the revered Zurich Canon. Tell me, Executive Director of Global Operations Lyris, will you report me as is your sworn duty?"

"The story about them and the Secaucus attack ...it...was made up."

"I know. Do you think I'm a fool?"

Denali doesn't wait for an answer. He turns his attention to the displays, where his men rampage through the patricians' homes. They enter the master bedrooms and murder the wives with headshots while they sleep. They kill the staff members. Within minutes, the teams have erased the remainders of the Wilmington, Townsend, and Lockwood families.

"My compliments, commander. These men are well-trained. Now, find Townsend's eldest son."

"We're already working on it."

"Excellent. Lyris," Denali says, turning, "I don't believe you answered my question."

"I don't…you're not a fool, Denali. But why kill them if you knew the truth? They were innocent."

"Oh, they were hardly innocent. Trust me, none of us are."

"So, you murdered them in cold blood?" Lyris asks, his tone harsh enough to cause the patrician to narrow his eyes.

"No, *you* did. You signed their death warrants when you released their names to the media…and it was about time. I didn't think Raimius was ever going to issue that order. He used to be more predictable."

"You knew," Lyris whispers.

"Knew? Lyris, you need to open your eyes if you want to run Intercorpex. I was counting on it."

A cold truth causes Lyris to shiver. He will be leading a weakened Intercorpex with Denali Keating as puppet master and him as his marionette. The administrator-general position will be almost ceremonial without the strings cut.

"This is your plan to get the regents to remove Raimius?"

Denali laughs. "This is only the first domino to fall. The fallout from these murders will lead to a series of events that will shake the foundations of Intercorpex and the global corporate community. The end state will result in the removal of Raimius as administrator-general and your ascension into his position."

"What events?"

"You'll find out soon enough," Denali says, slapping Lyris's shoulder. "You look shaken up. Let's have a drink in the study. My men will clean this mess up."

"At once, sir," one of his men confirms.

A million questions rattle around Lyris's mind. Is Denali behind Liberteum? Is what's been happening the work of the terrorists, or is it a clever misdirection while his men execute his master plan? What are his plans for Intercorpex?

"How can I help you without knowing your intentions?" Lyris asks. "I won't know what to do when the time comes."

"You said you wanted to run Intercorpex. That position requires decision-making in the absence of information. Play your role and trust your instincts. The rest will take care of itself."

"And if I fail?" Lyris asks, his voice cracking.

The smile disappears from Denali's face. "Then you'll end up just like those bodies downstairs."

CHAPTER FORTY-SIX

INTERCORPEX

Ferry Point Recreational Park
Throgs Neck Geographic District
New York City Municipal Corporation

This is an excellent place to dump bodies, but only if you want them found. Zyree glances back to where they parked fifty meters away. The popularity of this recreation area guarantees a steady flow of traffic from the superhighway off-ramp that loops under the beginning of the Commerce Bridge. Once named the Whitestone, it's the sole suspension bridge spanning this part of Long Island Sound. The other was severely damaged following the collapse and subsequently dismantled.

"The bodies were found within the limits of the New York City Municipal Corporation. That makes it a public safety investigation," the PSS captain says.

"The importance of the victims makes it critical to America Incorporated, which puts it in our jurisdiction," the BCS agent retorts.

"Under what auspices?"

"Are you kidding me with this? Under what auspices? How about those dictating that corporate security always has authority over public safety?"

"Not this time."

"I should have made popcorn," Malkor muses as they watch the grown men quibble from fifteen feet away. "Do you think law enforcement argued like this before the collapse?"

"I guarantee it," Zyree says, looking around.

Public safety erected privacy barriers, but it appears that the bodies were dumped next to a concrete bridge support. A vehicle could have pulled up where the off-ramp disappears under the bridge, paused to dump the bodies, and moved on without causing a ripple in regular traffic.

"We should intervene," Chiana insists. "Standard operating procedure dictates—"

"I know the regulation," Zyree interrupts, not wanting to hear her quote it. "Not yet. I want to see if this turns into a donnybrook."

"A what?"

Zyree turns back to her. "You don't get out of Asia much, do you?"

"Whatever. I know what the word means. I just didn't hear you."

The chief inspector smiles. He knows that her biocomp put the definition up on her contacts.

"Malkor, what's the line of sight on that camera?" Zyree asks, pointing back at the entrance to the parking lot.

"Incoming and outgoing from the parking lot, and mass transit drop-off," he states. "I'm betting the field of view is too narrow to have caught anything."

"Assuming they were brought here in a vehicle. This is called 'Ferry Point,'" Chiana says, despite the bodies being a considerable distance from the water and seeing no place to moor a boat.

The yelling continues. More agents and guardians join the fray. The PSS has the numbers, but the BCS has the training and swagger. The ratio is about five to one. They are only one insult from turning this into a full-scale melee.

"Two Bytecoins say the BCS takes them," Malkor offers.

"You're on."

"You guys are morons," Chiana says in disgust.

"If I have to get an executive mandate, I will," the stuffy BCS agent decrees.

"It takes the BCS an hour to figure out how to put your pants on. We'll have our mandate first," the captain retorts.

"Watch yourself! I'd hate to have to bring you in."

"I'd like to see you try, tough guy. We have three dead patricians lying there. This is our investigation!"

"Okay, there's our invitation," Zyree says to Malkor, hearing the magic words he was waiting for. "Excuse me, gentlemen. I hate to interrupt your lovers' quarrel, but I'll be assuming command of the scene now."

"Who the hell are you?"

"Chief Inspector Zyree of Intercorpex Security. My colleague here is Inspector Malkor. The perpetually angry woman behind us is Chief Inspector Chiana. Now that you've confirmed that the victims are patricians, the investigation is ours under the auspices of the Zurich Canon. Chiana can recite the exact paragraph for you. She's obnoxiously good at that."

"Asshole," she mutters as Malkor unsuccessfully stifles a laugh.

"How do we know you are who you say you are?" the senior BCS agent asks.

"My flashy good looks and hip uniform aren't enough proof? Have your superiors call Zurich. The man you want to speak to is Commissioner-General

Jurghen. Yes, he's as German as the name sounds so don't piss him off. Now, if you'll excuse us, we'll be investigating the corpses that you're letting decompose while you argue."

Zyree brushes past the agents and skirts the privacy curtain. He moves slowly, giving his biocomp the chance to process and identify anything his eyes miss.

"You don't see this every day," Malkor says with a whistle. Zyree bends forward and cocks his head to get a better look at their faces.

The three older gentlemen are lined up next to each other. They were positioned, not just dumped. All three lie face-up and have a look of surprise on their faces. Whatever they were doing before they were killed, they weren't expecting to get shot.

They're dressed in typical patrician formalwear, and their bronze coats of arms around their necks in lieu of a necktie are still present. Although not intrinsically valuable, criminals have been known to take them as trophies when a rare murder occurs. Not in this case.

"Yannen Townsend, Namyn Wilmington, and Nygehl Lockwood," Chiana says.

"The families of the *gentez-minorez* fingered in the Secaucus attack," Malkor says. "Retribution?"

"It looks like they each took seven or eight rounds. That's a lot of retribution. Turn one of them over, Malkor."

"I get all the fun jobs," he whines, complying. Rigor mortis has set in, making the body difficult to move. "How long do you think they've been here?"

"Eight or nine hours but we'll need a medical examiner to determine that."

"I just arranged for ICX Security to dispatch one," Chiana informs them.

Zyree rubs the stubble on his chin. "We need to find out where they were before the attack."

"They all have residences in Manhattan. They were probably there."

Zyree looks up at the bridge and then over at the adjacent park. That doesn't sound right. This recreation area serves the South Bronx area and isn't easily accessible from Manhattan. There are ten thousand places and two rivers to dump a body. Why this spot is a question he can't answer, so Zyree keeps his thoughts to himself.

"Wow, these are some serious exit wounds," Malkor says, still checking the bodies.

Exit wounds are larger than entrance wounds because the round becomes unstable as it forces its way through tissue and muscle. The size of these exit wounds means the bullets cavitated after entering their bodies.

"High-velocity rounds. Probably a rifle at short range, but not point-blank. These men were executed."

"How do you know that just by looking at them?" Chiana asks.

"The number of rounds that hit center mass; a lack of visible gunshot residue…you know, investigator stuff."

Chiana thrusts her chin out. "Liberteum killed them. They're killing their accomplices in the attacks."

"That's a rushed conclusion."

"Damn, Zyree, do you need a map to put this together? I think you need to go back to watching that kid and leave this to someone used to these types of investigations. You deal with the occasional suspicious death. I deal with the Yakuza, the Triads, and many other Asian crime syndicates that predate the collapse."

She has a point. But Liberteum isn't the only one who may have wanted these men dead. Not after what the global media has been reporting. He isn't willing to have an argument based on the evidence. If she wants to chase her tail, he plans on letting her.

"We were issued a joint mandate to hunt Liberteum. You investigate these murders, and I will work on tracking Liberteum down in Manhattan. Agreed?"

"Agreed," Chiana says, beaming.

Zyree and Malkor walk away from the bodies and past the still-bickering agents of the two rival America Incorporated agencies. They stop arguing long enough to see Chiana still working on the scene.

"You're seriously going to let the Ninja have this one?" Malkor asks. "These are the worst patrician murders we've seen in decades. You're either losing your edge or know who it was."

"I know who it wasn't. If Liberteum had killed them, they'd get left in the underground and not under a bridge in the Bronx that requires vehicle transportation to reach."

"Good point."

"This investigation will be time-consuming. I don't want to be looking the wrong way when Liberteum strikes again."

A priority notice from Zurich flashes on their contact lenses. It's longer than the regular updates, so the two inspectors read the entire message. After Zyree finishes, he knows that things are about to take a turn for the worse.

"Damn…"

"I see it too," Malkor says. "The families of the murdered patricians were found dead in their houses. You called it: This rules out Liberteum."

"Chiana won't think so. The alternative is too scary to consider. These murders could lead to a patrician war, and that's the last thing we need if Liberteum succeeds."

"Succeeds in doing what?"

Zyree thinks back to his conversation with Teman in that dingy urch bar when he brought up the meaning and possible origin of the name "Liberteum." The chief guardian dismissed it, but that may have been premature. Zyree is beginning to think that the terrorists are determined to live up to their moniker.

"Freeing the world."

CHAPTER FORTY-SEVEN

AMERICA, INC.

Shareholder Hall
Corporate Hill Governance District
Washington-Arlington Municipal Corporation

Fiolla stares at the sweeping façade of Shareholder Hall after the conveyance pulls up, and she climbs out. It's not often that executives are dispatched to Corporate Hill on official business. Modern meetings and correspondence are conducted at the speed of electrons. Face-to-face meetings are reserved for high-level confabs, and the practice of hand delivering messages died when the postal service went the way of the dinosaurs.

The staff was surprised when Fiolla arrived at the chairman's office with an envelope embossed with the swooping eagle of their corporate logo. Valen's message herein is being treated like the Dead Sea Scrolls. The schedule is immediately cleared, and she is ushered into the spacious office.

"There was no requirement to deliver this in person, Executive Fiolla," Chairman Hammond says.

"Chief Executive Valen didn't want there to be any misunderstandings."

Hammond opens the envelope and removes the tri-folded paper. Whatever he wrote inspires an amused smile. Hammond folds the message, replaces it in the envelope, and tosses it on the desk.

"He'll be present at Saturday's hearing," he says to Boardmember Zeykala, who lurks behind her. "Thank you, Executive Fiolla. And thank the chief executive for me."

"I will, sir."

"I'll walk you out," Zeykala says.

Fiolla nods, but she wants nothing to do with her escort out of the building. She subtly stretches her normal gait and increases her pace. The two women turn the corner and climb the marble stairs to the main level. With nobody around them, Zeykala makes her move.

"I admire your loyalty to Valen."

"I'm loyal to America Incorporated. Valen is my chief executive officer. We should all be loyal to him."

"Of course. Am I to assume you'll show the same level of dedication to the next chief executive?"

"When Valen *retires,* and a new CEO is named, yes."

"That's good. Loyalty is a valuable asset that few possess…other than to themselves, that is. I just want to ensure that yours isn't misplaced. Valen is going to be removed on Saturday. You may be in denial, but I assure you, it's unavoidable."

"If you say so."

"You disagree?"

Fiolla purses her lips. "I don't have a crystal ball. I have no idea what's going to happen."

That's not what she wants to say, but she holds her tongue. A confrontation with Valen's archnemesis isn't in anyone's interests, especially hers. Fiolla recognizes this as an attempt to milk her for information, so she's desperate not to fall into a trap by saying too much.

"You know, Fiolla, Corporate Affairs is one of the most difficult groups in the whole corporation to work for. You need to know a lot about everything to do your job well. You're responsible for extinguishing fires by interacting with every department and subsidiary to douse them."

"I understand what my job description entails, Boardmember Zeykala."

She smiles. "I checked into you. You're well-liked. Your peers characterize you as good-natured, approachable, tough in a crisis, and fair in mediating disputes. I didn't expect such glowing reviews."

"And I didn't realize you were moonlighting in Human Resources," Fiolla says, forcing a smile.

"I know you don't like me, but there's no need to be hostile," Zeykala says, grabbing her arm and stopping in the middle of the corridor. "I'm paying you a compliment."

"Thanks."

"I think your talents are being wasted. Has Valen ever talked to you about a promotion?"

"I haven't been at the White House long," she admits.

It was a weak justification, but her only answer to the bright red warning light indicating where this conversation is heading. Fiolla starts again across the lobby's polished marble floor for the door. Zeykala keeps pace, much to her chagrin.

"I see great potential in you," she continues. "You're the kind of executive that will help lead this corporation into the next century."

"I like to think that as well. Thank you for your company, Boardmember Zeykala, but I must return to my duties. Have a pleasant day."

"Fiolla?" she says as the door swings open. "Opportunities come and go in the blink of an eye. Don't throw away a promising career by keeping yours closed too long."

CHAPTER FORTY-EIGHT

LIBERTEUM

"The Cellar"
SoHo Geographic District
New York City Municipal Corporation

There is only one access to The Cellar from the underground. A short tunnel leads to others, like branches on a tree as you move away from the trunk. Michele waits at one of the intersections while the bar is scouted. What makes the place unique is that it has street access. It's one of the urch speakeasies that do.

"Rykos is there. He's getting grilled by Gyell, who's wondering what he's doing sitting in an underground urch bar," Jasper says, his face tense with concern. "Are you sure you want to go through with this? It smells like a trap."

Michele exhales and looks down the tunnel. "Yeah, I'm sure. Meet me at the rally point and have the tools ready. We may have to perform some quick surgery to get those biojacks out of Rykos."

"You think he's going to come with you?"

She shrugs. "We're going to find out."

"Good luck," Jasper says with a shake of his head as he disappears into the adjacent basement and back the way they came.

Michele traverses the tunnel and steps quietly into the dimly lit bar through the access carved into the wall. She scans the patrons, looking for anyone who seems out of place. None of them do, except Rykos, who sticks out like a neon sign. Urches and Ivies might as well be from different planets in both dress style and demeanor.

Gyell nods when he notices her gliding over to his makeshift bar. Despite being chummy with select guardians, he doesn't like outsiders in his establishment. Even Rykos's father has been here. Public Safety and Security let him operate out of this location because they believe he gives them information on urch activity. Some of the info Gyell provides is legitimate to maintain appearances, but a substantial percentage isn't entirely accurate. Disinformation can be a powerful tool.

"Know this, Rykos," Michele says, coming up behind him, "if this is a trap, I will kill you where you sit."

"Good to see you, too," he says, turning on his stool. His eyes flicker to life when he sees her.

"I'm serious."

"So am I." He flashes an almost adoring smile. "This isn't a setup. Nobody knows I'm here."

Michele grabs his right arm. The jagged scar from their first biojack removal is still visible. There is little doubt that corporate authorities replaced the old one with a shiny new one when Rykos returned. He probably has more than the ones they previously removed.

"*Everyone* knows you're here."

"Ya want sometin' to drink, Michele?" Gyell asks, not understanding her intentions and wanting to avoid blood spilling in his saloon.

"No thanks, Gyell."

"Ya use my place and don't pay me for it? Dat's just wrong. Ya lucky I owe ya pops my life."

"He saved you twice, if I remember correctly. For your troubles," she says, pulling three slugs out of the hip pocket of her tight black pants. She slides them across the makeshift bar. Satisfied, Gyell checks on his other customers.

"That guy knew Quarren? I wouldn't think they traveled in the same circles down here. They're very different."

"You meet and befriend all manner of people if you stay in the underground long enough," Michele explains, feeling for her knife and gun before taking a seat on the stool next to Rykos. "My father saved him from a group of urches looking to rob him. Then he saved him from the PSS a couple of years later."

"Quarren got around."

"You have no idea. Why did you want to meet me, Rykos?"

Rykos turns to face her. "I want my father back."

"I'd like to help you, but I don't have him."

"Don't lie to me. You guys captured him during a raid."

There is a fire and steely determination in his eyes. It's a far cry from the young man she met at the rave and held as a captive in the Broad Street Station. He's not the confused boy her father coaxed during their talks. He has nerve now, either from his experiences with them or what came after.

Michele presses her lips together before speaking. "He was captured in a place called the Bastille, that's true. It was Haven's stronghold. He has him."

"And Haven works for you. Order him to release my father."

"I'm afraid it's more complicated than that now. There have been some changes since we last saw each other."

Rykos gives her a suspicious look. Then the light bulb clicks on. His face contorts into a mix of disbelief, realization, and frustration. He must have been encouraged when Farron set up the meeting. Now the hope he was harboring flickers out.

"Haven went rogue, didn't he?" Rykos asks, shaking his head. "Well, that was predictable. He clearly hated you. Do you know where he's keeping my father?"

"No, not for certain."

"You can't have that many hiding places down here. Tell me where you *think* he is."

Michele's eyes narrow. "Rykos, even if I could help you find him, I don't know that I would. I don't owe you anything."

"No, you don't," Rykos says, catching her off-guard. "I owe you."

"For what?"

"Letting me live, for starters. And for Quarren's tutoring. I wasn't lying when I told Farron that he was right about everything. He opened my eyes and validated my suspicions about the world."

There's a long pause in the conversation. Quarren left quite an impression on him during their short time together. Her father had that effect on most people. It was his superpower.

"What do you want from me, Rykos?"

"I want you to help me get him back. We both know that you have a better chance of finding Haven than the PSS does."

"What makes you think I want to help you?"

"You wouldn't have agreed to meet with me otherwise."

Michele knows that Rykos is sharp. Most people wouldn't have made that connection with Farron or would have made it far later. She is willing to help, with strings attached. She can explain that in due time. Right now, the focus needs to be on getting him to take that first step.

"It's not that easy. Staying in contact with an employee would spell disaster. Communications are too easy to trace. We'd be exposed. If you want your father back, you'll have to do it my way. You're a smart guy. You know what that means."

Rykos inhales, swallows hard, and nods. "I do. I'm willing to make that sacrifice if you promise to help."

CHAPTER FORTY-NINE

AMERICA, INC.

The White House
Corporate Governance District
Washington-Arlington Municipal Corporation

The images are appalling. Valen knew these men. He's attended various meetings, galas, and functions with them. It's difficult for him to see their faces contorted in a mix of surprise and agony. It's harder still to not focus on the mutilated skin from the bullets that pierced their torsos.

"I thought Intercorpex Security took over this investigation. Where did these photos come from?"

"New York Public Safety and Security took these before the BCS and ICX Security arrived. Had they known their place, we may have uncovered more information."

Virtari never misses an opportunity to pass the blame onto somebody else. With the amount of time he spends promoting himself and the BCS, Valen is surprised Human Resources didn't place him in marketing as a registrant. They're almost as ruthless.

"What else?"

"We have the final count of the patricians' murdered family members: seven at the Townsend residence, five at Lockwood's, and three at Wilmington's."

"Seven?"

"His grandchildren were visiting," Virtari clarifies.

"The wives of all three patricians were murdered in their beds," Cayem adds. "Nygehl Lockwood lost both of his sons and his daughter. Only the eldest Townsend son seems to have escaped harm."

"How did he manage that?"

"He was out of town," Virtari says.

"We're trying to locate him, but he must have heard what happened and went dark. He could be anywhere."

Valen stares at the junior agent. "If commandos killed my family, I would too."

"Sir, I'm not sure the term 'commando' applies here. We are looking at the real possibility that Liberteum has increased its reach," Virtari concludes.

Valen scans the faces around the situation room conference table. Nobody is refuting Virtari's explanation. They either believe he's correct or are afraid to challenge him. Fear stifles honest discourse.

"These murders weren't all conducted in Manhattan. They were conducted in exclusive communities. Manhattan may be within reach, but the Townsend Estate in Montclair is about twenty miles away. You want me to believe that underground terrorists did that?"

"That is the conclusion Chief Inspector Chiana of ICX Security came to. I'm just repeating what she reported to us."

"Director Virtari, I'm not interested in Intercorpex's opinions. I want to know what you think."

"It's not my investigation, sir."

Valen's eyes narrow as he leans forward. "Humor me."

"Yes, I agree with her conclusions."

"I understand. You informed me that every ingress and egress from Manhattan was monitored. How did Liberteum leave the island to execute these attacks?"

"They stole the transponders from the PSS and—"

"You said that wouldn't matter—that they wouldn't get past your enhanced security cordon."

"Then perhaps they have accomplices in those areas."

"The BCS has allowed Liberteum to develop assets capable of conducting a covert night raid miles from Manhattan? They have commandos who can murder the families of the elites and slip back into the shadows without a trace?"

"I'm not sure what you want me to say."

"Say that you will assist the Intercorpex investigation, carefully weigh the facts, ask hard questions, and not accept their bullshit conclusions without verifying them."

"Yes, sir." Virtari's words were the right ones, but his eyes suggest that the CEO should have improper relations with his mother.

"Ladies and gentlemen, whoever did this wanted to send a message. It's one thing to kill patricians, but the perpetrators murdered their *families* as well. I want to know who and why, and I want it fast."

"Yes, sir," the staff around the table utters in unison.

"Where are we with locating Chief Guardian Teman?"

"There's nothing new to report, sir. Not so much as a blip on any of his biological tracking devices. He had Level Five monitoring. That fifth device is implanted deep in his tissue. It cannot be easily found or removed."

Valen looks around for an explanation that isn't coming. "So, why can't we track it?"

"He could be in a Faraday cage," the Bureau's technology advisor says from the far end of the table. "It's a mesh enclosure designed to block transmission and reception of electronic signals."

"Okay, what you're saying is, he could be anywhere?"

"Unfortunately, yes," Virtari concludes.

This security briefing is already double its usual length and far more disturbing than usual. Events are spiraling out of control. The BCS isn't making any progress on any of them. Valen needs something to break his way. One victory will make a difference.

"All right. I want to hear solutions to these problems the next time we convene. Find some."

Valen strides out of the Situation Room and heads up to the Oval Office. He's greeted with the impatient sound of his digital assistant before he makes it two steps.

"Chief Executive Valen," she says, using her seductive Russian-accented voice, "you are late for a VidLynk with the CEO of Chicago and have upcoming meetings with the Indonesia Corporation trade delegation and agricultural subsidiaries about improvements to crop yields."

"Cancel my meetings for the next two hours, Halie," he orders, placing his palms on the desk and hanging his head. "I'm going for a walk in the park. Have Executive Fiolla meet me there."

"As you wish, Chief Executive."

CHAPTER FIFTY

INTERCORPEX

"The Cellar"
SoHo Geographic District
New York City Municipal Corporation

The Cellar is in the SoHo geographic district. It's a part of the city where even a modest increase in foot traffic is noticeable. This area has always had a reputation for being urch central. Even though the PSS dragnet has decreased their numbers, Zyree assumes the cellar-dwellers have eyes everywhere.

"I don't like this, Boss. We should wait for support."

"What support, Malkor? We don't have a team and can't ask the PSS or BCS. Even if we could, time isn't on our side. Rykos is biojacked, and Liberteum won't risk staying exposed for long."

"Well, at least let's go in loud."

Modern non-lethal measures to subdue and incapacitate are effective. In most cases, "going in soft" means employing these measures to immediately pacify a group of people before they can resist. It comes with a downside: An attacking force announces its arrival. The alternative is to "go in loud," meaning with guns blazing.

"I almost wish Chiana was here to quote you the regulation on that," Zyree says, studying the hidden entrance to the urch bar from across the street.

"Boss, I hate to be a killjoy, but we have no eyes or ears in there. Do you really want to waltz in to find ourselves outmanned and outgunned?"

"I've been there before. I know the layout," Zyree argues. "It's not that big."

The Cellar is where Zyree presented to Teman the information they'd collected on Liberteum. Although its existence is an affront to corporate policy, the chief guardian allows the bar to operate unmolested in exchange for information. It was nearly empty the first time Zyree was there. It may be again.

"Knowing the layout isn't going to keep us from getting shot."

"I guess we'll just have to rely on your quick wit, then," Zyree says, leaving their reconnaissance spot and crossing the street with Malkor hustling to catch up.

Zyree pauses at the cover to the stairs and counts down from three with his fingers. He yanks the door open and descends quickly into the basement. He tries not to think about Malkor being right – this is a bad plan, but it's their only one.

The urches in the poorly lit watering hole immediately react. They have a sixth sense for when something doesn't feel right. Two members of Intercorpex Security walking into their favorite hangout causes most of them to scramble for the exit at the back of the room. The ones closest to the inspectors huddle against the wall in fear.

A woman at the end of the bar pulls out a weapon and points it at Zyree. Malkor levels his gun at her simultaneously with the chief inspector. The standoff is on. Zyree closes the distance slightly to get a better look at her in the pale light. She's the same brunette from the photos of the rave. Bingo.

"Put it down!"

"Not a chance."

"Be smart. Nobody needs to die today. You have no cover. If you choose to fight, you'll lose. You can't get us both," Zyree says, moving in a wide arc to get a better angle as Malkor moves up along the bar.

Rykos steps in front of her, acting as a human shield. That was unexpected. The analysis pops up on Zyree's contacts: fear and determination. He assumed she would take him as a hostage. Instead, the kid is protecting her.

"What the hell are you doing, Rykos?"

"I'm getting between you and the only person that can save my father," he says, his voice calm and even.

"I was right. You are a member of Liberteum."

The woman lets out a quick laugh from behind him.

"No. I'm negotiating for my father's release."

Zyree's eyes narrow. He finds that hard to believe, but the analysis in his peripheral vision shows no deceit.

"Assuming that's true, this isn't the way to do it. Now, you're going to step aside by the time I count to three, or you're going to become an unfortunate statistic."

"That's not going to happen, Chief Inspector. You'll have to shoot the son of the chief guardian of New York City and hero of the corporation."

"One…move, Rykos."

The woman refines her aim. Zyree hopes that she's not a good shot, but deep down, he knows better. The pair shuffle toward the back exit that leads to the underground. Time is running out.

"Two…"

"Be smart, Rykos. I'll drop both of you before you get there," Malkor ominously adds, tracking their movements with his weapon.

"If ya say three, ya partner gets da first slug," a voice bellows.

The bartender has an old shotgun trained on Malkor. Zyree swings his gun around to cover him. Malkor closes his eyes in frustration over getting tunnel-vision and forgetting to cover the bartender.

"Drop the weapon, friend," Zyree commands. "This is no concern of yours. We're not here for you or your business."

"Dat girl over dere is my bizness. Now yous gonna walk outta here da way ya came and not come back," the bartender says.

"That's not going to happen."

"Then ya gonna die." He turns to the woman. "When I meet your pops, I'm gonna tell him we's even."

Zyree does the mental math. If her father was the man that he saw at the station… He squeezes the trigger and puts a round in the bartender's chest. The bartender reflexively fires the shotgun as the barrel falls. The sound of the blast is deafening as the slug pounds into Malkor's torso, knocking him to the ground.

The chief inspector pivots on the balls of his feet and takes a knee, swinging his weapon in the direction of Michele and Rykos. She pumps two rounds in his direction, both close but high, forcing him to roll and seek cover in a booth. Another two bullets splinter the wood next to his head. Zyree hazards a glance and catches the two of them disappearing into the passage.

"Shit."

Zyree crawls over to Malkor, who is still splayed on the ground. "You okay?"

"Damn it! I told you we'd get shot."

"We didn't get shot. *You* did," the chief inspector says, feeling his partner's clothing for any blood indicative of a wound.

"So much for relying on my quick wit," Malkor says, grimacing.

"Your armor took the shot."

"Yeah, but it still hurts like a sonuvabitch."

The energy-dispersing plating works best with lower velocity projectiles like those fired from the bartender's shotgun. It works but is less effective against the high-power rifles Liberteum used on Broad Street. Still, it doesn't feel good.

"Can you move? We need to go after them."

"Yeah, give me a minute," he says.

Zyree helps him up to his feet after fifteen seconds. He bends forward at the waist, fighting the pain. A minute is all they can spare. With a few blinks of his left eye, he opens a line to the war room at the NOC.

"Yeah?"

"Duckballs, tell me you have a biojack fix on Rykos."

"Stand by," the technician says as Zyree hears the clicking of a keyboard. "Yeah, I've got…Why is he moving away from you?"

"Things didn't go quite as planned. Where is he?"

"Sixty meters to your east and moving north. Subsurface based on the interference."

Zyree turns to Malkor, who is gritting his teeth. "Recovery time is over. Let's go."

CHAPTER FIFTY-ONE

UNDERGRADUATE RYKOS

Underground
SoHo Geographic District
New York City Municipal Corporation

We hustle through a series of basements and short tunnels. I don't know how Michele manages to move so fast down here. I can't see a thing and have already tripped twice and slammed into four walls.

"Have we lost them?"

"No," Michele says, stopping at the intersection of two different routes and firing up a small torchlight. "You know those guys?"

"The talkative one was Chief Inspector Zyree of Intercorpex Security. He showed up right after you left me at the subway station. I don't know who the other one is."

Michele pulls a knife out of the sheath tucked into her back and I gawk at the intimidating blade. "What are you doing?"

"You're transmitting."

"They're Intercorpex. Biojacks can only be monitored by the PSS," I argue, not wanting to get sliced open again in a dingy tunnel.

"Yeah, and two armed Gestapo clad in body armor just happened to stop in for a drink."

"What's a Gestapo?"

"Never mind. Do you want your father back, or were you lying?"

Michele moves her face inches from mine. I stare into her determined eyes.

"I do."

"Then, as you business types like to say, this is the price of admission. It's that or you can stay here and wait for them. Choose."

I present my right arm. On cue, she grasps it and places the tip of her blade against my skin. I turn away. With a flick of her wrist, she makes a crescent-shaped incision. I bite my lower lip to fight the pain as she lifts the flap of skin and digs out the microchip with the knife. I glance back at it. I've never seen a biojack in person before.

It's amazing what that small encapsulated device does. Without it, there is no functioning in the corporate world. Biojacks are identifications, geolocators, financial transactions facilitators, and a set of digital keys. They are powered by a small battery that is recharged by kinetic motion, body heat, and the movement of blood through my circulatory system.

"I have three more," I warn her.

"Yeah, but you don't want me taking those out. Jasper can do that. Let's hope they're only monitoring your primary one."

"What do we do with it?"

"We leave it here. We're at a junction. That will force the men chasing us to separate to cover both routes. They're getting closer. Come on."

"Which way are we going?"

"Left through the basements. Right leads to an old sewer being monitored by the PSS. It's how they captured so many urches in this area."

We move through the bowels of the city. There are a few doors, but most of the transitions are holes broken through walls. Some of them are large enough to squeeze through standing. Others require us to crawl or even slide on our stomachs to get through. I don't know how urches live like this. I'm already exhausted and we haven't gone far.

Michele reaches through a small hole and pushes something away on the other side. She slides her petite frame through. I struggle to shimmy into the almost pitch black room on the other side. Standing up, I walk into some sort of boxy container and curse before the overhead lights come on and I see what I hit.

"This is as good a spot as any," Michele says, looking around at the crowded basement.

Wood crates are everywhere. Most of them are marked "fragile" and are stacked and leaning around the room. I brush the dust off one of them, searching for identifying markings.

"What is this place?"

"This part of the city used to be full of art galleries. This is what's left of one."

"Okay, so why are we staying here?"

"Someone is gaining on us. He must have night vision optics. This will level the playing field. Take this, stand here," she orders, positioning me behind some crates near the entry.

"And do what with it? Sit?"

She places her finger over her lips and takes ten steps away. No sooner does she get there than a figure slides through the opening we just came from and charges into the center of the room.

"Don't move a muscle," the figure says to Michele as he trains his weapon on her. "Where's Rykos?"

Now I get it. I grip the folding metal chair and swing it quickly. It catches him square in the back and he crumples forward. "Right here."

Michele pulls her weapon and aims it at him. In a flash, Zyree pops to his feet and swings his hands in a scissor movement that breaks her grip on the gun. It skitters across the dirty concrete floor. In an equally quick motion, he draws a knife and squares off against her.

"Not again," she moans.

He lunges before she can reach for her own blade. Michele parries the thrust away with her arm. She stomps down on the instep of the man's foot and lands a hard right to his face. Stunned, he withdraws the knife enough to allow her to perform the same disarming move he used on her. He gives Michele a surprised look that she rewards with a slight shrug.

Zyree moves in with a couple of quick punches that Michele blocks. He returns the favor when she counters. I want to intervene, but don't know what to do. These two have fighting skills I couldn't dream of. Barring any other option, I retrieve Zyree's weapon and point it in the direction of the two combatants.

Each continues to look for a way to hurt the other. Zyree throws a jab that lands on Michele's cheek, but she finds his head with a quick combo in retaliation. Zyree swings hard, looking for a knockout punch that she ducks. She crouches and sweeps out his legs from underneath him. He grabs her arm as he starts to crash to the ground. Now off balance and unable to fight the momentum, she goes with it, springing forward and tucking into a roll.

The move causes Zyree to lose his grip. He springs up off the floor and turns as the momentum from Michele's gymnastics move carries her to her feet. Zyree charges at her when she pivots, revealing the gun she lost. Zyree freezes in place and stands erect with an angry grimace.

"Kneel. Interlace your fingers behind your neck." He does as he's told.

"Damn, you're good," Zyree says, shaking his head. "Did Haven teach you how to fight?"

"No. They're skills I picked up throughout a misspent life. Shut down your biocomputer."

Zyree cocks his head. "I forgot the password."

Michele's face is welded with determination. "I won't ask again. I can cut it out if you wish."

"That won't be necessary," Zyree says before uttering a series of commands that theoretically shuts it down. I have no idea if it's actually off.

"Take your contacts out," I command, more to let the two pugilists know I'm still here than for any practical reason.

"Look at you getting all bossy, Rykos. They're no good without the computer."

"Then you have no need for them. I'm sure your vision is fine."

"Twenty-twenty," he says, pulling them out of his eyes and dropping them.

I grind them into the floor with my foot before stepping back. Even if he left his biocomp on, at least he can't control it.

"I'm told you're Chief Inspector Zyree."

"I am. What's your name?"

"Michele, but I'm betting you already knew that."

"I actually didn't. I only knew your father's name. Rykos probably told the BCS, but they don't share information. Michele is an old name—not one you often hear these days."

She nods. "How did you find me?"

"I didn't. I found him," Zyree says, looking over at me.

Michele was right. Intercorpex is somehow monitoring my biojack. I want to know how he saw through the lies about my escape when the PSS and BCS didn't. He tested me for gunpowder residue in the triage area that day. The thought sends another shiver through me. I hope he doesn't mention anything about our meeting in Central Park.

"Why were you looking for him?" Michele asks.

"Because I was hoping he would lead me to you. Or to Haven."

"What do you know about Haven?"

Zyree stares up at her. "Probably more than you do. I was his mentor and his friend. I spoke at his funeral when we buried him."

"You have poor taste in friends. Haven is unhinged. Why is Intercorpex looking for us?"

"Seriously? You attacked the exchange twice and are going to do it again."

Michele smiles. "And you're going to stop us?"

"It's my job to try," Zyree says before a wary look of resignation creeps over his face. "Or, it *was* my job to try. Your killing me will only force Intercorpex to send an army of inspectors to hunt you down."

"We've faced worse odds. You're wrong about one thing: I'm not going to kill you, Chief Inspector," she says, turning her attention to me. "He is."

"What?" I ask, shocked.

"I have no quarrel with this man, Rykos. He's only doing his job, as misguided as it is. So, I'm putting his fate in your hands."

Her words crash into me with the force of a train. Do I have to make this decision? I watch her for a long moment, hoping she's joking. Her impassive stare tells me otherwise.

Shaking, I take a couple of steps over to Zyree and put the muzzle of his gun to his head. I glance back at Michele with pleading eyes. I get no reprieve. She studies my every move intently while keeping her weapon trained on our quarry.

If this is some kind of test, it sucks. I don't know what the right or wrong answer is. Nothing in my life has prepared me for this kind of decision. There's no turning back from this if I pull the trigger. No amount of clever deceit will allow me to return to society, much less as a corporate hero.

This is a moment of truth. Everything I've done has led me to this moment. I'm the one who wanted this; I invited it to happen. I strengthen my grip on the weapon. Forcing doubt out of my mind, I take a deep breath and steel myself to do something I never would have imagined.

CHAPTER FIFTY-TWO

AMERICA, INC.

The White House Executive Park
Corporate Governance District
Washington-Arlington Municipal Corporation

Unlike the leaders that predated corporate reign, the chief executive does not drive around in an armored limousine or have a swarm of guards following him wherever he goes. While there is security at the Chief Executive's Mansion, America Incorporated doesn't see threats against leadership that occurred before the economic apocalypse.

"You have shadows," Fiolla says, noticing the two armed BCS agents standing fifty feet away.

"And an overhead drone courtesy of Director Virtari. Given the murdered patricians, he thought the security detail was a prudent measure. I'm starting to feel like the American president."

"I'm not sure it would make me feel any safer."

"Trust me, it doesn't. I just finished a long security briefing in the Sit Room," Valen says, turning to stroll along the cobblestone paths. "Between the murdered patricians and other disconcerting issues, I can't shake the feeling that I'm missing something."

Fiolla looks around. "Sir, do you think it's a good idea to talk out in the open like this?"

Valen gives her a devilish smile and slides his hand into his pocket, pulling out a small black device. This disruptor is larger than the one Farron carried. It's either an older generation or more powerful. Either way, anyone eavesdropping won't hear a word they say.

"What do you mean by 'missing something?'"

"Raimius started by blaming us for the attacks in New York and Secaucus. Then, all of a sudden, global corporate media outlets start reporting that evidence points to the upper and lower patricians being responsible."

"Including our own media," Fiolla says.

"I know. Then the bodies of three patricians are dumped in the Bronx and everybody immediately blames Liberteum."

"It could still be designed to discredit us," Fiolla concludes. Valen winces and grinds his teeth.

"Is it? Why link patricians to the attacks, then? It gains Raimius nothing unless he thinks I'm working with Keating and Covington, which makes no sense. And even if he *does* think that for some reason, it's a dangerous game to play."

"You think it's something else?"

Valen turns and heads toward a bench. He sits, taking a moment to admire the park's beauty. Fiolla joins him, eyeing Virtari's "security detail" spies. He is having Valen watched, and that makes her uncomfortable on several levels.

"It hasn't been publicized, but there were terrorist attacks in Moscow, the United Kingdom, and German corporations. Add to that an urch uprising in Paris and a worker riot in China. What do you get?"

"Coincidence?"

"That's one hell of a coincidence. Fiolla, who gains if there's global unrest?"

"Intercorpex," she says, connecting the dots. "That doesn't mean that any of this is related."

"Raimius has always sought to expand his power. He fancies Intercorpex as a global government more than a marketplace. What if he's trying to make that dream a reality?"

Fiolla presses her lips together and closes her eyes. "That's a stretch, sir. He wouldn't be that reckless."

"Are you sure? Two groups are most affected by an increase in exchange power: corporations and patricians. By assigning blame for the attacks, he has divided the patricians. By supporting terrorists, he's weakening the corporations most likely to resist him."

"China, the United Kingdom, France, Germany, Russia, and us."

"Exactly."

"Sir, I respect your ability to war-game scenarios, but it takes a lot of suspension of disbelief to reach a point where you believe that Raimius is capable of orchestrating this. He might covet power, but there are other ways to get it."

Valen takes some time to reflect on her objection. The man is so methodical in his thoughts that it can be infuriating to have a conversation with him. She's beginning to think he's lost interest.

"Corporate power is a zero-sum game. Total gains or losses are balanced by the total losses or gains of another. If Raimius wants to enhance the global hegemony of ICX, it comes at the expense of corporations and patricians."

"Who are both being targeted in this series of incidents," Fiolla says, catching up. "It makes sense on a theoretical level, but do you have proof?"

"No. It's pure speculation at this point," Valen quickly answers. He doesn't play fast and loose with the facts to get them to conform to his worldview. "I can't fight a war on two fronts. First, I need to survive Saturday's hearing. Then I can worry about Raimius and his thirst for world domination."

"Not to add to your burden, sir, but Boardmember Zeykala was chatty with me on my way out of Chairman Hammond's office."

Valen remains silent as Fiolla recaps their conversation. He gets angry once she finishes.

"That's a bold move, even for her. Now it's my turn. I need you to set up meetings with board members," he says, rubbing his chin. "I want to talk to the ones in Zeykala's camp. If she thinks it's appropriate to entice my people, I will make a run at hers."

Valen is not usually emotional in his decision-making. He can remain calm during the fiercest of arguments between his executives and still render a logical, thoughtful resolution. Fiolla isn't getting the feeling that this is one of those times.

"What good will that do?"

"Zeykala will expect me to go on the offensive before the hearing. Why disappoint her? Only I won't be talking to the people she thinks I'll target. Thank you for telling me about your conversation with her," he says, turning to Fiolla. "It gave me the direction I was looking for. As the Chinese strategist Sun Tzu once said, 'You can be sure of succeeding in your attacks if you only attack places which are undefended.'"

CHAPTER
FIFTY-THREE

THE PATRICIANS

Safe House
Tribeca Geographic District
New York City Municipal Corporation

The domicile will have a swath of threadbare carpet by the time this night is over. Farron is wearing it down with his incessant pacing. He disagreed with Michele's decision to meet with the kid. He never should have told her that Rykos reached out to her. Then again, he never thought she would be reckless enough to agree to meet. At this stage in the game, there is too much at stake and nobody knows that better than Michele.

"They're here," Adiz says from his workstation.

The hacker has been monitoring the closed-circuit surveillance in the building. Farron watches as the trio boards the elevator. He can't believe his eyes. Could she have made a more boneheaded decision?

This is probably the last place Rykos expected to end up. Urches aren't known for spending much time aboveground. There's little doubt that he expected to be taken to an abandoned cellar or tunnel deep in the scummy recesses of the city. It's where she should have taken him. Instead, Michele and Jasper accompany their guest up to the unfinished domicile.

"Have you lost your damn mind?" Farron shouts at Michele after he opens the door and the three of them step inside.

"I'm sure most people will say so," she responds with a wink, brushing past the patrician.

"No, I mean what were you thinking bringing Rykos here? This is the last place the kid should be!"

Rykos folds his arms across his chest. He just realized that Farron is more involved with Liberteum than he let on during their conversation. It's one thing to arrange for a message to reach a terrorist leader. It's another when she's living in one of his domiciles.

"Settle down, Farron. Where did you expect me to take him? Valhalla? The Alamo? Where in the city is safer for us than this place?"

Jasper sees the question in Rykos's eyes and leans in to his ear. "They're codenames for some of our underground strongholds."

"It's better than bringing him here," Farron continues. "He could still be transmitting."

"He's not. Jasper took care of his biojacks."

"You don't know if you got them all. You kidnapped him after the rave. He could have biojacks that he doesn't even know about."

"I scanned him for transmitters," Jasper says, collapsing into an ergonomic chair next to Adiz. He looks at Michele and back at Farron, realizing he inserted himself into a verbal crossfire. "I removed all his biojacks. End of story."

"How much does he know?" the patrician demands.

"I don't care what you guys are planning, Farron," Rykos says. "If Intercorpex goes down, so be it. All I'm interested in is securing my father's release."

"Isn't that special. And then what? You expect us to let you back into the world so you can tell your daddy and his cronies what you saw here?"

"I can't go back," he says, lowering his eyes.

Before Farron has a chance to ask, Michele explains what happened in the tunnel. Their patron intently listens without interruption. It doesn't alleviate his concerns, but he's more at ease.

"Okay. How do you plan on getting Haven to release him? You don't even know where he is."

"Adiz?"

"I can wager a guess. Michele arranged this sanctuary and built Valhalla. Haven created the Armory, the Motor Pool, the Bastille, and the Alamo. Since the Armory and Bastille were both raided, they're out. The Motor Pool is a terrible place to bring a captive, so that leaves the Alamo."

"You need to be sure," Michele says.

"I would check it out for myself, or maybe one of you can, but who here thinks that's a good idea?" Adiz answers with an almost annoying level of sarcasm.

"If you know where he is, let's go get him."

Jasper looks at Rykos and shakes his head like he's a moron. "It's not that simple, Rykos. Your father is the chief guardian, and they murdered Freya. Haven isn't going to just give him up because we ask."

The guardians caught Freya infiltrating the EOC. Rykos wouldn't think his father was involved in that, but his guardians were acting on orders from somewhere.

"You guys blew up half the city. I'm sure you can break him out."

"You don't understand. The Alamo has that codename for a reason," Adiz explains. "It's not impenetrable, but it's designed to be very costly for anyone storming it. A rescue attempt would be suicide."

"I assume you have a plan then?" Farron asks Michele.

"The beginnings of one, yes."

"Finish it quickly. We're running out of time." Farron passes Michele and heads for the door before stopping. "You'd better hope you're right about this, or we'll all pay the price."

CHAPTER FIFTY-FOUR

LIBERTEUM

Safe House
Tribeca Geographic District
New York City Municipal Corporation

The door closes behind Farron. Michele glances at the time on Jasper's workstation and grimaces. Ten p.m. Time has never had much meaning to her. In the underground, there are few ways to tell night from day. Most food raids happen while the city's employees sleep, so urches develop a sense of when the world above them is still. Outside of that, it has no relevance.

"Is he afraid I'm transmitting and he's leaving just in case?"

"Yeah, probably, but he owns the building. He would be implicated just the same."

"Things seem a little tense between you," Rykos observes.

Michele offers an almost imperceptible nod. "I'm convinced that Narik Covington tipped off the PSS about Haven's position. He and Farron are old friends, and he's defensive over it."

"There's no doubt that the twerp did it," Adiz snorts as he types away at his terminal.

"Is that why Haven is no longer with you guys?"

"It was his excuse. The real reason doesn't matter. You've had a stressful day and must be tired," Michele says, taking him by the arm. "Let me show you to your room."

Michele leads Rykos across the living area and down the short hallway to a spare bedroom that isn't being used. Like the rest of the domicile, it is unfinished but still features a bed and typical bedroom furniture.

"I never would have looked for you guys here."

"Nobody would. That's the idea. Stay away from the windows. They're tinted, but we don't need any of the drones hovering around the city taking an interest. I think you'll find the bed comfort—"

"Why did you agree to meet me?" Rykos blurts out. Michele looks at him blankly. "And don't tell me it was because of my brilliant plea about getting my father back. What do you *really* want from me?"

"What do you really want from us?" she fires back.

"I asked first."

Michele taps the weapon holstered on her hip. "And I'm the one who's armed."

"I already told you."

"You want your father back even though, by your admission, you don't have a warm relationship with him."

"You don't trust me?" Rykos asks, sitting on the edge of the bed.

Michele joins him, savoring the feeling of being off her feet. She aims to leave enough space between them to keep it from being awkward. It doesn't work.

"I don't trust anybody, least of all the only son of the chief guardian who's willing to rip out his biojacks and leave a comfortable life to join us without a second thought."

"I'm doing this for my mother. My father and I aren't close, but she means everything to me. Their marriage…isn't good right now, but she's in pain. Deep down, she always feared something like this would happen. She pleaded with me to find a way to get him back. I agreed."

Michele studies his face for signs of deception and finds none. Rykos may be conflicted, but he's not a liar. He is devoted to his mother. Michele admires that. Her mother died when she was very young.

"Why would she think you could do what the PSS and BCS can't?" Michele asks, struggling not to lower her guard.

"She thinks my story about what happened in the subway station is bullshit. She thinks I'm with you guys."

"With us?"

"Or at least sympathetic to your cause."

Michele perks up. It's what she wants to hear, which also puts her on guard. When something seems too good to be true, it usually is too good to be true.

"Why would she think that?"

"I've always been rebellious. Balin – the guy I was with at the rave – he and I used to spend hours sitting on this rock in Central Park trying to make sense of the world. He never fully bought into corporatism. I found myself agreeing with him."

"What happened to Balin?" Michele asks, understanding that his fate was her doing. She was the one who decided to leave him behind when he became belligerent before Haven shot him.

"I don't know where he is," Rykos says, lowering his eyes. "They took him. I haven't seen him since that night."

There is worry and fear in Rykos's expression. Those two emotions can turn simmering resentment of the system into full-blown hatred. Every member of Liberteum has traveled that path.

"I don't think you realize how special the capability of questioning the system is. Most employees don't have those critical thinking skills. The ones who do become urches."

"And join Liberteum?"

"Some of them. You said you warned us about the raid because you were mad at your father. Is that true?"

"Good memory. Yes, it's true. My turn. Why did you kiss me before you fled the station?"

Michele feels her cheeks burn hot as she blushes. It was an impulse she still doesn't understand. Urches don't typically get involved in relationships. Their needs are more primal and are satisfied as such.

"I didn't think I would ever see you again. It seemed like a good idea at the time."

"And the punch?"

Michele grins. "Same reason."

"What do you think now that we're both here?"

Rykos gazes into her eyes, and she returns his stare. He starts to lean forward, and she's tempted to kiss him. It's a bad idea. This isn't the time to get carried away by emotion.

Michele draws her knife and places the tip of the blade against the underside of his chin. He stops cold. That should dispel any notions of romantic pursuit.

"You've lost too much blood from cutting out your biojacks," she says, standing and replacing her knife in its sheath. "Get some sleep, Rykos."

Michele leaves the room and closes the door behind her. She leans against the unfinished wall in the hallway as she grapples with an unfamiliar emotion. Rykos can be a critical part of her plan. His involvement could be the difference in the success of Archimedes. But this is more than that. She walks back to the living area, wondering if there is another reason she wants him around.

CHAPTER
FIFTY-FIVE

INTERCORPEX

Global Network Operations Center
Manhattan Financial District
ICX New York Exchange

It's the same routine Lyris has maintained for years now. He followed it the mornings of the Manhattan and Secaucus attacks. It will be the same one he follows for the next one. With America Incorporated's and Zyree's failure to capture the terrorists, it can't be counted out.

"Good Morning, Wyeth," Lyris says, climbing the metal stairs up to the raised workstations overlooking the NOC floor.

"Morning, Director," he says, placing his mug of coffee down and peeling his eyes off the display with a GlobalNet site loaded.

"Anything to report?"

"Frankfurt volume is at an all-time low leading up to close. Beijing volume was also down before handover."

"Fallout from the murders," Lyris concludes, using the biometric eye scanner to log into his system.

"Has Chief Inspector Zyree reported in?"

"With a little luck, he's lying dead in a ditch somewhere. Zyree doesn't follow procedures. If he checks in, it won't be with me. Even Chiana hasn't heard from him."

Wyeth's head pops over the divider on the platform. "I thought those security types always looked after their own."

It didn't take Lyris long to figure out that Chiana and Zyree despise each other. She's everything he isn't: competent, trustworthy, and reliable. The glossy veneer that one success put on an otherwise lackluster career will only cover his shortcomings for so long. She is the future of Intercorpex Security and knows it. So does Lyris.

"Not in this case, apparently. Chiana is running lead on the Bronx patrician murders. Is AME News still running stories?"

Wyeth points up at the far left display on the wall of the NOC. "Are you kidding? They've barely talked about anything else."

"I haven't been watching. Who are they blaming?"

"Liberteum are the prime suspects. Journalists are sticking to the narrative, but their body language speaks volumes. They aren't convinced."

"Typical. The media get their marching orders from the parent company."

The vision of Denali murdering the patricians has haunted Lyris for the last thirty-six hours. His admissions were equally terrifying. He *wanted* Raimius to blame him publicly even though he wasn't responsible. Then he has three distinguished patricians of the *gentez-minorez* over for dinner and executes them and their families. It's sadistic, but it's also nonsensical.

Lyris struggles to understand why he would do that and what he's hoping to gain. It's only a matter of time before Intercorpex Security figures out where the victims were when they were murdered.

The murders have forced Raimius's leak out of the spotlight. His plan to implicate the Keatings and Covingtons is backfiring. Lyris rubs his chin. Was that why Denali did it? Did he know the killings would draw attention away from him? If so, it's a bold move. Murder is an egregious breach of the Zurich Canon.

"Hey boss, the GlobalNet is buzzing with news of everything from murders to riots to worker uprisings in countless corporations. It seems like the world is falling apart. Are we going to be okay?"

Lyris asked Wyeth to take a leap of faith with him. It was a big ask, and he obliged by following every instruction flawlessly. Now he's looking for reassurance, and Lyris owes him that much. He just can't do it here.

"I haven't forgotten our conversation, Wyeth. Whatever challenges face us, we face together."

"Okay," he says with a nod.

He hustles down the stairs and ventures onto the NOC floor. Lyris watches as he speaks to some of the technicians and their supervisors. He's rallying the troops for another trading day, and he's good at it. He would follow his orders unconditionally. That may come in handy someday.

CHAPTER FIFTY-SIX

AMERICA, INC.

The "Alamo"
Manhattan Island
New York City Municipal Corporation

The three sharp claps cause Teman to force open his swollen eyes. His vision is depleted from the trauma to his face. He doesn't know how long he's been here, but it feels like an eternity. Everything hurts. Every movement he's forced to make is agony. Every punch makes him want death to come sooner.

"Break time's over, Chief Guardian," Haven says after entering the brick and steel prison. "In case you were wondering, I was out checking our security. I poked my head around at street level. Do you know what I didn't see? A guardian. Not one. I mean, you'd think I'd see at least one if they were all out looking for you."

Teman starts to say something but his jaw aches, and his neck screams in pain when he moves it. He stops. There's nothing to gain from it. Haven could have seen three squads of guardians march over their heads and not tell the truth.

"Hoist him back up," Haven commands.

"How long do you plan on keeping him alive?" Nyvar asks, hesitating.

"I don't know. Why?"

He points at Teman. "He's in bad shape. He might not survive another beating."

Haven nods.

"My colleague here thinks you're about to die, Chief Guardian, so let's chat while you still have some use of your jaw."

Haven grabs a wood chair, spins it, and sits in front of Teman. He rests his beefy arms on the top of the backrest and just stares. The chief guardian tries to glare back, so he knows he's not broken. But he is. It's impossible to convey strength through a battered face.

"Sucks being on the receiving end of this kind of abuse, doesn't it? Have you ever received any kind of training in this? No? Of course not. You're only a guardian.

Nothing more than a glorified babysitter for all the sheep bleating on the streets above."

Teman lifts his head. He forces words out despite the pain. "I don't need your ramblings."

"You're my prisoner. You have no choice. You see, Intercorpex inspectors undergo intensive training. Language schools, shooting scenarios, investigative techniques…all easy stuff compared to TORT school. It stands for Torture Resistance Techniques, but those who survive it call it Camp Slap Happy. It's three days' worth of physical beatings and psychological torture. You don't know what to expect going into it, regardless of how many stories you've heard. Sometimes the torturers want information; sometimes it's punishment; sometimes they beat you just for fun. Regardless of the reason, you know what kind of man you are by the end."

Teman doesn't move. He doubts Haven is lying about that. He can't compare his training to Intercorpex Security's because there is no comparison. They are two different organizations with two vastly different missions.

"Do you know what kind of man you are, Chief Guardian? I doubt it. You're soft, just like the employees you serve. You don't know anything about sacrifice."

"You're wrong," Teman mutters.

"How? Tell me you know what it means to struggle. You rely on your corporate masters for everything from the cradle to the grave. What kind of life is that? Have you ever even stopped to think about it?"

Teman allows his head to hang.

"No, I didn't think so. Your mind can't comprehend freedom. I didn't understand it myself until I left Intercorpex Security. I sacrificed. I faked my death, gave up everything, and challenged myself to survive under your largest city. Do you want to know why? Because I could. For the first time in my life, I could do anything I wanted."

"Good for you."

"It is, isn't it?" Haven asks, his voice higher as he perks up. "All I wanted was to live out my days in peace with the others who chose to reject your oppressive system. But you and your corporation couldn't leave it alone. After all, urches are a threat to your beliefs. I mean, if you're willing to surrender your humanity, why shouldn't we, right? You love to thump your chests about how great the world is, how you solved all its ills. Do you know what the truth is? You're all just as despicable as the idiots who led the world into an economic apocalypse."

"And you're going to fix that?" Teman strains to ask.

"No, no, no. That's Michele's thing. I respected her father. He taught me what being free meant. Gave me purpose. His daughter was the one looking to change the world or some bullshit like that. I hate her for corrupting him."

"You tried to kill her?"

Haven smirks. "She had it coming. She thinks you can all be reformed. I'm more of a realist. Michele may collapse the system, but she'll never *change* it. The people in it are too dependent. I came to terms with that a long time ago. None of you can be saved. I hope I live long enough to watch as you all starve and murder each other in the streets after it happens."

Teman remains silent. It's a revelation. He figured Liberteum was united in its purpose, but things aren't as black and white as he thought.

"What happens…if the system…doesn't collapse?" Teman asks, struggling to move the words out of his mouth.

Haven shrugs and then grins. "Then I'll kill as many people as possible, starting with you."

The words send a shudder down Teman's spine. Where is Zyree when he needs him? He's the kind of guy who shows up for the rescue just in time to save the day. It's a partnership that shouldn't have been taken for granted.

"It's time to show you the same respect for life and liberty that you showed Freya," Haven says, getting up off his chair and moving it out of the way. "String him back up."

CHAPTER FIFTY-SEVEN

UNDERGRADUATE RYKOS

Safe House
Tribeca Geographic District
New York City Municipal Corporation

I wake up to the smell of breakfast and fresh-brewed coffee. I dress and venture out into the main living area to find scrambled eggs, bacon, toast, and strong java poured into expensive mugs. My three hosts are living it up in their time above ground. This must be a treat for them, especially Michele, who was born in the dank, dingy underground and knows little else.

The distractions of this pampered existence haven't blunted their focus. This isn't a vacation for Liberteum, no matter how pleasant the accommodations are. Adiz is more fidgety than usual. Jasper keeps getting up and moving around the room to burn off nervous energy. Michele rubs her temples to relieve the stress headache.

"It's almost eleven. What's he waiting for?"

"He'll come through," Jasper assures her. "He knows we need the public key for this to work."

"Public key for what?" I ask. Jasper looks over at Michele, who nods as she continues her massaging. He launches into the explanation.

Intercorpex uses a modern version of PKE to communicate with patrician computers running their trading software. Public key encryption is a form of asymmetric encryption that eliminates the need to securely send an agreed-upon secret key to an intended recipient. In wide use since well before the collapse, this version splits a key into two smaller ones.

The first is made public, and the second is kept private. Messages from the patricians are encrypted using the public key provided to them once they log on to their systems. Their biometric credentials, usually a fingerprint, retinal scan, or both, are then encrypted and sent to Intercorpex, where the information is decrypted on their Wall Street computers using the private key.

Michele stands and starts pacing after he finishes. "I hate relying on something totally out of our control."

"It's the only way we keep this a secret," Adiz concludes. "We'll never get past Intercorpex's intrusion detection measures otherwise. Even if we did, they change their private key every twenty-four hours. Jasper's solution is the best chance for success of phase two."

"I hope you're right," Michele sighs. "It'd be a shame to come this far to find out everything we've done is pointless."

"What comes after phase two?" I ask from the living area sofa.

"Phase three," Adiz replies sarcastically.

"You watched phase one," Jasper adds.

"Yeah, while chained to a column. I meant, what is this all for? If your goal is to take down the system, simply crippling the exchange won't work."

The hackers look at each other, then at Michele. She stops her pacing directly in front of me. "Why not?"

"Because corporatism is more than a stock market. Employees serve the parent company, not Intercorpex."

"And who does America Incorporated serve? The patricians. And they need the exchange," Adiz argues.

"America Incorporated serves itself."

"So, how would you change the system, Rykos?"

I shake my head. "You can't change it. People are too dependent on it."

"He sounds like Haven. Why is he even here?" Jasper asks. I scowl, not liking that comparison one bit.

"Are you sure about that?" Michele presses, ignoring her hacker.

"Yes."

"I'm betting you're wrong." She turns to stare out the smoked glass windows at the street below. "What if people could no longer depend on the system?"

That sounds familiar. My mind drifts to the rock in Central Park. Balin hated corporatism. He would wax philosophical about what the world would look like if it suddenly didn't exist. Those conversations were all hypothetical. The people in this room are determined to make it a reality.

"You won't get that just by destroying Intercorpex."

"That's true. How familiar are you with the actual man Archimedes?"

"He was an ancient Greek scientist or something."

"He was a mathematician who lived in Syracuse during a time of war. The city was under siege for months before his death. Can you guess how it finally fell?"

"I don't know," I admit. They don't teach this in modules, so I hazard a guess. "The army stormed the gates and overran the defenders guarding the walls?"

Michele shakes her head. "They were victims of overconfidence. The citizens went to a festival instead of preparing for an attack. They weren't paying attention when a small party of Roman soldiers scaled the walls under cover of night and took control of the outer city."

"And you're counting on nobody paying attention now. I get that."

It worked for their first attack. Nobody realized what Liberteum was capable of. But now, the exchange and the corporations are alert, even if they don't want to admit what happened publicly. Someone *will* be paying attention. They can count on that.

"The story doesn't end there. The main fortress behind the inner walls remained firm. The city was weakened but not taken. After another eight-month siege, an Iberian captain named Moeriscus decided to save himself by letting the Romans in. He opened the gate during a diversionary attack."

"You must have access to a lot of books," I say. "So which part of that story is happening now?"

"We scaled the wall in phase one. Now we take the outer city."

"And what happens after that?"

"Phase three: Create a diversion while our modern Moeriscus opens the fortress gate. Then watch it fall once and for all."

CHAPTER FIFTY-EIGHT

INTERCORPEX

One Guardian Plaza
Municipal Governance District
New York City Municipal Corporation

Interrogation rooms aren't built for comfort for a reason. Of course, Zyree is usually on the other side of the table and the cameras. He closes his eyes again and adjusts the ice pack a guardian gave him to quiet his throbbing head. It isn't working any better than the pain relievers he took.

"How's your head?" Malkor asks from the wall he's leaning against on the other side of the interrogation room.

"Shhhh," Zyree says, placing his index finger over his lips. "Not so loud."

"I can't believe she kicked your ass."

"She didn't kick my ass. Okay, well, she kinda did. She's got crazy good fighting skills. She would have kicked yours, too."

"Whatever. You're lucky to be alive."

"You know, I'm not so sure luck was involved," Zyree says, leaning forward in his chair. "I learned something."

"Not to get pistol-whipped by a teenager with your own weapon?"

"Yeah, that, but something else, too. Rykos had a gun to my head in the underground with a golden opportunity to finish off the man who uncovered his secret. All he needed to do was pull the trigger."

Malkor thinks it over for a moment. He's searching for any plausible explanation for why Zyree is still breathing that doesn't defy understanding.

"He's the son of the chief guardian. Maybe he hasn't been indoctrinated as a terrorist yet."

"Maybe. Then why didn't Michele kill me?"

"Michele? That's the name of the hot terrorist in the picture?"

"Yes, Malkor, she's the hot one," Zyree says, rolling his eyes. "Liberteum is a group of vile terrorists determined to destroy the global economic system. I'm hunting that group. She's its leader. Why didn't she finish me when Rykos didn't?"

"Where are you going with this, boss?"

"I don't know. I'm not thinking straight. But…I'm trying to figure out Liberteum."

The uneasy feeling Zyree has isn't from his pounding head. There is much more to that group. He can feel it. Without a reasonable way to articulate that, even to Malkor, he needs to keep it to himself for now.

A public safety guardian wearing a rank Zyree has never seen walks into the interrogation room and closes the door behind him. He sits down at the table with a tablet computer. He looks up at the camera monitoring the room and makes a slashing motion across his throat. This conversation will be off the record. Zyree isn't sure if that's a good or bad thing.

"I'm Constable-Guardian Dzamko, acting chief guardian until Teman returns."

Zyree cocks his head and winces at the pain. "Constable-Guardian? I've never heard that title."

"It's special."

"You're a little old to be a guardian, aren't you?"

Dzamko's mouth curls. "That's why I'm special. Constable ranks are reserved for guardians with a long, distinguished service but who are unfit for duty. Given our institutional knowledge, the higher powers decided to keep us around to perform functions that may require additional expertise."

"What was yours?"

"I ran the major crimes unit for fifteen years. I'd welcome you to One Guardian Plaza, Chief Inspector Zyree, but I know you've been here before. Your superiors in Zurich confirmed your identities. Commandant-General Jurghen was unfazed about your activities."

"We're given great autonomy in our operations," Zyree explains.

"So I gathered. I read in your impressive file. Chief Guardian Teman spoke highly of you in his summary. He said if he had listened to you, he would have had fewer funerals to attend."

"Constable Dzamko, I hate to be rude, but I'm tired and banged up. Are we free to go?"

"Not just yet. Some questions need answers. Let's start with my first: How did you manage to walk into a meeting between Liberteum and the chief guardian's son? The second question is: what on earth was Undergraduate Rykos doing in an urch bar with them?"

"Good questions," Zyree says without adding color.

"And ones I don't expect you to answer," Dzamko says, not missing a beat. "The next order of business is a request from the BCS. They're demanding to speak to you."

That gets his attention. They have the authority to question ICX Security in situations like this. "Are you turning us over to them?"

"Hell no. Those prima donnas can pound sand. If they want to talk to you, they can find you themselves."

The comment makes Zyree chuckle. He winces at the pressure that reverberates through his head. "No love affair with your fellow agency, Constable?"

"You witnessed our dispute at the Bronx murder scene. I've been dealing with turf wars like that for decades. What do you think?"

Zyree already likes this guy. He's a straight shooter willing to bend the rules and break them when warranted. It's a very un-guardian-like approach. Teman took risks, but that was partly because Zyree was blackmailing him with knowledge about Rykos. Constable Dzamko sports a hearty disdain for the rules born from age and experience.

"If you know that I'm not going to answer your questions, and you're not holding me for the Bureau of Corporate Security, why am I still here?"

"Chief Inspector, I'm too old to play games. I'm interested in results. You had a good relationship with Teman. You teamed up to thwart the most serious terrorist in the Corporate Age. I'm hoping you'd be interested in working together again."

"To find Chief Guardian Teman?"

"And figure out what the hell is going on. I know the murders of those patricians are Intercorpex's responsibility, but something doesn't feel right about them."

Zyree glances over at Malkor and notices his wolfish look. He pushes himself off the wall and stands behind his boss.

"You don't think it was Liberteum?"

"No, I don't. I believe that it's a means to an end, though, and the result won't be good for either of our organizations."

"Are you asking to share information?"

Dzamko leans back in his chair. "We've been chasing our tails searching for Liberteum. Chief Guardian Teman was overzealous and got himself captured because of executive pressure. I don't care how you found Liberteum at that urch bar, but I know it wasn't luck. I want to cooperate because we need your help."

"Is this an official request?"

A smile creases Dzamko's lips. "Are you the type of man who cares?"

Zyree wants to agree. An alliance makes sense, but Chiana could recite every regulation he's breaking. Then again, what she doesn't know won't hurt him.

"I'll agree to it under one condition: Our cooperation stays between us. You're not the only one with rivals you can't stand to work with."

Dzamko smiles and nods. Zyree reciprocates. Maybe this unexpected detour to One Guardian Plaza wasn't a waste of time after all.

CHAPTER FIFTY-NINE

THE PATRICIANS

Keating Family Brownstone
Manhattan Upper West Side Geographic District
New York Municipal Corporation

Farron inhales and exhales a few times. This used to come naturally. After the attacks in New York, it's gotten much more challenging for him to keep up appearances. He's been putting this call off for a while. He knows he will need to answer for that.

Calls that terminate in any executive office are filtered through access lists. The patrician isn't sure that this one will make it through. If it clears the switchboard, it will be announced to the recipient, who will likely deny the unknown intrusion. The only reason he has any confidence in connecting is that the audio-only VidLynk is secure.

"Hello? Who is this?" Fiolla asks.

"It's me."

"Farron? How did you manage to place a secure VidLynk from an unknown IP?"

"I have my tricks," he says. "I'm just happy that you accepted it. I wanted to hear your voice."

"Likewise. I want to see your face, but this is audio-only. What has taken you so long to contact me?"

"I've been a little busy, courtesy of AME News."

He hears the quiet sigh. He can almost imagine her crossing her arms. That wasn't a valid reason to be incommunicado, and she knows it. Farron can't tell her the real reason.

"We've both been busy. The board of directors is looking to oust my boss."

"I've heard. Valen's a strong CEO. He'll be okay."

"I don't share your optimism. Do you have something you want to tell me?"

It wasn't a question. It was a demand. "Like what?"

"I asked if you were a member of Liberteum and warned you not to lie. You said 'no.' Fine. Now I'm hearing news stories that your father and Shalius Covington were involved in the attack in New York."

"Please tell me you don't believe that, Fiolla."

"What do you want me to think? It makes sense. I'm wondering if I was wrong to trust you."

This has always been the tough part of Farron's task. Fiolla is emotional and under tremendous stress. It can't be easy to distinguish truth from propaganda in this world. Maybe it's never been. That's why he called her. He needs to keep her playing the game for a few more days.

"Then Raimius has won."

"What's that supposed to mean?"

"He planted the leak to cast suspicion on my family and the Covingtons."

"He wouldn't be that reckless," Fiolla snaps. "Who told you that? And don't you dare say that you can't tell me."

"He was that reckless, and it's working. Even you don't believe me anymore. And I shouldn't tell you but will anyway. It came from Executive Director of Global Operations Lyris."

"What? No way."

"Lyris already confirmed it. We have him on video admitting to it in our Greenwich mansion. He orchestrated the first leak about the *gentez-minorez*. Raimius used that to blackmail my father. When that didn't work, he tainted us with a scandal."

"Why would Lyris tell you that?"

"Let's just say that my father has a special relationship with him. That's all I can say. He would kill me if he knew I told you that much."

"Why was he blackmailing him? What was your father planning to do?"

"Stop Raimius from working with Talya Bettancourt and her proxies from ousting Chief Executive Valen."

Farron hears Fiolla stop breathing after a sharp inhale. She understands the implication of what he leveled. The administrator-general interfering with an internal corporate matter in this way would be unprecedented and extremely dangerous.

"Why is Raimius working with Talya Bettancourt? Why interfere with America Incorporated's leadership?"

"Valen's the only CEO with the balls to stop him from expanding Intercorpex's power. He's entered into an unholy alliance with Bettancourt to solve that problem. If Valen is removed, Raimius has more freedom to accumulate the power he covets, and Bettancourt gets a lackey in the White House. Win-win, which is why Valen needs to stay in power at all costs."

Farron stands and starts pacing around his living area. This domicile is nowhere near the building Michele and her hackers are holed up in. He's always liked this one. It may be a favorite out of all his residences.

"The board is split, but Zeykala thinks she has the votes for removal. Any advice?"

"Fiolla, you are a strong, beautiful, intelligent woman and a capable executive. The only one who doesn't realize that is you. You don't need my advice. Valen knows what to do. You just need to be there to help him. I'm sorry, I have to go."

Farron feels a pang of guilt. This is getting harder for him. He knew there was a chance of that. His father certainly knew it based on their conversation at the mansion following the attacks.

"Farron…I'm sorry that I accused you of…."

"It's fine."

"No, it isn't. I keep doubting you. I don't know why."

"It's something we need to talk about, but not today. Talk soon," he says before ending the VidLynk.

Farron collapses back into his chair. He reaches for the Russian vodka on the small table and drains the glass. It all comes down to this. Tomorrow is a huge day, and there is nothing more he can do except sit back and watch. His father's scheme has miraculously gone according to plan. He hopes his variant of it finds the same success when the time comes.

CHAPTER
SIXTY

INTERCORPEX

Global Network Operations Center
Manhattan Financial District
ICX New York Exchange

Heels clicking on metal risers announce Lyris's visitor before she arrives. Dressed in her form-fitting black Intercorpex Security uniform, Chiana is a beautiful woman. She might even be better looking than Nevala. He has a thing for Asian women.

Chiana stands in front of him, erect and confident. "I was told you would like an update on the murder investigation. I'm still in the preliminary stages—"

"Take a walk with me, Chief Inspector."

She allows Lyris to slide past her and follows as he heads down off the platform and past the NOC floor.

"Director Wyeth," Lyris says, connecting with the NOC's communication system. "Cover the floor. I need to step out."

"Sure thing," he says over the channel.

"What's the status of Chief Inspector Zyree? Is he okay?"

"My apologies, Director, but I'm not sure what you are talking about."

"You haven't heard? He was found unconscious by the PSS in a SoHo basement."

"What was he doing there? And how did the guardians find him?" Chiana asks as they reach the corridor that leads to the museum.

"I was hoping you would know."

"You assume that Zyree and I talk to each other. We may have the same title, but we're *not* close."

"You don't have a high opinion of him, do you?"

"May I speak freely?" Chiana asks, getting a nod in return. "He's a dinosaur. I understand now why some corporations have termination policies. Why keep ineffectual people around?"

Lyris rewards her with an encouraging chuckle. "I didn't realize Zyree was that old."

"He's old enough to be set in his ways. Security must constantly evolve, Director. Threats change, and so do the tools and techniques needed to defeat those threats. You adapt, or you perish. Zyree refuses to do that."

They enter the Hall of Horrors through an access door inside the arch that leads back toward History Hall.

"Turn your biocomp off. This place is best experienced without text popping up on your contacts," Lyris explains, prompting immediate compliance. He looks around the room. "I like coming in here. It reminds me how far society has come."

The dim lighting sets the mood as they stroll past images of human suffering and hopelessness. The long, curved gallery showcases all the major crashes and economic events stock markets endured. They pass holograms of planes hitting the skyscrapers of the World Trade Center, depictions of The Cleanse, and the fallout from the global economic collapse.

"These were dark times."

"Yes, they were."

The pair wanders through the hall, past the pedestal with its single flame that continues to burn. They walk through open black lacquer doors that lead to Genesis Hall.

"No tours today?"

"We haven't opened the museum since the attack."

The pure white of Genesis Hall stands in stark contrast to the darkness of the gallery that preceded it. Holographic displays depict the rise of corporations in a more upbeat presentation designed to showcase the benevolence of the entities that trade on the Intercorpex exchange. Even the struggles and massacres like the Valentine's Day Holocaust and Bloody Monday are portrayed positively.

"I think the architect gives too much credit to the corporations here," Chiana opines. Lyris raises an eyebrow, prompting her to continue. "Intercorpex is the most stabilizing force the world has ever seen. We did what the League of Nations and the United Nations never could: ensure a lasting peace."

"I'm all for changing the name from Pax Corporicana to Pax Intercorpex," Lyris says, staring at a woman after his own heart.

"That's something to think about when you become AG."

"What makes you think I will?"

"You're head and shoulders above any candidate for the job. I know the regents pretend they're omnipotent, but they're part-time bureaucrats. You know the exchange and have the leadership experience needed to usher us into the next century."

"How are you not running ICX Security?" Lyris asks, stopping at a display.

"Jurghen won't retire, and I'm too junior to assume command. Zyree is way ahead of me in line, courtesy of his Medal of Gallantry. Perhaps that's another indignity you could correct after your promotion."

This woman knows what she's doing. She's buttering Lyris up, and he's keenly aware that it's working. The only question is how far she's willing to take this.

"Zyree running ICX Security would be a disaster. Unfortunately, replacing him would be hard to justify, especially for a new administrator-general. It doesn't matter how talented or deserving you are."

"Shame."

"Of course, anything is possible if Zyree isn't around to assume that command."

Chiana snaps her head around. "Why wouldn't he be?"

"Liberteum is a dangerous foe," Lyris says with a shrug. "They're violent and deadly. We've already lost an inspector fighting them. Another loss would be…."

"Tragic." Her grin makes the word anything but sincere.

"Can it be arranged?"

Lyris doesn't know this woman. He's taking an enormous risk by making that suggestion. There could be consequences if her hatred of Zyree isn't as intense as his. But he knows it is, and in these dire times, chance favors the bold.

"Sir, to be clear, are you suggesting…?"

There was a reason Lyris chose to bring her into the galleries. The museum has no audio or video surveillance that will record this conversation ever happening. Her biocomp is the only thing that could have betrayed him, and he had her switch it off.

"We both want you to be the next commissioner-general. Chief Inspector Zyree is the only man standing in the way of that happening. Until he isn't."

CHAPTER SIXTY-ONE

AMERICA, INC.

The White House
Corporate Governance District
Washington-Arlington Municipal Corporation

An attendant comes with the coffee service and pours each of the two men a cup. Valen takes his black while Hammond puts enough sugar in his to keep a toddler jumping off the walls for a week. The big man leans back into the sofa. Valen sips the coffee until they're left alone in the office. He's thrilled that the BCS agents were ordered to wait outside the room.

"I was surprised you asked me to come," Hammond says. "This may look like you're attempting to exert influence."

"Is it any different than Zeykala treating board members to fancy dinners or *Prima* Bettancourt hosting a gala for them at her Chesapeake estate?"

"No, I suppose it isn't. Going after Zeykala's support on the board was a bold move."

Valen takes another sip. "This isn't a time for being timid."

"No, it isn't. Zeykala expected you to go after the undecideds. You're a strong CEO and a persuasive man, and she can't afford to present anything other than a united front. She's panicking because her vote count is soft."

"How soft?"

Hammond sets down his cup into its saucer on the table. He clasps his hands together and stares at them. Valen patiently waits, but he's ready to start screaming on the inside.

"The vote could still go either way. Zeykala's supporters assured her that your pleas fell on deaf ears. Privately, they've expressed concerns about a change in leadership right now. The issues with Liberteum are bad enough, but intercorporational events are more worrisome."

"You're talking about what's happening in Russia, Germany, France, and the UK spheres?"

"Bombings, murders, riots…it's scary stuff that conjures up memories of a dark past. The threats to corporatism are playing out globally, and the board realizes that."

Fear is a powerful motivator. For centuries, the Church used it, quoting scripture and professing tales of a spot in Hell reserved for sinners. It's historically been an effective tool for tyrants and despots to regulate behavior. America Incorporated does not overtly use fear as other corporations do. Fear of termination keeps employees in line. This fear over world events is a double-edged sword.

"Zeykala will try to use that fear as a tool to remove me."

"She already is, my friend. She believes the global unrest and your failures against Liberteum are the keys to your undoing."

"Where do you stand?" Valen asks, earning a glare from Hammond. "It's a fair question. You called the hearing."

"I had no choice. You know that I'm your most secure vote. That said, why did you call me here?"

Outside of Fiolla and a small handful of others, Hammond is the only person Valen trusts right now. He explains his suspicions about Raimius, laying out the theory about how this is all being orchestrated by forces looking to advance their agendas. He's as skeptical as Fiolla was.

"Raimius is a power-hungry control freak, but I can't imagine he would go to this extreme. Do you have any proof of this?"

Valen hangs his head and shakes it while he stares at his shoes. "No. It's hearsay."

"Is the BCS investigating it?"

"Virtari accepts anything ICX Security has to say on any matter without question. Convenient, isn't it?"

"Valen, you're in danger of spitting out more conspiracy theories than Raimius. Do you honestly believe Virtari is being persuaded into inaction by Talya Bettancourt? There's never been any love lost between the two of them."

Director Virtari is one of the most powerful men in the corporation. He runs the Bureau of Corporate Security with an iron fist and commands absolute loyalty from his agents. Their training conditions them to follow his instructions without question.

His strength causes friction with other powerful people. Valen has had a number of struggles with Virtari, as have board members and *Prima* Bettancourt. The man is a walking, talking contradiction. He has powerful enemies, staunch support, and is loved, hated, feared, and worshipped all at the same time.

"Except now they have a common enemy. That's been a unifying factor throughout world history. Virtari hates me. If the *prima* is making promises to him that he can plausibly deny, what's the downside?"

Hammond nods slightly. "It's an elegant theory, but without any proof, I can't take action."

"I'm not expecting you to."

"Then what are you expecting?"

"If Intercorpex or the patricians are seeking more power, it's going to come at our expense. I can't move pieces around the board to block them if I'm not in the game."

Hammond should have been made CEO of America Incorporated. He plays the political game better than any executive in the entire sphere of influence. It was a surprise that he wasn't chosen when his time came. It was impossible to undo that travesty, so he was made chairman and ensured Valen's predecessor was retired early. That paved the way for his ascension and the ongoing conflict with Zeykala.

"Then let's make sure we keep you in it. I'll take the temperature of some of the fence-sitters and see where they stand. I'm an impartial third party."

"Impartial?"

"So far as they know, yes," Hammond replies, beaming. "Just keep doing what you are doing, Valen. There's nobody I trust more to navigate these waters than you."

CHAPTER SIXTY-TWO

INTERCORPEX

The Empire Building
Midtown Geographic District
New York City Municipal Corporation

The views from the observation deck of the Empire Building are spectacular. The America Tower may be the island's tallest structure, but this view is better. From the tree-lined boulevards to the gleaming skyscrapers that rose from the ashes of a beaten city, this vantage point captures the most majestic views.

This building was a burnt-out shell like most following the Great Collapse. It is a historic landmark and was one of the first skyscrapers rebuilt by the new corporation. The early America Incorporated executives used consistency to cement their authority. Thus, the Empire State Building was only slightly renamed when the term "state" lost its meaning. It never lost its view or status as an integral part of the city's skyline.

"You realize that Liberteum hides underground," Malkor says, coming up behind Zyree. "You're not going to see them from way up here."

"We can barely find them down there. You really have to hand it to America Incorporated. They rebuilt New York into a marvelous city."

"Yes, they did. Are you here to admire the scenery or hide from Lyris?"

"Neither. I wanted a change of perspective," Zyree says, continuing to stare uptown past Central Park.

"Still bothered that Michele and Rykos didn't kill you?"

"Yeah."

"Well, I hate to ruin your serene escape from reality, but Lyris is looking for you."

"I bet he is. I checked in with Zurich as soon as Constable Dzamko released us from One Guardian Plaza. That was my only obligation."

"How did that go?"

"Jurghen laughed at me harder than you did."

"They laugh at you, and then end up hanging medals around your neck."

Zyree scowls. The problem with receiving laurels is too many people are content to rest on them. He doesn't care for accolades or climbing the ranks. It's why he excels at what he does. Inspectors who crave attention or rewards often begin making the wrong decisions.

"I don't think there will be medals passed out this time."

"Why do you say that?"

The chief inspector moves along the ledge and massive fencing around to the south side of the building. The downtown view is equally impressive. Wall Street is obscured by skyscrapers, but he knows it lies just behind them.

"Distraction. The attack last week was a black swan event. Unfortunately, corporations, patricians, and the exchange haven't learned the right lessons from it. They're focusing on the trees at the expense of the forest."

"I'm not following you, boss."

"The attacks failed…unless they didn't. Everyone focuses on the bombings and ignores the trading interruptions. I can't get past the feeling that severing the data center links and interrupting the ITQS was a part of Liberteum's master plan."

"You think blowing up the station was Plan B?" Malkor asks.

"I think they were covering their escape, and it worked. The intrusion into Intercorpex's network is the key piece to the puzzle. Nobody is paying attention to that except us."

Zyree returns to staring through the fence at the gleaming buildings on this brisk but beautiful day. It's a shame more employees don't bother witnessing this. The observation deck is almost completely devoid of visitors.

His last statement isn't completely true. Ortan is paying attention, but he hasn't spoken to him since he left Iceland. If he's uncovered anything, he hasn't shared it. In the meantime, patricians are getting murdered, Valen and Raimius are an insult away from dueling with pistols at dawn, and major corporations are seeing attacks, bombings, riots, and uprisings. The world is a mess.

"Okay. What's our play?"

"Michele said they are going to destroy Intercorpex. Part of me believes her. We have to stop them before they try."

"How? We've lost the kid," Malkor says.

"We didn't lose Farron Keating. Rykos was searching for Farron and wound up meeting with the leader of Liberteum in a dingy urch bar less than a day later. He's involved in this somehow. It's time to open an investigation and track Farron Keating like a bloodhound to see what he does next."

CHAPTER SIXTY-THREE

UNDERGRADUATE RYKOS

Safe House
Tribeca Geographic District
New York City Municipal Corporation

The shouting from the other room stirs me from sleep. It's a male voice, not Adiz, Jasper, or even Farron. I rub my eyes, climb out of bed, quickly dress, and slink into the hallway. I lean up against the wall and stay out of view as I listen to the argument. Michele is having a tense standoff with someone with his back to me.

"You don't get it! We're under investigation. The stakes have gone up," the man argues.

"Narik, you knew the risks when you got involved in this," Michele reminds him. "Did you actually think it would stay a secret forever?"

Narik Covington…he's the man I saw with Farron in the pictures. It looked like they were good friends. It makes sense he's involved in this.

"Yes, and so did my father. Public knowledge wasn't supposed to happen this soon. It could ruin everything he has planned."

"To use an old adage, shit happens. I'm not interested in your father's political power plays. We have a mission to accomplish it. That requires getting to the Alamo. The only way we make it is if Farron drives us."

"There's no way I'm allowing it."

Michele's eyes narrow. "You don't get to make that decision."

"The hell I don't. The Keatings are also being investigated. He can't risk being seen with you."

"It's an administrative investigation based on a media report, Narik. Even if they are taking it seriously, they aren't watching you."

The patrician stands erect and folds his arms across his chest. "You're assuming. I said no, and that's the end of the discussion. The Alamo is close enough for you to take the tunnels. Or arrange your own transportation. You have vehicles with transponder codes."

"The Motor Pool is in Midtown, and Haven controls it."

"Then I guess you have a problem. Farron isn't taking you."

Michele takes a menacing step toward Narik. "We made a promise to Rykos."

"*You* made a promise to Rykos."

"We need him. It was always part of the plan."

A part of what plan? What the hell is she talking about? I was right. There is more to my presence here. We made a deal, but I never thought it was one she was counting on.

"That plan was abandoned. Michele, Quarren was a wise man. He survived by choosing his battles. Don't fight me on this."

"I learned a lot from my father, including how to deal with bullies. Isn't that why you sold Haven out?"

"I didn't sell Haven out to anybody," Narik shouts.

"Yeah, right. Farron has already agreed to this, and I don't answer to you. We are fulfilling our promise. Farron, get Rykos, and let's go."

"I can't let you do that."

Narik flicks his wrist. A mechanism pops out of his jacket in less time than it takes to blink. He points a small gun in Michele's face.

The response is immediate. Adiz and Jasper draw their weapons and Farron wisely backs against the wall. I'm in the wrong spot if bullets start flying. I retreat deeper into the hallway.

"You can't get all of us," Michele warns, sounding calm for someone who has a gun pointed at her.

"No, but I will get *you*."

It's time to act. I take a deep breath to calm my nerves and burst into the room swiftly and quietly. I snatch a weapon off the end table next to the sofa and swing the gun up in one motion. It stops when the muzzle presses against the back of Narik's head.

"The hell you will."

"You must be Rykos," he says without moving. "Do you even know how to work that thing?"

"You'll find out when you realize you're walking toward the light."

"This changes nothing. I squeeze this trigger harder, and your leader dies. I'm going to count to five."

"I will count to three," I say, digging the muzzle deeper into his flesh. "Then I'm going to ruin Farron's carpet. After that, I'll walk over to One Guardian Plaza and explain how the Covington family is behind everything. That they're using the myth of some phantom terrorist group to confuse the truth about their involvement. That it was their security forces all along. Fact or fiction, Intercorpex will seize the opportunity to strip your family of their status and punish you for violating the Zurich Canon."

"You think they'll believe you?" He doesn't sound quite so confident now.

"I can be quite persuasive. Ask the BCS. Three...two..."

Narik complies, slowly lowering his arm. Michele covers him as Jasper disconnects the weapon from his arm and frisks him. He shoves the patrician over to the sofa and forces him to sit.

Farron pushes himself off the wall and stares at his friend. Narik stares at him with hateful eyes.

"You're going to get us killed."

Farron shrugs. "It's a possibility, but a deal's a deal. We're getting Rykos's father back. That's the end of the discussion."

"Jasper, it's time to start the music," Michele commands after glancing at the clock.

I check it myself. The market opened fifteen minutes ago. Jasper sets his weapon down on the desk beside him, and Adiz joins him at the adjacent workstation.

"Enter the encryption code."

"Done," Adiz confirms.

"All right...spinning up one trading application instance...logging on...and accepted. Okay, here we go. Initiating biometric validation...."

"Moment of truth," Adiz says, leaning back in his chair as the two men watch their displays.

Michele doesn't take her eyes off Narik. She only closes them for a moment as if saying a silent prayer. Even I'm caught up in the moment. I've never been a part of something bigger than myself. I'm starting to understand the attraction of Liberteum.

"We're in!" Jasper exclaims, and everyone in the room exhales. "He came through with the encryption."

"Better late than never," Adiz says.

"Execute a trade," Michele commands. "Something small."

"Let's sell one hundred shares of CHN...and, order confirmed. This is fun, Farron. No wonder you guys spend all your days doing this."

"The novelty wears off," the patrician moans.

"Trade executed," Adiz says, spinning in his chair to face Michele and slapping Jasper's hand.

"Ramp up the trades. Don't get too eager. Stick to the plan. I don't want to tip them off too early. Set to continuous executions once the volume gets high enough, and then make your way to Valhalla. We'll meet you there when this is over. Come on, Rykos. Let's go and surprise Haven. Farron?"

Farron moves to the door, and I join him. He nods at Narik. "What about him?"

"Yes, what about him?" Narik mocks as Adiz covers the angry patrician. "You need me, Michele. Like it or not, we're partners in this."

Michele looks at Farron, who nods. He's right. The Covingtons have access to resources she might need, especially with Haven running around the city. The benefits of keeping him close outweigh the liabilities.

"Take him with you, Adiz. If he gives you any problems, shoot him."

CHAPTER SIXTY-FOUR

THE PATRICIANS

Keating Family of the Gentez-Majorez Estate
Greenwich Geographic District
Southern Connecticut Municipal Corporation

Abbot has poked his head into the study a couple of times. Denali would be more annoyed had he instructed his loyal servant to leave him undisturbed. But he didn't, so the checks were appropriate. Denali has been left in solitude to watch the upcoming show outside of those brief interruptions.

He brings up a VidLynk and selects a name from the address screen. This is the first of multiple critical conversations he will have today. Maybe the most important. If this fails, half of his plan goes with it.

"Are you in place?" Denali asks when the video connects.

"Ready to go when you give the word," Shalius says from his domicile in Washington.

"Is your son taking care of the matter?"

The elder Covington scowls. "I haven't heard from him."

"There seems to be a lot of that going on. Could Farron and Narik be together?"

"Possibly. I don't know."

Denali rubs his chin. Out of the two boys, Farron has always been the irresponsible one. His being incommunicado is an irritation but not an unexpected development. Narik is another matter. It means something could be wrong. Denali pushes the doubts out of his mind.

"What are you going to do?"

"I have entrusted the transactions to another family member," Shalius says, checking something off-camera. "She has a brilliant mind and wants a larger role in the family's dealings. There is no way she'll let me down."

"Okay. I'll keep you posted."

"I'll be waiting, old friend."

Denali ends the connection and turns his attention to the ticker. A few strange trades have been popping up, but nothing that would raise alarms. Good. If this is the beginning, Farron successfully convinced Liberteum to start slowly. Denali didn't think they would. It's not a group that understands the value of patience.

The doubt creeps back into his mind. If Liberteum has commenced their plan, why hasn't he heard from his son? His instructions were clear. Timing is everything, and once again, Farron is jeopardizing the mission. He had better have a good reason for his lack of communication. Denali pulls another address off the screen.

"Your secure VidLynk has been connected," a polite computerized female voice informs him. "Audio-only, per your recipient's request."

"I didn't expect to hear from you."

"Is everything in place?" Denali asks, unsurprised that there is no video for this interaction.

"Yes," the woman says.

"Will there be any problems?"

"As I explained previously, the situation has been handled."

Polite words from someone who finds such graciousness revolting. She meant to say more along the lines of "weren't you listening," coupled with "how dare you question my competence." There is no harm in checking up on the situation. She has less to lose than either Denali or Shalius. Or so she thinks.

"It's an appropriate question."

"You have your tasks to be concerned about. Rest assured, I've taken care of mine."

"Then don't let me hold you up."

The call ends, and Denali leans back into his plush chair. He has worked hard for this day. Now it's time to see if that work has paid off. His bishop will take their queen off the board. Once that happens, the world will change. He will be the man responsible for changing it.

CHAPTER SIXTY-FIVE

AMERICA, INC.

Shareholder Hall
Corporate Hill Governance District
Washington-Arlington Municipal Corporation

Modern business is nothing if not punctual. Tardiness is viewed as an affront to courtesy, so every meeting starts on time. As a result, attendees are expected to be early. The modern adage is, "If you're early, you're on time; if you're on time, you're late; if you're late, you're screwed."

Valen scans the room. The entire board of directors is occupying seats behind elevated polished wood counters. They extend at forty-five-degree angles from either side of the marble and wood rostrum that has space for two – the chairman and the *prima*. A sizeable corporate logo graces the wall above it.

"Let's bring this hearing to order," Hammond says as he crashes the gavel down on the sound block at precisely nine a.m.

Board meetings are held in the heavily remodeled Senate chamber of what was once the United States Capitol. Seats behind the CEO are lined up for shareholders who want to attend the hearing. Other than Valen's closest advisors seated directly to his rear, executives have been relegated to the galleries above.

Except for a single microphone, the adjacent table to his right is empty. He presumes that it's for questioning material witnesses the board might call to testify to his dereliction of duty. Valen can't wait to hear who they drag up there, although he already has a good guess who they will be.

"This meeting aims to address concerns levied by board members against America Incorporated Chief Executive Officer Valen about his job performance over the past month."

"Point of order," Valen says into the microphone, ending Hammond's introduction.

"I'm sorry, Chief Executive Valen, this is not the time for opening remarks."

"I'm not making one."

"Then why are you making a 'point of order?'"

"I'm looking for a correction to the stated purpose of the hearing."

Hammond exchanges a look with his fellow board members. "I'm afraid I don't know what you're referring to."

"Me neither. I don't understand what 'job performance over the last month' refers to. Trade deals are turning record profits, our stock is performing well, and productivity is near an all-time high. Our subsidiaries are—"

"Are we going to sit here and listen to the chief executive's resume?" Zeykala interrupts.

"If the issue before the board is my job performance, then yes."

"You know why you were brought here," Zeykala snarls.

"Does Boardmember Zeykala have the floor, Chairman Hammond?"

"No, she does not," Hammond says, grinning slightly. He knows what game Valen is playing. He turns to Zeykala, who is seated at the counter to his right, closest to the rostrum. "Please refrain from interrupting these proceedings without recognition."

The rebuke unsettles Zeykala. She's an intelligent woman with a short fuse. Valen is exploiting that weakness by getting her emotional and frustrated. The more off-balance she is, the less she can anticipate and react to what happens next.

"You are well aware that this is about your failure to locate and eradicate Liberteum," Zeykala says, ignoring the chairman's instruction.

"I'd say she wants your job, Chairman Hammond, but I think we'll all agree that she has designs on mine."

The room bursts into muffled laughter. Valen isn't here for a comedy routine, but the quip gets his point across. Zeykala's face flushes with anger as she leans forward in to her microphone.

"I'm glad you find humor in this, Chief Executive Valen, because I don't."

"You're out of order, Zeykala. Sit down," Chairman Hammond barks, and she reluctantly complies.

"Liberteum wasn't stated in the purpose of this hearing as the chairman read it. So, I guess we're *not* assembled to discuss my job performance. This is about the difficulties of tracking down and destroying a cunning and elusive group of anarchists. Is that statement correct?"

Valen shares a knowing look with Hammond as Zeykala fumes. *Prima* Bettancourt has the rigid posture of someone constipated on a toilet.

"Yes, it is," Hammond clarifies.

"Good, so let's talk about Liberteum. Let's talk about them in context of my responsibilities. Then we'll move on to how our efforts have prevented other attacks.

Then let's find out what suggestions your witnesses and the other board members have about what could realistically and cost-effectively have been done better."

Satisfied, Valen leans back in his chair as his eyes focus on the rostrum. His opening salvo hit its mark. He reshaped the narrative and forced Zeykala to be careful in her questioning. As they used to say in the United States, it's "game on."

CHAPTER
SIXTY-SIX

INTERCORPEX

Global Network Operations Center
Manhattan Financial District
ICX New York Exchange

Downmarket days are nothing new. Markets, by their nature, go up and down. This is different, though. In the forty-five minutes since New York opened, early gains carried over from Frankfurt have been wiped out by a steady downward trend. The IGI being down over one hundred thirty points this early in the trading day is a cause for concern, and Lyris isn't bothering to hide it.

He calls up the Intercorporational Global Index analytics and settles into his chair. The candlestick chart pops up, and he enlarges it. Similar to a bar chart, this one features thin vertical lines showing the period's trading range and thicker lines showing previous opens and closes to illustrate trends.

"You okay, Director?"

"Look at the board and tell me what you see, Wyeth," Lyris says, gesturing to the front of the spacious NOC.

"We're down."

"Yeah, but in a volatile market, buying and selling causes prices to fluctuate. Any decline in prices is offset by momentary jumps when buy orders are submitted."

"That's right," Wyeth says, leaning closer.

"Okay," Lyris says, bringing up a separate bar graph of order counts. "Where are the buy orders?"

Sell orders outpace buys by a ten-to-one margin. It's displayed in vivid color. Wyeth is surprised that operations haven't reported it.

"What the hell? Could the patricians be liquidating because of the murders?"

"Sure, but patricians are opportunists. We'd see buying as prices drop, especially for larger corporations. Look at America Incorporated."

"AME is down big. The market could be reacting to Valen's hearing on Corporate Hill."

Lyris presses his lips together. That would be an expected result. Stock markets have never liked change. The slightest bit of upheaval can make for a hectic trading day. Only this is anything but an expected result.

"Look at China, the UK, and German corporations. They're all down. There haven't been any system or network anomalies, right?"

Wyeth shakes his head. "The network is clean. NetEng has been running continuous diagnostics since the New York attack. There have been some typical equipment failures, but nothing out of the ordinary."

"And intrusion countermeasures? Encryption protocols?"

"Archangyl hasn't reported anything, and ITQS encryption is rotated every twenty-four hours. I supervised the procedure myself last night. Everything checks out."

Troubleshooting exchange problems is an art as much as a science. When an issue is identified, technicians look for other symptoms. Root causes are traced by knowing how systems interact and their effect on each other. Unfortunately, the process becomes impossible when there's a lack of symptoms. It's like trying to complete a puzzle with most of the pieces missing.

"Is there anything that can cause this that you can think of?"

"Just ornery patricians," Wyeth muses.

"Help Desk, has there been any increase in call volume?" Lyris asks over the integrated communications system.

"Director, Help Desk. Call volume is normal."

"Compile a breakdown of all complaint topics and report back."

"Yes, sir."

"You still suspect something is wrong?" Wyeth asks, getting a nod from Lyris. "What do you need me to do?"

"Check for anything, and I mean anything, out of the ordinary."

"You got it," Wyeth says before bounding down the stairs.

Lyris leans back in his chair and watches his displays. People could easily dismiss this as paranoia. It wouldn't be the first time he's been accused of that. But the attacks changed his outlook. He's being more cautious, and something in his gut warns him that something is very wrong.

CHAPTER SIXTY-SEVEN

THE PATRICIANS

Shareholder Hall
Corporate Hill Governance District
Washington-Arlington Municipal Corporation

After a quick fifteen-minute testimony from Chief Executive Safmor in New York that didn't help Zeykala's cause, she moved right to her superstar. Virtari took the stand and, for the past half hour, has prattled on about all the things he would have done differently had he been the one allowed to pursue Liberteum instead of the PSS.

Shalius Covington has watched from his office as the hearing unfolds. Now it's time to play a more active role. He quietly enters the hearing through the double doors and slides to a spot along the wall. Chairman Hammond has not asked Valen to refute a single statement, nor has he interjected during the testimony. He yawns loudly, causing the old patrician to smile. It's intended to let everyone know he is still in the room.

"Are we boring you, Chief Executive?" Zeykala asks, admonishing him. He grins. "Please continue, Director Virtari."

"As I was saying, I have asked Chief Executive Valen on several occasions to allow me to assume control of the search for the terrorists."

"When was the most recent time?" one of the board members asks.

"At the America Tower a few days ago. The chief guardian of Public Safety and Security of New York City was present. I argued that corporate security is better trained and equipped for these types of search operations."

"And what was Chief Executive Valen's response?"

"It bordered between derision and apathy."

The crowd breaks into a murmur, but it has nothing to do with the tone of Virtari's answer. All eyes turn to Shalius, who makes his way up the center aisle towards the rostrum. He stops between the tables Valen and Virtari are seated at. They both stare at him blankly.

"Can I help you, sir?" Hammond asks, equally confused by the patrician's behavior and violation of decorum.

"I'm very sorry for the intrusion, Chairman Hammond, but I have come to claim my chair."

The words sounded great coming out of his mouth. He's longed for a lifetime to utter them and marked the occasion by dressing in his finest silk suit and Italian leather shoes. His silver hair makes him as distinguished as the family crest gleaming at the opening of his high-collared white dress shirt.

"I'm sorry?"

"My chair. I would like to be seated."

"Shalius, there are seats to the rear of the—"

"*You're* in my chair, Talya," he interrupts.

Valen wears an amused smile. There is a cacophony of conversations breaking out in the room. Most of the board members exchange bewildered looks.

"Have you had a stroke or something? This seat is reserved for the *prima* patrician."

"I assure you, I'm in perfect health. I'm also aware of the position of the occupant in that seat. You seem to not be aware that it's mine now. You sold a substantial part of your position in America Incorporated this morning, and I have increased my stake. I am the new *prima*."

"You must be mistaken," she stammers as another wave of gasps and whispers reverberates through the room.

The Bettancourts have been the largest holders of AME stock for as long as anyone can remember. Under normal circumstances, any challenge to that claim would be ridiculous. That Shalius Covington would be bold enough to make it in front of his peers and the board of directors rattles her.

"No, I'm not. Check for yourself."

Chairman Hammond beats her to it. "It looks like he's right. You sold twenty-five percent of your stake in America Incorporated."

"I think it's despicable that you hauled me in here to destabilize our stock just so you can repurchase more later at a lower price," Valen says over the sharp gasp in the room.

"I did no such thing!"

Half of the board and the gallery is staring at her. The other half corroborates the information on their tablets.

"The transaction report says otherwise," Valen continues, rechecking his tablet. "If that's not what you're doing, explain why you began dumping large numbers of shares right before this meeting."

"Your attempt to embroil me in some sort of conspiracy is unconscionable. I have not made any trades today. Any insinuation that I have is a complete fabrication."

"This is the Intercorpex transaction report as of one minute ago."

Chairman Hammond sends the transaction report to the large display mounted above the rostrum for everyone in the room to see. The same document is forwarded to each board member's display. The chamber erupts into muffled chatter as Hammond slams his gavel several times to quiet the observers.

"That's not possible!"

"Twenty-five percent is a hefty amount, *Prima* Bettancourt," Hammond says. "It wouldn't take much for any member of the *gentez-majorez* to accumulate enough shares to have a majority stake."

"You orchestrated this!"

"Yes, I did," Valen says. Gasps suck all the oxygen out of the room, and Shalius turns to look at him. "I hacked into your account while sitting here, defeated the biometric key, and executed trades while you questioned Safmor and Virtari."

Snickers echo around the room, prompting another smash of Hammond's gavel and stern looks at the patricians on the floor and the executives in the gallery. Shalius bets he wishes this were a closed hearing.

Talya sneers. "I didn't mean you were doing it yourself."

"Yes, of course, then I must be in league with Intercorpex. Everyone knows about my close personal relationship with Administrator-General Raimius."

"The market. It's…it's down almost…the IGI is down three hundred," one of the board members stammers in shock and disbelief.

"And falling fast. AME is falling right along with it."

"You are the chief executive officer!" Zeykala shouts, coming to Talya's defense by attempting to reassign blame. "You are the captain of the ship, and it's sinking. Why shouldn't we vote to remove you right now?"

"So, now I'm not only responsible for Liberteum, but for our stock collapsing because of irresponsible trading by our largest shareholder?"

"You are the chief executive officer!" she shouts again.

"I am, yet I'm still sitting here for a hearing everyone has concluded is a witch hunt to prove gross incompetence. So, Boardmember Zeykala, I'm not sure what you want me to do. It's hard to manage a situation while I'm answering questions before the board. Unless Chairman Hammond dismisses me…."

"Under the circumstances, maybe it's best if—"

"Point of order," Zeykala screeches. "Chief Executive Valen was brought here specifically for his failings leading up to this debacle. There has never been a more appropriate time to hold this vote."

She's desperately trying to turn this around. Zeykala knows that Valen will never be invited back if this hearing is adjourned. Not with the allegations leveled against Talya Bettancourt.

Hammond looks conflicted. He has the perfect excuse to recess this hearing. There is no way a majority of the board would find his decision to table a vote inappropriate under the circumstances.

"I demand to be seated as *prima*, Mr. Chairman," Shalius states evenly.

"Chief Executive Valen, ending this meeting with the specter of having to repeat it later would place this corporation in an even more precarious position. We will continue after a short recess so that Chief Executive Valen can coordinate an executive response. The board will assemble in my office to settle the question of Shalius Covington's claim. We will reconvene at ten after ten."

Hammond slams down the gavel and offers Valen an apologetic look. Shalius doesn't care about that. He has a rightful claim and plans on seizing it. That's all that matters in the center ring of this circus.

CHAPTER SIXTY-EIGHT

LIBERTEUM

Safe House
Tribeca Geographic District
New York City Municipal Corporation

The trio climbs into Farron's conveyance in the small parking garage under the structure, with him behind the wheel. His driver isn't going to be joining him on this trip. Farron pulls the vehicle out into the street and starts heading south and east. Rykos stares out the tinted glass. That must come in handy for avoiding the prying eyes of street cameras and overhead drones.

"Do you remember how to drive?" Michele asks playfully.

"You had better hope so. Obvir has been with me for a long time. I haven't taken the wheel in a while."

Silence fills the car as they glide with the other traffic. It's a strange sensation for Michele. She isn't used to vehicular transportation. Rykos eyes the rapid-fire tapping of her foot on the floorboards.

"Is Archimedes going to work?"

The tapping stops. "There's only one defense against it, and that's what we're counting on."

"You still haven't explained how it's going to change anything. What comes after this?"

She smiles. "Something amazing."

"You're not going to tell me, are you?"

Farron eyes her in the rearview mirror. She meets his gaze for a split second before staring out the window.

"No, I'm not."

"Can you at least tell me what my role is?"

"Who says you have one?" she whispers.

"I heard you arguing with Narik. You also wouldn't have made the deal to get my father back unless there was something in it for you."

"You're right," Michele says, turning to Rykos. "Scary things are about to happen. Employees won't know how to interpret or react to them. We have always wanted an intermediary. I need you to be our voice – our translator."

Rykos shakes his head. "I don't know what good that will do."

"You know exactly what good it will do. You're a hero of the corporation, or whatever ridiculous title they conveyed on you after your release. You're a known entity, especially in this city."

"I can't convince anybody of anything."

"I don't need you to convince people. I need you to explain things to them."

Now it's Rykos's turn to stare out the window. Whatever he thought Michele needed him for, it wasn't this. It will make him the voice of a terrorist group. He will also be its face. People will look at him as the leader, not the spokesman. She understands how dangerous that is.

"I don't think it will have any effect."

"Why not?"

"Have you ever heard the term 'bounded rationality?'" Rykos asks.

"No."

"It's a business term used to explain the decision-making process. It means that the rationality of individuals is limited by available information, the cognitive limitations of their minds, and the amount of time they have to make a decision. It's the reason corporations are so successful in controlling their employees. They limit information, teach employees to think a particular way, and restrict the amount of time to contemplate choices by imposing arbitrary deadlines backed by punitive actions."

"You see, Farron?" Michele says, staring at the patrician, whose eyes are still welded in the mirror. "I told you he'd be good at this."

"What do you mean?" Rykos asks.

"You made the argument we'd want you to. I didn't pick you because you're the chief guardian's son or just some random kid. You're special. You know how you're being controlled and how to explain it to others."

"You're asking a lot of me."

Michele nods. "And you're asking a lot from us. The last thing I want to do right now is confront Haven. I agreed to it, knowing the risk. You'll have to take a leap of faith in return."

Rykos stares down at his hands. He stretches his fingers out and wiggles them. Michele is tempted to grab his hand to get him to stop, but the action could be misconstrued. That and she might not want to let his hand go.

"I'll do what you ask, but I don't know the result. Employees are conditioned to respect and follow the corporation and its executives from birth. They won't change their thinking no matter what you do or what I say. They don't rationalize things that way."

Michele can almost hear Haven uttering those words. That was his argument. She spots the museum coming up on the right. They're almost at the Alamo, and the conversation will have to wait until this rescue mission is over.

"You're missing one key thing about bounded rationality, Rykos."

"What's that?" he asks as Farron stops the conveyance.

"When we're done, people will be making emotional decisions, not rational ones."

CHAPTER SIXTY-NINE

INTERCORPEX

The "War Room"
ICX New York Exchange
New York City Municipal Corporation

Constable Dzamko is a man of his word. Since Zyree's return to the war room, the PSS has been tasking resources and sharing whatever information they need. Although the constable questioned it, he didn't decline the request to trail Farron Keating with one of his drones. Zyree smirks, knowing that if the BCS and PSS cooperated this well, he wouldn't need to be here.

"I'm going to repeat it…this corporation has the neatest toys," Duckballs gushes as he watches the video streaming in from an overhead drone.

"Any activity?"

"Nothing yet. The conveyance is still parked in the garage. There hasn't been any foot traffic in or out of the building."

"Aerial Ops is telling me that the drone is almost out of power and will need to transfer its duties," the attractive guardian says over the VidLynk. "Another will be on station before that happens to ensure no coverage gap."

"Good," Zyree says with a respectful nod that she returns.

"The PSS just sent over the details on the structure," Bird's Nest says. "It was designated as a patrician residence in 2081 by the New York City Municipal Corporation. Units are sold off individually. Farron Keating purchased his domicile about five years ago."

"So, he lives there?"

"His primary residence is listed as a domicile in Gramercy off Lexington Avenue. There's no evidence he lives in this building."

"Patricians are known to keep multiple units in the city," the guardian explains. "Most of the *gentez-majorez* have at least two."

"Must be nice. Anything else?"

"There have been several work permits requested from the corporation...okay, this is interesting. It looks like...it looks like Farron bought other units."

"Other units? How many?"

"Uh...all of them. I think he owns the entire building."

"Have you ever heard of anything like that?" Zyree asks the guardian.

"No, owning an entire building is peculiar. It's not unheard of for patricians to procure multiple units to combine them, but that's only typical for uptown brownstones."

"Brothel? Harem?" Duckballs asks, earning a look from Bird's Nest.

"It could be a guest residence for friends from overseas."

"A whole building?" the guardian questions. "Not likely."

"What if it's a guest house for terrorists?" Zyree asks, earning everyone's attention. "Maybe that's why the PSS hasn't found Liberteum. They're searching below ground when they should be looking above it."

Nobody speaks. It's an insane theory, but nobody challenges it. There was never a reason to consider such an idea until now. That only makes sense if Farron is involved. Zyree thinks he's deep in this.

"Farron's conveyance is leaving the garage," Bird's Nest says, turning his attention to his display.

"Can he see the drone?"

"Possibly, but he won't know the camera angle, and the skies are full of them," the guardian says.

"The windows are tinted," Bird's Nest observes. "We can't see inside."

"Can we at least get audio?"

"Checking... No, there's interference," the guardian says, frustration growing in her voice.

"He has a disrupter. The patricians know how to maintain their privacy in a city with this much surveillance. Is Constable Dzamko there?"

"I'm right here, Chief Inspector. I heard what you said about Liberteum possibly being above ground. It makes sense. It also answers questions about why we couldn't find them. We just never considered it a possibility."

"I wouldn't have either," Zyree admits.

"I have units in the area. I can send them over to check out the building."

"Let's hold off on that, Constable. I don't want to tip our hand. If Liberteum is holding Teman, it won't be there. There's too much of a chance of him broadcasting from a missed biojack. Let's see where Farron leads us. Sound like a plan?"

"I'm okay with that."

The door swings open, and Malkor enters. He waits until he closes it behind him before speaking.

"The market is tanking. Everyone in the NOC is stressed out."

"Do they think it's an attack?" Zyree asks.

"No. From what I heard, the trades are legitimate," Malkor says.

Zyree waits for the other shoe to drop. There must be something more. Malkor wouldn't have rushed up here otherwise.

"But?"

"Patricians are reporting that they aren't making the trades the system says they are."

"How is that possible?" the guardian asks.

"It's not," Bird's Nest interjects. "All trades are encrypted, and the interface can only be accessed following biometric and login verification. Those can't be spoofed or bypassed."

"What if they could?" Zyree asks, thinking out loud.

"How?"

"Constable, do you think you can get me the utility information for Farron's building? I need electricity usage patterns and broadband data capabilities."

"Sure. We're on it."

"You think Liberteum could be behind this?" Malkor asks with a raised eyebrow.

"I have no idea. It could be nothing, but it's worth looking into while we wait for Farron to get to wherever he's going."

It sounded good coming out of his mouth. Too bad it's a lie. Something is wrong. He turns back to the drone footage and doesn't fight back the feeling that Liberteum is making its move.

CHAPTER SEVENTY

AMERICA, INC.

Shareholder Hall
Corporate Hill Governance District
Washington-Arlington Municipal Corporation

The hearing adjourns, and the room begins to buzz. It's loud enough that she would have to shout into her tablet for a VidLynk. That won't do, so Fiolla moves into the corridor and starts wandering to find a quiet space. There are countless patrician offices here, and many will be occupied.

She finds a quiet spot off the large foyer and makes her VidLynk request. It will get routed through the White House switchboard. Whether that is a good or bad thing remains to be seen.

"I'm a little busy here. What do you want, Fiolla?" Lyris asks after making the connection.

"You know what I want. The market is plummeting, and there's not so much as a peep from the exchange. What's going on?"

Lyris sighs. "It's normal market activity."

"You call this normal? AME's value is plunging."

"Did you expect to hold a hearing to remove your CEO and not have the market react?"

"Only it's the whole IGI that's tanking. There should be an inverse correlation in stock movements. Everyone should be up except us. Don't insult my intelligence by hiding behind that excuse. What's *really* going on? Is there another attack on your systems?"

Lyris stops typing and stares at her for the first time. "I resent that implication."

"I don't give a damn what you resent."

"Our systems are functioning normally. Archangyl hasn't detected any internal or external network or software threats."

Fiolla knows that the Archangyl intrusion detection system is unbeatable. It's artificial intelligence that supposedly cannot be spoofed or defeated. That didn't stop

Liberteum from finding a way around it. There is no reason to believe they couldn't replicate that success.

"You're telling me that the patricians are making these trades?"

"My operations staff are selectively auditing them in real-time. They're legitimate transactions. Now, if you don't mind, a dozen other corporations are asking the same questions."

Fiolla hears a tone, and Lyris diverts his eyes away from the VidLynk. They go wide with surprise.

"I have to go, Fiolla," he says, disconnecting the VidLynk.

"That bastard just disconnected me," she mutters, punching her tablet to send another VidLynk request. It's denied immediately.

Fiolla takes a cleansing breath to calm her nerves and leans against the wall. She tries to connect to Farron, and the request goes unanswered. He might be busy, especially considering what is going on in the market. Still, time is of the essence. If anyone knows what's going on, it's him.

She spins away from the wall and nearly bowls into Aris Fontainbleu. The aging patrician is staring at his antique tablet with a concerned look.

"My apologies, sir."

"Don't worry about it. I have bigger concerns than getting bumped into by a beautiful woman."

"Anything I can help with, sir?"

"I doubt it unless you know what is going on with Intercorpex. I got an e-note from my grandson. He manages my family's financial affairs with one of my granddaughters. He asked if I traded any America Incorporated stock. I didn't."

"Why would he ask that?"

"Because he got a transaction report from the exchange that says I did."

The revelation hits Fiolla like a hammer. She closes her eyes. Of all the days, please not today. There's no way that's a coincidence. Something is very, very wrong, and it's coming at the worst possible time.

"Talya Bettancourt claimed the same thing. Sir, this may be an inappropriate request, but may I see the transaction?"

"I have nothing to hide," he says with a shrug, showing the report on his tablet. "I can't understand how this would happen. It's my login, but I've been here all day. This tablet doesn't even have biometric capabilities."

Fiolla checks the report to see if he's mistaken. He isn't. According to this, he has executed five separate transactions since market open totaling…her mouth drops.

"Sir, what percentage of your stake in AME is this?"

"Almost half," he says. "It took my family a long time to accumulate that much. I instructed my grandson to buy more depending on the outcome of this hearing. That's why he contacted me."

"Outside of the *prima*, are others experiencing the same problem?"

"A couple of patricians said there was some issue, but I never made the connection. Do you know what's going on?"

"No, and I wish I did. I just got off with the global director of the exchange. He assured me that nothing is amiss."

"Well, clearly, something is."

"Thank you, sir," Fiolla says with a slight bow. "I will let you know if I uncover anything."

"Thank you, young lady."

Fiolla closes her eyes. Valen told her that he knew Zeykala's and Talya's weaknesses. Could this be a ploy to somehow expose them? Did he somehow arrange a problem to postpone the hearing and elevate Shalius Covington as *prima*? Or is there something else happening?

She types a message on her tablet. There is only one way to find out.

Talya not lying. Problem with trading.
Denied by ICX. Market plunging.

The response is almost immediate. It's also as upsetting and confusing as the problem itself:

I know. Find out who they're going to blame first.

CHAPTER
SEVENTY-ONE

THE PATRICIANS

Keating Family of the Gentez-Majorez Estate
Greenwich Geographic District
Southern Connecticut Municipal Corporation

Everything is going according to plan. Shalius made his move and rattled the America Incorporated board of directors enough for them to call a recess. Liberteum is rattling the market and causing a panic. Outside of the radio silence from his son, Denali couldn't be more pleased.

He stands, desperately needing to stretch his legs and burn off the tension seizing his shoulders and upper back. He thinks about a walk in the garden before changing his mind and descending the stairs to the sublevel. The walk can wait.

Denali enters the command center and positions himself in front of the digital deployment map. He then stares at the unit status board. It hasn't changed much. Some are still undermanned, meaning the recruitment isn't going as well as he hoped. He could take it out on the commander, but a week isn't enough time to expect considerable progress.

"Can I help you with something, sir?" Commander Lacune asks after noticing his presence and striding over to him.

"Things are happening quickly. Are the forces in place for the next mission?"

"Most of them, sir. I'm still working out logistics plans for several units. Everything will be ready in the next day or two."

"That should be sufficient."

"I have an update on your planes if you're interested."

Denali's eyes light up. "I very much am."

Lacune sends a series of images from his tablet to the display on the wall. Instead of glamour shots of the magnificent machines, it's close-ups showing the repair work.

"We have procured the parts for the engines. Mechanics are working night and day to make them serviceable. One jet is fully operational."

"That's excellent news."

"We may have an issue getting all three airborne. The other two have significant structural damage and metal fatigue that may keep them grounded."

"Make it happen, Commander. Whatever it takes. We will need them, and soon."

"Yes, sir. I will instruct them to redouble their efforts."

Denali nods and turns to leave.

"You know that I follow your orders without question."

The patrician stops and turns as the room falls silent. "I do."

"May I ask what this is about? It's difficult for me to strategize, arrange logistics, and position personnel if I don't understand the overall plan."

Denali clasps his hands behind his back. "You don't need to know."

"You're right, sir. I am speaking out of turn. My apologies," Lacune says with a respectful bow of his head.

The patrician grimaces. He's right. Lacune should know more than he does. He commands the army, and Denali will need that army before this is over. The details are above his pay grade, but the strategic objectives can't be kept a secret any longer. Not for him or any of the men and women in this command center.

"Do you play chess, Commander?"

"I know how to play, but not well. I'm better at real-life than games."

"The two are often the same. Serious mistakes or blunders decide the outcome of most chess games. That isn't unlike life."

"I suppose that's true. Are you treating what's happening as a game?"

Denali smiles devilishly. "In a manner of speaking. This is a game with deadly consequences and not one we want to lose."

"Are we winning?" Lacune asks.

"It's far too early to know. We are still moving pieces to the right squares and developing our position. We have done it faster than our opponents, and we control the center of the board. That is most important."

Lacune averts his eyes briefly before they light up. "Intercorpex. You mean the attacks in Secaucus and Manhattan."

 Denali nods.

"By pieces, you mean our units?"

"And Liberteum, my son, other patricians, and even Director Lyris. We have powerful pieces," Denali says, gesturing at the unit status board, "and we have pawns. Each serves its purpose if used correctly."

"I understand, but how do you know how our opponents will respond?"

"Because I know them and how they'll react based on experience. I know their capabilities and what resources, or pieces, they have to move. Human beings like routines and rarely deviate from patterns of behavior. It makes them predictable. In chess, thinking one move ahead is sufficient for winning if you guess with perfect accuracy. I calculate a few moves deeper to account for other reasonable possibilities. That's where you come in."

"Your knights?"

"And rooks. This army allows me to force our opponents to take action when needed."

"The attacks on the overseas corporations," Lacune concludes.

"If you check your opponent's king, he must get out of check. Thus, it's a forcing move."

"I'm still not sure I understand, sir."

Denali inhales deeply and scans the faces in the room. "You will. Eventually, you will see the whole board."

"And the planes?" Lacune asks, pointing at the pictures on the display that still aren't painted the flat black Denali wants.

"They are my queen. Bringing the queen, the second most valuable piece in chess, into play early is a bad idea because it can be lost while the other side develops lesser pieces. If used properly, the queen can cause serious damage. Ours will."

"Sir? What's the most valuable piece on your board?"

Denali beams. "I am. I'm the king, and I will not be check-mated. Ever."

CHAPTER SEVENTY-TWO

INTERCORPEX

The "War Room"
ICX New York Exchange
New York City Municipal Corporation

Malkor steps into the room and eases the door closed behind him. He strides across the room and slides up alongside Zyree, who is staring at the aerial feed of Farron's car on the display. The inspector crosses his arms.

"You know, it's only a matter of time before Lyris realizes you're in the building. He's gonna come up here to chew your ass."

"He's too busy watching the market melt to bother me right now. What's the count now, Bird's Nest?"

"Help Desk reports fifty-seven tickets for incorrect transactions and climbing."

Zyree turns to Malkor. "Trades are being made, but the patricians claim they aren't making them. With modern encryption and biometric logins, there's no way these are fraudulent trades. Something else is going on."

"Liberteum?"

The chief instructor shrugs. "If it is, Farron is the best chance we have of finding them. He's in our crosshairs, and I want to keep him there. Where is Chiana?"

"Surveying the Wilmington crime scene."

"Good. The farther away from us, the better. Where is Farron now?"

"The Bowery," Duckballs reports.

"Where the hell is he going?" Zyree mumbles.

"The Bowery is a robust entertainment district," Bird's Nest muses. "Not that I get the chance to go there."

"I doubt he's catching a comedy show at ten-thirty in the morning."

"He just pulled into a parking structure," Duckballs says. "It's the...New York Museum of Business."

"Constable, is there something special about that place?"

"No," Constable Dzamko answers over the VidLynk. "It's just a museum. Before the collapse, it was known as the New Museum. It featured the cutting-edge art of the time. The building next door was razed to make way for the parking structure and rooftop garden."

"Bird's Nest, I need you to put a map of the Bowery up on the primary wall display."

He complies, and Zyree walks over to study it. He can't believe they would stay in the museum. So, where would they go? There's nothing there.

"Do you want me to zoom in?"

"No. Constable, can you bring up the subterranean map and see if there's any way to transit out of that museum?"

"Sure. Hold on… You think they're heading somewhere below ground?"

"Yeah, but I don't see any obvious targets."

"Okay, the Bowery is an old section of the city. There are a lot of defunct sewers and modern maintenance tunnels. Sensors are monitoring the ones we've uncovered."

"I don't think they're going far," Zyree says, tracing the streets on the map with his finger. "Otherwise, there was no point in driving. Constable, can you stage your assault teams in the park between Forsyth and Chrystie?"

"I can have them there in fifteen minutes."

Zyree nods and returns his stare to the map. He steps back and rubs his growing stubble. Where are they going? And more importantly, will it be too late when he finds out?

CHAPTER SEVENTY-THREE

UNDERGRADUATE RYKOS

New York Museum of Business
Bowery Geographic District
New York Municipal Corporation

Farron kills the electric motor, and we all climb out of the conveyance, each carrying a torchlight and weapon retrieved from the storage compartment. Michele leads us across the lowest floor in the parking structure and stops to look around. There are cameras, but most are trained on the entrances and vehicle travel lanes. None of them are pointed at the double doors of a machine room.

Satisfied, she quickly defeats the lock. It seems odd to me until I recognize that it's connected to a stairwell that leads into the subbasement of the museum. She strides confidently down the corridor. There is no surveillance here, and she seems relatively confident that we won't run into any maintenance workers.

"For the record, this is a terrible idea," Farron whines.

"There are only three routes into the Alamo," Michele explains. "The first two are the primary tunnel and secondary tunnels. Haven no doubt has them both heavily guarded. The third is the emergency escape tunnel, which he only *might* have guarded. So unless you want to grab a shovel and start digging a new one, this is our best chance."

"That's not what I meant. I know you made a deal, but this is an awful risk."

"It's also multitasking. Each phase of Archimedes was designed to be executed under cover of a diversion. Haven was taking care of those. I intend to make him useful to us once again. We can save Rykos's father, distract the PSS, and take care of our Haven problem all at once."

"Or die trying," Farron mumbles.

The patrician isn't cut out for this. I don't know why Michele would bring him along, other than needing transportation and one more body with a gun. There is safety in numbers, although not much in this case.

"Then don't go. Stay here, or go back home and wait it out with your father," Michele says, defeating the lock of another set of double doors that I assume is one of the museum's maintenance areas. "Otherwise, quit whining and focus."

Farron nods, and we enter the mouth of a dark maintenance access tunnel that leads west out of the building. "This tunnel is monitored. Once we trip the sensors, we invite the PSS to hunt us down. I'm willing to take that chance to honor our arrangement and rescue your father."

"But?" I ask.

"But if you go back on our arrangement once we free him, I will hunt you down. Do you understand?"

There is no sarcasm or exaggeration in her voice. She means every word. I wonder if she arranged for Liberteum to carry on without her if this fails. I mean every word, too. Michele has more faith in me than my father does.

"I will honor our deal. You have my word."

She glances over at an apprehensive and unconvinced Farron. "Okay, let's go. We'll have to move fast. The longer we're here, the better the chance we're found."

We activate our torchlights and walk down the maintenance tunnel. This is clean and tidy compared to the places I've seen in the underground. The walls are whitewashed, and there is overhead lighting that workers can activate.

Our footsteps echo loudly off the walls of the long, straight tunnel. Utility pipes are suspended over our heads in the otherwise empty tunnel. A lone metal standing cabinet marked "Tool Storage" is bolted to the wall ahead. I'm caught off guard when Michele stops at it.

"Hold this," she says, handing me her torchlight.

I dutifully point it as she opens the unlocked cabinet and removes tools and the middle shelf. I'm about to ask what she's doing when she pushes the lower half of the back panel and rotates it counterclockwise. I aim my light inside the cabinet and see the access to a dark crawl space.

"No way…. You guys never cease to amaze me."

"It opens into a walking tunnel in fifteen meters."

"Ladies first," Farron says, not enjoying a minute of this.

Michele slinks her way into the narrow opening of the pitch-black earthen tunnel. After admiring her for a second, I follow, with Farron pulling up the rear. We slide on our stomachs until we reach the part that widens. I'm glad I'm not claustrophobic.

"Okay," she whispers, "this leads to the south side of the crypt."

My eyes track the beam of light down the tunnel. "Wait…crypt?"

"The Alamo is constructed in the crypts below St. Patrick's Old Cathedral. The basilica is seldom used, and the entrance to what lies below it was sealed during the second revitalization project. Creating a secure stronghold was one of my father's first engineering projects when he fled to the underground. Once he tunneled to it, we turned it into habitable space."

"People live there?"

"I spent most of my childhood there."

I exchange a look with Farron, and he shrugs. How did she turn out this normal? Well, as normal as an underground terrorist can be, anyway.

"Okay, what's the issue?"

"I can't be sure where Haven is keeping your father. There are multiple rooms built out of the crypts on both sides. Some are connected. We can get to the central corridor that runs the length of the church undetected, but once we move the stone, Haven's men will spot us."

"Will they turn on you?"

Farron lets out a laugh. "They already have. Take your best guess, Michele."

"He could be anywhere. Hardening this place against attack was Haven's responsibility. I don't know what modifications he's made."

"Are any of the rooms reinforced with an extra layer of brick or metal?" I ask.

"One or two. Why?"

"My father has a Level Five biojack. There's no way Haven would ever find it, let alone remove it. He's transmitting. Since the PSS isn't crawling all over this place, the signal isn't getting out."

"Okay, then he's probably in the northwest corner. Getting there is a risk. If we're wrong, this will end in an ugly firefight."

"Then let's hope we're right. I haven't come this far to turn back now."

"Okay," she says, checking her weapon. "We have the element of surprise. Let's hope it's enough."

We move down the tunnel as it narrows before reaching a stone slab blocking the access point. Michele takes a deep breath and pushes on it. The stone dislodges, and she slides it to the right as quietly as possible. She pokes her head out and moves quickly but quietly into the hallway. Farron and I follow suit.

Overhead lights illuminate the hall, probably from the basilica's electrical panel. Michele gets her bearings and begins to creep down the hallway.

We freeze when we hear men laugh on the other side of one of the heavy doors. We sneak past, continuing until we hear Haven's voice. We stop short of the opening and move alongside the wall. Michele flashes a single finger, then a second. When the third goes up, we burst into the room.

CHAPTER SEVENTY-FOUR

LIBERTEUM

The "Alamo"
The Nolita Geographic District
New York City Municipal Corporation

Haven is enjoying this. The chief guardian is unable to protect his shattered body from blows. Not that he has the will left to. Every punch is theatrical. Haven teases him with some and blasts him with others to maximize the psychological effects of the abuse.

"I have to admit, Chief Guardian," Haven says as he winds up for another strike, "I'm a little surprised that you're still alive."

Three shadows cast from the light behind him dance on the floor as three figures barge into the room. Haven drops his fist but otherwise remains frozen in place. Nyvar jumps for the rifle leaning against the wall.

"You reach for it; you die, Nyvar," Michele says with conviction and authority.

"How the hell did you get in here?" Haven asks.

"I crawled."

Haven nods and then grins. "The emergency tunnel. I knew I should have booby-trapped it."

"You knew you couldn't. That's the last thing you'd want to deal with if you had to get out of here in a hurry."

"And you would have known I didn't have the manpower to guard it. Very clever, Michele. I never thought you would have had the balls to come here. What do you want?"

"Him," she says, pointing in Teman's direction.

"No, I don't think so."

"Nobody asked for your opinion, asshole. I should just kill you now for what you did to him," Rykos says, staring at his father.

"Look at you, Ivy, growing up so fast. You're right. You should kill me, but you won't. Not if you plan on making it out of here alive."

Haven walks over and puts his chest against the barrel of Rykos's gun. "Let's see if you're a killer. Go ahead, do it while you still have time. Oops, too late."

Three men swarm into the room. A chorus of shouting and threats erupts in the cramped space. The frantic cries and pleas bounce around the chaotic room as the air thickens with tension.

"Put it down!"

"Drop it!"

"Don't make me shoot you!"

Haven twists and jerks the weapon out of Rykos's grasp. Two seconds later, the muzzle is pointed at his head. Michele reacts and moves hers within an inch of Haven's temple. The shouting dissipates as everyone in the room has the others covered.

"I've read about this before," Haven says with a stifled laugh. "What did they call it? A Mexican standoff?"

"Take…him…down," Rykos says through a clenched jaw.

"You're not in a position to be making demands, Ivy," Nyvar retorts. "He has a gun to your head."

"And I have one to his," Michele adds. "So, in the interest of self-preservation, I suggest you do it."

"Go ahead," Haven instructs Nyvar. "Dear old dad is as good as dead anyway."

The rope is given slack, and Teman's restraints are removed. Nyvar drops him onto the steel chair. He reflexively moves his hands behind the chair back for Haven to bind them. This time, he's left untied.

"Well, this will be a nice family reunion, although a short one," Haven mocks.

Teman stares at the figures in the room. His eyes are swollen, and his vision must be blurry from the beatings. He tries to focus and swallow hard, wincing at the pain it causes.

"Rykos?" he manages to say.

"Hello, Father."

CHAPTER SEVENTY-FIVE

AMERICA, INC.

Shareholder Hall
Corporate Hill Governance District
Washington-Arlington Municipal Corporation

The hearing is gaveled back into session after the board of directors, and the attendees return to their seats. Only the *prima's* seat remains unoccupied. Shalius Covington has a legitimate claim, but Talya Bettancourt insists no shares were traded. It is something that Intercorpex will need to adjudicate. Any decision will require an investigation that could span days or weeks. Hammond has decided to move on with this hearing without either patrician seated.

"Where did we leave off?" Hammond asks.

"We were wasting time listening to people who hate me parade up here with their reasons," Valen says before anyone can answer.

"You don't think we're entitled to hear opinions about your leadership?"

"You can hear all the opinions you want, Boardmember Zeykala. None of the courses of action they present would have led to the satisfactory result you're looking for."

"So, you admit that your approach has failed?"

Valen shakes his head. "I admit that I haven't succeeded *yet*."

"It's the same thing!" Zeykala screeches.

"Only in the minds of simpletons."

"That's enough," Hammond snaps. "Keep this professional. Chief Executive, you know this is a hearing to determine your accountability on the matter."

"Thank you, Chairman Hammond. The agenda has changed so often that I've lost track," Valen says, causing another wave of snickers to fan out through the room. "Let me simplify things: As chief executive officer, I'm one hundred percent accountable. That's not even a discussion."

"If Valen admits he's responsible, we should immediately move to sanction," Zeykala argues, eager to hold a vote.

"What exactly am I being punished for? Not catching Liberteum in a week? Is that the criterion this board is measuring against? Everyone hoped to quickly finish this business. Perhaps Virtari's slash and burn techniques may have been more effective."

"May have?" Zeykala asks.

The trap is sprung. Valen needed her to commit to a plan of action to show the board how irresponsible his strategy is. By baiting Zeykala, he hopes to end this ridiculous meeting once the other board members realize that.

"We have the benefit of hindsight but not the gift of foresight. We cannot peer into the future and know what the result would have been. So, we turn to historical examples to provide guidance. Boardmember Zeykala, are you saying you are longing for a repeat of the Catharsis?"

"I'm stating that I want the objective met."

"We all want the objective met. I'm asking if you believe the Catharsis was an effective means of achieving a goal."

"It got the job done."

"Yes, with wide-ranging and debilitating consequences. Would you be willing to sacrifice the good of the corporation to bring one plan to fruition?"

"It doesn't matter what—"

"Would you?" Valen barks.

Zeykala glances at her colleagues, who stare at her with keen interest. "I don't answer to you, Valen."

"No, you answer to our shareholders, many of whom are in this room. Yes or no? Would you make that sacrifice?"

Valen has her boxed in. There is no correct answer, and Zeykala knows it.

"I would not," she says, thrusting her chin out.

"You would never sacrifice the corporation?"

"No."

Valen taps on his tablet and sends the latest quote for AME stock to the display above their heads. It isn't pretty. The large red number and down arrow sear into the retinas of the executives and patricians in the room. It doesn't have the shock value felt during the attack but is a reminder that they live in volatile times. Boos rain down from the gallery as Valen inches his mouth toward his microphone.

"Boardmember Zeykala…the fact that we're still in this meeting while our stock is down one hundred thirty-one and still plummeting demonstrates that you already are."

CHAPTER SEVENTY-SIX

INTERCORPEX

The "War Room"
ICX New York Exchange
New York City Municipal Corporation

The tension has ratcheted up with each passing minute. Almost thirty of them have passed since the first sensor in the maintenance tunnel near the museum was tripped. Zyree knows that it was Farron and whomever he is traveling with. Why they haven't seen another is what's eating at him.

"Are the other sensors in the Prince Street maintenance functioning?"

"They're reporting as online, Chief Inspector," a guardian on the VidLynk from the RTCC assures him.

"They could be stationary," Constable Dzamko offers.

"Not likely," Zyree says, tracing his finger along the map. "Where is the next sensor in that tunnel located?"

"Lafayette Street, where it meets the pedestrian lowline."

The explanation pops up on Zyree's replacement contacts. Lowlines are modeled and named after a subterranean park built before the collapse. They are pedestrian walkways below street level to shield commuters from inclement weather. Natural light is reflected into them from above, and the vegetation creates a relaxing ambiance. Over two hundred of them were built in the city, mostly connecting major SpeedRail stations, city attractions, and dense commercial areas.

Zyree blinks the information away. There's nothing remarkable about the area between the museum and Lafayette Street. There aren't many building accesses off the maintenance tunnel, and they'd also be monitored.

"Bird's Nest, switch to an overhead view."

A drone feed comes up. That's when Zyree spots something and flicks his finger at a structure.

"Constable, does this drone have ground-penetrating radar?"

"Absolutely. What are you thinking, Chief Inspector?"

"What do you know about this church?" Zyree asks.

"The Basilica of Saint Patrick's Old Cathedral? It's been around since the early nineteenth century. It hosts the occasional wedding but no services. Why? You don't think they're in the basilica, do you?"

"No, but they could be under it. Have the drone scan the grounds around the church. Malkor?"

"Yeah, boss?"

"Find transportation and get the gear loaded. Don't let Lyris see you."

Malkor nods and charges out the door.

"Okay, we're getting some results."

Zyree moves back to where Bird's Nest and Duckballs are seated and watches the two guardians now split-screen on the VidLynk.

"There's something under there, but it was once a cemetery and could be nothing. Feeding the raw data into the computer and routing the drone to circle the area. There's a linear void running from Prince Street to the church."

"I'll be damned," Duckballs says when the extrapolated results stream onto his display. "A tunnel."

"What's underneath that church?"

"Nothing," Dzamko says. "Just a...crypt."

Zyree grins and Dzamko returns it. He turns to one of his guardians.

"Captain, move the men from the park and dispatch additional guardians into an airtight perimeter around that basilica. Seal off at Broadway, Houston, Bowery, and Spring Streets. I want an inner perimeter at Elizabeth and Lafayette. Have aerial ops arrange redundant drone coverage."

A chorus of "yes, sirs" sings out from the room.

"You're creepy, Chief Inspector," Dzamko gushes.

"I won't pat myself on the back until we get confirmation. We'll meet you over there."

"The command truck will position on Mulberry, south of Prince."

"Malkor, you'd better have our ride ready," Zyree says after blinking to open an internal communications channel.

"Three minutes."

"What do you need us to do?" Duckballs asks, disappointed that their action might be coming to an end.

"Keep working with the PSS. I still need an answer about utility usage from Farron's building. Once you get it, correlate it with market activity and see if anything matches up."

"Will do. Good hunting, Chief Inspector."

CHAPTER SEVENTY-SEVEN

UNDERGRADUATE RYKOS

The "Alamo"
Nolita Geographic District
New York City Municipal District

I may have my differences with my father, but nobody deserves this treatment. That's especially true when it's at the hands of someone like Haven. My father being tortured and beaten fills me with an almost irrepressible rage. I want to blow a hole through Haven's head. Unfortunately, none of us will get out of here alive.

"Rykos…wh-what are you doing here?" my father stammers.

I force my thirst for revenge aside. I stare at my beaten and bruised father, who speaks through a battered jaw and stares at me through swollen eyes.

"I came to get you."

He wouldn't have lasted much longer. The fierce determination in his eyes is gone. It's the first thing many people notice about him. The iron will that drove him to put duty ahead of his family is now a casualty of the sustained abuse.

There have been days when I wished this on him. The praise he'd heap on Varella filled me with resentment. His treatment of my mother made me cringe. Seeing him like this, my heart doesn't ache for him – it hurts for her.

"How?" he asks.

"It's a long story." I don't want to have to explain it. Not now.

"Why don't you want to tell it, Ivy? I'm curious how the two of you linked up again."

"It's not important, Haven," Michele argues, inserting herself into the conversation.

"Oh, I disagree. It must have been important to risk landing yourself in this situation. You've worked your whole life to make your plan a reality. Now you're throwing it all away for what? To save this piece of garbage? Why?"

"I made Rykos a promise."

"Then you made a deal with the devil."

"Rykos is not the devil."

"Okay, fine, he's the devil's son," Haven says. "Like always, you're missing the point. You're wrong if you think he's buying into your grand vision. He's going to turn on you."

"You don't know me," I argue.

"I know your father – probably better than you do. I know what he's done in the name of the corporation. The lives he's taken—"

"My father protects the people!" I shout.

Haven lets out a sarcastic laugh, and even Nyvar snickers. "That's right…he's a *guardian*. He protects the system. If you think otherwise, you're more naïve than I thought, Ivy."

"He's performing a job, Haven," Michele says. "He doesn't know any different."

"Exactly! That's exactly my point. The corporation conditioned him to perform a function like some factory robot. When he's no longer of any use, he'll get discarded like the mindless trash he is. That's why your plan will fail, Michele. These people don't know how to live. They never will."

Michele tightens the grip on her weapon. I don't know if it's a reflex, anger, or she intends on using it.

"You're wrong, Haven. The smallest spark can ignite the largest fire."

"If you believe that, you're a fool."

"My father did nothing to deserve this," I shout, pointing to the beaten body slumping in the chair.

"Nothing? Ask your 'protector of the people' what he did to Freya. You remember her, right Michele? The woman you once called a friend. He tortured her in the basement of that building, and then he murdered her in cold blood."

"That's not true!" I protest.

"Ask him yourself, Ivy. Look into his face and ask him what happened to her. He'll tell you the same thing he told me once he opened up. Her life was worthless because she wasn't one of them, so he killed her."

"Father?"

"I protect…employees."

I recoil slightly. The response wasn't what I expected. I saw Freya. She was energetic and lovely. I want to hear a denial that he killed her. Or a justification as to why. Instead, I get defiance and something else….

"You joined…Liberteum?"

"I'm here to rescue you. It was the only way," I say in a soft voice that's sincere but not regretful.

"So…you became…a terrorist?"

"It's more complicated than that. They're not terrorists. They are more than you think they are."

My father fights to lift his head. There's something about the way he's staring at me – a glare like nothing I've seen before. I've seen disappointment and even disgust during our arguments. I've never seen this. It's hatred.

"You," he gasps, barely able to force out the words, "are not my son."

CHAPTER SEVENTY-EIGHT

LIBERTEUM

The "Alamo"
Nolita Geographic District
New York City Municipal District

Michele glances at Rykos. He looks wounded but keeps a stiff upper lip at his father's brutal slight. He mentioned they had a complicated relationship. Suddenly, it feels like it's much worse than that. There is a deep resentment under the surface that finally emerged. As angry as Quarren got with her on occasion, he never disowned her.

Now is not the time for hashing out family relationships. There are too many guns, too much anger, and too little a chance anyone survives this. She will need Rykos's head in the game to have a chance at surviving. She tries to refocus him before Haven can exploit the rift between him and his father.

"What's your plan, Haven? Kill everyone until nobody is left?"

"The people of this world aren't worthy of mercy. They stand by and allow their corporate masters to exploit them. Death is the best thing for them."

"By your logic, they are suffering. That makes death the mercy you claim they don't deserve."

Haven is about to respond when one of his men bursts into the room. He stops when he sees them with guns drawn on each other. Michele has seen him before but can't remember his name. He's just another of Haven's young, impressionable foot soldiers.

"Whoa."

"What is it?" Haven snaps.

"I...I just got a report from Koltayne. The PSS is closing in on the church from every direction."

"What! How many?"

"Dozens, at least."

"You brought them here!" Haven shouts at Michele, tightening his grip on the weapon he has trained on Rykos.

"I did no such thing."

Michele works it out in her head. The sensor in the maintenance tunnel alerted the PSS, but why would anyone have been tracking Farron? If they are, it means their safe house was compromised. That's unlikely. It must be something else.

"Rykos is transmitting. That's how they found us."

"His biojacks were removed."

Michele takes a step toward the primary tunnel leading out of the crypt.

"Where do you think you're going?"

"Haven, if you want to stay here and die, that's your business. We're leaving with the chief guardian."

"The hell you are."

Haven swivels his gun out of Rykos's face and levels it at Teman's head. Everyone tenses up again, taking closer aim and readying for the worst.

"If you pull that trigger, you die right here and now. All that talk of revenge dies with you."

"Haven?" the young kid prods, desperate for instructions.

"Tell Koltayne to give constant updates," Haven says without taking his eyes off Michele. "There's only so many ways they can breach this crypt, and I need to know which one they try."

"What if they sever the line?" he asks.

"Military TA-312 field phones are old technology. The wire that runs through the tunnel. They can't cut or intercept it. Carry out my instructions."

The boy nods and heads out into the main hallway. Haven glances at his henchmen.

"You guys go arm yourselves to the teeth and prepare the defense. If Brother Varyck upstairs can't convince them we're not here, we will have to kill as many of them as we can. Nyvar and I will handle things here. Go."

"You got it."

Haven glares at Michele. "You're not leaving. I'm prepared to die today. You aren't. Not until your precious Archimedes plan is finished. And I can guarantee that your entitled patrician, this punk Ivy, and the chief guardian don't want to die. So, get comfortable. It's about to get real."

CHAPTER
SEVENTY-NINE

INTERCORPEX

Global Network Operations Center
Manhattan Financial District
ICX New York Exchange

Having a technical issue is one thing. Once identified, an army of experts can devise a course of action to deal with it. When you don't understand the problem or where it originates, the result is a feeling of helplessness. That's where Lyris is right now.

He rubs his temples as he stares at the big board from his workstation above the NOC floor. The market is plummeting. It is almost as bad as the day of the Manhattan attacks. They understood the cause of that. This is different. Nothing appears to be wrong except the result.

"Director Lyris?"

"Give me good news, Wyeth."

"We've confirmed a problem," Wyeth says, causing Lyris to perk up. "Patricians aren't making a majority of these big trades."

Lyris scowls. "That's not possible."

"The Help Desk spoke to dozens of them. They did not authenticate to execute these transactions. They sent the logs to prove it."

Lyris closes his eyes as his head pounds. "NetEng, run a diagnostic on all network equipment and circuits."

"Sir, we've already done that three times."

He slams his hand down on the desk. "Then do it a fourth! And then do it a fifth. Keep doing it until you find something."

"Yes, sir," he answers meekly.

A notification pops up on Lyris's display. He expects Raimius, but it's Nevala on her line. A connection is made, and her beautiful face is racked with concern and fear.

"Nevala?"

"Lyris, Raimius is having an aneurysm over here. What's going on?"

"I don't know. We're still trying to determine if there is actually a problem."

"Work fast. There must be one. The IGI is sinking faster than it did a week ago."

"I know, Nevala, I'm watching it."

"Raimius is going to be calling you any minute. He's going to fire you if you don't have answers."

Wyeth hustles across the NOC floor, stopping only to confer with network engineers. He finishes and races up the stairs for the elevated workstations.

"Thanks for the heads-up, Nevala. I have to go."

"This is bad, Lyris. We can't find the problem, but what if we apply filters to the trades? We can sift—"

"There is nothing to filter. These transactions are from authenticated accounts. We can't arbitrarily accept some and deny others. It's market manipulation."

"We can try circuit breakers," he offers. "By pausing trading, we may be able to turn this around."

"Those can only be applied to specific symbols. Everything is down. We have stocks approaching zero," Lyris says, pointing to the displays on the wall.

"Can we halt trading? It's not unprecedented."

Lyris leans back. They have never ceased trading, and he can't order that until every conceivable option has been explored. It's a death sentence for his career.

"It's unprecedented for Intercorpex."

Wyeth looks down and presses his lips together. Another idea pops into his head. "We can have patricians manually place their orders."

Lyris shakes his head. "The high-speed traders will storm the NOC with torches and pitchforks."

"Yeah, but they don't seem to be affected by this. Keating and Covington are among the *gentez-majorez* buying big blocks of shares. Covington may have a majority stake in AME now."

That is interesting. Lyris leans forward. Thanks to Wyeth, the problem is now coming into sharper focus. It's the Intercorpex Trading and Quotation System itself. The second, more meaningful part is that Denali is probably behind this. He warned that Lyris would know what to do when the time came. He may have been wrong about that.

A notification pops up indicating that Raimius is requesting a VidLynk. The director ignores it. There is nothing to be gained from a conversation with him right now.

"What do you want me to do?" Wyeth asks after watching the notification disappear.

"The problem has to be somewhere. Have Development scrub the ITQS code for differentials from the previous version. Search every line for inconsistencies. There has to be one."

"And if there isn't?"

"Then it's the end of Intercorpex."

CHAPTER

EIGHTY

THE PATRICIANS

Keating Family of the Gentez-Majorez Estate
Greenwich Geographic District
Southern Connecticut Municipal Corporation

Abbot enters with a degree of urgency. He often slips in and slips out, light on his feet as if he were emulating a cat. Not this time. He swung the door open brusquely and marched straight up to Denali. This must be important.

"Sir, your terrorists appear to be in trouble."

"How?"

"I am getting word that the PSS and Intercorpex Security surround them."

That gets Denali's attention. "Where?"

"Old St Patrick's Cathedral. It's just south of Houston Street in the Nolita Geographic District in Lower Manhattan. The area has been cordoned off, and the PSS is closing in."

That's not what Denali was expecting to hear. At least it isn't from any place that could be linked to the Keating family. The bad news is that he still has plans for the group. Or, at least, part of it. The more troubling aspect of this is that Farron should be reporting the situation. His silence has gone from being an irritation to something of paramount concern.

"Where the hell is my son, Abbot?"

"Farron has not contacted us."

"Is he with Liberteum?

Abbot shrugs slightly. He's not a man who often uses physical gestures to convey a message. "The exchange manipulation wasn't conducted at that location. He would have no reason to be."

"Abbot, send Lacune up here. Then find my son. Start with the obvious locations. Once you do, send someone over with a tablet and force him to VidLynk me at gunpoint if you must."

"At once, sir."

Abbot departs the study, and Lacune arrives a couple of minutes later. He's slightly out of breath from the sprint up here from the command center.

"Commander, are you monitoring what's happening in lower Manhattan?"

"Yes, sir. The PSS has mobilized a considerable force down there. Here is the intelligence we've been able to gather thus far."

Lacune doesn't bother asking for permission before sharing a map to the main display. The red lines of the cordon are augmented with detailed information on personnel counts and vehicle dispositions. In the center of the square is a dot at the basilica. There is no information on the number of Liberteum terrorists there.

"It's a classic siege operation, much like the techniques they used at the Chinatown urch rave. I would expect them to forgo the non-lethal munitions this time."

"Can we intervene?"

A surprised look flashes across Commander Lacune's face before he suppresses it. "We can, but they have a massive numbers advantage. Our men are highly skilled but are likely to take significant casualties. And then there's the expected fallout."

"You mean having to explain why my army attacked a corporation's public safety and security organization to save terrorists."

Lacune nods. "It would be difficult to justify, and there is no doubt that the PSS or BCS would link them to the Keating family. Our men are distinctive in appearance and capabilities."

"What kind of casualties would we expect?"

"It depends on the circumstances," Lacune says, his eyes shifting up as he runs scenarios in his head. "Expect the outcomes to range from fifty percent with partial success to one hundred percent and mission failure."

Denali frowns. That won't do. He has expended considerable energy and resources training these men to perform specific tasks. He cannot afford to waste them like that, especially without the expectation of success. Liberteum isn't worth it.

"What about an extraction?"

The commander looks up, mentally considering the possibilities. "The odds of success increase slightly, but the costs would still be high and couldn't be done covertly either. Not from there."

"From elsewhere?"

"It would depend on the location. For it to be a consideration, the terrorists would have to exfiltrate the church."

Denali stands and moves to the wet bar to pour himself a drink. "They call it the Alamo."

"My history is a little rusty, but that was a last stand, wasn't it?"

"Not that rusty. It was a watershed moment in U.S. history. Except for one boy who left to beg a general for reinforcements and explain what was happening, every defender was killed."

"Then I find it unlikely that the terrorists would flee. It sounds like a location where they will go down fighting and inflict as many casualties as possible."

It's a reasonable assumption, but Denali doesn't like relying on assumptions.

"What forces do we have in the city?"

"We have seven twelve-man units stationed in safe houses within the municipal borders. We can have more there in just under an hour."

"I don't think this will take that long. Position two teams near the cathedral to monitor the situation. Have the rest ready to move as the situation develops."

"Objective?"

"Exfiltration, if practical. Avoid contact with the PSS and do not inflict any casualties."

Lacune gives him a deadly serious look. "And if that becomes impossible?"

"Come get me. I will make that call."

"Do I have the authority to move teams around the city as I see fit, or should you be consulted?"

Denali is about to take offense to the question until he realizes why it was asked. In attempting to absolve Commander Lacune of responsibility for causing a conflict with one of the world's largest corporations, he subverted his command authority. Now, Lacune is unsure what his duties are.

"You are their commander. I have dictated the rules of engagement but have no intention of micromanaging your command of the army. Use whatever teams you feel are necessary and position them as you see fit to accomplish the mission. If a situation arises that leaves us no choice but confirmation, that is my order to issue and yours to carry out. Understood?"

"Yes, sir."

Commander Lacune leaves smartly and pulls the door closed behind him. Liberteum's location being compromised is an unexpected development. That location should never have been found. There must be something more to it. Denali needs to understand what that is and fast. The clock is ticking.

CHAPTER EIGHTY-ONE

AMERICA, INC.

Shareholder Hall
Corporate Hill Governance District
Washington-Arlington Municipal Corporation

Fiolla tries not to draw attention as she quietly enters the chamber. She couldn't have picked a worse time. The room is dead silent. Tension chokes the air like a suffocating blanket of smoke. She glances at Zeykala, whose face has turned bright red. Whatever just happened is about to set her off.

"How dare you accuse a member of this board of subversion?"

"I'm not accusing you. I'm stating it for the record," Valen thunders. "I want you to answer a question: Why are we still in these proceedings while our stock price is collapsing and Intercorpex is on the precipice of dragging us into a recession?"

Fiolla glides up the center aisle and slides into a seat directly behind Valen. She pauses to catch Zeykala's glare and shudders. Fortunately, it's not meant for her. She's trying to burn a hole into Valen.

"We're getting off track here," she says to Chairman Hammond.

"I agree. Let's move to our next witness on the—"

"Point of order," Valen interjects. "Since I can't get a straight answer, I request that Zeykala be required to testify."

The room erupts in chatter. Most executives don't get to see how corporate politics are conducted at this level. They don't understand the nuances and the constant positioning. Every word must be carefully crafted, and every statement must be made for a tactical or strategic purpose. Valen is the undisputed master at this.

"That's an…unorthodox request."

"From what's happening on Wall Street to the question over who our *prima patrician* is, everything today is unorthodox. My request should be honored. Boardmember Zeykala should be required to speak to the allegations."

"Give us a moment to confer," Hammond says, gathering the board members behind the rostrum.

Valen leans back and turns to Fiolla. "Any news?"

"The exchange claims there isn't a problem when there obviously is one."

He rolls his eyes and shakes his head. "Any thoughts on this being the work of Liberteum?"

"Not by Intercorpex. I don't know what the BCS or PSS are saying."

"Okay."

"You look concerned, sir."

That's an understatement. Fiolla thought he was more in control of these events than it appeared. If that was once true, it no longer is.

"I've given Hammond two solid opportunities to end this madness. He's passed on both of them. Nobody would blame him for adjourning, considering what's going on. Something's wrong."

"Is he trying to look impartial?"

"Maybe," Valen says, turning back to watch his friend. "If that's the case, he's doing a bang-up job of it."

Hammond is an ally. There really should be no cause for concern. He provided information before he should have and met with Valen in the Oval Office to strategize. There could be a logical explanation for not wanting to end this hearing, but Fiolla doesn't see it. There is no love lost between the chairman and Zeykala, so he can't be on her side.

Valen turns back as the confab breaks up and the board members take their seats. Feeling helpless, Fiolla pulls out her tablet and types a quick e-note to Farron.

I need your help.

Hammond clears his throat before leaning in to his microphone. Valen already knows what he's going to say. His response to the verdict will mean everything in this hearing.

"The board has decided that it would be improper to have a member testify. It sets a dangerous precedent and could result in an undue burden on future requests."

"Isn't this hearing setting a dangerous precedent, Chairman Hammond?" Valen argues.

"You're out of order, Chief Executive."

"We're already playing fast and loose with the rules of decorum here, sir. The testimony from the CEO of New York City and the director of the Bureau of Corporate Security was not subjected to cross-examination."

"You are not entitled to cross-examine," Zeykala interjects. "This is not a courtroom."

"Isn't it? Am I not on trial for the actions against Liberteum? If this is simply a hearing, why does everyone in this chamber know what motion will be made?"

If there is one universal truth in the world, it's that people hate having their hidden agendas exposed. Hammond nervously looks at the board members, who return awkward glances.

"With your permission, I would like the floor to speak in my defense," Valen says, leaning back and awaiting an answer to the challenge. Hammond would be crazy to deny that request.

"Granted. You have the floor."

"Point of order," Zeykala says. "This hearing—"

"Denied. Please proceed, Chief Executive Valen."

He stands, breaking another rule of decorum. He needs everyone to see him and listen intently. A masterful oration can change hearts and minds by appealing to emotion, and he's drafting this one in his head.

"It's ironic that we're in this place. It was once home to the Senate, one-half of the legislative body of the United States government. At the height of its military, economic, and political influence, that nation was the world's premier superpower.

"Historians have studied their collapse for generations. Scholars argue that the people were entitled, privileged, and complacent. The people lost the American spirit that inspired the first two hundred and fifty years of its existence. They wax eloquent about how its citizens forgot what it meant to work hard and sacrifice.

"All of that is true, but the true root of their demise was accountability. Whatever happened to holding people responsible for their actions? Blinded by ideology, Americans stopped holding their leaders accountable. Politicians paraded endless scandals past the public to denigrate opponents instead of seeking justice. The courts became instruments of the political morass they were created to hold in check.

"After a nation that once fancied itself a 'shining city upon a hill' collapsed, corporatism corrected its many deficiencies. Citizens long ignored by their governments became employees with a vested interest in success. We became united in purpose because our successes and failures were shared. We were accountable to each other, from the chief executive to the janitor who mops the floors.

"I believe in this system with every shred of my being. Above all, I firmly support holding executives and employees accountable for their actions. When a CEO is failing this great corporation, that individual *should* be called in front of the board to answer for it. Only that's not what this is."

Valen surveys the faces around the room. Executives in the gallery and the patricians behind him are riveted. He has their undivided attention. Now to drive the point home.

"What we are seeing here today is a cleverly camouflaged coup d'état. This is not about accountability – it's about power. Corrupted board members have placed devotion to themselves and their agendas above the needs of our shareholders, employees, and prosperity as a corporation.

"What happens here today will have a lasting impact on this corporation. New generations of employees will regard corporate power with suspicion and ambivalence, just as they did with the leaders before the Great Collapse."

Valen pauses, letting his words soak in. He expects Zeykala to interrupt his monologue, especially considering the damage it's doing. She doesn't. The board sees the same thing he does – a room full of executives and elites who understand and agree.

"I assumed this position with the singular goal of maintaining America Incorporated's tradition of excellence. We have experienced our share of setbacks, the problems with Liberteum included. However, no reasonable person can argue with the overall results. It has been my honor to serve through the good times and the bad. Our founders set us on the path of success, but we are entrusted to continue walking it. This magnificent corporation lives and thrives because of our actions. It can also die through them.

"So, let's stop calling witnesses armed with their personal political agendas. If you believe the failure to apprehend Liberteum given the limited time is my failing the corporation, then remove me. If you realize that the role of the chief executive is much bigger, and have confidence that we will eliminate this threat, then your decision is clear."

Applause starts from the gallery and ripples to the patricians seated behind him. It grows in intensity until it becomes thunderous. Hammond refrains from smacking his gavel on its block and lets it continue. Board members gawk and shrug at each other. When the ruckus shows no sign of dissipating, Hammond finally attempts to restore order. It takes another forty-five seconds for the silence to return.

"I think we have heard enough. We are faced with deciding whether to allow Chief Executive Valen to continue his duties or remove him from his position. We will decide that now," Hammond says. "Would somebody like to make a motion?"

CHAPTER EIGHTY-TWO

INTERCORPEX

Near Old St. Patrick's Cathedral
Nolita Geographic District
New York City Municipal Corporation

Malkor stops when they reach the command truck in the Nolita district. The neighborhood earned its name for being north of the old Little Italy section of the city when there was such a thing. Like most districts, it kept its pre-collapse name for continuity reasons. The corporation changed the names of most landmarks but didn't bother with regions or city neighborhoods. Zyree has no idea why. This whole area has been reconstructed and is probably home to mid-level managers of subsidiary corporations. It's nice but lacks the prestige of other parts of the island.

Zyree can see part of the basilica from this spot. Unlike the cathedral in Midtown that it shares a name with, this structure is considerably smaller. Constable Dzamko pulls up with a team of guardians, and the men shake hands. Malkor sets about unpacking the gear as Zyree joins the constable in the back of the command truck.

"Report."

"Sir, we've established a perimeter around the basilica and are quietly beginning evacuation of the buildings within those confines. Assault teams are posted in the maintenance tunnel, and teams are searching the subfloors of surrounding structures."

"What about the basilica?"

"No noticeable activity."

Dzamko turns to Zyree. "I hope your magic contacts have told you something we don't know."

"Nope, this is a gut feeling."

"That doesn't inspire confidence, Chief Inspector. There will be hell to pay if we're wrong about this."

"I know the stakes. It's the best lead we have, so let's verify it."

Zyree exits the truck and hustles down the metal stairs. He looks around the area. Lower Manhattan has thousands of tunnels, sewers, and old structures. It is a good place for urches to hide.

"What are you thinking?" Dzamko asks.

"We should go knock on the door and see who answers."

"You want to announce that we're here? That's nuts!"

"If they're in there, they already know. If we're wrong, we can take a moment to atone for our sins."

Dzamko shakes his head and lets out a laugh. "You're my kind of crazy, Zyree. After you."

They walk up the sidewalk on Mulberry, past Prince Street. Along with its grounds, Old Saint Patrick's occupies almost two-thirds of the next block. Zyree bounds up the stairs and stops at the heavy oak doors. He knocks as loudly as he can and waits, scoping out the front of the building.

"You know, if Liberteum is in there, we probably won't live much longer."

"At least everyone will know they're here."

The door swings open, and a young priest answers. "Can I help you?"

"We'd like to come in and look around if that's okay," Dzamko states, giving the man a once-over to see if anything is off.

"Of course. God's house is open to all. Please," he says, gesturing them in.

It's a beautiful sanctuary featuring ornate, cream-colored stone and high arches. The basilica is almost too majestic to be a terrorist haven. Long wood pews face the altar in even rows, with a wide center aisle separating them. It's all illuminated by light pouring in from large windows on either side of the church.

Zyree strolls over to the ornate wood carvings below the enormous stained glass window. He casually scans the stone floor, and nothing seems out of place. There is no sign of any entrance to the crypts below.

"Is there something wrong?" the priest asks.

"We had a report of criminal activity in the area. There's nothing to be concerned about, Father," Dzamko says.

"It's 'brother,' actually. I'm only training for the priesthood. I have yet to be canonized."

"Of course. We're sorry to disturb you, Brother. We'll be on our way."

The two men walk toward the door as Zyree counts down from three silently in his head. When he reaches zero, he spins on his heels, draws his weapon, and drops to a knee. The sudden move catches the "brother" off guard. He panics and reaches for something in his pocket. Zyree recognizes the butt of a pistol before his contacts tell him. Zyree levels his sights and squeezes the trigger three times, putting a tight shot group right in the middle of the man's chest. He falls backward onto the marble floor, his weapon bouncing out of his hand when he hits it. Dzamko rushes over as blood oozes from his mouth, and he stares at them with dying eyes.

"Command, tango down."

The sanctuary floods with guardians a moment later, weapons drawn. He turns to the team leader.

"Search for any access to the crypt below."

"Yes, sir."

Dzamko touches Zyree's shoulder as he stares at the corpse. "How did you know?"

"Magic contacts," Zyree says, pointing at his eyes. "Random information displays on them all the time. Some of it's useful. Priests in training are called seminarians, not brothers. And you are ordained into the priesthood. Canonization is reserved for saints."

"I think you should be canonized after this."

The constable searches the man's body. There is nothing in his pockets other than spare magazines for his weapon. He pulls back a sleeve and sees the familiar torch of Liberteum tattooed on his forearm. Dzamko retrieves the man's weapon and studies it.

"3D printed."

Zyree nods. "He was a sentry. They know we're here now."

"Sir, there is no entrance to the crypt below from here," the lieutenant says.

"Clear everyone out."

"Tunnels are the only way in or out. Makes sense. We need to access one to get down there," Zyree says as they walk up the center aisle toward the exit.

"No way. We're not running the same gantlet Teman did a week ago."

"You have a better idea?"

"Actually, I do. We borrowed some neat gadgets from our BCS rivals. Let's go play with them."

CHAPTER EIGHTY-THREE

LIBERTEUM

The "Alamo"
The Nolita Geographic District
New York City Municipal Corporation

There is one truth to playing chicken: Someone needs to flinch. It's the only possible outcome. Nobody can hold the status quo for eternity. Michele edges toward the chief guardian, intent on helping him out of his chair.

"We're not staying, Haven. You can fight this battle on your own."

"You're not in a position to make demands."

Michele stares at him. This has become a circular argument.

"Rykos…you fight…with them," Teman mumbles, breaking the tense silence.

"I'm not here to fight anybody, Father," Rykos explains. "I made a promise to Mother. I'm trying to make good on it."

"I…don't care. Traitor."

"Go ahead and hit him, Ivy. That's what I did when he got mouthy," Haven says, enjoying the moment.

Someone flinches.

"You bastard!"

Rykos charges at Haven, but he's ready for it. Instead of shooting him, he brings his gun down on Rykos's head. The expert blow leaves him dazed and turns his legs to jelly. He drops straight to the ground. Haven trains the weapon back on Michele as he goes to kick Rykos. She takes advantage of the distraction to shift positions as Farron covers Nyvar. When Haven glances up, he's staring down the barrel of her weapon.

"Unh-unh," she admonishes. "Drop. Your. Weapon."

"I don't think so. We're all friends here. Except maybe for Rykos and his father. They seem to hate each other."

Rykos stands and rubs his head. He reaches for Haven's gun but is too slow. He yanks it away and shakes his head.

"Trai…traitor. Traitor," Teman keeps mumbling, sounding like he's taken leave of his senses.

Michele glances over at Farron, who gives her a hesitant look. This wasn't how any of them imagined this going down. She is searching for a way out of this that doesn't cost them their lives. It's a stalemate, and the PSS is closing in to kill them all.

"I think your father might kill you if I gave him this gun, Ivy. Do you want me to put him out of his misery before he tries?"

"My name isn't Ivy. It's Rykos."

"Who cares? We're all going to die together."

"Haven! They're moving something up against the western wall," a soldier bursts into the room and shouts.

"What? A truck?"

"No, something smaller."

"At least we know how they're planning on breaching. Go get ready."

The man scampers into the main corridor. Haven glances over at Nyvar, who reads his eyes. The breach will happen soon. This isn't a fight Haven wants to pass up.

"It's decision time, Michele. Either we shoot each other, or we fight what's coming together. What's it going to be?"

"You'll put a bullet in my back the first chance you get," she says.

"I wouldn't trust me either, but what choice do you have? We're surrounded. There's only one way left out of the Alamo, and you'll have to get through my men to use it. You have no options."

Haven will shoot all of them the first chance he gets. He doesn't need them to defend the Alamo – he needs human shields. He's counting on the PSS not wanting to kill their leader. If you're damned if you do and damned if you don't, then do. She tightens the grip on her weapon and moves her finger to the trigger.

CHAPTER EIGHTY-FOUR

INTERCORPEX

Near Old St. Patrick's Cathedral
Nolita Geographic District
New York City Municipal Corporation

Zyree's mouth hangs open as he watches a guardian work the wireless control panel. It's not because he's in awe of the sheer power of Dzamko's "neat gadget." It's because he has never seen something more underwhelming. Children's toys are more intimidating than that thing.

"A miniature robot? Seriously?"

"What's wrong with it?" Dzamko asks.

"Nothing, but I expected something a little more…you know, impressive."

"Like what?"

"A vehicle-mounted rail gun, maybe? What are you going to do with that little thing?"

"Zyree, my grandmother used to say that good things sometimes come in small packages. You'll see."

"You could have told me you were conducting an operation!" an annoying female voice screeches. Bad things sometimes come in them, too.

"You were busy," Zyree tells the spawn of Satan, who materialized from the depths of hell directly behind them.

Chiana is dressed in her own fitted red and black body armor that matches their newly donned equipment. Instead of a rifle, she has two holstered handguns. He's surprised the "ninja" doesn't have some Japanese kanji or a pair of katanas to complete the image. It doesn't matter if she's Chinese.

"Not for this. You need backup."

"He has backup," Malkor says, not pleased that she's here.

"You're running a separate investigation, Chiana. This doesn't involve you."

"You just didn't want me here," she argues.

Zyree smiles. "That too."

"Who's the cartoon character?" Dzamko asks in a whisper still loud enough for her to hear. Zyree almost laughs.

"Chief Inspector Chiana, Intercorpex Security. Who the hell are you?"

"Constable Dzamko, the acting chief guardian of the New York City Municipal Corporation," he responds coolly, turning to Zyree. "I don't like her. Do you want me to get rid of her?"

"More than anything," Zyree says, knowing that there will be hell to pay back in Zurich if he does. "But let her stay."

"We're ready, Constable," the guardian with the controls reports.

"Watch this," he says with a grin. "Okay. Blow it."

The guardian taps his tablet, and several seconds pass. Then the robot explodes. The force of the blast directed at the brick wall is orders of magnitude larger than the robot itself. The foundation evaporates into pulverized red dust. When the cloud settles, a six-foot hole has been ripped into the crypt.

"Okay, that was impressive."

"Send it in."

Dzamko gestures them into the command vehicle. A guardian pilots a drone through the hole and is greeted with muzzle flashes from the end of the hallway and the side rooms.

"Liberteum confirmed."

"Ya think? Find Teman. He must be in one of these crypts."

Zyree stares at the display and points. "He's probably in one towards the back where the fire is coming from."

The guardian starts wrestling with the joystick. His movements are becoming more urgent.

"Come on…come on… Damn! I'm taking too much damage, sir. The drone's attitude controls are failing."

"Prepare to breach!" Dzamko commands. "Will a splash compromise the building's structural integrity?"

"No, sir. It's armed with AP."

"Then you know what to do, Lieutenant. Get it done before they use Teman as a human shield."

Zyree grabs Malkor by the arm as he starts to follow the constable out of the truck. "You're not going to like this, but you have to hang back here."

Malkor's brow crinkles, and his jaw tightens. "Why?"

"You need to represent Intercorpex if something goes bad in there."

He shakes his head. "I'm not letting you go in there without backup."

"I have backup," Zyree says, sounding unconvincing.

"You need someone who doesn't want to see you dead."

Zyree forces a smile. His partner has a point. He can't count on Chiana to have his back. He trusts Dzamko and his guardians, though. That should be enough if he sticks close to them.

"I'll take my chances. I'll make it up to you later."

"You're the boss," Malkor says, unhappy but professional enough not to protest further.

Zyree claps him on the shoulder and joins Dzamko and Chiana outside. The guardians are maneuvering a tracked vehicle mounted with a steel shield toward the hole in the foundation. This guy doesn't do anything halfway and isn't taking any chances with his men's lives. He would like to think that the drone will get them all. He knows better.

CHAPTER EIGHTY-FIVE

THE PATRICIANS

The "Alamo"
The Nolita Geographic District
New York City Municipal Corporation

Everything is different than it was fifteen seconds ago. Explosions have that effect. The air is choked with dust as thick as beef stew. The deafening noise rattled their eardrums, and the concussive blast knocked everyone to the ground. Liberteum is no longer pointing guns at each other. They have a new enemy in their midst.

Farron rolls onto his side as weapons open up in the corridor. First one, then several. Their staccatos hurt his ringing ears. He begins climbing to his feet before losing balance and dropping to a knee. He shakes his head to clear the cobwebs.

"What are they shooting at?" Michele shouts, already standing and covering the door.

Haven crawls over and lies in the doorway. He rocks forward on his hands and the balls of his feet and peeks into the corridor.

"They breached the foundation wall! It's a surveillance drone."

Farron stares at Teman. He's the only person in the room who understands the tactic. He was knocked off his chair in the breaching blast and moved his arms to cover his head. Michele notices his reaction and dives away from the door, dragging Farron to the ground with her.

The world erupts in flames, flechettes, and a thunderous noise amplified in the confined space of the crypt. The brick wall between them and the corridor takes the brunt of the explosion. Haven's men firing at the drone from the end of the hall weren't so lucky.

Teman is the first to recover and crawl over to one of Haven's men, who was blown into the room. The chief guardian retrieves the man's handgun from its holster. Rykos watches in horror as he forces himself up to his knees and points his gun at him.

"Father? Father, it's me!"

"Rykos?"

"Yes. Let's get you out of here."

Rykos climbs to his feet and takes two steps toward his father.

"Traitor!"

Teman fires at almost point-blank range. Rykos doubles over, clutching his abdomen. He stares back at his father through wounded eyes. Haven was right after all. That thought shakes the patrician to his core.

Farron has always been indifferent toward others. He's a member of the elite and was raised by his father to believe that the world is there to serve them; that the only priority is the family and its wealth. That's changing. He feels invested now – in Michele and even now in Rykos. Nobody understands complicated relationships with a father more than he does.

The chief guardian lifts the weapon again. Farron feels emotion course through him as his adrenaline surges. He has always been a wallflower. He has always stood off to the side while others do the heavy lifting. No longer.

Farron's feet move faster than his mind. They move quickly toward the door. He smacks Teman hard across his head with the butt of his weapon before he can fire a second shot. The chief guardian collapses and curls into a fetal position as gunfire erupts from all around the crypt. Rykos has been spared, if only for a couple more minutes.

"Aw, hell. My father…shot me," Rykos says as Michele applies a dressing to the wound and places her hand over it.

"That was predictable," Haven taunts. "I should put you out of your misery."

He's raising his weapon when a soldier bursts into the room.

"They're coming! They have some sort of mobile shield wall! We won't be able to stop them."

"I'd say it's your lucky day, Ivy, but you're finished. Fight or die, Michele. If you flee, it will be the last thing you do. Death awaits you at the end of the tunnel. Be a leader, for once. Defend this place."

Nyvar tosses a rifle to Haven, and they man the door, alternating positions to fire salvos down the corridor. Rykos is in agony. Farron rushes over and squats next to Michele. He shakes his head when he sees the kid's midsection colored crimson with blood.

CHAPTER EIGHTY-SIX

UNDERGRADUATE RYKOS

The "Alamo"
The Nolita Geographic District
New York City Municipal Corporation

Michele grabs at my clothing, and Farron helps pull me to my feet. The pain is overwhelming. I can't walk. All I want to do is lie down and sleep. My legs buckle. I try to collapse to the ground. Despite being two sizes smaller than me, her iron grip around my waist keeps me upright.

"If we move him, he could die," Farron says.

"If we stay here, he definitely will. It's our only chance," Michele says, sliding my arm over her shoulders.

"Haven has someone waiting for us at the end of this tunnel."

"I know. We'll deal with it when we reach him. Let's go."

Every step is agonizing. Michele and Farron hurry me through a dark tunnel leading away from the crypt. The clatter of gunfire becomes distant echoes. I'm not sure if that's because of the distance or my head getting fuzzier from the blood loss.

The light at the end of the tunnel is real and not a celestial metaphor. We reach a small set of stairs that leads up to whatever is above. It takes every ounce of my strength to place one foot in front of the other, and I grit my teeth as we make the ascent. Then Michele and Farron stop cold.

"Don't move!" a kid who doesn't look much older than me shouts, menacing us with a rifle.

"Easy, Koltayne," Michele says calmly and evenly. "It's me."

"Michele?" he says with genuine surprise. "Haven instructed me to kill you on sight. I don't want to do that."

"I'm sure he did. He had the opportunity to do it himself back there. He didn't. I don't want to fight you, but I will if you don't help us."

"What's happening?" he asks, contemplating his options as the popping of gunfire resonates from the tunnel.

"Guardians breached the Alamo. Haven and the others are making a stand, but Rykos is hit. We're leaving with him. You should come with us. The Alamo is lost."

He stares at us, his mind busy pondering the decision. I know how it feels to be stuck with competing loyalties…it's a tough position to be in. Everyone's life boils down to a series of critical decisions. This is one of his.

"I'll get the first aid kit," Koltayne says, slinging his rifle over his shoulder and retreating to another room.

"Where are we?" Farron asks.

"It's a church building just to the north. It serves as an office," Michele says, helping Farron lay me on the ground. "We're lucky the PSS didn't secure it."

"Move your hands, Rykos."

I comply, and she exposes the wound. I don't have to see it to know it's gushing. I feel the warm, viscous liquid pouring out of my abdomen and onto my clothing.

"He's losing a lot of blood," Farron observes.

I stare at the joists above my head. My vision is starting to go. Everything is foggy. Wherever they are taking me, I won't make it. I just want to lie here and be still.

"Leave me. I'm only slowing you down."

"Shut up, Rykos," Michele says.

"If the bullet hit his stomach, he's going to go septic long before—"

"No! I didn't risk my life to let him die now. We'll find a way to save him."

I'm drifting. The pain numbs as I fight the need to sleep. So weak…

"The PSS will have this whole area sealed off. We'll never get out of here with him."

Michele prepares a modern bandage. She inserts it into my wound, causing me to wince in pain. When she pulls a string, it expands and plugs the hole but doesn't completely stop the bleeding. She pulls another out of the aid box and tucks it into her pocket.

"Help me lift him. Koltayne? Is this place still rigged to blow?"

I'm lifted to my feet, and my arms are draped over their shoulders.

"Yeah, to cover an escape."

"Good. Set the timer for five minutes."

"Five minutes? We'd better move fast. This thing will be seen from space when it blows."

"It's…not long…enough. Just leave…me," I say.

Michele pivots, leaving me to rest my weight on Farron. She grabs my chin and holds my face up as she looks into my eyes. Then she kisses me. Like before, it is magical. This time she doesn't hit me afterward.

"Don't you dare give up on me. Do you understand?"

I nod. Did that just happen, or did I imagine it? I can't tell the difference anymore as I feel myself moving beneath me. My breathing is getting quicker and shallower. Is this what death feels like? I need to try to hold on.

CHAPTER
EIGHTY-SEVEN

INTERCORPEX

The "Alamo"
The Nolita Geographic District
New York City Municipal Corporation

A throng of men falls in behind the tracked robot with the massive black titanium shield. Chiana and Zyree let the guardians take the lead to fire their rifles through a pair of ports. A guardian near the rear of the tracks uses a joystick to navigate the rolling metal wall over the debris on the street. He jolts forward down the sharp incline that leads into the underground burial space. The corridor runs the length of the church. The shield fills the space with only inches to spare on each side.

"Constable, permission to launch gas," a lieutenant shouts over the blasts of gunfire.

"No, Teman will choke to death before we can reach him. Use concussion grenades."

The men pull their weapons out of the firing ports, and two different guardians fire concussion grenades through them. The sound is deafening even through their ear defenders. The fire from the crypt ceases, but only for a few seconds. Then more bullets bounce off the shield.

"They're firing from a room on the right and the far back room on the left," a guardian reports, staring at his camera feed.

"Lights!"

Two intense beams of light illuminate the darkened, dust-choked hallway. The response is immediate. The first volley from the terrorists takes out the light on the right side.

"I'm hit!" a guardian behind them shouts as he collapses to the ground.

Zyree looks up to see the stone roof getting pock-marked. Ricochets. The clever bastards are exploiting the two-foot gap between the shield and the ceiling by bouncing rounds into them.

"Stay low and close to the shield!" the chief inspector shouts.

"Move forward," Dzamko commands.

The tank shield lurches deeper into the crypt. Seeing their predicament, the terrorists fire with more urgency. Men peel off and clear other crypt chambers as they pass them. So far, nothing.

"Tango to the right!"

Zyree stacks in tactical formation against the wall with Chiana and another guardian. Three concussion grenades are launched into the room, and the shield robot lurches forward, exposing the entrance enough for them to squeeze through. Rounds strike the wall next to the doorway as they rush in, staying low to avoid the fire. Zyree's visor identifies the muzzle flash, and he engages the target, silencing the weapon and ending the life of the man wielding it.

He turns just as Chiana lowers her weapon in his direction and fires. His armor absorbs the hits, and he sprawls across the floor. Zyree's training kicks in, and he rolls behind the stone slab that dominates the middle of the crypt. He snatches his handgun from his hip holster and trains it on the avenue of attack. Chiana makes the mistake of being predictable. In her haste to finish him, she emerges around the corner. He pumps two rounds into her armor. The impacts knock her off balance. Caught by surprise, she retreats towards the corridor.

She stops, crouches, and spins in one fluid motion. Her weapon barks three times, forcing Zyree to roll back behind the slab. The guardian who entered the room with them decides to act. He sneaks up behind her and buttstrokes her to the head with his rifle. Chiana crashes to the ground. Zyree scurries over on all fours and jumps on her back.

"What the hell was that all about?" the guardian asks.

Zyree slaps on a set of electromagcuffs and confirms that she's unconscious. "I don't know. Leave her here. We'll deal with whatever this was later. We have bigger problems right now."

"Bomb!"

The urgency in the voice out is unmistakable. Zyree grabs the guardian, and they dive over the stone slab and crash to the ground on the other side. The blast shakes the building. Zyree looks up, wondering if the foundation will continue to hold the structure above them. When the sound dissipates, an eerie silence replaces it.

"You okay?"

"Yeah. I think so."

They rush past Chiana to find guardians sprawled along the ground next to the battered shield. The mini tank took the brunt of the explosion but paid the price. Both tracks are mangled. This thing is dead.

"Constable, are you okay?" Zyree asks, helping him sit up.

"I'm getting too damned old for this."

Dzamko surveys the damage to the shield tank. He scowls and pulls the two steel pins on the support braces. Showing remarkable agility, he brings his leg back and kicks the shield over.

Zyree raises his rifle, expecting a fusillade from the terrorists. Nothing happens. They creep closer to the back wall. A couple of guardians take position behind them. When they reach the last room, he nods, and they burst in.

Except for three bodies on the floor, the crypt is empty. Two are dead terrorists. The third is wearing a guardian uniform drenched in blood.

"Dzamko! Over here!" Zyree shouts, hoping they aren't too late.

He rolls Teman over, expecting the worst. His face is battered and barely recognizable. Dzamko takes a knee as his men provide security.

"Teman, can you hear me?" he asks.

He checks for a pulse and stares at Zyree with troubled eyes.

CHAPTER
EIGHTY-EIGHT

AMERICA, INC.

Shareholder Hall
Corporate Hill Governance District
Washington-Arlington Municipal Corporation

Silence grips the room. Some board members stare straight at Valen. Others set their sights on Hammond. A few look at each other. Long, agonizing seconds pass. Nearly sixty of them. They are all waiting for the one board member who matters to speak.

Zeykala clears her throat, shattering the stillness of the room. "I move that Chief Executive Valen be immediately removed from his duties and a temporary caretaker be appointed until a permanent chief executive is named."

"There is a motion on the floor," Hammond croaks amid a wave of grumbling. "Do we have a second?"

There is another tense silence. Zeykala sits back and waits. Finally, she stares at one of her peers.

"I second Boardmember Zeykala's motion."

"We have a motion, and it has been seconded," Hammond says. "We will perform this vote by show of hands. Recorder, please note the results for the corporate record. All in favor of the motion, please raise your hands."

They go up, some faster than others. Everyone in the room does a silent count. Fifteen.

"Opposed?"

Another fifteen raise their hands.

"Will the recorder please read the result?" Hammond asks.

"In the question of the motion to remove Valen as chief executive officer and name a temporary replacement, the result is fifteen votes in favor and fifteen against. Chairman Hammond, when a tie exists, you are obliged to vote on board matters to break it."

Hammond hangs his head. A tie is the last thing he wanted. The chairman is rarely called upon to vote. It's doubtful that even he can remember the last time there was a tie in this chamber.

"This is a tough decision. It's not as straightforward as either Boardmember Zeykala or Chief Executive Valen has led us to believe. We should not be using the failure to capture Liberteum as the sole reason for removal. It would also be disingenuous to ignore that reality simply because of past successes.

"What concerns me is what these failures mean. We have heard testimony from Chief Executive Safmor and Director of Corporate Security Virtari. They have lost confidence in Valen's leadership. To be effective, the chief executive must have the support of employees, executives, and this board. It's clear to me, Valen, that you no longer have the support necessary to lead this corporation."

Hammond turns his head towards a smug Zeykala. He returns his eyes to Valen before delivering his decision. There is no anger or joy in them. They are devoid of all emotion except one: regret.

"As a result, I vote in favor of the motion."

The blood drains out of Valen's face. Politics has always been a dirty business, and corporate politics is no different. He was blindsided. Not in a hundred years would he have expected Hammond to stab him in the back.

"Chief Executive Valen, you are hereby relieved of all executive leadership responsibilities. Human Resources will be directed to designate your new title as Chief Executive-Retired. You will be permitted to retain your residence in the White House until the transfer arrangements of personal effects can be determined. Access to confidential corporate briefings and restricted areas, including the West Wing and Situation Room, is revoked."

"Chairman Hammond, I move that Boardmember Zeykala be named Chief Executive Pro Tempore of America Incorporated," one of her allies on the board motions.

"Seconded."

"All in favor?" A majority of the hands goes up.

"Opposed?" Only a few hands dart up. "Abstain? Would the recorder announce the result of the vote?"

She recounts the question and the results: twenty-three to three with four abstentions. The motion carries, and Valen's worst nightmare has become a reality. He lost his position to the woman in the world who deserves it least.

"Congratulations, Chief Executive Pro Tempore Zeykala," Hammond announces, getting polite applause from the board. The response in the room is something completely different.

A cacophony of jeering and boos quickly drowns out a smattering of cheers. The contempt for the decision grows more vitriolic. The reaction of the patricians is less riotous, although they look upset at the railroading. Hammond smashes his gavel, but the clacking sound of wood on wood is lost in the clamor.

"With no other business, this hearing is adjourned," he shouts, unheard by everyone except those closest to him.

Valen continues to sit erect in his seat. He's not ballyhooing about the miscarriage of justice. He only glares at Zeykala, who returns his stare with a devilish one of her own.

The rancor swells, and so does the hostility. Those who support the decision are in the minority. They recognize that and begin to find the exit as the threats become more vicious. Insults and accusations that this hearing was a farce are hurled at Hammond and the board members.

Valen stands and straightens his tunic. He surveys the angry faces in the gallery above. Without a word or gesture, he turns to face Fiolla and nods in a silent show of gratitude. She's wounded and angry. Every ounce of that emotion is worn on her face.

The pot boils over. Fiolla sees pushing and shoving erupt in the gallery above. Seconds later, the first punches are thrown. She can't tell who struck first, but it doesn't matter: The result is the same. The riot spreads when a tablet computer is hurled at the rostrum. It's the first drop of the coming deluge.

Valen walks back up the aisle towards the doors in the rear with a quiet demeanor that keeps him above the fray. Board members begin to take cover behind the counter as objects rain down on them. Uniformed BCS agents usher them out of the room. Fiolla decides to flee the melee before she gets caught up in it.

No sooner does she reach the exit than she's grabbed and slammed against the far wall. A hand clasps over her mouth. Fiolla stares wide-eyed into the hateful eyes of Director Virtari.

"We have unfinished business. Do you think crossing me was a good idea now? There's nobody left to protect you."

Fiolla crashes her fists on his arms. His grip on her only gets tighter. With a hand still clasped over her mouth, he grabs her throat with the other. His grip is like a vise. She gasps as his hand cuts off the oxygen to her mouth and blood to her brain. She can feel herself getting woozy.

"Understand something, Fiolla. You're next. It may not be tomorrow or next week, but I promise you, Zeykala will sign your termination papers. Then I'm going to put a bullet in your head myself."

The fight in the gallery spills into the hallway. People emerge bleeding from open head wounds. Others are venting their frustrations on the building itself. Men and women expected to work together are brawling as corporate security agents struggle to restore order.

Virtari releases her with a shove against the wall. Dazed and gasping for air, Fiolla slides down it and collapses into a ball on the floor. With everything that's happened and her life in jeopardy, all she can do is cry.

CHAPTER EIGHTY-NINE

INTERCORPEX

The "Alamo"
The Nolita Geographic District
New York City Municipal Corporation

Zyree doesn't like relying on his biocomp. It's a tool that many of his peers rely upon too heavily. Technology is an asset until it results in an erosion of skills. That's a forgotten lesson from the Great Collapse. The first to die were those who couldn't survive in life without electronic or mechanical assistance.

In this case, the computer detects Teman's breathing before Dzamko can break the news. Given his condition, the chief guardian probably wishes he were dead.

"He's alive. Barely. I'm Constable Dzamko. You're safe now, Teman. We're going to get you out of here."

"Constable, we've got gophers," one of the guardians says. "This tunnel heads north."

"Command, we found a tunnel north through the graveyard." He pauses to listen. "I don't care what the drone's ground-penetrating radar hasn't found. I'm staring right at it. They used the explosion to cover their retreat. Double the perimeter at Houston Street and start a search of every building. Yes, every last one!"

"Rykos," Teman says, managing only a whisper. "Rykos…"

"He's not here," Dzamko assures him.

"No…my son…I killed…I killed him."

"They took him, Teman. He's not dead. We'll get him back."

"No…I shot…dead."

"He's going into shock," Zyree says. "We need to evacuate him."

"I need medical services in here now!" Dzamko shouts, the urgency in his voice apparent.

"My son…."

Teman starts to sob, but no tears form. Zyree just stares at him. It could be shock. It could be something else. Faint gunfire sounds from outside the crypt. Dzamko looks at him before his comms channel comes to life.

"They're firing from the rectory! Heavy weapons…they're shooting at everyone! We're taking fire at the command vehicle!"

Zyree darts down the battered hallway and climbs over the mangled shield tank. Dzamko is right behind him as they charge up the incline to the street, ready to fire. The terrorists are fleeing the rectory, engaging guardians to the north at the intersection of Houston Street. They move and fire in short, effective bursts. They aren't spraying and praying like amateurs. Aimed shots are finding their marks. A moment later, they disappear down a cross street.

"Tangos are heading west on Jersey. I want a hard perimeter set up at Houston and in front of that shopping center on Crosby Street."

"Our hammer to their anvil?"

"That's the plan. We need to pin them down before they make it underground."

Zyree nods and the two men are running up the street when a brilliant flash precedes a shockwave that knocks them off their feet. Zyree ends up face-down on the asphalt as another blast rolls over him. It diminishes to a grumble as he gets blanketed by debris. When the air clears enough to see, he finds the small rectory reduced to a smoking hulk.

"You okay?" Zyree asks.

"These guys and their explosions," the constable moans, checking himself for injuries. Gunfire erupts from down the street. "The command truck can handle this mess. Let's go."

The area is chaos. Guardians are everywhere. Some are covering the crypt, and others are racing toward the ruined rectory. Zyree and Dzamko have another plan. They sprint toward Jersey Street and drop to the prone position when bullets snap over their heads.

"Damn it," Dzamko grumbles, gritting his teeth. "Command, I need a force to come up Lafayette from the south. We need to keep them pinned here."

"Roger. Drone footage shows a total of seven tangos. I say again, seven terrorists entering a building to your east."

A man emerges and fires out of a blown-out window. The barrage stitches the brick wall directly above Zyree's head. He returns fire, forcing the terrorist to retreat into the building. Dzamko rises and then takes a knee.

"We've got them cornered in the building."

"Don't be so sure. Liberteum doesn't do anything without a plan."

Dzamko checks in with command as his guardians swarm around the structure. The streets have gotten quiet. There is no gunfire. Liberteum isn't even trying to keep the PSS out of the building. That's not good.

"There are no egresses out of that building except…it has access to the pedestrian lowline," he says, his eyes growing wide. "Command, route three teams to the lowline below Lafayette. Do it now!"

"You know where they're heading?" Zyree asks.

"I have a good guess. Come on. I know an alternate entrance we can use."

They sprint across Lafayette Street at full tilt and find the commuter access to the lowline. Zyree has never seen one here. It isn't a characterless, tile-and-steel pedestrian thoroughfare. It's lush with countless trees, flowers, and even waterfalls. Natural light is reflected in from the street level above, reducing the need for artificial lighting. It's a beautiful and serene space.

"You move pretty well for an old guy. They should rethink removing you from active service," Zyree says, noticing that the constable is barely winded.

"Perish the thought," Dzamko says, noticing employees walking back and forth down the lush corridor.

"Command, clear everyone—"

"Get down!" Zyree shouts, dragging the constable to the ground as two armed terrorists appear directly across from them in the entryway.

The chief inspector scrambles to a short stone wall with dirt and a thriving lemon tree. Bullets chip away at the planter and strip the tree bark. Several employees go down. Others scream and run for their lives. Liberteum isn't reserving their fire for the guardians. They're shooting at everyone.

A terrorist lays down suppressing fire as the others bolt toward the SpeedRail entrance. The guardians coming from the south seek cover. Zyree sees an opportunity. He rolls out from his position, lines up the red dot from his sight, and drops the man with a headshot. That's how you beat body armor.

"Command, they're heading for the SpeedRail!"

"Roger. Moving teams into position."

Gunfire erupts in the brown line of the SpeedRail. A dozen dead or severely wounded bodies are lying on the ground. The intensity of the gun battle in the station increases sharply. Then there's a sharp blast. The concussion almost knocks the two men over. The firing ceases, outside of occasional bursts that grow softer and more distant. They made it through the first perimeter.

Zyree and Dzamko find eight guardians at the top of the escalators. Four of them are dead and the other four are gravely wounded. The metal security gate has been blown open. The chief inspector starts to administer aid as Dzamko surveys the carnage.

"Command, we have a team down at the station entrance. Get this line shut down."

"We're working on it, sir."

"Don't work on it. Get it done," he scolds.

"They're on the platform," Zyree says, hearing the exchanges of fire below as he applies a tourniquet to a guardian's leg.

Two men arrive to tend to the wounded. Zyree and Dzamko make their way down the broken escalator and into a hail of gunfire. Zyree's contacts flick off as his armor takes two rounds. He collapses on the metal stairs, sliding down them on his back.

Dzamko spots the target on the platform and drops him with a well-placed salvo before ducking the return fire. "You all right?"

"Goddamn, that hurts," Zyree says, lying prone on the steps while trying to massage his ribs through the battered armor. With the abuse it's already taken, energy dispersion plates are almost useless.

"Can you move?"

Zyree nods and then struggles into a squatting position while staying low. He peeks over the edge of the escalator at the remains of the firefight. People are lying everywhere, most of them covered in blood. The carnage is sickening. Liberteum is leaving a horrendous body count in their wake while only suffering minimal casualties.

Both men turn their heads when they hear the whooshing sound and electric hum of the oncoming train pulling into the station. This is going to be very bad. If that train stops at the platform, a lot of people are going to die. Dzamko recognizes the same urgency.

"RTCC, damn it, shut down the brown line of the SpeedRail!" he pleads into his throat mic.

"We can't do it from here. We're working with Transportation Operations. They're slow to respond."

Dzamko pokes his head up and ducks just as the escalator gets peppered with more rounds. "They won't shut the train down in time. We're the only two left on this side of the tracks."

Zyree shrugs. "Then it's up to us."

The sleek electromagnetic SpeedRail glides in and stops with graceful precision. The doors open, and travelers step out, having no idea what they're walking into. The terrorists' rifles shred the closest people to pieces. They climb over the bodies and enter the train as passengers scatter and recoil in horror.

Zyree pops up when the last man boards the train and engages the guardians on the opposite platform through a shattered window. He grabs Dzamko and they dash down the remaining steps and dive through the closing doors at the train's rear. The constable makes it through cleanly, but Zyree's ankle gets stuck. The terrorist shooting is fifteen feet away. He turns as the door sounds an alarm and reopens, freeing his ankle. It's too late. The chief inspector is prone and exposed in the doorway with his rifle sling pinned beneath him. He can't move it.

The man aims and moves his finger to the trigger. His head explodes, and brains splatter behind him. Zyree glances up to see Dzamko searching for other targets.

"I'm glad you shoot as well as you run. I owe you."

"I hope we survive this so I can collect."

The doors close, and the train accelerates. There's little cover in these cars. The slight bowing of the seating obstructs an otherwise clear line of sight to them from the terrorists positioned forward. The dead bodies stacked up at the door absorb the gunfire from the front. Dzamko joins Zyree in the prone position, as low to the floor as possible.

"This was not a good idea," Zyree grumbles as a shot ricochets off the floor mere inches from his face.

"Command, we're on the SpeedRail. Shut this damn thing down!"

The train begins its deceleration for the next stop, and the terrorists at the front of the train open fire on the platform. There's nothing either man can do about it.

"Constable, this is the RTCC. We have video confirmation of four tangos at the front of the train."

"Roger. We're pinned down aft," he shouts over the sporadic gunfire.

"This SpeedRail just became an express. Transportation will shut it down at a designated stop. We have a surprise planned."

"What stop?" Zyree asks as the train lurches forward and accelerates.

Dzamko turns to him. "Library Park."

CHAPTER NINETY

LIBERTEUM

Houston Street SpeedRail Station
Nolita Geographic District
New York City Municipal Corporation

The trek from the rectory has been challenging. The short tunnel into the youth center was followed by the need to traverse several cellars to an old maintenance tunnel. That led to a utility tunnel that fed the original subway system. That was the easy part. Koltayne and Farron push and pull Rykos through a ventilation shaft that pushes fresh air onto the modern transit platform. They emerge through a vent into a maintenance room and wait in the darkness for the rushing air and distinct sound the electromagnetic train makes in the tunnel.

"This is our only chance," Michele says when she hears the train pull into the station.

"Stupid is what it is," Farron argues.

"Can you think of a faster way to get to Valhalla?"

"I can think of ones with fewer cameras."

Urches avoid going near SpeedRail stations because of the heavy surveillance. Cameras and biojack monitors are spread everywhere in the renovated mass transit hubs. They are designed to safeguard employees while encouraging urches to keep their distance. That doesn't mean they always do.

"They won't be watching the feeds. Haven will have their undivided attention by now. We'll make it."

"How do you know that Haven isn't already dead?"

"I know Haven."

They step out the door onto the platform. Michele takes a moment to admire the space. The few stations she's seen in her travels are breathtaking, and this one is no exception. Built to reflect a neighborhood's character, the architects and designers gave each station a personality. This one features entertainment-themed murals, faux neon lighting, and an artsy vibe.

The platform isn't crowded. A few dozen employees wait behind the pulsating safety lights along the edge as the sleek train screams into the station and then slows smoothly before stopping. The doors open, and several employees disembark. Farron and Koltayne climb aboard, carrying Rykos between them. Michele follows and surveys the occupants. There is no blending in with this crowd. The quartet immediately draws the attention of everyone on the train.

"The SpeedRail system is automated. They can shut down any train, line, or even the entire system with a simple command," Farron warns.

"Let's hope they don't have reason to."

Michele sits in one of the gel-covered plastic seats that run the length of the train at curved angles. Koltayne and Farron set Rykos down between them as the employees look on with heightened suspicion and growing fear.

Rykos grows paler from blood loss and the toxic fluids leaking from his intestines. He's conscious, but his eyes are glassy, and he's drifting in and out.

"We'll never make it to Valhalla. Half these people are probably reporting us," Farron whispers.

Michele pleasantly smiles back at the employees staring at them. She's trying to remain an oddity they'll go home and tell their families about tonight. It's not working.

"We don't need to make it there. We only have to get to Grand Central. We can arrange for the Emissary to pick us up."

"It's too risky for him, and Rykos will die without immediate surgery. We need to get off at University Square."

The square is home to the main campus of New York University, one of the training grounds for middle-tier employees of America Incorporated. It is half the distance to their stronghold but a strange place for Farron to want to disembark.

"Why?"

"You're an urch," a large man in a corporate tunic says, pointing his index finger at Michele.

"Easy, Koltayne," Michele says when she notices him slowly reaching for his weapon."

Two others join the boisterous man. None of the three are executives or employees who work directly for the parent company. The higher up the food chain employees are, the deeper the resentment of urches. Michele knows that she has one chance to get them out of there.

CHAPTER NINETY-ONE

INTERCORPEX

SpeedRail Brown Line
Midtown Geographic District
New York City Municipal Corporation

Dzamko and Zyree are one with the floor as the SpeedRail begins to decelerate. Heavy gunfire from the platform rips the lead cars apart at window level. Terrorists dive on the floor. Glass and shards of metal rain down as the carnage dances towards them before shifting back to the front.

The train stops and slams down onto the track. The SpeedRail is a maglev system that uses superconducting magnets to suspend the train above a U-shaped concrete guideway. Zyree knows that they cut the power to the rail.

"Go!" Zyree shouts.

They jump up in unison and make it about a hundred and fifty feet before Liberteum recovers. They shelter at a pair of doors near the middle of the four-hundred-foot train. The terrorists have good situational awareness. Two are firing at the platform, one is covering the train, and one shoots out the driverless train's windshield.

"Hold fire!" Dzamko commands into his throat mic.

Weapons from the platform go silent a moment later. Nobody moves or talks. The silence is eerie following all the firing. A thick layer of cordite drifts through the air as each side takes stock of the situation.

"There's no place to go, Haven!" Zyree shouts, shattering the tense quiet.

"Zyree? Is that you?"

The chief inspector stands, keeping his weapon pointed to the front. It would be an easy shot with a rifle, but his men would drop him a second later. Liberteum is caught in a trap. There is no reason for Zyree to trade his life for Haven's.

"Damn, man, it is you. Fancy meeting you here."

"The tunnel is blocked. The station is surrounded. There's no escape this time, Haven. Give it up, or I get to bury you again."

"Still bitter about that, are ya? No escape," he says derisively. "You have always lacked imagination. Before you do something stupid, open that duffle on the seat a couple of feet in front of you."

Zyree glances at the drab canvas bag. It could be booby-trapped. If it is, the guardians will annihilate the front of the train. It'd be an even trade.

"Go ahead, look inside it," he urges. "It won't bite you."

Zyree peels back the flap. The main compartment has explosives and a timer that isn't ticking. It reads one minute and is holding.

"This won't stop me from shooting you, Haven."

"This will."

He raises his arm out in front of him and brandishes a dead man switch. That's their contingency. The device is nothing more than a reverse detonator – instead of pressing a button to trigger the bomb, releasing pressure will if Haven becomes incapacitated or is killed. If he goes down, they all die. So do all the employees on this train.

"It turns out that the explosives training Intercorpex Security gave me has paid major dividends. Timers are boring, so I spiced things up. Oh, and there's an equilibrium trigger on that. It'll blow if you have a heroic streak and try to dump it out the window. Let me go, or I send this train and everyone around it straight to hell."

"You're not going anywhere."

"Then shoot me. I dare you."

Haven was never prone to bluffing. This isn't the man he once knew, but Zyree knows that hasn't changed. Haven will kill everyone on this train, including himself, without hesitation.

"Tell the men in the tunnel to back off," Zyree says to Dzamko. "We need to evacuate this train before we engage him."

Two of Haven's men climb out the window, and then a third. Haven smirks as he sits and swings his legs through the shattered windshield frame.

"See ya around, Zyree."

"RTCC, instruct the teams in the SpeedRail tunnel not to engage the tangos moving north for the next ninety seconds. Restore power and open the train doors."

Seconds tick by before the power begins humming. The lights still functioning illuminate, and the climate control system clicks on. Those aren't the only things that started. Zyree glances down at the timer. It has begun its countdown.

"Get in here," Zyree screams at the men on the platform when the doors open. "Get as many wounded as you can and get out of this station! You have…fifty-two seconds."

The two dozen men on the platform pour through the doors and collect wounded employees. Dzamko marshals ambulatory passengers to the exit to fend for themselves. As fast as things are moving, it's too slow. Zyree checks the timer. Thirty seconds. They won't be able to save them all.

"Help me with him," Dzamko says.

They pull an older man covered in blood to his feet and drape his arms over their shoulders. Dzamko looks around and grimaces. He nods, and they maneuver out the door and lug him down the platform. Gunfire echoes in the tunnel as they climb the escalator stairs. The RTCC must have ordered the guardians to engage the targets when they realized the bomb was active.

Zyree and Dzamko are almost to the top when they hear the rumbling of the explosion. It grows louder and louder until its force slams them in the back, catapulting them out of the station. The two men and the wounded employee land hard on the concrete sidewalk outside. Dazed, Zyree rolls onto his back and stares at a sky growing dark with thick black clouds. Fitting.

CHAPTER NINETY-TWO

THE PATRICIANS

Keating Family of the Gentez-Majorez Estate
Greenwich Geographic District
Southern Connecticut Municipal Corporation

The world outside the thick stone walls of this massive Greenwich mansion is descending into chaos. The silence and stillness within its walls don't mean all is well. Denali's eyes are welded to the ticker scrolling the market data streaming out of New York. It has created tunnel vision where nothing outside it exists. Even Abbot entering with Commander Lacune doesn't break the spell.

"Sir, we have a situation," Lacune says with a healthy amount of urgency in his voice.

Denali pries his eyes off the display. "What is it?"

"The siege was broken in Nolita. Liberteum fled the area on a brown line SpeedRail and is currently trapped in Library Park Station."

"Trapped?"

"They are surrounded, and the PSS has men on the platform and the train."

Denali grimaces. It's too soon. "How the hell did they end up on a SpeedRail in the first place?"

"A running firefight with guardians through part of lower Manhattan and into a lowline. From there, they fought their way onto a northbound train."

"Extraction possibilities?" Denali asks.

"Limited. May I?"

The patrician nods. Lacune sends video streams from his tablet to the display. Denali scans them. The outside of the station has a couple of dozen guardian vehicles.

"We have teams on the perimeter and two adjacent to the SpeedRail tunnel. Unfortunately, there is no way to reach them on the train. Liberteum will need to find a way out of this on their own."

The three men watch people begin pouring out of the access. They are frantic and panicked. Lacune zooms in on the activity. Then a massive explosion shakes the camera and the blast knocks the figures down like bowling pins. Thick clouds of black smoke billow out of the station's entrances.

"My God."

Lacune holds his hand over his ear. Denali lets him listen as he watches the scene play out.

"Liberteum is engaged in a firefight with the PSS in the tunnel north of Library Park," Lacune says.

"Can you intercept them?"

"It would require contact with the PSS."

Denali knows what that means. He doesn't need the terrorists anymore but would prefer to use them over the alternatives for his next phase. This decision, like many in life, requires a risk-reward analysis. What people want and get are often two different things because they can't bear the risk. He is Denali Keating, not most people. He gets what he wants.

"Commander, tell your teams to protect my investment."

"Yes, sir. I will report as soon as we have word of the outcome."

"You have an incoming secure VidLynk from Shalius Covington," Abbot says, skipping using his complete formal name. Denali nods, and Abbot taps his display. He leaves with the commander.

Denali checks AME News while the VidLynk session gets encrypted. There is nothing on the explosion at Library Park. There haven't been any reports on the explosions and gunfire at the old cathedral or the lowline. Typical.

He shifts to another display. The market is approaching rock bottom. Denali shakes his head. Could the course of action be any more obvious? Does Intercorpex need an engraved invitation to do what must be done?

Shalius's face fills most of the VidLynk. He's not in the *prima's* office on Corporate Hill. That's a little surprising. Denali would have thought he'd be measuring it for new curtains by now.

"Are congratulations in order, *Prima* Covington?"

"Regretfully, no. With the chaos in the market, Intercorpex has been slow to provide America Incorporated with updated shareholder information. Nothing is settled."

"Well, they're quite busy over there," Denali says, curling the corner of his mouth. "Are you still buying shares?"

"As fast as I can. Talya is doing the same, no doubt."

Denali clenches his jaw. He's right about that. Talya is going to be very unhappy. She will take her ire out on him, but that's a problem for another day.

"Is Intercorpex going to let the market go to zero?" Shalius asks, leaning in to the camera.

"No."

"No? Because it sure looks like they are."

"There will be an intervention," Denali says.

"You sound certain of it. Should you be?"

It's a fair point. Denali has to put on a brave face, but he isn't sure of it at all. In the next thirty minutes, he will know if the faith he placed in Lyris was warranted.

"Not every chess move works as planned."

"You're not the one who will be bankrupt if it doesn't. I've wagered my family's fortune on this gamble. You need to ensure it pays off."

Now Denali is starting to get annoyed. "You only have financial exposure. Mine is far greater, and you know it. Every plan requires adaption. One way or another, we will both get what we want. That much I can guarantee."

Shalius nods. He likely disagrees but doesn't look willing to further press the issue.

"Very well. I will leave you to it."

Denali ends the VidLynk. There will be plenty of time to stroke his friend's ego later. How hard and for how long will depend on what happens next. He stares at the ticker covered with red symbols down more than eighty percent of their value. The end is near. What the hell is Lyris waiting for?

CHAPTER NINETY-THREE

INTERCORPEX

Global Network Operations Center
Manhattan Financial District
ICX New York Exchange

The situation is growing increasingly desperate. Technicians are running around the NOC floor in a panic. They are searching for a problem that doesn't exist, and all Lyris can do is watch. Not that the market crashing is the only thing happening in this city.

It feels like a throwback to the worst day in Lyris's life. Liberteum disabled their primary and secondary circuits in massive explosions that rocked the city. Once the hack of their systems ended, they failed over to London and saved Intercorpex. There are unconfirmed reports of explosions and gunfire only blocks north of Wall Street, and the market is again in freefall.

The two things could be related, or they might not be. Lyris can only watch from his workstation as events unfold. It's a helpless feeling. Well, there is one thing.

"Sir, the IGI is going straight to zero. We need you to perform some of your magic," Wyeth pleads. "We need to do something while the market still has some value."

"Like what? What do you want me to do?" Lyris snaps.

"You know what."

It's not unprecedented. The New York Stock Exchange halted trading several times in the wake of terrorist attacks and economic catastrophes. Intercorpex consolidated worldwide markets into three exchanges to standardize operations. They removed risky options trading and eliminated dark pools. Those measures were taken to avoid the calamities that led to the Great Collapse. Despite all that, here they are…

"Director Lyris, Intercorpex Security. We have reports of a massive explosion in the Midtown Geographic District."

"NetEng, is there any impact on our network?"

"Negative. All circuits are communicating nominally."

"Where the hell is he?" Lyris hears Raimius shout in his shrill voice from the entrance to the NOC.

"Roger, Security. Continue to monitor, but we have bigger problems right now."

Everyone on the NOC floor stops what they are doing and turns to gawk at their visitor. The administrator-general is larger than life. His presence is akin to Zeus coming down off Mount Olympus. To Lyris, he's the grim reaper with a scythe coming for his soul.

"What are you doing to my exchange, Lyris?" the administrator-general barks, stopping in front of the raised platform.

"My job."

"Look at the IGI! Something is wrong," he screams, pointing at the big board.

"All trades are clearing. They're real transactions. There's no hack, no spoof, and no outside influence. Start with the patricians if you're searching for someone to blame."

"Don't give me that! You're the executive director of global operations. Don't tell me that patricians could be responsible for this debacle!"

"I'll repeat it more clearly," Lyris says, choosing words sure to annoy Raimius. "Every trade we have reconciled has come back—"

"I don't want to hear your excuses. You…you are hiding the truth, aren't you?" he screams, wagging an accusatory finger.

"Excuse me? What truth?"

"Don't play coy with me, Lyris. You want this market to crash to make me look inept so you can take my job. You want me to fail as administrator-general. It's why you're ignoring my VidLynk requests."

"I didn't take your requests because I was confirming whether there was a system issue."

"And I said don't lie to me!"

"Raimius, there isn't a coup being planned in the dark recesses of the building. Don't spew your insane conspiracy theories in front of my staff. You're distracting from ongoing monitoring during a crisis. Now, get off the floor."

Raimius recoils at the harsh retort. "Your job is to run the operations of this exchange, and you're failing. You are all failing. I should fire you all, starting with you, Lyris."

The executive director folds his arms across his chest. It all comes down to this. He needs to make a stand in front of everyone. Enough is enough. If he doesn't act, Raimius will destroy him. If he does, Denali could do the same. Wyeth is right: There is only one option left to save Intercorpex.

"Then do it," Lyris challenges.

"Don't test me."

Lyris swallows hard and takes a deep breath. "Attention in the NOC! This is Executive Director of Global Operations Lyris. Effective immediately, close the exchange to trading."

"No! Don't you dare!" Raimius threatens, first to Lyris and then to the staff manning the rows of workstations.

"Take the ITQS off-line," Lyris states calmly.

"Belay that order. Under the authority granted to me as administrator-general, I am removing Executive Director Lyris from his position. Director Wyeth, you are now acting executive director of global operations."

Everyone in the NOC looks around with uncertainty. Lyris looks over at his colleague and steps backward in a symbolic gesture of yielding control. Wyeth straightens his tunic and faces the staff. He works closely with these people, and they respect him. If he asked them to follow him into the fires of hell, they'd bring marshmallows.

"Attention in the NOC," he croaks. "This is Acting Executive Director of Global Operations Wyeth. Director Lyris has been removed from his position, and I have assumed control per order of the administrator-general."

Raimius watches with satisfaction as the scene unfolds. Everyone awaits the next order, which should be to remove Lyris from the NOC floor. Raimius is handing him Intercorpex's most coveted position on a silver platter. Very few would ever pass up an opportunity like this.

"We have all been through a lot together. We've seen hard times and even survived nearby explosions. Whatever the future brings, we will face that together. That future starts now. Shut down the exchange to trading."

"No! Stop!" Raimius screams to the staff.

"Follow my orders, everyone," Wyeth says. "It is on my authority."

The floor bursts into a flurry of activity. This staff is well-trained, and they set about their tasks with ruthless efficiency. This procedure may never have been used, but that doesn't mean Wyeth doesn't conduct drills to practice it. As a result, everyone knows the sequence of events.

"ITQS offline."

"Matching engine offline."

"I order you to stop!" Raimius bellows. Nobody is listening to him.

"Reconciliations halted."

"Symbols are frozen at last price. Clearing the board."

"Wyeth, you are relieved of duty!"

"You can't do that, Administrator-General. You aren't authorized to remove me while I hold both director positions in this NOC."

Lyris smirks. The man knows his protocols. He's one hundred percent correct. The big board reads no data for all ticker symbols on the IGI and GCSI. The display scrolling exchange transactions has gone dark.

Raimius's eyes burn with hatred as they settle on Lyris. There is no going back to the way things were. When the dust settles, only one of them will remain. The other will likely be dead.

"Acting Executive Director Wyeth? This is Trading Operations," a voice announces over a seldom-used loudspeaker in the NOC.

"This is Director Wyeth."

"The exchange is closed."

CHAPTER NINETY-FOUR

LIBERTEUM

SpeedRail Green Line
NOHO Geographic District
New York City Municipal Corporation

As interest grows, a small crowd starts to gather around Michele. None of them are overtly hostile, but they don't look happy either. If she doesn't win them over, their odds of getting off this train are nil.

"Yes, I'm an urch. My name is Michele, and I'm the leader of Liberteum. This is Koltayne, and he's Farron Keating, a patrician of the *gentez-majorez*. This man between us is Undergraduate Rykos, hero of America Incorporated."

The man blinks, trying to process that information. He looks at his friends, unsure what to think or do. Michele's words sound like the start of a bad joke.

"I'm betting you didn't expect to ever see the four of us together," Farron adds, trying to lighten the mood. It doesn't work.

"You're murderers. I know what happened downtown."

"We just came from there. The man causing all the mayhem is named Haven, and he used to be a part of my group."

"Used to be?" another man asks.

"He tried to kill me a couple of days ago, and I wasn't pleased, so we parted ways. Haven is more than a murderer. He's a psychopath. I hope the PSS puts him down like a rabid dog."

"Our stock is crashing. They all are. The news keeps saying the patricians are causing it...are you responsible for what's happening with Intercorpex?"

"Yes."

"Were you responsible for the first attack?" a woman asks, joining the group.

"Yes, we were."

"That's not what we were told," another man argues, trying to reconcile what Michele is saying with the facts he thinks he knows.

"There will be lots of things you're told about what happened today that won't be true either. I just admitted to dozens of crimes against the corporation. Ask yourself who has more reason to lie."

"What are you doing on this SpeedRail?"

"We are trying to get Rykos medical attention."

"Why not take him to a medical center?"

"Because if we do, the Bureau of Corporate Security will take him away and torture him for information until he's dead. I don't want that to happen."

"How do we know you didn't do that to him?"

"Because I would have left him in the underground to bleed out instead of getting on a SpeedRail."

"We've seen the videos on the news about what you people are doing to us. Assaults…and the poor woman who was raped…you're animals!"

Farron fidgets in his seat. This could get ugly very quickly. Right now, it isn't looking good.

"I've seen the videos," Michele says to the surprise of the gathering. "I was horrified. Then I saw something that didn't make sense. One of the assailants was someone I knew—someone captured by the PSS during a raid last week."

"Are you saying it was fake?" the first man asks suspiciously.

"It looked real to me," the woman argues, still clearly upset at the images.

"It looked real to me, too. I don't know who produced the videos. I do know that the assailant was in custody at the time of that assault. He couldn't be involved. That makes me question all of the videos."

"That sounds far-fetched."

"I agree. Look, I know what you've all been told about us. I'm not asking you to believe me or what I stand for. I don't expect you to accept why we're doing what we are. You will get to make that choice for yourselves soon enough. But this man is important to me, and he's dying. If I don't get him to a surgeon, he'll die. I can't live with that."

Tears begin to well in Michele's eyes. A single one manages to escape and run down her cheek. It's a strange sensation for her. In the underground, crying is a weakness avoided at all costs.

"We're getting off here," Farron says, standing.

He helps Koltayne lift Rykos to his feet, and they drape his arms over their shoulders. Michele uses her eyes to plead with the crowd around them.

"Please…please, let us save him. That's all I ask of you."

The group exchanges looks. Their emotions and their conditioning are conflicting, and it's causing indecision. Michele knows that they can't fight their way out of here. It'd be a losing battle, and Rykos will die.

The woman moves out of the way. A man follows her. A couple of seconds later, they have a clear path to the door as it opens.

"Thank you. Somebody is going to interview you about what happened on this train. Don't lie to them. Relay everything exactly as it happened. When you do, ask yourself if I'm as evil as they want you to believe."

Michele follows the men onto the platform. They lurch toward the exit as the train doors close and it accelerates towards the next station.

"My friend is usually in the medical training building. I just hope he's there today," Farron says.

"Rykos dies if he isn't. He doesn't have much time left."

"You were amazing back there. You care for him, don't you?"

Michele doesn't want to talk about it. She felt vulnerable, and her feelings for Rykos could be viewed as a weakness. The golden rule of the underground is you never give anybody an opening they can exploit. This is no time for feelings.

"Yes, but that's not what saved us."

"What did?"

"The awakening that we've been working for. People are so used to lies that they don't know how to react when they finally hear the truth."

CHAPTER NINETY-FIVE

INTERCORPEX

42ND Street & 6th Avenue
Midtown Geographic District
New York City Municipal Corporation

Fire crews and rescue teams hurriedly perform their work. Men and women come and go out of the smoke-filled SpeedRail station, searching for survivors as they combat the flames. The damage the bomb did will pale in comparison to the human toll Haven exacted today. The consequences of this incident will ripple through both America Incorporated and Intercorpex.

"Are you okay, Chief Inspector?" Dzamko asks, handing Zyree coffee in a paper cup.

"Thanks," he says, graciously accepting it. "I'm fine. What a mess. There's going to be hell to pay for this."

"We've already seen one of today's ramifications. Valen was removed as CEO of America Incorporated."

Zyree doesn't involve himself in the inner workings of the world's corporations. He's never met the former CEO but has been impressed with his job performance. It's a loss for this corporation.

"That's surprising."

"It gets worse. Zeykala is the new acting chief executive. Her first directive put the BCS in charge of safety and security operations in New York. That means we technically work for them instead of Chief Executive Safmor."

"Can you fight it?"

"No. I can't do anything even when they turn this city into a bloodbath. I guess it should be expected. We have dozens of dead employees and guardians with almost nothing to show. At least we got most of the passengers off the train. It could have been much worse."

"That's something, I guess. Maybe the only thing," Zyree says, staring at his coffee.

"There's no sign of Haven. He found the irrigation tunnels under the park. We thought we had him corralled in the sanitation tunnel that serves the library and then we lost him. Tactical teams will continue the search until the BCS takes over operational control."

Zyree scowls. That's twice he's failed to finish them. "He could be anywhere by now."

"This area of the underground is heavily monitored."

"You're assuming he stayed below the surface. I'm not sure you should do that anymore."

Dzamko nods. "You knew him?"

"Yeah. He was an ICX inspector that supposedly died in a training accident years ago. Now he's…he's not the same man I knew."

"I would hope not. Speaking of colleagues, what happened with you and that ninja back at the crypt?"

Zyree had forgotten about Chiana. "I have no idea. She tried to kill me. I don't know why."

"We have her in custody but aren't authorized to keep her. The guardian's helmet camera caught the whole thing if you need evidence for your organization."

"Thanks. I'll submit the footage when I report to Zurich. Commissioner-General Jurghen can figure out what to do with her."

"I can stall for twenty-four hours if you need time. Do you have any intel on what happened to the exchange?"

"What are you talking about?"

"I would have thought your fancy contacts informed you."

"My biocomp blinked out in the SpeedRail station. It's toast. What's going on?"

"Intercorpex halted trading. The IGI had lost more than three-quarters of its value. Some symbols went to zero before the exchange went dark. The last official word is that there were no anomalies, and the crash was caused by normal market activity."

Zyree scoffs. "Yeah, right."

"There's one more thing. I finally got the utility report for Farron Keating's building in SoHo."

"Let me guess: Electrical usage far exceeded typical usage, and data transmissions rates were through the roof."

"I said you were creepy. How did you know?" Dzamko asks, surprised at the accuracy of Zyree's conclusion.

The chief inspector wants to kick himself. As if letting Haven and his band of gun-toting misfits slip through his fingers wasn't bad enough, he fell right into their trap. While he chased Haven through the city, Liberteum brought the exchange to its knees. This Michele woman is brilliant.

"I don't know how they did it, but Liberteum took down the exchange from there. Can you get some people to secure the building?"

"I can pull a team from the search. Haven is the BCS's problem now. Do you want to accompany them?"

"Malkor can go," Zyree says, facing his loyal compatriot. He nods but is still pissed that he missed the action on the SpeedRail. "Coordinate with the PSS and let me know what you find. I'll meet you down there."

"You got it. Try not to get into any running firefights while I'm gone."

Zyree stands and grins. He'll be hearing about that for a while.

"Are you sure you're okay?" Dzamko asks.

The chief inspector stares up at the darkening skies before turning back to him. "I'm not sure any of us are. Want to take a walk with me, Constable? I want to see something."

They make their way through the mass of emergency personnel toward Times Square. It's midday, and employees have streamed into the famous intersection to see the sight for themselves. They are milling around, staring and pointing at the massive displays that grace the sides of the skyscrapers.

While there are still plenty of bright advertisements like before the crash, countless displays are dedicated to the exchange and performance of AME stock. Each employee is constantly exposed to it, especially at the "crossroads of the world."

They are all dark now. The tickers wrapping around the buildings surrounding the intersection of Broadway and Seventh Avenue show no data. Instead of the latest quotes for symbols in the IGI and GCSI scrolling across the LED screen, there is only a terse statement proclaiming that the market is closed. No wonder people are spooked. It must be a strange sight in a society where business is life.

"This is eerie," Dzamko says. "Zyree, what is all this about?"

The sky opens up in a deluge. It's a fitting metaphor. The storm has finally arrived.

"Free the world. That's what Liberteum's name means. They just took a big step toward their goal."

Zyree wonders if this is their end game or if there's something more. He stares again at the empty ticker display. It doesn't matter what comes next. For the first time since twenty-four-hour operations began, not a single share is being traded. Liberteum got what they wanted.

"What's their goal?"

"To show us a world without Intercorpex."

ACKNOWLEDGMENTS

I try to write the best stories I can, but without the people who read them, it's meaningless. Thank you to all who have read this novel. I sincerely hope you are enjoying this series, and I cannot begin to express my appreciation for investing your time in me. My core group of dedicated readers anxiously awaiting my newest release inspire me to work even harder. Thank you for providing endless motivation.

Reviews are essential to authors. In today's crowded marketplace, it's a crucial means for readers to discover books and decide which world to dive into. Please take a moment and leave a review my novels. I greatly appreciate your support!

I was asked not long ago if I intended to write strong female characters in this saga. The short answer is no, it wasn't planned to mirror societal shifts. The characters just happen to *be* strong women. The same applies to Kylie Roberts, Chelsea Stanton, Tierra Campos, and Victoria Larsen. They are fun to write, and I enjoyed giving Michele, Fiolla, Zeykala, Talya, and Ilaria the spotlight in this novel.

The incredible women in my life are a source of that inspiration. My wife Michele is the world to me. I cannot begin to express how much I appreciate her support in pursuing my dream. To my beloved mother Nancy, and my sister Kristina, thank you for always being there during this journey.

America, Inc. is more than a series. It's a saga, much like life itself, has many players, subplots, and hidden agendas. It is written as a cautionary tale. We are all the stewards of freedom and liberty and must be constantly vigilant for assaults against them. It takes a guiding hand to help bring that to life. A special thanks to Michael Waitz at Sticks & Stones Editing for another superb effort. One of these days, I will learn the lessons he tries to teach me. Other bad habits I may never be able to fix.

Another big thank you goes to JD&J Designs for another fantastic book cover. How do you express the idea of "bounded rationality?" I didn't know either. Thankfully, they had the creativity to develop a concept and the patience to work with me until I got the cover I wanted.

ABOUT THE AUTHOR

Mikael Carlson is the award-winning author of the novel *The iCandidate* and the Michael Bennit Series of political dramas. He also has written two other ongoing series: Tierra Campos Thrillers and Watchtower Thrillers. His newest series, America, Inc., is a retelling of the futuristic dystopian Black Swan Saga that serves as a cautionary tale of life in a world following a global economic collapse.

A retired veteran of the Rhode Island Army National Guard and Unites States Army, he deployed twice in support of military operations during the Global War on Terror. Mikael has served in the field artillery, infantry, and in support of special operations units during his career on active duty at Fort Bragg and in the Army National Guard.

A proud U.S. Army Paratrooper, he conducted over fifty airborne operations following the completion of jump school at Fort Benning in 1998. Since then, he has trained with the militaries of countless foreign nations.

Mikael earned a Master of Arts in American History in 2010 and graduated with a B.S. in International Business from Marist College in 1996.

He was raised in New Milford, Connecticut, and currently lives in nearby Danbury.